THE
CAROLINIANS

THE
CAROLINIANS

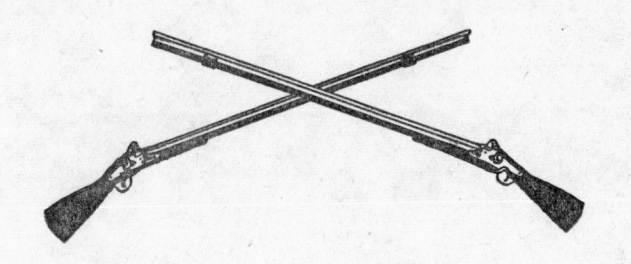

BY JANE BARRY

Doubleday & Company, Inc., Garden City, New York

With the exception of actual historical personages,
the characters are entirely the product
of the author's imagination
and have no relation to any person
in real life.

FOR JOHN AND CLINTON

THE
CAROLINIANS

1

THE DUST rose gray and ugly, hanging in the unmoving air, enveloping, impenetrable; the mules kicked it up at every step; it fanned like a wake behind the wagon.

In the stillness and blinding heat there was no sound but the creaking of the axle and the monotonous jangling of trace chain and singletree. The wagon lurched over the stones in the road, threatening to overturn, or even to fall apart, for the wood pins holding the sideboards were nearly rotted out, and the axle bolt was rusted and worn thin. A man's heels, in scarred dusty boots joggled up and down over the tailboard.

The man on the wagon box, the girl beside him, did not speak, did not look at one another. Naked to the waist, the man hunched over the reins. His face, with its deep-set gray eyes and aquiline nose, was Indian-dark from wind and weather, expressionless and impassive. A lock of jet-black hair hung wetly over his forehead and the sweat ran on his shoulders. He was curiously, childishly, smooth-skinned, with a long swell of muscle in forearm and chest; wiry, but with more than an intimation of great physical strength in the young, cleanly built body. He rode with one moccasined foot propped on the dashboard. Beside it, his rifle angled up and out at the hot white sky.

At his side the girl, little more than a child, kept her eyes averted. Her hands were clasped loosely in the lap of her faded black bombazine dress; the garment was too small and fitted her badly. Framed in the scarlet shawl which covered her head, her face was thin, sallow. It was a fragile, delicately boned face which, with more flesh upon it, would have been exceedingly pretty. Apathy showed in the sag of her narrow shoulders; the eyes, bent to her rough work-worn hands, were sharp with anger.

They had long ago finished talking to one another, said all there was to say, found no further necessity for looking at one another, seeing as how each knew how the other's face looked. The silence between them was not a strained silence, but it was not easy either; it was more a dullness of spirit which rose about them like a miasma contained in the wall of dust kicked up by the mules. The heat and the dust and the merciless jarring of the wagon had sapped every last drop of vitality from them, and there was nothing to do but let the body jolt to the wagon's jolting and suffer the sun and breathe the dust and wish it was all over.

Now, with an insistence which a thing with no will of its own ought never to possess, the booted heels behind them had begun to scrape, ever so softly, against the tailboard, and in cheerful conspiracy the road became rougher, the wheels more susceptible to jar, so that even over the sound of harness and axle, they could hear the booted heels talking, gently, sweetly, like a scraping of mice on a plank floor.

On a long curved hill the man reached out and braked the wagon a little. The mules were not hurrying, but they did not lag, keeping up a steady plodding pace. The cool steep mountain lay behind; ahead the land was rolling and hilly, burned dead from lack of rain. It was October, but there had been no respite from summer, and the leaves still held to the trees. The land withered and drew in upon itself. Nothing moved in the static landscape but the wagon and the mules and the booted heels.

2

UNDER THE DUSTY OAKS, on the hill above the road, Sabrina Quantrell sat astride the big roan horse, holding him back in the shade, watching the wagon curve with the curve of the road. Near the base of a tree, where the earth was cool, a blue hound lay with his forepaws stretched straight out before him. He panted methodically, stoically, and the water dripped from his tongue.

The girl sat looking down at the wagon on the road. She, horse, dog, were bound by a kinship of darkness and stillness: the patient hound with his yellow eyes gone dreamless, and the big roan with his narrow head and gentle mouth, and the girl, sitting straight out of long habit, but wanting to droop and lie over in the heat, like the strawbells did in the woods in summer. She was tall and long-legged, and the line of her body was easy and graceful in the saddle, like the whole lower half of her was slung casually from the broad straight shoulders and narrow waist. Under the thick and frankly disordered chestnut hair her handsome oval face was cool and serene, the wide-spaced gray eyes quick and alert. She had a high forehead and high rounded cheekbones, and her rather severely carved mouth with its well-defined upper lip bespoke a self discipline and firmness which nothing in either her eyes or the set of her head suggested. In these, rather, was a willfulness, almost a mischievousness, so that there was about her a curious authority, half tranquil and composed, half wildly independent, like a painter cub submitting to the terrors of existing among humans, but not adapting to it. She wore a rough linen shirt and short boots, and her striped cotton skirt was tucked up around her.

Her interest in the wagon, cursory from the time it had come into view, became riveted as the mules neared the bottom of the hill. A little closer, and she could tell for sure, but that looked much like her brother hunched over the reins. He'd gone off on foot, saying it would be three days at most, and here she'd looked for him a full week. A long three days she had to chide him with.

Now she was sure. Without being asked the little smile came to her mouth. She urged the roan forward, out of the dark vacuum of shade and took him out and over the brow of the hill at a full lope.

She had to angle now, to intercept the wagon. The dust puffed itself up big under the roan's hooves; then he cleared the ditch at the roadside and came up short.

She looked into her brother's dark, perspiring face. But before she had a chance to say anything he spoke, in that soft polite voice of his, like he didn't know her very well, like he was warning her.

"Morning, Brina."

"Morning, Brant." For the first time she looked fully at the girl beside him, not having even thought about the girl before this, recognizing her only in the moment of greeting: little Authie Stoner from off the mountain, orphaned and poor as a church mouse and a bride of three months. "How you, Authie?" she said.

"All right, thanks, Sabrina," the girl said in a hard tight voice. She still stared down at her hands.

Uncertainty stamped Sabrina's face; she kept her tone light, half teasing. "I've seen more cheerful faces any sunny morning you can reckon," she said.

Her brother's eyes stopped her. He said, "I reckon Authie's had a spell of hard luck." He jerked his thumb briefly over his shoulder.

The worn canvas covering had shaken away from the sprawled body in the back of the wagon. The head lay bent at an awkward angle. The eyes were closed in the swollen purple face, the tip of the tongue protruded between the thickened lips. The long lank dark hair, heavy with grease, had picked up slivers of straw and debris from the wagon bed.

Sabrina put her hand heavily on the roan's neck to steel herself. Still she could not take her eyes from the burden her brother drew, and it seemed to her, when the first sickness had passed, that Hanson Stoner's brutal pock-marked face, a face she had known all her life, had attained a ghastly dignity, a subtle refinement, in the finality of death.

She said in a low voice, "What happened, Brant?"

Again he jerked his thumb, this time at the girl. "Authie found him hangin' this morning. We're on our way into the settlement."

Now Authie Stoner looked up at Sabrina, as if she searched for something. Pity is degrading, pity is condescension. Sabrina's face, she saw, mirrored sympathy and shock. Almost immediately she looked away again, as if she did not dare to meet the older girl's eyes. But she spoke, still in the hard tight voice, as if she would choke on the insubstantiality of words. "I ain't beggin' pardon for Hanson," she said. "He drunk too much and he talked too much. I reckon I can guess what happened. He come into the settlement Friday night and got drunk and said something couldn't only be settled by killing. Because he weren't no King's man." The tightness went out of her suddenly, she sagged on the wagon box as if she had been shot.

Sabrina was hotly conscious of dust, dryness, sweat. "You mean . . . you don't think Hanson did this himself . . . you think someone else did it?"

And the girl said scornfully, "Hanson didn't have either guts or

12

brains to kill himself. But he was my only kin. No matter how I felt about him, he was my only kin."

Beyond and past her, Sabrina and Brant Quantrell looked at one another. But his face was still blank and emotionless, and it was Authie Stoner who responded to Sabrina's silence.

"Brant here, he's a King's man, but he come through and cut down Hanson's body and offered to bring me . . . us . . . into Benton's Crossing, all out of the good of his heart. Yes, and milked my cows afore he done it."

And Brant said, with the little flame of ironic amusement curling the edges of his voice, "It was I couldn't stand to see you mourning over Hanson that way, Authie."

She understood, dry-eyed. "So I didn't care a cob for Hanson. I didn't love my own pa much, but I was sorry when he died. When my pa lay dyin' he give me to Hanson, on Hanson's forty-third birth date it was, and here I am just turned seventeen and Hanson was the only body I had left in the world."

Now Sabrina was moved. "Who you think did it, Authie?"

Her head came up, quick, feverish, flashing. "Your people done this, Brina, yours and Brant's, and this favor you doin' me now don't take the sting out of that. Hanson used to say we wasn't beholden to no English King ever again, no matter how many wars was to be fought over it. He held to that thought, held to it so hard some King's man got riled enough to kill him for it. And all we'd ever did was keep our peace."

Anger stirred in Sabrina also. "No, Authie, you didn't keep the peace. My father kept the peace here and you cannot deny it."

The girl's voice softened a little, but the flat hard vehemence which was almost rebellion stayed with her. "He ain't kept it now," she said.

There was silence. Sabrina's sympathy for the girl swept her again, but it was tempered by embarrassment and confusion. She had never got used to the hill people; she found them either cold and indifferent, or full of violence and revenge, with no emotion in between. Whatever the rule of the hills, if it could be said to be a rule, it would always end up blood for blood. But you had to say something, you had to offer something, no matter how small. Always, with these mountain people, she had the peculiar feeling that she must agree, speak softly, placate. "I'm so terribly sorry, Authie."

The girl nodded. "I reckon I know that without bein' told. I'm beholden to you, Brina, and Brant too."

As if the mention of his name had shaken him awake, Brant Quantrell picked up the reins. "I reckoned we'd ought to stop by the house."

Sabrina shook her head, almost in relief, he thought. "Father went into the Crossing early this morning. It's Council day."

He said, impassive again, "You hear that, Authie?"

"I heard," the girl said. "Council meetin'. That means they'll all be there. Aiken Sheller and Mr. Lyons and Dr. Malcolm." She spat the words out. "And Alwyn Quantrell. All the King's men, poundin' tables in the inn and talkin' empty talk. Today I'll give them something to talk of. They can talk of a dead rebel today." She did not look at either of them again, returning obstinately to the study of her clasped hands.

Sabrina reached out across her, and for a moment her hand rested lightly on her brother's, where it held the mules' reins. "Come home as soon as you can, Brant."

For the first time warmth came to him. "I will. You know I will."

She swung the roan's head over. "Good-by, Authie. If you need anything. . . ."

"Good-by," the girl interrupted stonily. Now Sabrina saw there was a black bruise on her neck, like Stoner had hit her with the blade of his hand, maybe yesterday, maybe this morning, early. . . .

She let the roan take his own gait up the hill. The blue hound was standing under the oaks, waiting; his tail moved almost imperceptibly in welcome. Only once did she look back, but the wagon had headed around a bend in the road by then, and the last thing she saw was Hanson Stoner's joggling, lifeless heels.

3

THE SETTLEMENT LAY in a hollow in the foothills, white as a scar in the monstrous expanse of forest and mountain which shadowed and protected it, and the dusty wagon tracks of road wound down out of the Alleghenies to the hollow, following old Indian trails, old routes of march. This was, had been, a frontier town; nothing lay beyond the mountains but isolated settlements like itself, scattered farms, hillside cabins. The human roots which had taken hold here had been forced by fifty years of Indian hostility and French enmity to fight for survival, but roots which wrest sustenance through love of land spring firmly.

No man living could say whether the inn had come with the population, or the population with the inn; the inn had simply always been there, the early target of Cherokee lance and Catawba spear, the stopping-place for both French and English troops, the haven for traveler and settler and trapper. The life of the settlement was caught up and contained in its comfortable inn room: all things were here, food, drink, heat, coolness, argument, seat of government. When nothing else had stood in Benton's Crossing the Bear had been there, with the same narrow wooden shutters and heavy oak doors, refreshed over the years with white paint and a stone courtyard, but otherwise unchanged since the days of the Indian wars.

Around and about it, over the years, had grown up the general shop, the cooperage, the blacksmith shop, the church, the burying ground: the necessities. With man, hacking a way of life out of the wilderness, come horses, come cattle, oxen, mules, come women and children, come God, come death, and each requires the services of an artisan. The settlement grew, bounded at either end by narrow streams which rose from the same spring source, and became known in free translation from the Catawba, in old military dispatches, as the Place-of-Two-Creeks; then the shop came, and it was The Crossing, and with the coming of the church, Benton's Crossing. And where there had been only the stream and the inn, there were now the cooperage, with its confusion of dogs and flies and iron rims and spokes and wooden wheels, and the blacksmith shop, a little inferno of heat and glare and sound of file and ring of anvil and rising of steam. And the men came down from the mountains with their wagons and their horses, and after a time their women too saw a need in the wilderness, and beside the inn another artisan plied his craft. Inside Aiken Sheller's general merchandise shop it was cool and dim, and there was a dry-sweet-acrid odor of flour and wood and rope, spices and molasses and leather, tea and dry goods and dust. On the sloping porch men spoke and spit;

up the creaking steps women went to buy the stuff of existence, and there was never a hill man whose boot tracks could not be traced from Sheller's to the inn, from the inn to Sheller's.

Still, the houses were few: the Lyons family home, built of stone and set about with flower and vegetable gardens; the frame house whose builders had not seen fit to stay, now occupied by the territory's only physician; the little stone house beside the church which had been a labor of love for the men of the territory: they had built it for a permanent resident pastor. For many years there had been the circuit preacher, traveling his long and lonely route through the wilderness; marriages and baptisms were delayed or set to the time of his arrival, and in the periods between his visits, each man was preacher in his own household. So it behooved them to support unequivocally a man vowed to devote his life to their province, and they built first the little chinked log church with its wooden spire, and then the stone house, so that the good Reverend need not sleep his nights in the inn. And it was the first time in all its history that the inn shared what had been wholly its own: now there was another place of meeting, place of social gathering, and men wandering beyond any known frontier, men denied God but not Godless, came to sit in awe that there should be a church in this place.

In a country of forest, man kept his trees. Oak, willow, birch, aspen, pine, lived too in the settlement, casting their pattern of sunlight and shadow among the shops, sheltering coolly the long rectangle of man-made park across the road from the inn. Beyond this little row, this scar, there was only the vast silence of deep forest, staggering up the face of the mountains; the rolling yellow grasslands along the water courses; the colored fire of wildflowers ringing the foothills; the great stands of tall pine on the mountain ledges. Benton's Crossing had carved itself, from boundary of mill wheel and stream, out of the mountains, out of the forest, and whatever lay beyond the Alleghenies was endless frontier, only now beginning to know the first axe-bite of man's intent and dream. Under that towering range spread the territory dependent upon The Crossing, sparsely farmed, isolated, and the names of the mountain men stood forthrightly on the stones behind the church: Sheller, Albrecht, Post, Denning, Halpern, McCullough, Gresham, Whiting, Scott, Stoner, Dean, Ballentyne, Shaver: English, German, Scotch, Irish, and these names were the soul of the back-

16

country provinces of the Carolinas. Direct, hard, strong men bore those names, peaceful men who had kept the chaos of a war for independence at bay, the death which was a natural outgrowth of wartime at sword point, by the all too simple expedient of tending to their own affairs. There were other towns and settlements which looked upon Benton's Crossing as neutral. But in this year 1780, in this colony of South Carolina, mindful of what had made them (forest, Indian, hardship, land) they were not neutral. They too were at war, quietly, steadily, in their own way, wanting none of whatever small dignity is attendant upon neutrality, ready at a moment's notice to cry to the world, and die crying it, we are Englishmen, we are loyal.

The Provincial Council of the Crossing territory had sat little more than an hour when Brant Quantrell came in to break up the session with his grim news. Returned now to their table in the inn, they sat before the empty fireplace: Brant and his father, Alexander Whiting, owner of the Bear, Dr. Fraser Malcolm, trader William Lyons, shopkeeper Aiken Sheller. Where they had spoken easily, good-humoredly with one another that morning, meeting routinely, with no business of particular importance to be discussed, they were now silent and thoughtful. The tankards, the decanters, the glasses, sat untouched upon the table.

The Bear was dark and cool as a cave. At one end of the room was a huge stone fireplace. There were a long pine table and long pine benches before the bar counter, and a companionable grouping of round tables and wide-bottomed chairs occupied the remainder of the room. There was a feeling of space. Brass and copper sparked in the gloom. The stone floor was still wet from the scrub brush. The patina of use, of the oil of human hands, of boot tread, of fabric wear, were here; the smell was cold and liquid and dark, like ocean depth in summer.

Alwyn Quantrell sat at the head of the table, his clay pipe between his teeth. His hair, flowing on his shoulders, was as fine and silver as autumn frost, and he had a strong lined face and alert eyes. Something resolute and powerful, much of tremendous kindliness and warmth were in the fine craggy visage. He was tall, and his shoulders were still straight and full under the butternut waistcoat and linen shirt. His broad-brimmed black hat lay on the floor beside his chair. He smoked quietly, steadily, and the pungent smoke drifted like gray shadow in the dark corners of the inn room. After a time he said, almost wearily, "Well, what is it we must do now?" and his keen eyes went down the length of the table, studying the faces of his fellow council members.

The silence lay in the room. Fraser Malcolm stood up and began to pace, holding his tankard but not drinking from it. He wore a frilled white shirt and tight buff breeches and polished black riding boots; he was greatly aware of himself as a dim study in black and white and brass against the dark interior of the fireplace. But nothing with him was pose. He was wiry and dark and striking, and when he put a booted foot on an andiron it was with no thought of pretention, it was simply that it occurred to him to put his foot on the andiron, and he did it splendidly. His eyes were cold and black as obsidian; everything about him spoke of intelligence, almost of superiority, and he knew it and wondered at times what he was doing in Benton's Crossing. Now his sharp young face was turned to Alwyn Quantrell, and it bore nothing of answer to Alwyn's query. But because he hated the helplessness, the silence, he said, "I'm for burying Stoner and going home and forgetting about it."

Alwyn, watching him, shook his head. "What we do with Hanson Stoner has already been decided for us. What I would seek now is some assurance that this will not happen again."

At the end of the table, the Reverend Richard Jordan toyed with an empty glass. He said mildly, "And how do you propose we do that, Alwyn? What is there of assurance now that this has happened? Fraser would have us dig a grave and say our prayers and go our own ways again, and he may be right. We cannot, after all, maintain a constant vigil over our neighbors . . . only God can do that."

Seeing that both Brant Quantrell and Fraser Malcolm were grinning at him, he lowered his eyes. A circuit preacher who had given up his circuit to take residence in Benton's Crossing, he lived near William Lyons' garden plot, and was much given to meditation. His shaggy gray hair stood upright, as though he tore it frequently, when the mooings of Lyons' cows and the clucking of Lyons' chickens disturbed his thought. Round, cherubic, gentle but not meek, absent-minded but dedicated, he had replaced a tall and spare ecclesiastic whose eyes smoldered with fire and whose sermons reeked of brimstone and whose platform resounded with fist thumpings; he had brought to replace these promises of eternal damnation a pleasant liberalness which appealed to a people believing sincerely that the Great Jehovah belonged to New Englanders and had no place in their slower-paced, more tolerant mode of living. Richard Jordan had no fears for his congregation. He leaned heavily on the right arm of God as being all-embracing and all-sustaining, and what God could not settle in Benton's Crossing Alwyn Quantrell could. Therefore he was liberal, both economically and philosophically, not above charitably doling out the little he had to live on, not averse to telling God, with a sigh, if You don't take care of this for me, I shall have to get Alwyn Quantrell to do it. He rode the back country like a dragoon, was conspicuous at deaths and unobtrusively present at births, and he had a taste for claret. Now, seeing Fraser Malcolm's humorless laughter, he reiterated, for Malcolm was the thorn in his side.

"Prayer is often the solution to the seemingly insoluble," he said.

Alwyn Quantrell saved him. "Thank you, Richard, but I can't help feeling we've gone beyond prayer. My one thought is for the future. I know only that we must not let this be a beginning, that we must keep it an isolated instance."

Malcolm set his tankard down on the table. "I would like to call the Council's attention to a matter it seems to have overlooked. We've one definite and irrefutable fact to go on: Hanson Stoner was hanged this morning. I pronounced him dead and signed a certificate to that effect. But it strikes me we have all listened much too carefully to the hysterical ravings of an ignorant little mountain girl who says her late husband was hanged by what she calls 'King's men.'"

Alwyn looked at him gravely. "What are you getting at, Fraser?"

"What proof have we that Stoner was murdered by Loyalists? You know as well as I how easily death comes to these hill people, you know their laws of vengeance and killing for vengeance. Hanson Stoner was the most disputatious, contentious man who ever drew breath. . . . He must have had enemies on every farm in the territory. It's eminently more logical to believe he was killed over a land dispute, a trading deal, that child wife of his . . . maybe the possession of a dog, how in hell do we know?"

Brant Quantrell did not look up, and his voice was very soft.

"Why don't you say he was murdered by Indians, you want to go that far, Fraser?"

"What do you mean by that?" The young doctor's black eyes narrowed as he faced Brant.

And Brant shrugged, looking up now, with that calm, expressionless face and the softness still in his voice. "Authie says Loyalists did it. You say it was a vengeance killing. I say it could have been Indians."

Malcolm came and dropped down on the bench beside him, and the illusion of his power, his dark sensuality were gone. He seemed white, almost sickly beside Alwyn's son, for where Malcolm's dark wiriness only emphasized his slight build and pale skin, Brant Quantrell's dark wiriness served to point up the smooth play of muscle in the strong shoulders and arms, the clear, sunburned skin, the overpowering healthiness. The contrast went deeper than anything of flesh and blood and bone: as Malcolm affected the frilled white shirts, the black boots, Brant Quantrell carried to extreme the deerskin shirt, the moccasins, the battered old hat. They detested one another.

Malcolm's voice was soft now, and pleasant. "All right, you're the expert on killing. You tell us."

Nothing moved in Brant's face but the shadow of rage which passed briefly, darkly, across his eyes. He took his breath in slow and easy, relaxing, keeping his control, knowing Malcolm would have to say something like this, knowing Malcolm never lost an opportunity to insinuate, to refer obliquely to him as a killer of animals, and of men. But he knew too he could beat Malcolm at the game.

"Speaking as an expert then, if you want it that way, you ain't takin' one thing into consideration. Hill people killin' one another for revenge don't hang. They shoot or they knife or they bash one another's brains in, but they don't hang. Loyalists hang. They leave their mark just as sure as any Cherokee takin' a scalp. So I reckon you ain't got it figured, Fraser."

Malcolm tried to put the disgust in his voice and failed. "And you consider that a major point in your theory?"

"I reckon I got to." Brant looked down at the table again. "That, and the fact there was the tracks of at least ten men under that tree when I cut Hanson down."

The men began to murmur among themselves now, as if they

would all speak at once. They were with Brant Quantrell, Malcolm knew; they did not like Brant Quantrell much, but they respected his knowledge and his courage, they knew that long days in the mountain wilderness, in the silent forests, in the scattered Cherokee and Catawba camps taught a man things. He had made their decision for them.

Malcolm stood up and began to pace again. "All right, say I am wrong. Say it was not a revenge killing, say it was our people. Alwyn, you maintain we must keep it an isolated instance. How do we isolate, how do we even consider isolation? If this comes down to the murder of a rebel by Loyalists, it is a beginning. What's to prevent Hanson Stoner's friends, if he had any friends, from reprisal? Maybe they'll want to hang *me* in reprisal. Don't try to isolate me, Alwyn, because I'll kill for the sake of my own life. So where does it stop? We can't stop it."

"You are quite right, Fraser," Alwyn said. "We cannot stop it anywhere but in Benton's Crossing. Do you propose to do exactly what I say we must fight against? How long have we now gone about our own peaceful countryside armed? How many of us have found it necessary to use our arms? None of us, ever. I have been proud of our people. Now threat hangs over us, and you suggest we do more than arm ourselves? You suggest we *use* our arms?"

"I have never seen you armed, Alwyn," Malcolm said with great affection. "I make no suggestion. I merely believe we should not delude ourselves, that we should prepare, possibly, for the worst."

"Wait, now you go too fast, Fraser. What do you mean by the worst?" William Lyons, a man in his early fifties, dressed starkly in black, and with a calm, good-natured face, asked the question. He bartered fresh eggs, milk, and vegetables for hides and fur, traveling by horse through the mountains; intelligent, honest, steady, and level-headed in emergencies, he was respected by everyone but his wife and daughter, and having been born in Benton's Crossing his community lay next to God and King in his heart.

Malcolm answered him half in anger. "You don't have to ask me that, do you, William? You know damned well I mean civil war. And you know civil war means killing."

"Killing will never settle this," Alwyn interposed. "It would be futile to ask justice for Stoner's killers, even if we knew them. But we have all taken the pledge of allegiance to the Crown, and I say that the Crown would not have our support take the form of murder, or even of the most trivial persecution of the rebels among us. I would like very much to believe, to make you believe, that this is an isolated act of violence, a warning to us."

"Are there rebels among us?" Malcolm smiled a little.

"I prefer to hope not, Fraser, but you know as well as I the temper of our people. There are times when a man would swear to Indian blood to save himself from a Cherokee gantlet." But a terrible feeling of foreboding had come to Alwyn Quantrell. It sat heavily upon him, and he could not shake it loose. "We must admit the probability that Stoner's killing is a triggering off of bigger things."

For the first time Aiken Sheller spoke. "You are right, of course, Alwyn. God knows how we've managed to keep peace this long."

Alwyn turned in his chair and looked at him. Aiken Sheller too had been born in Benton's Crossing, born puny and grown to manhood puny. Knowing him so well, Alwyn had always found it a matter of quiet amusement that the watchword of Sheller's life was that he was a good Christian, a motto whose precarious foothold was the assumption that the saying in itself would accomplish the end, the purpose, and that one need not be a good Christian so long as one said he was. In a sense, the livelihood of the territory depended upon him, and the shop he had inherited from his father. But he was a fair man; he owed as much, perhaps more, to these men than they to him, and he stood with them and supported them.

Alwyn told him, "We would delude only ourselves if we turned away from this probability. But it would seem to me that here lies the fruit of the reason for the existence of a council such as ours. For six years now we have met, we have kept the peace. Aye, say it if you will, we have held ourselves aloof. We have judged, decided, acted, perhaps not always as well as we might have, but no man can say without fairness and understanding. No man has ever been denied his right to come before us, to state his case, to ask his due. No man ever shall be denied, as long as I sit upon this council, be that man Loyalist or rebel. It occurs to me that we could not save Hanson Stoner, but that we can prevent this from happening again."

"How do you propose to do that?" Sheller said. His glasses sat high on the high bridge of his nose. In moments of distress he was prone to whip them from his face, invariably, inevitably tearing loose a corner of his small wig in the act. This he did now in a gesture familiar to them all.

And Alwyn said quietly, "By waiting."

They looked at him with something of astonishment. Sheller said, "Waiting? Waiting for what? For this to happen again?"

The old man shook his head. "No. That would be far too conclusive a thing for which to wait. I would far rather wait and see *whether* this happens again . . . take no definite step, live with the threat. For it would seem to me that with the turn this war has taken, with the near proximity of our English troops, any man who rises against his neighbor now takes his own life in his hands. If it is known that military reprisal will be the reward for civil war, I think we can maintain this peace of ours. Tomorrow, when we bury Hanson Stoner, every man in the territory who has received word of this will be in Benton's Crossing. It would be a good time to let them know our feeling on this matter . . . tell them, as it were, in the form of the burying itself."

Richard Jordan reached now for the decanter of claret. A flush of enthusiasm came to his round face. "I see. You would have the attitude of the council made public in my funeral oration, then, Alwyn?" And he looked up again and saw that the young thorn which was Fraser Malcolm had presented its sharpest end to him. In the opposing camps of religion and medicine they had accepted one another as guests, but not as permanent residents: when Jordan's wife had taken ill with a tumor it had been Malcolm after all who was the logician, the prophetic, the omniscient, standing in the slope-ceilinged bedroom, rolling down his sleeves, looking Jordan in the eye, saying words Jordan never forgot: I know what you're thinking, you're thinking the one thing you can draw any comfort from now, that this is God's will. I don't know what it is, Richard, but it isn't God's will. She's going to die, she's in pain, and I can't do anything but drug her out of her mind. (Standing there, with the black level eyes glittering and the slim fingers busy with his cuff links.) All I can do is wish to hell I could put her out of her misery, but they won't let me do that. They let me put a broke-legged horse or a crow-torn lamb out of its misery, but I can't touch the human soul. I'll do one thing for you, Richard, and it's the greatest concession I can make. I'll go home and pray. Since that day, Richard Jordan had done a great deal of praying for Fraser Malcolm. And in this moment he did not avert his eyes, but looked steadily at the young doctor. "Warning men through God is all we can do," he said.

Alwyn nodded wearily. "Perhaps I have failed you," he said, "not only in that I find no solution to this, but from the very beginning." Their faces turned to him, mirroring their faint but open surprise. Alwyn said, "Failed you because I want the peace so badly. Those of you who have known me all my life know that this was not always so, that I took my part in the Indian uprisings and when we fought the French. But I have wanted most of all to live in peace. Peace comes hard, and never unbidden; it must be bargained and bartered for. We barter now. We barter with blood and lives, with the young lives that were to secure the peace for us, to exist here, to reproduce, to make England strong. For five long years we have been at war, and for two long years the war has been here, in the South. The peace comes ever closer to us. Our people, our English troops, surround and protect us, and we are sworn to support them. I would not see them here for all the world. I would not see the *need* of them here. But I cannot plead peace when there is no peace. I can only plead the eventual triumph of peace, at any cost, and now the thing which I fear most, the highest cost of all, threatens us. It has happened all about us, everywhere but here: civil war."

His sturdy fist moved slowly, clenched, with force, on the table. "Brother against brother, neighbor against neighbor, father against son. In the North these things have been taken for granted, an inherent part and parcel of the background of war. All through the South it has been taken for granted. Except for us . . . one infinitesimal, minute speck of dust on the face of the earth, one little known and little cared about frontier settlement, keeping the peace. How few we are here, how well we have stood together. But all around us in the back country, the mountain areas of every province in the colonies, do we stand together? Are we a homogeneous group? We are not. We cannot be. From Charleston to the middleland our English planters fear their own slaves. Our Quakers and Germans remain neutral, our Scotch-Irish are loyal to this notion of freedom. Our new Scots are with us to a man, and will fight as loyally for us as they did for themselves on their own highlands. And how do you hold, how keep civil peace among so many incongruous elements? In Georgia they have hanged we Loyalists as traitors . . . we, traitors, hanged by the true traitors.

And we turn on them in reprisal . . . burn their homes, destroy their crops, girdle their shade trees, fire their rice plantations." Now the heat, and the weariness came into his tone. "This is not war! This is vandalism, barbarism, and I will not see it here!"

Then the heat left him, and he said quietly, "Whom did I hear say they pitied the rebel commander who went to our General Prevost with a flag of truce and the suggestion that South Carolina remain neutral until the end of the war? You, wasn't it, Richard?"

"Yes," Jordan said in a low voice.

"Pity! I felt no pity. I felt what that man must have felt when Prevost refused even to see him, and demanded unconditional surrender. I felt his relief, his pride, at the chance to begin again, to fight again. He was the underdog, that rebel, he was the weak man with pride. And even with the new chance before him, he must have known he had gone down to defeat. They all must know it. For we are going to win this war, we Englishmen. We are going to look back upon this revolt, someday soon, as a rich and horrible moment in our expansion. Our troops hold every major coastal city from Charleston to Savannah, the coast is ours, our forces have overrun the South." He held them, steady, compelling, venerable. "Are we now, on the very brink of victory and peace, to lower ourselves in the eyes of the Crown by murdering one lone man . . . two men, three men . . . out of spite and anger?"

The silence lay upon them again. A little Negro boy came in, barefooted, soundless, and filled the tankards.

"No," Alwyn said, "no. In every province but ours, men who are not soldiers, men who are not ambitious enough to be soldiers, fight one another, kill one another. The whole back country seethes around us, and we have thus far stood staunch in our loyalty, above so loathsome a thing as civil war. We must stay that way." He picked up his glass. "Gentlemen, the King."

They drank. Looking up over the rim of his tankard, Brant could see how tired his father was after his outburst, not necessarily from the physical strain on body and fist and voice, but tired in his mind. He stood up and threw one leg over the wooden bench, as if he mounted a saddle. "We been here over an hour," he said. "They going to bust the door down if Lex doesn't open up for 'em."

He and Malcolm looked at one another in distaste. Malcolm said, "You'll come in for the funeral, then?"

"Why not? Might be interesting. Might be whoever killed Hanson will come up and tell us all about it."

"Wait a minute," Lex Whiting said. He stood up, a rotund figure in his white apron. "I was just thinking, Alwyn, Lavinia and I wouldn't be at all averse to taking Authie Stoner on here, if she's willing. We've only Leonard and Opium now to help out, and Lavinia could use her in the kitchen."

William Lyons nodded approvingly. "I'd be glad to take whatever stock she's got up there," he said, "and sell the farm for her."

"That would be the ideal solution, not only for Authie, but for us," Alwyn said. "If we can keep her in sight there's at least a hope that this may blow over before more blood is shed."

The little Negro boy had swung back the inn doors. The men of Benton's Crossing, so long denied the solace of the inn, started up from the park, from under the trees, from the smithy and Sheller's. Their mingled voices made a muted thirsty roar, like sea water in the afternoon stillness.

The council members filed out, but Alwyn stood in the doorway, pipe in hand, looking out of the cave of darkness into the dusty glare. The light lay like melted butter in the courtyard, where another little Negro boy sat flatly beside a wooden bucket of water, scrubbing unenthusiastically at the stones with a pig-bristle brush. Richard Jordan stopped beside him. Their voices came clearly back to Alwyn, Jordan's teasing, the boy's full of mournful acceptance.

"What in the world are you doing, Opium?"

"Wu'kin'."

"Your intelligence certainly encourages your indolence, Opium. You are the only boy I know can devise some method of sitting down at any task you undertake."

"You is standin' where I washed, Rev'rint."

Alwyn Quantrell smiled automatically. Men passed him now, entering the inn, but he still stood, looking out, half lost in his own trouble.

For it was trouble, to be wise and strong, to be, as it were, monarch, prophet, counselor. Sometimes he came to the disaster, sometimes the disaster came to him, and all disaster was as personal, as human to him, as the tragedies and disasters of his own life. That is a gift, a talent born in some men, that though they walk as men, mind transcends, mind binds to mind, mind absorbs and thinks and understands as other minds, nerves quiver in unison with the nerves of other men, heart accepts and feels without question what the other heart feels, eye sees the light and the darkness behind other eyes. And the whole is a rapport beyond science, beyond metaphysics, not in any sense of the supernatural or mystic, but in the frank and terrible knowledge of human need, human dependence upon humanity. And it is beyond understanding, beyond wisdom; it is nothing a man acquires or learns, it is something native to him; and it enslaves and imprisons him all his life; it roots him fast in the entwining, unbreakable coils of the human despair which springs about him, so that this gift is a gift which a man may well do without.

4

THE BURYING WAS OVER. Nowhere had a face betrayed. The sun beat down. Aster and goldenrod spilled around the headstones. The open grave was a raw sore in the heat. Richard Jordan's voice droned interminably. And Authie Stoner stood straight and unweeping in her black bombazine, and turned away alone, at the last, to her new duties at the inn.

The men left the graveyard in little drifts and gusts and eddies, bound for Sheller's or the Bear or the park, bound for talk and surmise and speculation: William Lyons; the smith, Sam Ashe and his son Hal; Mortimer Post, Race Halpern, Henry Johnston, Newley Ballentyne and his sons Newley, Arthur and John; Garlin Gresham and his son Harley; Del Shaver, the Deans, McCulloughs and Mosebys, the Reddings and Langs and the two old Lamouree brothers. They moved on the high surging crest of temporary excitement and elation. No birds sang. No breeze stirred. The leaves lay together, dry and dusty. Horses and mules breathed shortly under the trees.

Hooves sounded hollow on the hard, burned road, and the men looked up and saw the two women riding in, over the crossing. Brant, standing in the roadway, said, "It's Sabrina."

"Ah, no," his father said, "I told her not to come."

The men took off their hats now, or touched the brims with the tips of their fingers before turning into the inn. Under the oaks before Sheller's, the two young women sat their horses.

Alwyn Quantrell said, "I asked you not to come, Sabrina. And you, Honora, your uncle would be most displeased."

"It is my fault, Uncle Alwyn." The fair girl who rode with Sabrina reached down to him. "We were riding and suddenly we were here. I've no excuse to make for either of us." Her face was unearthly, ethereal, when she smiled. He could not be angry with Honora Brevard, who had grown up with his children, who had spent a good share of her growing up in his house. In the soft, almost frightened face there was a childish gentleness, an unawareness. The long light hair gleamed under her blue tricorn, and she rode straight and proudly, for she was niece and ward of the wealthiest man in the territory, and had been bred to the might and power of the highest Loyalist tradition.

"It's all right," Alwyn said, forgiving her out of the depths of an affection nearly as strong as that which he bore for his own children. "We shall be going back when the sun's down a bit."

Her face lighted like a flower unfolding in the sun. "Hello, Brant," she said. Her mare threw up its head, protesting the uncontrollable tightening of her hands on the reins. "We've come to ride you back."

"Bless your pretty heart," Brant said. But he did not look at her; he held his sister's horse's head. His voice lost itself under the voices of Honora Brevard and his father, but it was savage and came from behind clenched teeth. "I told you not to ride this horse, didn't I? Didn't I?" And Sabrina regarded him with love and amusement and slid down out of the saddle.

They waited under the trees in the park for the sun to lower, for their men to start home. Opium came and took their horses to the stable behind the inn. They sat companionably, the women, Brant, Malcolm, except for Alwyn, who stayed apart from them, thoughtful and withdrawn.

From a little distance he surveyed the young people: Honora Brevard sitting close to Brant on the bench, her gloved hand lightly on his arm; Sabrina beside her, with her floppy hat pushed recklessly on the back of her head; Malcolm standing, with one foot on the bench, barely touching Sabrina's skirts, bidding with silence for Sabrina's attention. Their voices, their attitudes, lay beautifully in his hearing and sight, and he observed with pleasure.

"We could have syllabubs." Sabrina, in a tone which implied she had given the possibility profound thought.

"Syllabubs. Of course. Fraser, you'll get us syllabubs, won't you?" Honora, the echo, hands clasped together in anticipation, like a child.

Malcolm, scowling. "Here comes Ballentyne, let him get them."

Alwyn watched Newley Ballentyne lumber up through the park, pink and jowly and intent. He was big and moved without grace, and he held his hat before him in his hands, not knowing what to do with either the hat or the hands. Alwyn's heart slowed in his breast, for this was the man who wanted his daughter, and who seemed determined to assuage his want with the actuality of the having. Well, no man was ever the father's choosing for his daughter, and no woman the mother's choosing for her son, and he was alone in this, without a wife to him, a mother to Sabrina, to help him. And he had told her long ago he would never stand in her way.

"Hello, you all," Newley Ballentyne was saying, still clutching his hat as if he were about to sink into the ground and had only the hat to cling to.

"Hello, Newley," Sabrina said pleasantly. She was slouched against the bench now, swinging her foot, one arm up along the back of the bench. Her hand moved as though of its own will and touched Fraser Malcolm's boot like a caress. Malcolm saw rather than felt the touch, and his eyes went sharply to her face and saw her looking up under the floppy brim of her hat, right at Ballentyne, looking like a vixen enticing the dogfox off to a ferny meadow in the spring, promising the dogfox something he wasn't due for and probably wouldn't ever get. The bitch, Malcolm thought, playing us against one another, or trying to. He moved his foot and said, "Newley, go get the ladies some syllabubs from the Bear."

"Me go?" Ballentyne said. "I just got here. Why'n't you go?"

For answer, Malcolm sat down beside Sabrina, crowding her. At his deliberation Sabrina's mask dropped. "Oh, for heaven's sake, Newley, go get them," she said irritably.

"Well, all right, if you say so," he said with dignity, and crushed his hat upon his head and lumbered off again.

Honora broke into a fit of giggling. "How can you stand him, Brina? Does he still come to see you on Saturday evenings?"

Sabrina shrugged, with a motion much like her brother's. "Newley's not a bad sort. Fraser, stop pushing me." Then she said, under her breath, "Fraser . . ." and sat suddenly quiet, rigid, looking down and away from him.

A dog came up importantly, lifted its leg against the rear leg of the bench, and looked at them with derisive eyes. Sabrina leaned forward and snapped her fingers. "Here, boy. Here, boy." The dog trotted off, ignoring her. They sat in stillness; Honora's head was close to Brant's shoulder now. A little breeze came fluttering along the ground and picked itself up and drifted across their faces. Two honey bees followed in its wake, as if they rode scent in the wind. The leaves stirred over their heads. Gratitude touched them as the little wind had. Sabrina studied her father, lost in himself, a short distance away.

Beside her, still scowling, arms crossed on his chest, Malcolm dug her with his elbow. "In case you've never seen Newley Ballentyne clearly before, take a look now."

She looked and saw Ballentyne, rolling like a sailor across from the Bear, a great hulk bearing ludicrously the cold, frothy cream-and-sherry drinks. "Don't laugh at him," she said. Her shoulders shook with laughter. Malcolm could feel the tremoring of her body as she laughed. Angrily he said, "New for you to laugh at Ballentyne, isn't it? I thought you two were as good as betrothed." And she kept shaking with the silent laughter.

The women sipped at their drinks. From time to time Alwyn looked soberly at them, not speaking. Once Brant drank from Honora's glass while she held it for him, flushed and smiling. Malcolm deliberately, gently, leaned against Sabrina. Newley Ballentyne, back to a tree, stood with lips pursed as if to whistle, studying the sky overhead with self-defensive importance. After a time Malcolm could stand it no longer. He seized Sabrina's glass, drained the drink, and thrust the glass at Newley.

"Get us another, Ballentyne."

He came away from the tree enraged. "Now see here . . ." he began threateningly.

"Newley," Sabrina said, "please be nice. You're the biggest, strongest man here, and you make me so happy when you take such good care of us."

He looked at her. "Well, all right," he said, and took their glasses and went off to the Bear again.

"Get rid of him," Malcolm said under his breath.

"You get rid of him, you're the one doesn't like him," she said coolly.

"You do? I don't believe you, Brina."

And she swung her foot and looked bored and sighed, as if at his vast stupidity.

"Get rid of him. Ask me to supper. Let me ride you home."

"No," she said. "My, that breeze feels nice."

"What's got into you anyway? Is Ballentyne coming tonight? Or maybe McLeod?"

She did not answer, but he saw her whiten with anger. When the silence fell between them he closed his eyes, seeing her as he had seen her for the first time in his life, eleven years ago, when he first came to Benton's Crossing. She had been fifteen then, with wide, startled eyes and a great mane of hair which hung to her waist, long-legged and perpetually inquisitive, but already showing signs of the aloof coolness which characterized her. At fifteen a girl child lives in a world of her own; the armor the knights wear has not yet rusted, and there is no such state as disillusionment. He knew this, and so was both amused and moved when, at fifteen, and the first time he had ever seen her, she had looked up at him on his horse in the yard of her father's farm and said, "I have almost reached marriageable age, you know."

He knew too that when she was sixteen, any mention of this dreadful incident (for it is the kind of incident fathers and brothers use to tease) would send her from the house and into the woods in a passion of restlessness (it did not make her cry, for she was Sabrina Quantrell, she was not just-any-sixteen-year-old). When she was seventeen she tried to ignore him, and when she was eighteen she was mistress of herself and treated him lightly, like an old friend, as if she had completely forgotten the shameful thing. But it was not shameful to him, and when she was eighteen, and ripe and handsome, he began to remember it again, and when he remembered, it stood like a thin gray shadow in his mind, moving wraith-like in his brain in the night, tormenting him subtly in the hot dawns and still nights. So that on a Sunday evening, after the church meeting, while the children played about the stones in the burying ground and the elders spread a picnic supper in the park,

31

he had walked her up through the burying ground and the screaming, racing children, and across the meadow where the daisies
rippled like foam over the grass and the bluebells spilled down the
banks like blue fire, and the mist lay so low in the hollows that the
bluebells seemed to grow in water, with one star palely imprinted
on the still-daylight sky. And he remembered everything of that
evening, that she had laughed easily and lightly with him, that they
had spoken of horses and dogs and her father, and near the end,
before it happened, he told her how he had gone out for Del
Shaver's wife's confinement, and right in the middle of the delivery
the bed fell apart, and they had become hysterical with laughter
in the lovely summer twilight, with the bluebells clinging about
their knees. And he did not touch her. And she said how she heard
if you could come up on a skunk and fall on him from the front, he
couldn't do anything to you and you could take him home and fix
him and have a real nice house pet, and he said how he'd had to
reopen Billy Lee Macon's gunshot wound because it was healing
from the outside in. And she said did he think it was possible that
red bone hound of McLeod's had somehow got mixed up with a
wolf, because you never saw such wolf-looking pups as that hound
threw? And he did not touch her. And just as they entered the long
cool fringe of wood beyond the meadow, beyond the bluebells, a
little black snake slid out from under their feet, and she ran in
blind feminine panic; ran so hard and so far that long before she
finished running she was laughing at herself, half in exhaustion,
half in the sheer joy of laughter, so that by the time he caught up
with her they were in the woods: in the deep-mossed, water-cool
stillness. The trees arched over them like a cathedral with a still,
lacy dome, a vaulted arch of green, deep darkness, and the nameless, numberless white blossoms trembled in the moss like tears.
And the world was hushed and fragrant of tree and leaf and flower
and moss; the earth overpowered in the rich dark fecundity of leaf
mold; the earth shaped the mind with its stillness and darkness
and coolness, so that a last bird song rang sweet as a bell in the
distance, and a last moment of sunlight did not fall, but rather
ascended, like a rosy transparent spire, from the mossy hollow. And
still he did not touch her; even reaching for her hands to raise her
from the gray moss where she had fallen, he did not touch her
really, for he laughed too at that moment, and there was only an
impersonal, companionable contact in the touching of hands. The

only thing he did not remember was when the laughter died, or why, but he could recall the instant like a sword in him when he succumbed to the overpowering, when he let his mind be shaped, so that there had been a painful, beautiful bursting of light, and he had moved swiftly (but not involuntarily, for there was purpose in him) and buried his face in the warm pliant flesh, in the hollow at the base of her throat, where the darkness and the fragrance of the woods lay like honey. And the magic hands that healed bruises and stitched cuts and cured fevers, that had cared for her all her girlhood, were still magic, still cared, but in a different way, a way of power and demand and certainty. But not with resistance to her own will, for when she put up her hands and repelled him and stood breathing deeply, looking at him, he let her. He stood, with his right hand clasping his upper left arm, as though he sought to hold back the flow of blood from a wound. He said, "You asked me once. Now I ask you. If you say no I will never ask you again."

And she said, with the last light lying like a pool in the hollow of her throat, where his face had been, "No."

They came back quietly, not speaking, not touching, save when he took her hand to help her over a fallen tree (impersonal touch again, but no longer companionable) and the bluebells stood unmoving on the slopes now, and dark, dark, and the star had lost its softness, and the first thing he saw, returning to the elders and the children and the supper under the trees, was Alwyn Quantrell's face, full of watchfulness. The first thing he saw was the anxiety fade, and the overt relief on the father-face at their innocent return.

Now, rebuffed, repulsed, toyed with, knowing she did not want him and yet would not let him go, he thought, but she is an old maid. Twenty-six she would be, and an old maid. Not that she was without suitors, heaven knew; there had been suitors since she was eighteen, tried, found wanting, banished (not by Alwyn, but by Sabrina herself). And now at twenty-six the field had narrowed to Newley Ballentyne, whose one great passion in life was cows, and the Scot, Ian McLeod, dirt-poor and lonely on his little farm and twice Sabrina's age. He, Fraser Malcolm, appeared out of the running, and what did it do to a man's ego, knowing he could not outrun such tortoise-runners?

There was Newley Ballentyne beside him again, red-faced and perspiring. He rose from the bench, hating Ballentyne and Sabrina and Brant and the simpering Brevard girl, and walked across the grass to Alwyn Quantrell and thought, here is the only face, the only man among us without deception, without artifice. He put his hand on the old man's shoulder. "Alwyn," he said.

Alwyn started and looked at him as though he had been awakened rudely, roughly. "Ah, Fraser," he said.

"What lies in your mind, Alwyn? It has been an unpleasant day, true, but now it is over, and the girl cared for. Surely you're not worried?"

Alwyn smiled up at him wryly. "We've gone along so well here, Fraser. So well. We have kept ourselves whole and strong, and no dissatisfaction has eaten away the edges of our unity. Until now."

"The prophet hints at defeat?" Malcolm said, trying to comfort him. "The prophet who lifts us all to believe that no such word exists?"

"But some of us are born to hold to our beliefs in the very face of a truth which directs otherwise."

Malcolm turned. His cold black eyes moved restlessly, penetratingly over the little group on the bench. "And some of us are born to adore cows" (how bovine in truth Ballentyne's moist brown eye) "and some to suffer, not knowing why we suffer, indeed, perhaps not even knowing we suffer" (his eyes were overlong on Sabrina) "and some to go through life treading dangerously close to the brink of unreality" (how beautiful, how full of love, Honora Brevard's shallow blue gaze) "and some" (the son's impassive handsome face) "to . . . forgive me, Alwyn, step easily along a path cleared and broken always by others."

The old man nodded, unoffended. "I wish I was not so tired, Fraser."

"I know," Malcolm said. He was filled with affection and regard. Why, he was old, Alwyn was old, and worn with a hundred cares, and they, selfish beyond all bearing, still looked to him to hold them together, to keep them in perfect functioning unity, to provide from some inexhaustible wellspring of strength the heart and soul of their day-to-day living, their cause. The cares he would sustain with stoicism, even with eagerness, but they, the selfish, the dependent, would kill him. But Fraser Malcolm hardened himself to the luxury of sentimentalism.

"Ride home to Brandyhill with us," Alwyn said.

"I cannot, I've a confinement due. When it's over I'll ride out."

They shook hands. He thought he had never seen Alwyn look so

34

sad. Saying his farewell to the women, he struck out at Sabrina, bending over her hand. "Your father asked me out for supper. I regret I must decline." And he felt the pride come back in him at her disconcerted eyes.

He was in the Bear, drinking straight corn whiskey, when he saw them go back, out of Benton's Crossing: Brant loose and easy in the saddle, riding close to Honora Brevard, so that they nearly touched, horse and horse, man and girl; Sabrina beside her father, the line of her body as supple as a young willow in the spring, as young as youth beside the tall, heavy-set old man; Ballentyne bringing up the rear with a wagonload of supplies from Aiken Sheller's, rawboned and slack-bodied behind his mules.

Now communication between them had been severed, the old man going home in the late afternoon, the young man relaxed in the coolness of the inn. For the old man, carrying within himself a heart too huge for any man, thought of the day, of the murdering and the burying, of the inherent threat which lay in the murdering and the burying; thought of the meadow-springing of emptiness and coldness and hatred which grow like winter wheat in the September of the mind. And the young man, eyes narrowed over his glass, had forgotten all this, and thought only of the woman, Sabrina, and yearned for the darkness of the summer forest in which they had once stood.

5

THE SKY was stained with dawn, like a great half pearl emerging from dusky seas, lit from beneath, so that soft golds and apricots washed over its polished surface, washed and receded and returned as faint blues, as pale roses. Transparent and virginal, the half pearl of the sky drowned itself in beauty, in coloring of petal and of earth and of sea, bearing like a chalice the tender hue, the gentleness, the lovely light. These were the times of day, dawn and evening, when the half pearl went back into the dusky mauve seas, that the old man loved best. He watched the sky from his front porch, standing with his hand on the rail, waiting until the first curved lip of sun appeared on the horizon before he turned back to his room.

A breeze still moved at the window, blowing back the curtains. He sat down at the little round table, groping under the pile of papers, and at last drew forth a journal covered in deer hide. His door was open. He could hear Jewel in the kitchen, stirring up the fire, setting some heavy object on the hearthstone . . . kettle or spider, he thought. She sang softly to herself, words he could not distinguish, or perhaps could not understand; or perhaps they were not words at all, but only the high, humming, tuneless crooning of her race, born of and nourished by untold generations in unknown jungle clearings. After a time he smelled the breakfast fire taking hold and heard the hollow clacking of a wooden spoon going round and round in a wooden bowl.

He opened the journal at random and read, thinking he should know it by heart after all these years, all this time.

"October 29, 1777—On this day called Meeting of the Provincial Council at the Bear, on Arrival of Rider with news of Great battle in the North wherein a vast Army of our General Burgoyne was defeated by an Army of the Rebels (their Northern Army, so-called) at a place named Saratoga in the Colony of York on October seventh. This news we were Hard put upon to Believe in, but the Rider assured that it was indeed true, and many Gallant Englishmen had been killed in the action. It is greatly feared that the Rebels have won a Decisive victory for their side. Decisive it may be, but Certainly Disastrous for us. I must now Procure maps and study the Strategy employed in this Battle. Colonel Allerton of Hardington says he Believes this will be cited as a Major Battle. I Grieve at the necessity of concurring.

"June 10, 1779—Today saw first Detachment of British troops in Benton's Crossing, on Recruiting mission. They appeared in good health and spirits, and we found their Confidence contagious. Some Loyalist troops were with them, and some of our young men make Ready to go also.

"August 5, 1779—William Lyons returned from Charleston on this day, and reports at the Council Meeting that the City is in Abominable condition and very Filthy. These Misfortunes we attribute to the military occupation and feel utmost Distress for our brave men bent upon Securing the Coast. Richard brought the Meeting to a close with a Prayer for the Crown and all our men now in Loyalist Regiments.

"August 12, 1779—This day it was my Pain to hear that my brothers-in-law, the brothers of my first Wife, have embraced not our Cause, but that of the Rebels, and that they have marched to join the Forces in the North. After much Debate with myself, went to their cabin and found it closed and all their Possessions and dogs gone, except for a puppy which lay dead of starvation in the yard. I cannot write more. I am very tired.

"February 16, 1780—Distressing news reached us today of Civil uprisings all about the Colony. It would seem the Whigs ambush us, or we ambush the Whigs, and there is great bloodshed and sorrow Attendant upon this affair. Thank God our majority is loyal. The Council today pledged to keep order in our Territory, but voted our women must not travel about without Armed Escort. A sad Progress toward Peace. A suggestion by Aiken Sheller that a local militia be Organized was voted down, with Doctor Malcolm leading the Resistance. While I first Believed it a good Plan, I find as I write this that I have Fought too many Wars, and Fraser is right."

For a long time he sat quietly, while the breeze died at the window and the curtains arranged themselves in motionlessness. Then he leafed through the journal, picked up his quill pen, and wrote steadily: "October 11, 1780—Yesterday buried Hanson Stoner in the Graveyard at Benton's Crossing. He died of hanging, in a Black deed performed by our own People. Mistress Stoner is now alone and must needs go in Service at the Bear, to which Alexander and Lavinia have kindly Agreed."

In the room behind his own he heard his sons, Brant and Timothy, astir, Brant's voice clear and refreshed with sleep, the little boy, the child of his old age, husky when he spoke, as if he slept even while waking. They would go to the chores now, the milking of the cows and the goat, the gathering of the eggs, the feeding of the chickens, returning to splash noisily at the wash basin by the back door, to douse their dark handsome heads and brush their teeth with hickory twigs, and come at last ravenous to Jewel's hot breakfast. These were the scenes, the sounds, the knowledges, the intimacies of family and home, of fullness and richness in the heart, which he knew so well and which were forever novel. And yet there were times when he heard the sleep-husky voice of the little boy with a pang which made his blood burn. For there had been a time in his life when he had thought it a pity a man always had his memories with him, dragging along behind, intangible as shadows and sharp as knives; a shame you couldn't turn memory off, that there wasn't some sort of bar you could drop decisively, some mental block, so that everything which went before in a man's life was forgotten. Now he knew that a memory could be as rich and sustaining as hope is, or a dream; that a man's soul could feed on it as heartily and as well as on that also-intangible hope of future which, attained or unrealized, was destined to become tomorrow's memory. He knew that when he heard the boy's voice, when the huskiness broke in the throat at last, and the laughter sounded clear in the morning full-awakeness.

He sat reflectively at the table, turning the pen over and over in steady hands. He had lived sixty-two summers and he was still vigorous and active, with all his limbs intact and his eyesight good and his heart strong, and he was thankful. But he died a little all the time now, as he had been dying for all the years since he had come into his land, and as he would keep dying until his breath stopped and his eyes glazed and the memory was shut off as he once believed it should be. And now he died a little more quickly, in fear, in uncertainty, in atavism; and he wondered if the day would come when he would hear with weariness, with displeasure, the words he had heard so often, all his mature years:

Ask Alwyn Quantrell. Go to Brandyhill and ask Alwyn Quantrell.

Before him, before he became the man they asked, the land had been his father's, and before that it had been wilderness and Indians had walked it and the countless furred and winged creatures of earth and sky had enriched it with their droppings and their bones. The house had been his father's, with its colored glass on either side of the door, and the veranda, with the ironwork the Spaniard Diego had brought from New Orleans, and the path worn smooth by three generations of Quantrells, coming up from the road a half mile away and going around the house and up to the barn, weathered gray and half hidden in lilac planted by his mother when she was still a bride. The house was in a little hollow. It was the barn which stood on the hill, indomitable on its stone foundation, dominating because it had been built before the house, and had been half-house and half-barn when it was built. His father, the first Alwyn, and the first Alwyn's bride, Caroline Amanda, and the little boy, Paul, who had a club foot and quiet eyes, and the oxen and the chickens and the horses had lived in it before the house was built in the hollow. After they came, Caroline Amanda had picked the wild berries in the thicket, and they had called it Brandyhill. That too was memory: that his mother had named this land with a name which had in it a sweetness and tartness and a sense of height and a rich wildness. And the earth was red and good here, and the corn grew tall in the hot summer nights and the melons spread their bristly green leaves and tangled vines, and the tobacco grew too, enough for a man to pack away for the pipes of the coastal aristocracy and live well on the profit. There was more fish, more game, than any hundred men could ever catch, shoot, salt, cure, store. The Indians did not bother them, the silent, suspicious, brooding Catawbas who were always near, always a threat. They came sometimes, and went, and came again because the white man genuinely liked them, because the innate sincerity which was in him reached them.

That first year, when they lived in the barn, the little boy, Paul, with the twisted foot was born, and the second year, after they had built the house, the little girl, Charity. Now they had the cabin, with two good strong rooms, and a kitchen and lean-to attached, and outside the land lay rich and moist and there was the time and the blessed solitude and the splendor of the land. Then Caroline Amanda's father died in Virginia and left her a little money; with it they bought clapboard for the cabin, laying it over the log so that there was a double thickness of wall; they ordered the grillwork and the colored glass and the door with iron hinges, and a pony for Pauly to ride.

But the child never rode the pony, the child's twisted foot had held him back, had given him mercilessly to the coiled brown copperhead under the rock shelf, and when everything that could be done was not enough, they sent for the wrinkled old Catawba with the stiff scalp lock who waved feathers and blew smoke and that was not enough either, and the child lay now in a little grove of pines behind the house.

Three months later Alwyn was born, and he was sound and healthy as the little girl, Charity, but his coming changed nothing for Caroline Amanda. She did not recover after Alwyn's birth, but she did not die, clinging to life as if somewhere in the days ahead, if only she might survive, that little figure with the twisted foot would rise from under its stone and come hobbling down from the grove with its arms outstretched to her. And out of her own tragedy she wrought far worse, tutoring, adoring, protecting the little girl from the world of snakebite outside the door.

But young Alwyn was his father in the house again, full of peace and gentleness, yet with a core of resolution and strength which was not in his father. Young Alwyn could whistle a bird until the bird came almost to his hand; young Alwyn could build a trap in the evening and be sure of a weasel in the morning. He could shoot straight and handle a bow as well as the Catawba boys who taught him; he could creep a snake and kill it before the snake knew he was there, and there was no twisted foot to betray him. From the time he could tell the corn from the weeds, he worked. As Charity studied and sewed and grew the flowers her mother loved and kept fresh bouquets on the little grave under the pines, so Alwyn hoed in the fields and built fences and milked and plowed and hauled stone, and read and studied. He did this by himself, for Alwyn would not force his son; when the boy was fifteen he began on what Charity had already forgotten, and the English took him to Latin and the Latin to Greek, and when he tired of it he played the fiddle and sang to himself, singing the things he had made for himself and the world that was Brandyhill, and when he was eighteen he sang for a girl who lived twelve miles away and whose name was Sarah Ann Yancy.

Alwyn and his bride and the thin wisp that was Charity were in the house when the old people died. Caroline Amanda went first, as old Alwyn had wanted it, quietly and with a faint smile, as if she could see what she had looked for so long on the path to the pine grove. Old Alwyn went on awhile, not losing his faculties, seeing the daughter he regretted grow drier and wispier and the son he loved take over the land. He did not smile when he died, but when Alwyn closed the still-warm eyelids, something in his father's face hurt him, deeply, inside, as if the father had turned toward the path, and the woman and the child waited.

Charity lived on, a roll of gray dust in the corner which Sarah Ann Yancy Quantrell's busy broom and sharp eye had somehow overlooked. Alwyn had been twenty when he married, taking Sarah Ann off the Yancys' little place, and away from three brothers who farmed and manufactured stump water and hunted coon. They were big, quiet, bearded men. Alwyn liked them. They never said whether they liked him or not; they never said much of anything, but they left a jug of the clear fiery liquor for him now and then and took him with them after coon on frosty moonlit nights. Now he could remember more clearly than anything that part of his prime: Sarah Ann's bearded brothers and the rime of white frost on the ground, and the dogs baying ahead of them in the winter moonlight.

They were married two years before Brant was born, a too big baby who gave Sarah Ann a good deal of trouble, but whose feet were perfectly formed. Brant was two, when, following the old pattern, the girl, Sabrina, came. But she was in no way like her Aunt Charity, the little roll of dust in the corner, and Sarah Ann vowed silently that she would never be. But Sarah Ann's vow could not be kept, silent as it was, for something had gone wrong inside her, and there was pain, and no doctor in the Crossing, and the infection grew and spread and finally killed her. Alwyn could remember that too: the long night of waiting for her to die, and the three brothers sitting behind the ironwork grill and the wisteria, smoking quietly, with the jug between their feet. After she closed her eyes they left the jug and went home, whistling for the hounds which were always swarming about their legs and which had strayed off to fight with the Quantrell dogs.

The terrifying prospect of the future lay before Alwyn. He had two small children in the house, one a baby in arms, and he had only Charity to care for them. Still, when he decided, wrestling with his sorrow in the darkness, that he would take the children into the settlement and find someone to care for them, Charity was adamant in her refusal to allow him to let them go. She surprised him by her show of spirit; he saw that there was still a spark under the surface of her defeat. "I will not fail you, Alwyn," she said, but her voice was soft and timorous when she said it.

That was the year he bought Jewel, because she had just lost a baby of her own, and could nurse Sabrina. Charity could not protest this, except to say mildly that a white woman. . . . And Alwyn said fiercely, find me a white woman with milk, then. And Jewel came, born in slavery on a coastal plantation and sent away because the child she lost was that of her master's son, but he never got used to the sight of the baby's fair head against the full black breast. He was still not used to it in his remembering.

He measured, or remembered, things by the year. It was the year Joe Harley got shot by that drunken mule skinner. It was the year Ian McLeod came. It was the year we got Jewel. It was the year the Brevards came, with their little niece and their forty slaves, and built their fine brick house two miles distant. But he had something else by which to measure that year, and he did not like to remember. A drummer came through mending pots, a man in his late forties, lean and hungry-looking and with the mark of drink on his tight mouth. He ate with them and mended a kettle in return for his meal. He had a wagon, covered over with canvas, and two mules, and when he went, Charity went with him.

She left a message in her frail spidery hand, on the family Bible. It did not say much. It said, "I told you once I would never fail you. Now I have failed you." He never heard from her again. He would have liked to hear from her; he often thought of her, he often hoped she was happy, but he thought the chance of that was slim. He might have cursed his dead mother, but he did not do that either. He thought even if he knew Charity were dead, or that the drummer beat her on Friday nights, or that she too had taken to drink and mending pots, he would feel better about it. But he never knew.

On a summer evening he went to see his dead wife's brothers. Coming up the rise to their cabin, he felt hot and awkward, not nervous but awkward, for he had not been here since Sarah Ann died. A fox barked his queer strangled bark on the ridge behind the cabin. Limpid and pure in the moonlight, the song of a mocking bird rang down the pathway beaten smooth by Yancy feet. Then the dogs began to bark, and Trace, the young hound, came to him growling, tail rigid, and Alwyn spoke reassuringly to him and went on, with the dog sniffing at the horse's hooves. The three men, Joe and Luke and Darby, sat on the sagging stoop of the cabin. Joe, the eldest, was busy with the oldest of the hounds, searching him for ticks. At the corner of the house the puppies whimpered and fell and worried at one another's ears. Alwyn dismounted and pulled off his hat and stood before the three men in the moonlight.

"Good evening," he said.

Joe looked up from his search of the old hound's flank. "Evenin', Al'n."

Alwyn took a deep breath. "I came to tell you something," he said.

They waited. Joe went back to his search.

"You boys know I've been lonely since Sarah Ann died," Alwyn said. "It's not right a man should be alone when he's still young and when he's got two small children in his house. Children ought to have a mother to take care of them, not be brought up by a man and a slave."

They did not say anything. Alwyn took another breath and plunged on. "I'm aiming to ask that young widow in the Crossing to marry me and I wanted you to know about it first."

Joe tugged. The hound whimpered.

"You can't say I wasn't good to Sarah Ann, and kind." He wanted to say, you know I loved her, but he thought that might be saying too much. "But it's not right, with the children. And I wanted you to know."

After a moment Joe straightened and looked at him. "You want a drink, Al'n?"

"I'd be grateful," Alwyn said.

They handed him down the jug and he tipped it up and felt the liquor run down his throat like liquid fire. He handed the jug back and they took it silently. Then Joe said, "You figger you gonna find time to do a little huntin' this fall, Al'n?"

"I'll find it, all right," Alwyn said.

They were silent.

"I've got to be going back. Thank you kindly for the drink."

He was halfway down the path when Joe called. "Al'n."

He went back.

"Them pups is jest weaned. Trace's strain. You want one?"

The puppies huddled and cried in the moonlight. Alwyn dismounted again and caught a pup up in his hands; it shivered and wet on his palm. When he looked up, Joe had gone back to searching the dog. Luke and Darby sat with their feet on the rail, smoking. He carried the puppy down the path, feeling its warm bonelessness. He did not hear the fox any more, but the bird still sang, and the puppy went to sleep in his hands.

Before the month was out a circuit preacher (whose name was Richard Jordan and who would soon come to stay) wandered through and married Alwyn and Ellen Bowie, who had been married at seventeen and widowed at nineteen. She had taught school in a settlement in the north of the colony, and he was pleased about that, for it meant not only a mother for his children but a teacher as well. She was nine years younger than he, plain, but with a skin like a baby's and eloquent dark eyes and a quick smile. Her slight teaching experience and the grief of her widowhood had given her a maturity and tranquillity that Alwyn thought sat well upon her. There was none of Sarah Ann's sharpness and fire here, but there were firmer, more lasting things.

They lived quietly and well through the years of the children's growing. Sarah Ann's offspring were dear to Ellen's heart; she tried desperately to have a child of her own, but when the trying was too little she took it cheerfully and with resignation, giving herself, giving too much of herself, to Brant and Sabrina. No son and daughter of their generation were freer to do what they wished when they wished. Brant had gone early to learn what lay in the mountain fastnesses, Sabrina had learned early her role in life of welcoming him home. But the summer that he was eighteen and she sixteen, the stupendous thing occurred. Ellen fainted in the garden and was carried to the house by her stepson. To the distracted ministrations of her family she made no response; to the calm attentions of Jewel she finally rallied. After they put her to bed it was Jewel who made the announcement: it was time people had eyes in their heads and knew something about something. Here they all were in the same house day after day, and she was the only one knew Missy Ellen was going to have a baby. She bet Missy Ellen didn't even know it.

Alwyn was stricken. After fourteen years of marriage one did not go about fainting and having babies when heretofore there had been no fainting and having of babies.

But it was true. With an eighteen-year-old son, a man of a son working at his side, he was faced with the unbelievable prospect of fatherhood again.

Because he had been young when Brant and Sabrina were born, he had been proud. Now he could find no pride in what he had done. He was fifty-two years old and he was to father another child. It was as if he had perpetrated a terrible crime upon the body of the woman, nine years younger than himself, whom he still looked upon as a companion child to his children. Suddenly he could not bear the joy in Ellen's face and the bright flush of color where the first slackening of flesh began on her cheekbones; had he been less

44

sensitive he would not have felt the warm embarrassment which made him keep Brant at arm's length now, nor feigned the gruffness with which he invariably spoke to the women of his household. It took a long time for the shame to die in him, but at last, seeing his daughter and his wife and Jewel busy with small clothes, with the endless preparation, his expectancy mounted. The men of Benton's Crossing poked easy fun at him and the women asked after Ellen, and near the end the excitement communicated itself to him and Ellen Bowie became the most cherished thing in his life, and beyond the mere littleness of loving.

On a late spring day, a month before the baby would be born, he rode into the Crossing and smoked a pipe with Fraser Malcolm and made final arrangements and came back to Brandyhill in the evening, leisurely, full of contentment, with the sky rosy behind him and a mocking bird beginning and the overpowering fragrance of half spring, half summer about him.

The gray thread of supper smoke rose into the windless air and he took pleasure, riding through the open gate and into the yard, in the way his house lay upon his land, and the first candlelight in the windows and the green burgeoning of the garden plot. From somewhere beyond the barn he heard the faint silvery sound of the goats' bells. He dismounted and stood, holding the reins, looking at the green rows of the garden flanked by the turned earth, and then the silence came hard, crushing him, and he saw Jewel in the kitchen doorway, and he had never seen another human being look as Jewel looked in that moment.

After a time he took his pipe from his mouth and held it in his hand and drew breath into his lungs heavily to speak, and before he could speak heard the long, indrawn, wailing rage of the baby. And he moved, his feet like great unfeeling lumps of flesh and bone which carried him unknowing, and pushed past Jewel and went into the kitchen and down the hall to the front room and looked down at Ellen Bowie Quantrell's face and saw she was dead.

Brant said, "She shouldn't have done it. We were here, all of us. We were in the barn, an hour after you left, and Jewel was baking. She wanted water and went for it. I don't know whether it was carrying the water, or whether she fell, or what." And he could say nothing more, his mind swollen with remembering, with the finding of his stepmother's slight little body, distorted with the child she carried, and the overturned bucket, and the lifting her

45

and the seeing her blood, which was not in him, come pouring over his hands.

Because Richard Jordan was ill with fever, John Brevard read from an Episcopalian prayer book, and Alwyn, standing in the pine grove where both his wives lay, stood without support, firmly, standing long after it was over and turning away only when the hand touched him and he looked up, thinking it was Brant. Only it was not Brant, it was Joe Yancy.

"I left you a jug," Joe said.

"Thank you, Joe. I'm obliged." But he did not touch the jug. Late in the afternoon he went into the kitchen and looked down at the baby in Jewel's arms and remembered Jewel holding Sabrina.

"What are you feeding him?"

"Goat milk." Jewel held the baby possessively. "He takin' it good. He got a good strong stomach."

But it was not a baby Jewel held. It was an alien red strangling shapeless thing, hardly flesh and barely bone, which he viewed for a long moment as less human than a puppy. Then the terrible compassion, the hot surging of grief and of tenderness welled in his heart. He got down on his knees and looked long and hard at the sleeping baby, and touched it, and broke at last.

Now, in his sixty-second year, he sometimes thought he could feel all the death he had known, like a faint, not unpleasant twinge deep in his loins when he sat at his table and reread and made entries in the years-long record he kept. Of what use for men to record death, birth, war, the first day of spring, the setting out of onions; of what use to write it all down? Why, for the sake of re-reading it, of course . . . the old endless circle, curving and curving upon itself. . . .

"Hoo, hoo," Jewel said. "Breakfus'. Al'n, you hears me? Breakfus'."

"I'm coming," he said. There, a good sign, an omen of fortune to rise with vigor from the recording of his existence, to think with amusement that the twinge he had identified as a labor pain portending the arrival of death was only a gnawing of hunger after all. And he went down the hall and into the kitchen, seeing the old, routinized, loved scene: Jewel slapping at eager hands, the steam rising from the blue bowls, the tall pitcher of strong black molasses, the used, known surface of the pine table with its familiar scars and markings, his sons (big son, little son) fresh-scrubbed and hard-bodied, waiting for him.

"Why, where's Sabrina?" he said.

The little boy laughed. His laughter was clean and young and his eyes were mischievous. "She had to catch that colt and take him back to pasture. You know what, Father, that colt's getting just like a dog, it follows her around all the time. She says he's a nuisance. Do we have to wait?"

"Nuisance," Brant said, "she enjoys it. Damn it, who let that dog in?"

"Let him stay," Alwyn said. "No, of course don't wait." He sat down and the big blue hound whose eyes had filled with guilt at Brant's tone, looked with relief on Alwyn. He dared lie under the table, close to Alwyn, for he too grew old now; his amber eyes said, we must stay together, you and I. . . .

The little boy said, "Can I help you make the butter, Jewel?"

"You kin not. Last time you was too slow with the salt an' she got all rancy-like. You works outdoors, boy. You better git at that hoein' 'fore the sun gits too high."

They ate in silence, in hunger. The hound dreamed luxuriously of running an enormous rabbit, twitching and crying in his sleep. Sabrina did not return. After a time Alwyn said, "Did Sabrina have any breakfast?"

"She drank two cups tea," Jewel said.

"And she only went to put up the colt?"

"Well," Jewel said defensively, "she did say she might walk down to the falls."

And gone. Just gone.

"Aided and abetted by Jewel," Brant said.

"Now don't use them large words with me," Jewel said. "You only does it to torment me. Other times you can't think of no large words. You jest thinks of 'em when you wants to torment."

Alwyn finished his mush and turned his attention to his tea, blowing away the steam, looking over the rim and down the hall to the front door, a solid oak door painted white and flanked by the narrow leaded panes of colored glass. A long varicolored braided rug ran the length of the hall, and along its edges the wide boards were still dark from Jewel's soap and water.

The house was a clapboard center hall, painted white and built around the original chinked log. The logs, forming an inner wall, ran around the four sides of the two front rooms which branched off the hall. On the left front was Alwyn's room, with heavy drapes at the window and a smoothbore on the wall above his bed, the pine spool bed that his father and mother had died in. Behind it was the boys' room, with the wide bed and the two rows of clothes pegs and the high-backed chair which was a catch-all for Brant's books and papers and which Tag seldom sat on because it was heaped with Brant's treasures and therefore hallowed ground.

At the right front was the room that belonged to all of them, but which had become unused, a museum setting for the things which had been Alwyn's mother's and her mother's before her: the wing back chair and the cherry table, the solid brass spiral candleholders, the velvet drapes grown dusky with age. The patina of the years, of love, of gentleness, of care, lay upon these things; to preserve them, the room directly behind this room was the gathering place, the family place, where Alwyn could leave his papers on the floor and his letters cluttering the pine secretary. There was a fire laid but seldom lighted in the front room; a fire burned continuously, except in hot weather, in the family room, in the interior of the blackened fieldstone fireplace. Alwyn's squirrel rifle, with a brass lock and hand-burled chestnut stock hung over the narrow mantel. The big oval rug was worn and mellowed, so that its colors blurred softly. In the middle of the room was the round maple table where they ate on Sunday and on special days, and which became during the week a council table, an arguing place, headquarters for the silver polishing and the mending. They used the silver tableware on Sunday, the fine worn forks and knives and spoons which had been Alwyn's mother's too, and which matched the silver tea service. Weekdays they used utensils which had been made by Alwyn's father, with bone handles on which tiny carved rabbits fell to the hunter's gun and little foxes raced heavy-legged to hollow logs, pursued by hounds, and miniature squirrels surveyed the slaughter in the woods from leafless trees. It had mattered to his father, Alwyn thought when he used them, how he felt. His feeling, his mood, was reflected in the work. Sometimes man won; sometimes it was the fox or the bear who prevailed in the sheltering carved forests.

There were too in this room the Catawba relics which were Alwyn's father's, and the Cherokee lance which Alwyn had taken from a dead chief in the last uprising. There had also been a painting, *The Dying Moose*, which Sabrina had removed from the wall early in her youth. The painting was the work of her Great Grandmother Wylie, Caroline Amanda's mother. For more years than she cared to remember the bloody-breasted moose had hung on the wall, its head at an impossible angle, its eyes reproachful. She had never felt sorry for it. Had its eyes been filled with anguish, with the last, faint life-light, she might justly have removed it with horror, but its reproachfulness toward the hunter, whom Great Grandmother Wylie had mercifully not attempted to portray, struck her as merely comic.

The kitchen ran the length of the back of the house. It had been added in the middle life of Alwyn's father, and for some years had had a floor of hard-packed red dirt. Alwyn could remember when the wide pine boards were laid. His mother's pothooks still hung in the fireplace with its rough stone hearth, and there were the tavern chairs and the pine table, the tiers of shelves with their everyday dishes and the corner closet which held the bone china. The kitchen was a gathering place too, but mostly it was Jewel's, for she worked in it and bossed it and slept on a pallet in it.

A third of the kitchen was Sabrina's. When she was thirteen they had walled off a room for her, a small room, but one of her own, and it had a window in it, so she did not mind its size. From the window she could see the path to the woodlot and the pine belt, and far up the path, the little plot of graves. To the right were the corncrib and the barn, gray on its steep rise of ground and half hidden in the old lilac.

To the left of the rear hall there were narrow stairs which led to a low attic. The only closet was under the stairs, its ceiling sloping awkwardly, every inch of its space utilized.

There was a well house under the kitchen and a woodshed attached to the rear of the house. Beyond the house were the outhouse and the chicken house and the huge old round of maple, its top chopped and worn shiny from the axe, and the vegetable garden. Rough timbers fenced the rough sloping corral at the rear of the barn. Beyond this fence there were fruit trees, apple and peach and cherry, and beyond the fruit trees, where the woods began, there were wild berries: strawberries in the early summer and a thick tangle of blackberries in the later summer, growing close to the spring hole of cold clear water which bubbled faintly as it rose from the ground. South, toward Benton's Crossing, were the twenty acres of green, breathing corn.

It was a fine strong house and good beautiful land, Quantrell land through inheritance and use and love. And another day here, in which to give thanks for the strength to work the land. . . .

The little boy said, "May I be pardoned, please?"

"Where you going, Tag?" Brant was pushing his own chair back.

"I got to hoe, don't I? You going to hoe?"

"In a little while I'll help you. You see if any those squash still worth workin' with."

The blue hound got up with dignity and looked at Brant, wagging his tail. He had a thick muscular throat and eyes like horehound lozenges. "You want to go, Jim? Come on, boy." The tail moved faster now, but the hound went back to Alwyn. He wanted to be asked, but he wanted to stay with Alwyn; he wanted to be wanted, but he needed the responsibility of making his own decision. Brant went out the back door. A brown hound with white ticking, smaller than Old Jim, came out from under the porch, where he had been lying in the cool dirt, and followed.

Brant went up the path, hands in his pockets. He did not mind the heat in the country like he did in the settlement; here there was air moving, a coolness of breeze and water. Looking off at the mountains, he noted the waves of heat, watery and white in the distance. On the green slope of the pasture by the barn the horses grazed: Sabrina's colt, his gelding, the work horses, the horses bought or inherited from the Brevard stables. From the top of the hill he could see Tag, already standing with his hoe in the squash vines.

The purple vetch still bloomed in the meadow and made fine fodder for the cows. In the field beyond rose the dry shaggy spires of the bergamot, the harsh undelicate goldenrod, the branched purple asters, the creamy discs of the yarrow, each with its single garnet eye, the yellow partridge peas so loved by the fluttering coveys of quail. The ticked hound went ahead, young and lean-bodied, scent hunting, seeming not to see at all but only to smell, as scent hounds do. Where the woods were light and open the foliage of violet and columbine grew golden, far past flowering, and mossy rocks bore clubs of brown seed head. Here another spring rose and ran off as a narrow brook, washing over rocks to form small cataracts, falling into frothing pools. It wandered off to woods which deepened and darkened, where no light fell, so dark a wood, and so rich, that only the wild orchids grew there in summer, and the taller, more elegant fern. The earth was a cushion of pine needles, springy underfoot, and the silence was heavy in the ear, and no birds sang. As much as the forest was in him, as much as he loved the forest, he did not like this dark rich tract of his own land, whether through familiarity or sense of sharing it with his sister, who shared no other forest of his knowing. The darkness and richness of this woodland was too much; the stillness, the sinking softness underfoot, the perfect unmoving symmetry of thousand-bladed fern was a warning.

He knew where he would find Sabrina, lying flat on her stomach, with her hands in the icy running water of the brook. "Hello," he said, seeing that his noiseless coming, his shadowy materializing out of a shadowy woods had not even startled her. "Missed you at breakfast."

"I'm beholding," she said lazily. She took her hands out of the water.

"Why do you come down here, Brina, it's darker than a pile of black cats? Look, even the birds don't like it."

"But I'm not a bird," she said reasonably. He dropped down beside her and she rolled over and sat up and dried her hands on her skirt.

"What's the matter, Brina?" he said. His voice was ominously controlled. "You're pettish. Is it something I've done?"

"You? Of course not, silly."

"Then it's Fraser," he said.

"Your eyes are always where they pretend not to be, aren't they, and your ears too," she said softly. "Can you tell me, can you remember one word Honora said to you yesterday in the park? No, you can't. But you can tell me every word I said to Fraser and every word he said to me, and how I looked saying it and how he looked saying it."

"Onny never does say much," he said after a time, almost absently. Then he said, "I wish I didn't hate Fraser's guts."

"Well, he hates yours, I reckon, so you're even."

"He's always honing after you, Brina."

"Oh, why did you come down here?" Her voice was without complaint but weary. "Why can't you leave me alone? Not one moment's peace, not one moment."

The forest listened. Brant leaned back on his elbows; Sabrina sat upright, with her arms clasped about her knees. The hound waited for them, ill at ease, lifting his head now and then as if to snare a scent which did not exist on a wind which did not blow. She was glad he had come to find her; he did not regret his little journey into this forest he did not like. And they were silent, having made their excuses to one another: she for being there at all, he for coming to her. But she thought suddenly, What would it be like without Brant? What would it be like for him, without me? But is this enough for either of us, is this all? An unconscious, unrealized emptiness ate small painless paths interiorly into her heart, a gentle hypertrophy of which she was unaware and which was therefore indefinable to her, and nameless. She put her hand on her brother's arm.

"Brina, I'm sorry."

"So am I."

"Do you want to go back?"

"I suppose."

"I promised I'd help Tag."

"All right. Brant, wouldn't this be a lovely place to die in? It's so dark and cool and quiet."

He took her face between his hands. They saw each other as mirrors of each other, handsome, strong, deep-set gray eyes and long dark lashes, high-cheeked, sensitive bone structure. Only the mouths were different, hers wide and generous, his sensual, almost girlish. He said, "Remember when we were children . . . you and Onny and I . . . and we swore if one of us died the other two would kill themselves?"

She laughed, her face still imprisoned in his hands. "Haven't you released Honora from that vow?"

"Onny yes, myself no. Don't die here, Brina, I don't like it here." She let him lift her to her feet.

Around them the woods made a sound, in pity. "Come on, Duke," she said. The hound rose in obvious relief. He walked at their heels, subdued, scenting nothing, except the familiar scent of two people who belonged strangely to one another, who existed independently, interdependently, in a world circling precariously through a space of their own creating, like a thin, sullen star which may come to believe itself the only light in the universe.

52

6

DAWN IS KIND to small settlements which lie beneath mountains, softening the hard morning flaring of light in gray-shrouded cabins, laying fog mistily, like gauze in the hollows, vignetting with flattery the sharpness of cresting hills. To a man entering Benton's Crossing from the north, over the low-railed wooden bridge which spanned the near-dry stream, there would be an air of water color, of old dim paint readying itself to peel on old dim canvas; there would be rooster crow and door slam and faint gleam of lantern and candle; there would be cool wind lying like water in the low places and a fading of autumn stars in the sky and the leaves caressing one another with thin, dry, cicada-sound, and a leaping of raw gold as the bellows blew up fire in the blacksmith shop. There would be, as the eastern sky began that first anticipatory, tentative glowing of sunrise, a stamping of hooves, a ringing of iron, a bovine wailing for the pull of relieving hands, a beginning, a movement, a rising, which bespoke rebirth as surely as the coming of any spring.

Everything of peace and security lay here, lay trapped in the sight and feel and smell of familiar trees and houses and contours of land. For a time you forgot there was such a word as war; war was the farthest thing from a man's mind, seeing this little scar of a settlement looking like it had always been there, unchanging, forsworn by some elemental chemistry of dawn and mountain and wilderness never to change.

The mountains drew protectingly around it, and you didn't even think, maybe mountains aren't enough.

Coming out of the back door of the inn, yawning, belly full of hot breakfast, Brant Quantrell stood for a time on the stone step. Behind him, in the kitchen, Authie Stoner stood at a long plank table, whipping batter with a split sapling whisk. In the corner,

Leonard cracked eggs into a white crockery bowl. Brant closed the door on them and looked about the courtyard, between the inn and the stable.

A great willow grew in the center of the yard; its lower branches had been cut out, and in the shady spaces beneath it, grass grew greenly. Opium lay under the willow with his hands behind his head. He slept noiselessly. A golden bee hovered about him like a blob of honey suspended in space. Brant watched it taste hesitatingly Opium's eyebrow. Sunlight began to shaft heavily, hotly, through the willow branches.

He wasn't happy about having to come to town today, but it always made his father feel better when he came back and reported no, there hadn't been any trouble, or any hint of trouble. People had sort of quit talking about what happened to Hanson Stoner, like it was some sort of dreadful communal secret they didn't want to get out. And Authie seemed contented as a newborn baby in a bundle of wool. He sort of got the idea she was maybe elated Hanson had got taken off to the hereafter; it gave her a chance she would not otherwise have had to come down and live in a civilized part of the world.

He started down the alley between the Bear and the smithy, stopping to rub the chin of a black cat which arched against a trash basket. While he still stooped, liking the feel of the cat's sun-warmed fur, the sound of the men, the barking of dogs, came flowing around the corner and down the alley to him. He stood up and listened.

There was an excitement in the sound which infected him. He too needed the spur, the needle prick of the excitement; he too must join in whatever stirred the townsmen, in whatever brought them to gather in the road. He went on down the alley.

The men, and women and children, and dogs, burst like a blossom around the mounted British officer in full regimentals. Brant's eyes went over the newcomer, noted by the brevets that he was an ensign and not a very young one, and that his horse looked as if it hadn't had a decent fodder ration in days. "All right," the man kept saying wearily. "All right. All right. All right."

Brant went quietly to Aiken Sheller's side. They stood in the lee of sound and movement. "What's goin' on, Aiken?"

Sheller pulled off his glasses in that way which seemed to mark him a victim of excruciating pain, or at the least, desperation. "I don't know. I can't quiet them. *He* obviously can't." Brant vaulted up over the end of the sloping porch and stood with his thumbs looped through his belt, and at last caught the British ensign's eye.

The officer looked at him in weary gratitude. He had a thick roll of parchment in his hand. His regimentals were stained and gray with dust. "You Alwyn Quantrell?" he said.

Brant shook his head. His tongue moved around the inside of his mouth and lodged in a lower corner of his cheek. "He lives north, at a place called Brandyhill."

"Is this place Benton's Crossing?"

"Yes," Brant said, but to the men listening it sounded more like "yelt."

Something soldierly, something authoritative and superior and annoyed came to the officer. He straightened in his saddle. "Who are you then?"

"Name's Quantrell."

The ensign said, "My orders bear the name of Quantrell as president of your Provincial Council."

"Yelt," Brant said again. "Any help to you I'm his son?"

The officer looked interested. "You'll do. What I've got here's for every hamlet in the colony. You want to read it to these loyal subjects of the Crown? Or so I trust them to be." He tossed the roll of parchment over the heads of the men. Brant caught it with a quick, easy movement; he unrolled it, read, silently, to himself. After a moment he looked up.

Fear is the easiest emotion to raise in the face of anticipation, fear communicates itself: a dog snapped suddenly at the heels of the officer's horse; a child began to cry without knowing why it cried.

Brant read aloud.

" 'To all citizens now residing in the Colony of South Carolina, which Colony belongs in all its parts and parcels to His Sovereign Majesty George III of Britain: it is hereby proclaimed that the original proclamation requiring an oath of allegiance to the Crown, and the giving of parole to all those who do not sign the oath that they will not serve against the Crown, shall be superceded by the following proclamation to take immediate effect:

" 'All citizens now residing in the Colony of South Carolina are hereby ordered to commit themselves to active effort in the reestablishment of the Royal Government, and to sign a new oath of allegiance to the Crown, under penalty of being charged as rebels and traitors. All paroles are hereby discharged, in order that every person in the colony shall declare himself either hostile or favorable to the Royal cause. All who take up arms against the Crown shall be hanged as traitors, and all who do not declare themselves loyal shall stand trial as traitors and be dealt with accordingly."

"'Given unto my hand and seal at Charleston in the Colony of South Carolina on this 6th day of July, 1780. General Sir Henry Clinton.'"

In the road the people were quiet, stunned. Men looked at men and the minute seed of distrust, long dormant in the mind, began to move within its shell, to seek light and warmth. The British ensign sat his horse in silent indifference, looking at Brant dispassionately. What matter to him if neighbor should now fear neighbor, if man must pick his way carefully along the avenues of thought and speech, must guard with new vigilance not only himself but his entire family. On pain of death.

A clear high voice said, "Let us pray."

And they knelt in the dust, around the astonished British officer; the burst blossom about him settled as if its petals fell, and Richard Jordan said, "O Lord, guide us this day in the way of that which is right in Thy sight. Let us not harbor in our minds suspicion of any man, nor yet account ourselves responsible for that man's undoing in this time of stress. Give us strength to uphold the cause to which we now pledge ourselves anew. Keep the eternal spirit of Thy Son our Saviour forever in our hearts, and help us to rededicate ourselves to Thy service and to the service of our King. Let not blood flow among our people here, and hasten the ending of that vast flow of blood about us, that peace may enter our hearts and come again to our country."

Brant coughed.

Jordan said more slowly, biting out the words, "Give unto all men who have wavered in their loyalty the light by which to see clearly, the strength with which to walk steadfastly, that they may find their way with true acceptance to the loyalty and the protection of the Crown. In Christ's name, amen."

56

And the petals of the flower gathered together and rose to bloom again. Brant had not knelt, but he had prayed in a way: it could have worked, I reckon my father could have kept it working. He stood, one thumb hooked in his belt again. As if God gave a damn. Poor stupid general. Poor idiot king. "Aiken," he said.

Sheller was still on his knees.

"Git up, Aiken, and act like a loyal subject, will you?"

Sheller rose and came up on the porch.

"What are you prayin' so damn hard for?"

"I am giving thanks," Sheller said shortly, with dignity.

"Thanks." Brant's eyes were narrowed and depthless. Then he said soberly, "They're closin' in on us, Aiken."

"You young fool," Sheller said softly, "why don't you come down to earth and learn how white men live for a change. When you going to get over trying to think like an Indian? Don't you know this is better for us than a thousand-man militia unit in this territory. Can't you see this is peace for us? What's the matter with you anyway?"

Brant scratched the back of his head, tilting his hat forward over his eyes. "Well, I reckon I wasn't exactly lookin' at it that way. I reckon I was lookin' at it with the look says a man don't like bein' pushed. Don't like bein' pushed, ain't goin' to be pushed. We got two roads now. One's that peace you lookin' at, and you better put your glasses on tight now, Aiken. The other's hell around our heads if there's enough men don't want to be pushed."

Sheller made a sound of disgust. He gestured at the British officer, now dismounted and fussing with his stirrups. "We owe that man much. Your father will see it that way."

"Don't owe him any thanks for bein' so fiddle-footed." Brant slapped the rolled parchment into the palm of his hand. "July the General poked his seal on this and it's just gittin' to us." He set his hat back on his head where it belonged.

"For the love of heaven," Sheller said, "why don't you take that along home, so your father can see it and bring the Council together and set a day for signing?"

"All right," Brant said. "I will. I'll go."

He touched the rolled parchment studiedly to the brim of his hat, saluting the British officer as he passed.

Malcolm came to stand in the barn doorway. It was cool in the musty, hay-smelling barn; dust motes rose and fell where the sunlight shafted and filtered. A gray cat lay hunch-muscled on the threshold, tail snaking with eloquent grace, hunting eyes narrowed thoughtfully.

In the near stall Sabrina stood with a colt's nose in her palms. She talked to it, tilting her head to meet its eye, pursing her lips as though for some tangible contact. Malcolm was touched and repelled. He stood half in the searing sunlight, half in the coolness, like the cat, watching her, seeing the slenderness and strength in the set line of shoulder and clean narrowness of waist, the resolution (Alwyn's resolution) in the flat yet graceful set of foot upon the barn floor, the long shaft of thigh and leg, the length and slimness of which suggested speed, agility.

"Sabrina," he said.

She turned and smiled at him, a smile of formality, not without warmth but not entirely spontaneous. "How did it go, Fraser?"

"All right." He had come from the west pasture, from gelding Brant Quantrell's horse. Brant was still with the horse; Alwyn had gone wearily to the house. He, Malcolm, was also tired, and very thirsty. "Is there anything around to drink?"

"Come down to the house," she said.

"I'd like some cold water."

"We'll walk to the spring then. Don't you want to put something on your head?"

"I'm all right. Can I take this dipper?"

"Of course." She reached up and took the floppy-brimmed hat off a peg and set it on her head, hiding the fine shining dark chestnut crown from him, letting the ribbons hang on her shoulders. The colt began to follow them.

"Is he coming?" Malcolm said, squinting now in the sunlight.

"He's prone to follow me," she said.

"You shouldn't make a pet of him, Brina. He'll be good for nothing and he'll race all over you whenever he wants to. I've seen enough of horses for the day if you don't mind."

They did not speak, walking to the spring. The water lay stagnant in the heat and stillness, and they passed it and went on to the open woodland where the spring which fed the stream kept itself clean through its own bubbling. He brushed away the leaves at the edge of the water. They took turns with the dipper; the cold clear water dripped and lay blackly on Sabrina's dress and was absorbed by sunlight.

They sat in the shade. Old Jim, tracking them, came through the trees, not looking to see if they were there, but smelling them until he found them. Then he did not look glad at the finding, but only self-satisfied. It made her laugh.

"How old's Jim now?" he said.

She thought he really cared. "Let's see." She counted on her fingers, serene brow furrowed with attempt. "Eight, I guess he would be. He can still outhunt Duke or any other hound in the back country."

"I had a hound once," he said. "When I was a boy. He was a pretty thing. He chased horses. One day a mare kicked his brains out. I never wanted a dog after that."

He did care. Her face was suffused with a pink solicitousness, sprung from a divided rootstock: one half for the pretty dog who had been kicked to death, one half for the boy who had loved him. "I think it is lonely without a dog," she said.

"It's lonely any way you choose to look at it."

She sat with her arms clasped about her drawn-up knees. It was funny, sometimes his negative attitudes angered her, and sometimes they filled her full of softness and sympathy. "What's the matter, Fraser?"

He lay back on one elbow, chewing thoughtfully on a blade of dry grass. "What makes you ask that?" But he did not let her answer. He swung his head and looked at her out of the sharp obsidian eyes. "Do you ever get a feeling the whole world's full of terrible things going on all around and all of a sudden they're happening to you too?"

She nodded. "I expect you're talking about Hanson Stoner. About the war."

"No," he said. "About something bigger than Hanson Stoner. Maybe even about something bigger than the war. Because it's so damn hard to envision there being any war. That's the terrible thing going on all around."

"But you said you felt it was happening to you too," she said.

"Look, two weeks ago a man in our territory got himself hanged. Now we've all got to sign a pledge we're keeping faith with the King. We know up North they've been fighting, bloody, real fighting. We know it's all come South, it's somewhere out there, all around us." His free arm swung in an arc. "There's a tension in the air, Brina. Right here in this woods there's a tension. Something dark and impenetrable, something I can't explain. Don't you sense it? Don't you feel it?"

She nodded. "Of course I do. You don't live in the same house with my father and not feel it, Fraser, you must know that. Something is happening. Something will happen to us all before it's over."

He chewed at his lower lip. "This is either going to be an end for us or a beginning, Brina." Now he sat up abruptly. "Listen, let's say I am a patriot. All right, a rebel, if that's the word you have to have. I'm a rebel, and I live right here in Benton's Crossing and for the sake of keeping the peace I go along with the Loyalists. To all intents and purposes I'm a Loyalist. But all of a sudden they tell me I've either got to declare myself outright and sign my name I've declared myself or they'll hang me. Maybe I don't want to lie about it any more, maybe I'm tired of the whole mess, maybe I've got reasons I don't want to discuss with anybody, so when they come and tell me I've got to sign I'm waiting for them with a rifle. And maybe not just me, maybe a whole lot of men would rather be rebels. And that's the beginning. Or maybe, like I said, that's the end." Then he said, not in disgust, not even in disappointment, "You don't know what I mean, do you?"

She answered him with a query of her own. "You don't know much about women, do you, Fraser? Why should I not know? Whatever's in the air now, this tension, this closeness, call it what you will, storm coming up over the mountains, maybe . . . if a man, or a woman either can't feel it, then that man's a stupid man, and unfeeling, and maybe even uncaring. Women can feel things men can't feel sometimes. I doubt any man in Benton's Crossing's tried to feel what Authie Stoner felt the morning she found Hanson. I can do that. I can try to feel what she felt."

"That's romantic," he said.

"Nonsense, you know better. You know as well as I do that Hanson Stoner's a symbol now. A conscious symbol perhaps, but a symbol nevertheless. Of the war. Of what can happen."

"I feel trapped," he said. "I feel cut off and encircled and beaten. I feel like I crouched in the bushes somewhere and heard my own heart like a drum and waited for the wolves or the serpents or whatever the hell is out there to close in on me."

Her face in repose, almost somber, was sharply, clearly handsome and full of strength which had not yet made itself manifest. "I try not to let it frighten me," she said. "Why does it have to be? It used to be enough just to be alive. We didn't need this. We didn't even need to think about those battles in the North, and all those men dead. We didn't even need to dream it. We were almost the farthest west you could go, and we could subsist on that. Fraser, do you think we needed this war? Do you think the men who started it really had to start it?"

He lay back in the leaves and put his arm up across his eyes as though to shield them. "I think we needed it. And if the men who started it were fools, God give me the weakness of mind to be a fool."

"Fraser," she said, shocked, disbelieving.

He tore his arm away from his face. "Don't misunderstand me. You say you can try to feel what Authie felt when she found Stoner. Try to feel what these rebels felt, feel."

Now she did not answer, did not look at him, and something mocking came into his voice. "I had begun to admire your perception, Brina. Have you given up already?"

"Do you speak to my father like this, Fraser?" she said in a low voice.

And he said, "I don't need to."

"Don't need to or don't want to? You would convince me that so pessimistic a nature as yours can feel whatever guides the rebels? They're not pessimistic people, Fraser. They couldn't be and still go on and on as they do."

He sat up. "Listen, Brina, in England right now, right this moment, the England you swear fealty to, there are men who would see these rebels win what they want, who would wisely choose peace at any price. Fox, Burke, Pitt, who died on the floor of the House denouncing English domination of the colonies——"

"And are you one of those?" she said. "One of those . . . those pseudo-Englishmen?"

He saw the change come into her face, slowly, almost imperceptibly. The wide gray eyes widened a little, the lower lip drew down. Something in her, something in the face, shrank from him. "Of course not, goddammit," he said lightly, "I'm only trying to make you realize what a little bigot you are."

But she faced him down. She leaned across to him a little breathlessly, eyes serious. "Fraser, listen . . . Sunday, after church, Onny Brevard and I were standing out by the hitching rail waiting for Brant, and William Lyons came down the path with Aiken. We overheard him, we couldn't help it. William said he didn't like it at all you were riding off in the mountains so much. He said . . ."

"Go on," he said quietly.

"He said it didn't seem there could be so many people sick so much of the time."

He was silent; then he laughed. There was sweat on his upper lip. "William rides all over hell and gone himself. What's he talking about?"

"I'm asking you," she said. "All I know is it made me feel funny to hear him say a thing like that."

"Why," he said, "if you really want to know, there's a girl up on South Mountain . . ."

She smiled softly, amused, wonderfully sure of herself. Her face made him furious, deadly sick with desire. "What in the name of sin makes you think I want to talk about dogs or the war or Hanson Stoner?" he said.

"But you brought it up. What do you want to talk of?"

"Us," he said.

"Us," she echoed, as though in surprise.

"Stop looking like that," he told her. "Stop looking like a vacant, stupid unknowing female. I can't stand you when you're being female, Brina, and I can hardly stand you when you aren't being female. How much longer are you going to tell me I can't ask your father, how much longer are you going to waste us both?"

Now she did not smile and her serious face gave him hope. He moved closer to her and the vision came up in him like an explosion. "Sabrina, it's all well and good for us to talk of how we feel about wars and hangings, to go on living our little day-to-day lives and never going anywhere. But I'm not going to stay this way forever . . . maybe not even for long now. I know myself. I know how good I am. I know the day isn't too far off when I'll be the best man of my profession in whatever city I choose. . . . Boston or Philadelphia or New York. Nothing on the earth's going to be too good for me, Brina, or for you either. Because you can't just be a part of it, you've got to share it. I can't do it without you, Brina. . . . I've got to have you cool and gracious and serene to hold my house and my life and my world together, and if I have you I can have all those things tomorrow. I want to give you those things, and the sooner you accept them the sooner you'll have them."

The woods were very still. Her hat slipped off and hung by its ribbons. Her face was turned from him; he could see only the contemplative curve of her cheek. Then she said steadily, "But I don't love you."

"I know you don't. Now."

She shook her head. "It wouldn't be fair to let you go on hoping someday I might."

"Has it been fair to let me go on hoping all this time?"

"I didn't put the hope in you," she said.

Again he was angered, but he kept his control. "Sabrina, you are a very fortunate woman. You've managed, somehow, not to get yourself involved. And I know you're far too intelligent to take either Ballentyne or McLeod seriously. Because you can't tell me you don't want what I can give you one of these days: position and wealth and all the glamour of city living."

She drew a deep breath. "If I ever love anyone, Fraser, things like that won't matter. And I don't love you."

"No," he said, "you won't even let yourself be tempted. You're so bound up in your father and your brother and your way of life that any man you take will have to let himself be bound by those things too. I can't do that, Brina. You won't ever love anybody. You'd ought to take me because of that."

She smiled. "I reckon you might be right," she said, but with nothing of decision.

He lay back again, hands behind his head, staring up at the tatters of sky which pushed through the leaves. "What a fool I was to let you deceive me into believing you were a woman. Or even human. You, my dear Sabrina, are a tree which no wind will ever warp, a cliff of granite which never crumbles, the mountain towering over all the little mountains. Tell me once and for all, tree, cliff, mountain, no. And be done with it."

She rose in one long-legged, swift agile movement and stood looking down at him, tender, amused, flattered. But without any emotion which might pass as love. "Are you coming back to the house?"

"You can't even say no, then. Or won't. Your father and I are going over the assignments of territory. For the riders to notify the back country of the new pledge. Do we go back in peace?"

"I don't know," she said. The candor lay clear in her eyes. "You've disturbed me, Fraser."

He too rose. "With what? Talk of dogs, wars, or marriage?"

But she did not answer, turning away from him. He broke off a sapling and switched at his boot with it, not in anger or pain, but with a need to expend energy. They walked in silence, Old Jim following. But Malcolm still walked with hope, and Sabrina with a dread and alien something close to suspicion weighing like stone in her heart.

Brant leaned back in his chair, not really listening, not really caring, feeling the triumph clean and stinging-sharp, because all he had to do was look at Sabrina's face and know all the answers. He knew Malcolm, knew Sabrina so well that he could pretty well trace out which of them had said what in what tone of voice, and he was satisfied.

Through his satisfaction he heard suddenly his father's voice, controlled and quiet, but with a hesitancy foreign to that voice. He brought his chair back to the floor soundlessly, like a catamount came down on all four feet off a bluff, and listened.

"I don't suppose," his father was saying, "they'd have any objection to exchanging one or two of the assignments. Brant's, for instance." (And he kept silent, listening.) "He might change over with William."

And Malcolm arguing, "But it would take William miles out of the way. What difference does it make?"

Supper was over; its odors still hung hot and greasy and spiced in the room. Tag had gone to see to the stock. Sabrina and Jewel made a clatter of voice and work in the kitchen. The sound was distant and apart from the men, sitting at the round table in the family room, with the food and the white cloth cleared away and a decanter of last year's elderberry wine at hand. There should not have been a problem; it was strange Alwyn bid now to create a problem. But he had been busy on his land and had sent word to William Lyons to assign the back-country territories which must be notified of the new oath, and to set the day for the signing. And now he made as if to quibble with William's good work.

Brant said, "Where's he want me to ride to?"

His father looked across the table at him, eyes uneasy. "Northwest. Up into Clear Spring and Red Ridge."

Brant scratched his head, his eyes not saying anything back to his father's eyes. "Well, I don't reckon I'd like to go up there right now."

The anger, the dislike, edged Malcolm's voice. "You are planning to ride somewhere for us, aren't you?" he said.

Brant looked out the window. It was crystal clear in the east, under and around the thin drifts of cloud which moved over the trees. Dying sunlight lay saffron on the soft lower edges of the clouds. "Reckoned I would," he said evenly, "but I ain't going up to Red Ridge. McLeod could ride up there. I could give him a hand with his chores and do whatever he's got to do while he's gone."

"Is that agreeable?" Alwyn said, looking at Malcolm.

"It doesn't matter to me one way or another," Malcolm said.

Brant's chair scraped when he pushed it back. "You pick me out another ride someplace. Maybe strike out one of the older men and I'll take that." And he was not embarrassed or apologetic or even interested any more; he was just Brant Quantrell looking across the table into Malcolm's black gaze with his face inscrutable and bland and pleasant as a spring sky, so you didn't even know he was thinking.

Thought was for him a development, a slow maturing, rather than a rational argument to some problem posed. So with his attitude toward the war: that too had to develop, to mature. He saw Ian McLeod go off with some Scots Loyalists and get beaten at Moore's Creek Bridge in North Carolina . . . a futile little skirmish by a petty little creek, without purpose or direction or sense. But Ian lost an arm there. And it seemed to Brant a deed less of war than of some intense personal conflict which raged in other men and which he could not comprehend. McLeod was talisman of that conflict, lined and weather-beaten and foreign to him, saying, "You'll not go, lad, you'll not fight?" And the eyes full of a hate which he, Brant, could not fathom or touch, and which he took for some alien old-world trait, like the burr in McLeod's voice, or the kilt McLeod wore. . . . No, Mac, I don't reckon I got much reckoning to kill 'em or worry myself . . . and his eyes on the empty pinned-up sleeve of the homespun shirt.

All for freedom. Freedom was an alibi, a cloak and mask under which city men hid their hunger, their rapacity, their desire for what they had not earned. Brant Quantrell had been free all his life. How would city men speak to him of freedom, which they did not know; how dare, when he knew it so well? The holding back from the civilized chaos of war, the lack of response to the catchwords, the repugnance toward the jingoism, the emotional blindness to the viciousness and hate and stupidity which mark civil war were born in him, were things he could not help. Part of it lay in the very nature of the war; part of it was the inherent doubt that a spark lit by a few farmers at Lexington could kindle across the northern sky, eat south, until the towering red flame of war hung like a backdrop to all action, all existing; until the whole back country writhed under its weird light; until what was, had been, normal became, in this new perspective, abnormal.

The indifference, the repugnance which was past his understanding, grew in him as the wilderness did; for the wilderness grew in him, he did not grow in it, or perhaps he did not grow, but was wilderness, with silence and tree and mountain where heart should be, and mind, and senses. Raised as he was on the fringe of an untouched forest which stretched across the land, unbroken, for more than a thousand miles, he could no more help the mysterious beckoning, the subtle, formless, nameless response to the beckoning, than he could help being male, or young. In the short span of his life the settler's axe had violated, killed the forests around and beyond Brandyhill, so that what had been frontier in the French war was now civilization, something men pressing further west looked back upon from new frontiers. The flux, the thrust, the adventure, a whole continent of breathless solitudes, fermented in him like a yeast.

It had begun when he was sixteen, big for his age, pulled hard to maturing. At supper he said, "I'm going into the mountains . . . west," and felt foolish but forced.

Alwyn, looking searchingly into the dream-filled eyes, said, "Why?" But he knew, he too knew the lure of vastness and aloneness and wilderness which, by being conquered, conquered in turn.

"I don't know, but I got to go. I want to see it, that's all. It's there, and I want to see it. I don't know." And they were silent, father, sister, stepmother, for it was in them too, that lure, that knowledge of freedom unknown to any other men, any other nation, uniquely an American-pioneer-heritage factor, always there, just back of consciousness, always there beckoning. And you did not have to understand the beckoning to respond to it.

He went off into the enveloping green stillness alone. He walked in dark aisles of soundlessness on cool fragrant winds, trapped, hunted, fished, knew a loneliness which was in no way lonely. He lived in Cherokee and Catawba camps, learned Cherokee and Catawba ways, spoke their harsh speech, accepted the childlike improvidence of their future. He went as far west as the Mississippi and saw the French, and north into the Illinois country and saw the once-great nations of Delaware, Miami, and Detroit, drifted south again.

Up a river tributary, the year he was nineteen, he settled in a Catawba camp. Following bear track, anxious to do his share in the camp, he surprised a young squaw in a bay under glittering birches. He stood for a long time, watching her, with his rifle under his arm and the blood singing in his head, seeing the satin-smooth flesh and the slim young flanks, seeing the flash of fear in the dark liquid eyes when they found him. Seeing, at last, her smile, because he was young and hungry and would have something to trade. The Catawbas were poor now, and any sort of geegaw, a broken mirror, a piece of colored string, a little powder and ball meant much to them.

He stayed three months in the camp before the restlessness grew in him, and the thought of how Sabrina fared (thought even of Honora Brevard) and at last yielded to the desire for returning. And he went back, and by going cast a pattern his life would always follow. Caught up in the peace and security of Brandyhill he would be awkward, impatient of the restraints of civilization, ill at ease: because somewhere the young Cherokee men wrestled in the new meadows; somewhere on a summer day the camps were pitched along a running stream and the men laughed and told old heroic tales in the shade; somewhere, heads lifted to the first crisp scent of cold in the wind, the squaws had gone to gather nuts and berries, to take down the lodge poles and drift off to winter grounds.

He came and went, surrendering to the wilderness, surrendering to civilization, torn exhausted from the arms of one mistress to lie in the demanding arms of another, hanging, suspended, vacillating between the ties of family, home, and the long miles of mountain fastness, wilderness, to which he was also inextricably bound. When he was away he looked homeward and remembered; when he was

67

home he looked west and remembered. That same year, when he was nineteen and coming home again (interminably, constantly, uncontrollably coming home or leaving home) he stopped at the inn in Hardington, north of Benton's Crossing, and ran into Jared Millikin, who had once made a living taking Indian scalps for bounty. Nothing much might have come of it except that Keoweh, the Catawba girl's brother was with Brant, and Jared Millikin talked loudly on the inn floor and told lies and threatened, and after a time, not because of what Millikin called Keoweh or the girl, or the lies or the threats against his, Brant Quantrell's, Indian-loving life but simply because he was tired of listening, he picked up his rifle and shot Millikin through the heart. And Alwyn's old friend Colonel Allerton, who commanded the militia and ran the town, sent him on home, and he did not regret what he had done, he only regretted that he felt it had to be done.

It settled him, momentarily; momentarily because a week or a month or two months were momentary in his life. He was full of conscience in that momentary settling, or at least full of some indefinable thing which spoke and taunted and so served as conscience; when he was settled he tried to make peace not only with Honora Brevard but with himself and the way he felt about Honora Brevard.

Because he had staked a claim, staked it all unknowingly, unhappily, not meaning to. Or perhaps he had not really done it himself, perhaps it had been done for him by family, circumstance, Onny herself, a tacit agreement to which he had not agreed. She was the hurdle in his life which he had never quite cleared, and it had nothing to do with the approach to the hurdle or the skill in taking it, it had to do with something else. It had to do with something which made him believe that there really was no Honora Brevard, that she was a dream which occurred and reoccurred all his life (mostly when he was away from her). And it was a strange thing to him that there were men in the territory would have laid down and died for Honora Brevard and that she would have none of them, having evidently, obviously, chosen him, Brant, at an age when she could barely pronounce his name. She too pulled him home; maybe she had something to do with sending him off again, just by being there, waiting, when he came back to all the material things which were civilization; when he found himself faced with her, waiting, and saw her as some sort of rich and shining and beautiful device which civilization had created expressly to tempt him.

He welcomed the device when he came home. He shied from it long before it was time to go again.

He went back up into the Cherokee country and stayed for a time. (The Catawbas had years ago learned to live with the white man; the Cherokees could still be driven to rise, but the Cherokees knew Brant Quantrell and he was Benton's Crossing's insurance.) He preferred the Cherokees to the Catawbas, seeing they were still full of the old spirit and fortitude and fire, but he never liked the idea of their killing white men and when he went up this trip and found they had rum and cottoned to the idea of maybe setting out for a few scalps, he went out alone and brought in the man who had given them the rum and the idea, a Frenchman named Henry Deschamps, and fought it out with Deschamps. They moved in a circle of silent Cherokees, the boy wiry and strong and a lot cooler than the Frenchman, and when the boy had tired of the game he won it easily with the Frenchman's own trick, kicking Deschamps' legs out from under him and taking the knife in clean to the hilt under the rib cage. That was the second man he had killed up in the forest country where killing came easy and a man could get so he took to it naturally. He never had to prove himself to the Cherokees and he never had to tell them anything, but when he pushed off this time he was glad to find the companionship of a white man.

His good humor, with the finding of Pomeroy Hollister, was short-lived. An old man, bitter with his pretentious surname and calling himself Holly, Hollister lived at the crest of a mountain in the Red Ridge territory with a girl he had taken as his wife, a Cherokee whom he called Mary, but whose name was Dawn Star. And that was the first thing, the supression of so beautiful a name, that Brant Quantrell learned to hate him for.

Coming upon the garden plot, he had looked on the girl and for a time thought that this was what he had sought to find: that release which white men acquired in not only the cohabiting, but the day-to-day living with another race, and felt the virgin pure wellspringing of love in him. And he never understood it, but did not profit from this lack of understanding, did not learn that nothing of love is to be understood. There was Holly, past seventy, and the girl not yet twenty, little in stature and slim as a reed, with her face as still and placid and golden as a mountain pool, the fine dark eyes a little heavy-lidded, the mouth softly curving, the cheekbones high and rounded. And the wilderness was in her too; everything of clear water and forest darkness lay like reflection in her eyes. It enraged him. He could not accept without question her acceptance without question of Pomeroy Hollister; to that sour-bearded, lined, corn-whiskey soaked old man belonged a supreme triumph. And Pomeroy Hollister was the only man he ever feared.

Sometimes he thought the hammering of his heart would jar him to death, and sometimes his hands shook. Choice, with a deadly and jagged edge lay before him. If Holly had died the choice would have been simple, the choice would have been Dawn Star. He wished he had courage to kill Holly, but he did not have; he had only the humanness to admire Holly, to fear him, to hate him, not for what he had done to Dawn Star, but because he had done it first.

When Holly hunted he sat and watched the girl in the field until he could stand it no longer. He took the gourdful of water to her and she drank it, but when she handed back the empty gourd she said, "That is not for you to do," and he staggered over the raw edge of his own nerves and said fiercely, "How can you stay with him, how can you?" saying all the fruitless inane things he had sworn not to say, while she watched him in silence.

Don't say he has been good to you, what's being good?

He is old enough to be your grandfather, he is vile to you.

You can't love him any more than God Himself could love him.

With his breathing harsh and fast, and hope and hurt and fury in him.

And she said, "That is not for you to say, or for me. It puzzles me that love should be between squirrels, for I cannot love a squirrel."

And he did a terrible thing, dropping down before her, laying his face against her bare instep, where she stood in the soft garden loam. She was silent, not moving, not speaking, until some measure of control had come back to him, until the orgasmic shattering of the heart was over. Then she said, "It is better that you go."

Somehow he was standing, somehow he faced her. "It won't be forever. Sometime I can come back for you."

She shook her head slowly, watching him.

"You know what I say. Holly can't live forever." And he thought he saw a spark in her eyes. "What will you do when he dies?"

"Listen," she said. "Do you know what happens when death comes? Do you know the brown bird which sings like bells in the summer? You call it the wood thrush. Do you know it?"

"Yes," he said. "Yes, I know it."

"When it is time for dying my people say the brown bird comes, and sits on a near branch and does not sing. And someday when you are working in your field or walking in the forest, you will see the brown bird near you, and he will not sing. Then you will know that one of us dies, for the brown bird is a shy bird and does not come near unless he would tell you this. No, do not look this way, Brant. Is it not a lovely thing, to come so close to the shy bird? The omen of passing to another, happier place is a joyous omen, is it not?"

Her face glowed with a warm radiance. Again there was the dangerous emotional surging in him. "Does Holly believe that?" he said.

"What does it matter what he believes?"

"Then what does it matter what I believe?"

"It matters," she said.

But he did not understand. "Then I got to wait for the thrush. Is that what you're trying to tell me, Dawn Star?"

She smiled at him, and the smile was full of an ancient and awful sadness. "From the hour you came you have carried my heart in your breast. When you have forgotten Dawn Star, remember the brown bird," she said, and turned and picked up her hoe and bent to her work. And he too turned and saw Holly at the edge of the field, watching them.

He walked steadily, seeing the old man with the rifle under his arm rising like solid rock between him and the cabin. Now, he thought, now (feeling the sweat spring out on him) kill him, now while you got the chance . . . twenty paces, ten paces, and the embryo courage withering in the womb of the mind. . . .

"I'm goin' back, Holly," he said, looking the old man in the eye.

Pomeroy Hollister spit tobacco juice out of a stained and broken mouth. "Get too rough for you, boy?"

And he never knew to what the old man alluded, life, the lonesomeness, this primitive-wilderness existence, the girl. He did not want to know. When he left the cabin he carried in his shirt the blue-beaded bands he had seen swing on Dawn Star's breast a hundred times, binding the coarse dark hair at the end of her braids.

And he thought perhaps he had learned enough of life and death and that the returning to those things which, however transitory, were to him eternal, was the most sensible and therefore the most difficult solution. And those things were not really things at all, but a thing: father love and sister love and woman love, and a love of stability and sameness and dullness, a love of civilization, if he could educate himself to condescend to it.

In the autumn of '75 he went to Charleston with his father. In the city he did not listen much to the war talk, and was not blinded by whatever brilliance struck white off city living, off a civilization more civilized than he had known existed. He deplored the neat similarity of pastel brick houses, saw with something of unworldly wonder the cool white-columned mansions lying like diamond in their setting of emerald tree and opaline garden which they passed outside the city. He sat on the wharves and watched the spider tracery of masts and rigging on the sky and let his eye follow the powerful gliding of the gray scavenging gulls, and yearned for the still ponds and swamps of his own country, with the ducks rising on a frosty morning and the awkward blue heron crying their hoarse alarms in the dying summer and the sound of pines in the wind and foxes barking on the ridges. But he was in Charleston for a purpose. The first meeting of the General Provincial Council, of which his father was a member, had been slated, and he looked back and wondered if all the things his father had participated in and lived through and told him about had led to this: the French and Indian War, the Cherokee War (he had been fourteen then and could remember), the Great Slave Insurrection, which he could also remember but which had not touched them, nor the slaveholder Brevard. He was among the back-countrymen who had elected his father to the council, and this time, in Charleston, he saw and read the splendid manifesto which said the rights of Englishmen were their birthright and His Majesty's subjects in the provinces were entitled to the liberties and privileges of Englishmen. To insure those liberties and privileges, His Majesty's armies now wound bright and deadly through the South, intent upon a fleeing army of rebels, Patriots, Americans, who were no longer interested in the liberties and privileges of Englishmen but were filled with a fire to decide their own liberties and privileges.

And now this oath, this pledge to be signed, because if you were a rebel, Patriot, American, you no longer had any liberties and privileges, you were simply there to be hanged. If you felt it was worth being hanged for. The assigned riders of Benton's Crossing would carry the news to the back country; a rider would go up into Red Ridge, but it would not be Brant Quantrell. Suppose she was there. Worse, suppose Holly was. Something it would be to ride up to Pomeroy Hollister's door and say he'd better make the trek down and scratch his x on a document he couldn't read, conceived by a man he'd most likely never heard of; something to see what nine years had done to that still, golden face of Dawn Star's; something . . . ah, God, God, what did he care if nine years had left her as eaten away as a sandworn shaft of temple in some horizonless desert, what did he care?

It would be simple to say, casually, to Ian McLeod, don't bother Pomeroy Hollister, up Red Ridge way, he's too old to have it make any difference whether he signs or not.

Across the table at Brandyhill, across the wilderness token which was the girl, the thing he waited for, he looked at Fraser Malcolm, looked at city, town, civilization, ambition. And his face was expressionless, impassive, imperturbable, incurious, stoic, Indian.

7

ALONG THE RIDGE of the hill, where he had been scratching under the leaves, a little breeze ran. Old Jim worked the leaves aside to his satisfaction and followed his tail around several times before testing the coolness of the earth.

As suddenly as he lay down he stood upright again, looking over the crest, down the rock ledges where the dusty-leaved honeysuckle withered and grew yellow. The growl worked in him. He smelled Brant; he felt Brant's hand on him and knew it was all right. The growl died, but he stood rigidly, with his tail up. Brant dropped to the ground and the hand pressed his head and he heard and obeyed. Down Jim.

For a time they lay there, man and dog, looking down on the old mill road, the no-longer-used wagon track which had managed to leave only the imprint of itself in the second growth woodland where last year's leaves made a dun-colored blanket. After a while the women's voices came high and faint in the background and Brant said, "Come on, Jim," and began to inch his way down the slope, back the way he had come, still lying on his belly. When the crest of the hill hid him he stood up and ran, and the hound ran with him.

Sabrina and Honora were under the birches at the foot of the slope. They looked at him, their eyes curious and alarmed. "Be quiet," he said. "Don't make a sound," and the alarm grew in their eyes and they looked beyond him, up the slope, as if waiting for horror to materialize from the woodland. The dog waited, whining a little in his throat.

Sabrina's voice was low but calm. "What is it, Brant?"

"Under the hill, on the old mill track," he said. "British soldiers."

Honora had paled when he first ran to them. Now the color came back into her face, and her laughter was so high and carrying-clear that it frightened him. "British soldiers! I declare, Brant, that's the meanest thing you've ever done, giving us such a start." And he stepped to her side and took her arm and said, "Keep your voice down, Onny."

But she would not. "What on earth's the matter with you? Of all the. . . ." And did not say more because his hand, his beloved hand, was across her mouth, and his face looked as if he would strike her.

Sabrina was on his side; he had only to look at her to know that. Honora made no move to free herself, but her eyes, over the edge of his hand, were hurt and accusing. "You listen to me," he said, tightening his fingers at every other word, giving the words physical emphasis, "there's two companies of soldiers down on that road, headed for Benton's Crossing. They ain't going to find us first and sojourn along the way with two women, you understand me?" His hand came away.

She kept her voice down, but she was indignant. "How can you say such a thing? You mean we've no right to welcome our own people? I am English and they are my people, and they're yours too, and the least we could do is wave them a welcome!" Stepping back, her foot came down on Jim's tail. The hound's yellow eyes

74

rolled heavenward in hopelessness and desperation and acceptance and pain. He bayed.

"Oh Jesus," Brant said. "Shut up, Jim. You do what I say, Onny. We got to tell my father."

She came docilely, looking as if she would weep. He knew that look, knew also that it came not from his reprimand but because she had hurt the dog. She said nothing more as they hurried through the meadow, and after a time she put her hand out timidly and he took it in his own and squeezed it, and so they walked, hand in hand. She was not accustomed to such hurry; she felt faint from sweating and dizzy from sun. Excitement too played its part in her sudden physical decline. When she lagged he slowed his pace, not forcing her any longer, so that it was Sabrina who reached the farm first. The golden colt pushed its nose through the bars of the pasture fence when it saw her, but she did not stop, only picked up her skirt and ran.

Jewel was shooing chickens away from the back door. Amid the outraged clucking, her hand paused in mid-air, so that she appeared to salute. "Now whut?" she said. She had heard Jim belling over on the ridge.

"Where's Father?" Sabrina gasped.

"In his room. Catchen your breath before you goes pesterin'. You gonna tell me the trouble or not?"

"Brant saw some British soldiers on the mill track."

"That's somepin to run for?" Jewel said, but nothing could keep her away. She followed Sabrina through the kitchen and down the hall to Alwyn's room. She stood in the doorway, hand on hip.

Alwyn was standing by his shelf of books, holding an open book in his hand, scanning the page. His waistcoat was unbuttoned and his cuffs rolled back.

"Father," Sabrina said, "you'd better come. There are British soldiers riding into the settlement."

He closed the book with a little snap. His face broached questions she could not answer.

"Brant saw them," she said. "He's coming, with Honora."

When they reached the back door Brant and Honora had come into the yard. Tag too had seen Sabrina running and come down into the yard with a harness strap and a dish of bear grease still in his hand. Honora sank down on the doorsill with a sigh of gratitude. Her fair silken hair was disarranged and lay in loose curls on her

75

forehead. And she knew she should not have questioned Brant, for the first thing his father said was, "Did they see you?"

Brant shook his head. He would not say, for God's wonder, no thanks to Honora they didn't; he would not betray Honora. Her guilt became of tremendous importance to her in that moment, and she loved him for so loving a deception he practiced.

"How many?" Alwyn said.

"I reckon fifty or sixty. We'd never have known it, but Jim acted funny." The hound acknowledged this with wise eyes, and Alwyn's hand went instinctively to the dog's head. "Most of 'em infantry," Brant said, "with some dragoons ridin' their flanks."

Tag envied openly. He tugged at his brother's arm. "Git away from me with that bear grease," Brant said. "What do you make of it, Father?"

"I hesitate to say, son."

"You don't think it has anything to do with the new pledge?" Sabrina said.

"I doubt it."

"You going to ride into the Crossing?" Brant said.

"Indeed. We both should."

"We all should," Honora said. "Uncle John will want to go. You'll wait for him?"

"Me," Tag said, "I want to go. I want to see the soldiers too." But he knew it was useless even while he said it; the hot hope died even while it flamed. He submitted to Sabrina's arm about him.

"Not this time, Tag, not until we know what this is all about. Suppose you ride to Uncle John's and tell him Father and Brant are waiting for him to go into the Crossing. Maybe Aunt Margaret will come along and stay to supper with us. Help your father now, and don't be disappointed and maybe tomorrow you'll see the soldiers."

He set down the strap and the grease on the chopping block, his face composed but his child's shoulders bent in defeat. Sabrina whispered to him, "If you ride quickly, I'll get out the sugar drops after supper. You can have two." It was not like seeing British soldiers, but it was something. He had not had a taste of the well-guarded sugar drops since summer. So he ran and climbed the roan horse and rode bareback at full gallop down the road to Brevard Hundred.

Unlike Tag, Honora waited in full expectation of accompanying the men. When Alwyn had gone to change his clothing and Sabrina and Jewel to see to the first preparation for the evening meal, Brant took out his knife and flipped it with expert eye and apparent casualness into the earth at Honora's feet. She drew back startled, with a nervous little laugh. When he bent to retrieve the knife, his face close to hers, he said, "You ain't goin', Onny."

"That's for Uncle John to say." Her eyes were on the short dark hair at his temple.

"I'm saying. You stay where you're safe."

"You talk like they were rebels instead of our own people!"

"I ain't the trustingest soul in the world."

"I've noticed."

"I don't want anything to happen to you, Onny." And he took her hand and put it on his temple, where her gaze had been.

"You shouldn't go away and leave me . . . us . . . unprotected then," she said.

"You don't think Jewel'd let a strange foot on Brandyhill, do you?"

"It's not like having you."

"Listen, if those soldiers are as pretty as they looked to me I'd not have them in your sight. Promise me you'll stay here till we get back."

"I promise," she said softly, readily, faithfully, and felt a cold paralysis along her spine when he took her fingers to his lips.

The British infantry lounged under the trees in the park and the people stood about and watched it as if a red, caged animal, brought to be stared at, had been placed in their midst.

"Look at that," Malcolm said, leaning against the brick wall of the Bear, arms crossed. "You'd think they never saw a soldier before. You'd think they had an elephant cropping grass over there. How'd you like being stared at like that?" But he should have known better than to pose even a hypothetical question to Brant Quantrell.

"Wouldn't mind," Brant said, "long as I wasn't doin' nothing to be ashamed of."

He had ridden in ahead of his father and John Brevard. Leaving the gelding hitched behind Ashe's cooperage, he had walked along the main street, pushing through little knots and clusters of towns-people until he found Malcolm looking out over the scene with derisive mouth and jaundiced eye.

"Where's their officers?" Brant said.

"Inside beating on the table with tankards. Two of them. Lex asked to what we owed the honor of this visit and where they came from and where they were going and got told to mind his own affairs. Where's your father?"

"He's coming along. What you figure they want?"

"Supplies, food. Maybe horses. Maybe women. Sabrina's not coming, is she?"

"I ain't as big a fool as you reckon, Fraser." He went and swung open the inn door and peered in and closed the door again. "They're writing something," he said.

"Requisitions. They're figuring what they'll take from Sheller and probably from Lyons."

"Where's William?"

"He's gone up Little Dome to see Arley Hawkins about some traps. Here comes your father." And he stepped forward to help Alwyn out of the saddle. "Opium," he said in a controlled voice which penetrated and passed other sound, and said it again. "Opium." Opium came down the alley from the rear of the inn. "Take these horses around to the stables," Malcolm said. He eyed the horses frankly. "Never did believe in leaving good horseflesh around where anybody but your friends could see it."

Alwyn and Brevard went up the inn steps. Brevard was taller than Alwyn, with an open face and quizzical brow, quiet, plodding, with no spark and not much perception. Still, he seemed to radiate goodness and mercy, hale if not hearty, gentle somewhat as a beaten dog is gentle. Despite wealth and holding, despite beautiful wife and more beautiful ward, his face and bearing evoked pity, so that women liked him while their men tolerated him.

Alwyn pushed through the inn door at the same moment Lavinia Whiting came from the kitchen into the inn room with a tray of cold meat and cheese. He stood in the doorway until she had finished serving and had returned to the kitchen. Then he approached the table and stood, waiting.

The lieutenant was of an indeterminate age, with a lumpy com-plection and pink cheeks and a shock of light-colored hair which curled on the nape of his neck. His eyes were pale and wary, and all the skin of him which showed looked washed-out and sickly against the red of his infantry uniform. The dragoon captain appeared younger than his companion, narrow-shouldered in the green cavalry coat, with a sharp-featured handsome face and deep-set blue eyes under a prominent forehead and arrow-straight brows. It was a striking face, bold and self-assured. It looked at Alwyn uncritically, and the voice was without harshness.

"Yes?"

"Captain, I am Alwyn Quantrell of Brandyhill, president of the Provincial Council. Welcome to Benton's Crossing."

The dragoon officer leaned back in his chair and surveyed him for a moment. Then he laughed, shortly but not unkindly. "Why, we've found nothing but Provincial Council members in this settlement. Young man outside says he's a surgeon, he's a member. Man behind the bar, there, he's a member. Oaf in a wagon name of Ballentyne, he's a member. Not sure what a Provincial Council is."

Alwyn smiled, liking the honesty, the economy of speech. "Sir, we are men sworn to the Crown. In a manner of speaking, we set the tenor of the times in this territory."

White breeches showed. The dragoon lay back on his spine, legs spread, one arm dangling floorward. "Nay, sir, it's armies set the tenor of the times. By what wretched means do you eke out a living?"

Still Alwyn smiled. "The land, sir, and it's true enough, the land can be a wretched mistress when she wants. May I present my friend and neighbor, John Brevard?"

The dragoon came forward in his chair, gathering his legs under him like a cat crouching. "Brevard? There's a name rings bells in my head. You're no colonial, friend, and neighbor."

Brevard, at Alwyn's side, said, "Born English as you, Captain, colonial by choice."

"But with no refutation of birthright, I trust?"

"We are all Englishmen here, Captain."

The lieutenant half got to his feet. He was younger, Alwyn saw, than the dragoon. It was the creased and lumpy skin, the washed-out eyes, which made him look older. "You'll join us in some ale, gentlemen?"

They sat, and the dragoon pushed away the papers at his elbow and took a monstrous bite of yellow cheese. Little crumbs of it clung to his lower lip.

"Where's that black rapscallion I saw here a moment ago? Inn-keeper, there's to be meat and ale for my men. Meat, meat, why do you colonials cook a roast of beef beyond recognition? God, for some good English beef, with the blood running under the knife. Miserable cheese, not been aged properly. Fine pastry though, like bubbles in the mouth. Who's Brevard, from where do I know that name? You wed into the Withersbys, no? Beautiful women. Why here, Brevard, what's to be had here?" Now he tapped his forehead significantly. "Ah well, we've all our private shadows to avoid, I s'pose, except Bartholomew here, who's led a singularly dull and exemplary life. I've my shadows too, so I've no mind to quest after another man's. Name of Galton." And the hand was proffered abruptly to Alwyn, to Brevard, and as abruptly taken back.

Lex Whiting brought fresh tankards to the table but would not join them, listening intently as he contrived work for himself behind his bar. Lavinia came with pie still warm from the oven, exchanging greetings with Alwyn and Brevard, while the dragoon watched, listened, waited.

"You look well, Lavinia."

"I am stronger, Alwyn. Fraser says you're a better man at diagnosis than he."

"Ah, that's much for Fraser to say."

She went back to the kitchen.

"Here, what's this?" Galton said. "Why is she stronger and who is Fraser?"

They laughed. Alwyn said, "Fraser's the doctor you met outside. Madame Whiting's been ill and I suggested a visit with her Cousin Lucy in Charleston."

"Charleston, bloody filthy city. How we circled that poor rebel Lincoln and whipped him to shreds there. And those fool farmers who call themselves cavalry . . . we smashed them all up on the Waxhaws and waited to see how loud they could call quarter before we ran them through. Charleston's a feather in our helmets, gentle-men, right now Clinton's tickling the King's ribs with it. Say, what's this, a vinegar pie or I'm beaten to death, juicy one too, ain't it?"

Now Alwyn said it. "Is it presumptuous of us to inquire where your troops go?"

"Presumptuous. Not for you, gentlemen. Colonials are born pre-sumptuous. Why, first we've got to fill our hungry bellies and let our horses eat your grass . . . and there's not a great deal of that edible, dry, brown stuff . . . and stock up a bit, as your shopkeeper says, with flour and salt and a touch of pork. And then we're off to wherever our orders say. We've orders signed by Cornwallis' A.D.C. and passed on to that bold Tarleton of ours. He's a fighting cock, that one."

Alwyn said, "You're Tarleton's officer then?"

"Proud to be that, yes. Why man, man, Tarleton and cavalry are synonymous. Tarleton *is* Crown cavalry. You'll not find a cavalryman the world over doesn't make obeisance to that boy's name. You think he's about somewheres, do you? I'd not be saying where the terrible boy is at this hour, for he rises and descends like a wraith, and he's for leaning on your shoulder when you'd swear him twenty miles away. You'll not be questioning me further, gentlemen, I'm a rude man when I must be, and I must often, for I'm a professional soldier and I make my living by war. She too's a wretched mistress when she uses all her little beguilements to tempt me to a spot like this, where there's corn shucks in her mattress and not a silken sheet to cool me."

He got to his feet suddenly and strode toward the kitchen. Despite the pronounced limp, borne proudly from some unspoken battle, he strode, calling in that abrupt, brusque voice, "Another pie, madame, another pie," and pushing open the door.

But he did not enter the kitchen. He merely looked in, with all his weight on the good leg. "Well, bless me," he said, "the most edible things are kept in the kitchen. Bring me another pie, lass."

Authie Stoner, flushed, hair curling in the moist heat, brought the pie. Her face was a mask. Alwyn hoped Galton would not touch her, or if he did, she would play the game well. A vinegar pie upon the head was not a proud-gained wound. But after she set the pie down and inquired if there would be anything else and returned to the kitchen, Galton forgot her, eating prodigiously and with great freedom of manner.

"They do cook chickens well, though," the lieutenant Bartholomew said. "It's a crime they haven't a chicken cooked for us. I say, Quantrell, why is it there's no business at hand in this inn? They'd rather stand outside and stare at my men than quench their thirst?"

"We see so few soldiers," Alwyn said. "We are so cut off here and so many things of import happen around and about us. They watch you because they are interested." He took his pipe out and tapped it against a plate to remove the last trace of dead ash. "It is a fine thing you do, protecting and aiding us in our will to remain united."

"It is a foolish thing," Galton said. "Pah! We protect and aid women and children and old men. Young men, too, those without the spunk to protect and aid themselves. Women can always protect themselves, even if they have to do it with their own virtue, and children are small enough to hide, and an old man's feebleness ofttimes evokes enough pity to spare his life. Young men, though, that's another matter."

"We have given young men to Loyalist regiments," Alwyn said.

"Aye, and that's what tears me. Dilemma, dilemma, and what to do. It's only a soldier in the field stops to consider the pro and con of that, gentlemen. Take these Loyalist troops of yours. Why, bless them, their spirit's in the proper place, there's no denying that. See, they say, all raw and green and untrained, or if they're trained it's been marching about a village square left-footed with a rusty firelock on the shoulder; see, they say, here we are to support you. The spirit's fine, but they drag, how they drag about our necks. It's times like that I can't decide whether we're best off with 'em or without 'em."

"All soldiers must learn to become soldiers, Captain."

"There's naught original in that pronouncement, Quantrell. But I'm a professional soldier, and I'm for the experienced troop under my command. I've no time to rein in and stop to season green wood. Why, you lose wars that way, and the Crown does not lose wars."

"You are saying you are happier without us, then?" Brevard was put out at the cold appraisal.

"Bosh, who cares what I believe? I'm a professional soldier, and I do no more than abide to the letter of regulations." He pushed his chair back and regarded Alwyn from under one raised brow, the bold handsome countenance somehow mischievous. "Well, where's all your good Loyalists? Bring 'em in and let 'em stare at a soldier for a change."

"I say!" Bartholomew's lumpy face was red and indignant. "They're staring at soldiers now, if you don't mind, Captain. My soldiers."

"Aye, you'll make a good one yourself, if you keep that steel in its scabbard and out of your voice, Bartholomew. Well, open the doors and let the swine guzzle. There's that devil's spawn now, what's his name . . . here, boy, set down that tray and go across the street and call until you find Captain Galton's aide. Bring him along or I shall see to it you've not an ounce of skin left on you by morning, hear?" He smiled pleasantly.

The door stood open behind Opium's panicky exit.

"What now, won't they come and drink with their protectors? That's fine, like England, where a commoner won't take a drink with an officer of the Crown. Respect and awe, gentlemen, that's what this uniform demands, and so does the man who wears it if he's a professional soldier and does his work. Well, and here's a man wears the cloth. He'll drink with us, no doubt, for he's a professional man also."

Richard Jordan was moving steadily across the floor, sober and cherubic. The officers rose, acknowledging the introduction. But Jordan would not stay; he was serious, earnest, with no time for ale or claret, or for talk.

"I would have a service of prayer for you, while you are here," he said.

"Aye God, man," Galton said bluntly, "we've not time for such, we've riding to do."

"A half hour of your time," Jordan insisted. "It is for you, and for us, gentlemen."

"That's nearer the truth, that last. Services dull here in . . . what's the name of this place? . . . same old faces week after week, same old parson, same old God, even, eh? I've no taste for prayer when it's wreathing about my head like pipe smoke and I'm forced to kneel choking in it."

Jordan stood staunchly, staring at him. Galton went on, undaunted that he had not made some dent in the clerical armor. "Now prayer's fine in itself, Parson, a pretty thing to hear, and I'd lay down and weep at every bivouac if I believed I'd been forsaken. But there's prayer aplenty for Hal Galton: wife praying at home, and a son will be a soldier like his father someday praying at his schooling, and a mistress praying I'll make my fortune this war and come back to a peerage, and even an old mother praying I may be killed gloriously in the colonies, for there's no heroine in the whole of history like a mother who's given her son's life to the Crown and the country. You'll forgive me, sir, and understand my modesty. I am reluctant to pray for myself, for the name may fall too frequently on heavenly hearing, and wear itself thin."

And Jordan said steadily, "You have men who would pray, Captain."

"I have men who would be about the business of killing. Ah, here you are, Brunswick. Get what you can of that shopkeeper next door and find us some wagons. I note there's a fine garden farm down apiece, they'll have a wagon to give us. See what food's cooked in this kitchen and pack it."

The aide saluted, spun on his heel and was gone. Galton reached out and caught Opium's arm. "Here, boy, you'd not fear a gentle man like me. Well done, I say, and lucky for you I'll not need your skin after all. Here's reward and there's no need of biting her, she'll ring true enough."

Released, Opium bent for the gold piece which dropped at his feet. But he did not speak and his eyes were fearful. He raced for the protection of the bar. Galton laughed and got to his feet. Alwyn remained seated, and there was in his heart a first tremor, a fibrillation, of unsureness, of insecurity.

Several men had come into the inn, the cooper Sam Ashe, Newley Ballentyne and his father, Brant, Malcolm, McCullough, Dean. Between Malcolm and Ballentyne stood Garlin Gresham, a head taller than any man there, so drunk he could hardly stand. His beard was stained and matted, his mouth slack, and still he smiled. Alwyn knew he did not see the two officers, did not know there were soldiers in the settlement. His drunkenness forecast a singleness of unpurposeful purpose. But Malcolm had him firmly by the arm; Malcolm would not let him speak.

Galton stared at the men as intently as they had stared at his soldiers under the trees in the park. "Ah, the surgeon," he said, as if to himself, "and the tillers of the soil, and the town sot. All towns have one, there's no originality any more, more's the pity. Well, Quantrell, it's been a pleasant meeting, and we shall ride content, knowing you pray for us." Then he said, "I'll take your signed pledge if you please."

Somehow he had known it. Somehow it had been in his mind even while he rejected it, even while he gave negative reply to Sabrina's query in the yard at Brandyhill. Or was it pure coincidence: Benton's Crossing lying in their route of march, the knowledge of the new oath? He knew he would never know, and in a way he was glad that the document would be gone, out of their hands, out of the settlement, out of their lives.

He too stood. "There is one thing, Captain. Will you leave a receipt in our keeping?"

The black brow rose. "A receipt?"

"For the pledge, Captain. So that if the issue should arise we have proof that we have signed and given the pledge into the keeping of the Crown."

"By God." Galton breathed it, head on one side, eye like a falcon when it spots its prey. "Intimidation will get you no receipt from me. Let us hear no more of this. The word of a Crown cavalryman is sufficient unto itself." He held out his hand. "I am waiting."

Alwyn turned to Whiting. "Lex, bring the document."

Whiting's rotund figure disappeared up the stairs behind the bar. The floor overhead shook under his heavy tread. There was silence in the inn. Upstairs, something fell to the floor and shattered. Whiting came down with the heavy rolled parchment.

Galton unrolled it cursorily enough, glancing over it with indifferent eyes. "Alwyn Quantrell of Brandyhill. Brant Quantrell. Your son, sir? Where is he?"

Alwyn identified Brant with a forward movement of his head. Galton's eyes moved over the group by the door. "Ah, and Malcolm the surgeon, Fraser Alan Malcolm." Again he looked up. "And there's friend Ballentyne, whose wagon we shall need." The falcon eye rested with distaste on Garlin Gresham. "And where's the town sot's wavering whiskey scrawl?" Again he read, again he looked up. "What's your name, man?"

But Gresham was incapable of answering. And a sudden terrible truth came to Alwyn, but before he could speak, before he could utter any name he knew to be upon the document, Peter Dean, standing just behind Gresham, said, "It's Gresham. Garlin Gresham."

There was a quietness now, as the falcon eye moved up and down the document. "Gresham, eh? Then where's his name? I do not find it here. Come forward, Gresham."

Somehow Gresham tottered forward without support. His great hulk was bent as he searched for the axis of equilibrium. And a tremendous drunken dignity came upon him.

"Your name is not upon this oath," Galton said.

He was bewildered. "Shnot there?" he said.

Still Galton played. "You are a rebel? You refused to sign this?"

Gresham shook his head. The movement threw him off balance, so that he clutched at a table for support. "Kingsh man with besh of 'em," he said thickly. "Washn't here."

"It's true," Alwyn said. "He was not here."

"Indeed. And why not? Our understanding was you'd set a day for this good work. No such sacred document as this, bearing the names of the King's subjects, lies open upon a table that a man may wander in and make his mark whenever he chooses."

"But it was a matter of great importance," Alwyn said. "It was a question . . ."

"Importance," Galton echoed. "Importance? No single man's life or death is of importance, unless his name is written here."

Still Gresham groped in the fogged recesses of his mind. "Splain it, Al'n," he said, balance regained, dignity restored.

Alwyn fought to keep the desperation from his voice. "It is true, Captain. It was a family matter. His daughter. . . ." For a moment his voice faltered. "There was a child, you see, and it was necessary for him to get the father's acknowledgment that the child was his before Mistress Gresham became betrothed to another man."

"Spare me the details of your rustic revelries, sir, you know what Sir Henry Clinton has written here."

But Alwyn's desperation had reached Gresham. The fog was beginning to lift, and he cursed the thickness of his own tongue and somehow found speech. "Shtrue, I tell you, Cap'n, shtrue. Shwere we been, Ballentyne 'n' me, makin' las' plansh for my girl's good name . . . sho . . . so I wasn't here that day for findin' the youngest Macon boy that fooled my girl. . . ." It was too much for him; he sat down and fell over on the table.

Outside there was a stirring of men and horses. Galton's aide pushed through the door and looked significantly at his captain. "We're ready, sir. We've found three wagons in good condition and filled them. We'll wait on you, sir."

But Galton took his time. His hand moved out for the half empty tankard of ale beside Gresham's head and turned the tankard over. Gresham came up spluttering and conscious, leaning back in his chair, blinking.

"Rise, sot," Galton said.

He rose, and it seemed to Alwyn that his balance was better now. Galton signaled his aide with an imperious finger, and the aide came to him.

"Take this man into custody."

The men in the inn straightened as one man. Galton was not unaware of their faces, determined, angry. At the door he turned to

86

them. "You will remember there are sixty armed men in your town. It were well you kept your places."

Gresham was blind in the sunlight, standing between two infantrymen. He shuffled, and there was no longer any desperation in him, only incomprehension.

At the end of the park the infantrymen stood in relaxed rows, broken into two units, with the loaded wagons between. Around and behind them the green-coated dragoons walked their horses, turned their horses, laughed, with their bellies full and their brains singing with the strong ale. Galton crossed the road with his strong limping gait, drawing on his gloves as he went. When he reached the head of the column he conferred briefly with the little group of dragoons, standing, while they leaned to him from their horses. Bartholomew, silent and subdued, went to the forward unit of infantry.

Alwyn pushed his way out on the inn porch, seeing Gresham still standing in the road, between the two regulars. Glancing up, he saw Galton mount a big black with white patches, springing queerly from the leg with the old wound. Men, and women too now, had gathered in the park, amid the litter of mug and bottle and broken china. Galton lifted his hand and the dragoons closed in behind him, leaving the infantry flanks open. His bold head turned toward the inn, and Alwyn thought he could see the fierce shining of the eye.

"Gresham."

Garlin Gresham lifted his head as though it hurt him.

"Come down here, Gresham."

He moved carefully, feeling for steadiness.

"Stop right there, Gresham."

He stopped, in the middle of the road. He was an automaton, existing on the sustenance of command.

Galton said, "Run for your life, rebel."

Alwyn spoke but did not know it. He stepped forward, but Brant's hand came down on his arm like steel and held him. And Gresham still did not know, even when the dragoons wheeled out of the park and came down on him.

He waited dumbly, but had he not waited it would not have mattered. They were almost upon him before his feet moved, and even then they could not move quickly enough. He stood in the road chest high to the horses and saw them bearing down on him and stared at the onrushing blur of hoof and helmet, and did not even comprehend the rhythmic formation-draw of the sabers. But he heard the hooves after a time, a long time, and that was when he began to run, and there was now a grain of mercy in the fact that his back was to them and he could no longer see them.

He did not fall. There was no saving grace which let him go down under the hooves. They overtook him three quarters of the way down the road, just past Malcolm's, and the sun going west came white off the uplifted sabers. He made one little sound, of disbelief and surprise, and the surprise came clearly, audibly, as if he had expected to feel the hooves and could not understand not feeling them. The horses flowed around him, did not touch him. The icy anesthetic of the sabers froze him, before they struck him down.

Along the fringes of the road there was sound, as if wind moved in the trees, but the sound was not wind, the sound was human, rising, falling, like a wave cresting and flowering and washing back into itself again.

8

THE WATER HOLES where the stock came to drink were gray and scummy; bronze cattails speared their placidity. The surface inequalities of the land were open and sharp: the meadows, bounded by thickets and stone walls, rolled without softness in the harsh grasses. The sun went down heavily in a sea of thick mist. Wind stirred daily from the south, bringing with it the faint musty scent of stagnant water. The coolness had come. The sky promised rain and the earth waited, and the rain came. It was the last day of October.

Sabrina ran from the hen house to the back door, the egg basket over her arm. "There were only six eggs," she said.

Jewel did not turn around. "Is I supposed to be surprise at that?

It's like even them damn hens been gittin' it dinned into 'em they's a war on."

Sabrina put the basket down and took the woolen shawl from her shoulders. Her dark chestnut hair picked up the red from the morning fire, and the gold. In the dampness it curled, falling into deep waves from crown to shoulder. She pulled it back tightly, holding it in a thick club, taking a ribbon from the back of a chair, slipping it deftly around the club.

Jewel said, "Them damn hens. You wants somepin to eat?"

"No," Sabrina said. "No, I don't want anything."

"You goin' to town with Brant?"

"No," she said, still standing, still holding her hair back, although it was held tightly now by the ribbon.

"I ain't blamin' you," Jewel said. "Ain't fittin' to even stick you little finger out in. Them dawgs is scrabbin' round under the porch from one day's end to the next. Got more sense than Brant. What's he goin' off for?"

"I don't know," Sabrina said. "I reckon to see if Aiken's got anything . . . something."

Jewel turned from the mess she was stirring in the iron pot and looked at her. In the loose black dress her figure was breastless, hipless. "Keeps on, we be killin' that last goat an' the cow to boot." Then she said, "I got a little coffee."

"All right," Sabrina said. She sat down at the table, leaning her elbows on the scoured pine boards. Jewel put the cup down almost angrily. "Doctor Malcolm comin' for dinner tonight?"

"I don't know."

"You don't know, you don't know. You lookin' mighty peeky, Brina, an' no reason I kin think of for it. What's the matter with you?"

"I don't know," she said again. Then she said clearly, "Anyway it's the rain. Why can't it stop? Why doesn't it stop?"

"Well, all right," Jewel said, "if that's how you feels. I reckon it'll stop sometime. I reckon sometime sun'll shine an' hens'll lay an' house'll be so fuller meat we be throwin' it to them dawgs."

Sabrina sighed. A week ago they had given a cow to be driven along with other stock and foodstuffs from Benton's Crossing to a midland dispatching post, where the supplies were slated for distribution to British and Loyalist troops. After the cow, they knew, there would be other offerings and sacrifices: fodder, chickens, eggs, preserved vegetables and fruits. Occasionally British commissary agents passing through had confiscated necessities for the army; sometimes it was a family down on its luck which had to be fed and got off to a fresh start. There was a promise of lean times in Benton's Crossing, and the prospect of a long winter lay bleakly before them.

Sabrina said, "And I reckon we'll even get some white sugar again, won't we?"

"White sugar." Jewel sniffed. "Only ones eatin' white sugar is them damn Englishmens."

"Jewel."

"I ain't keerin' any more," Jewel said. "I'm sick'n tired handin' out food to them Englishmens. Not only that, but havin' to listen to 'em tellin' if you don't hand it out them rebels goin' to take it away from us anyway an' maybe burn us out the house doin' it. I ain't afeered of rebels an' I ain't to war with nobody, an' I'm sick'n tired givin' things away." She pushed the wooden spoon around the edge of the pot vehemently. Her eyes found the window. "There go Brant an' you daddy too. Now why can't they take that boy an' git him out from under my feets for the day?"

"Where is Tag? Have they all eaten?"

"Tag milkin'. They all eaten while you out messin' with that colt. You goin' to help me clean that closet today?"

"I thought you were going to let it go till spring."

Jewel turned and looked at her. "Oh you did, did you? I know you, come spring, you be off in the woods near as bad as Brant. Sides, it ain't even winter yit, not real winter. You gittin' lazier and lazier, Brina, you gittin' jest like Brant, and it wouldn't take much for Tag to catchen it too. You daddy and me, we's the only ones got any ambition around here, and you poor daddy got most of it in his haid."

"Jewel, that's dreadful. What's got into you?"

"What's got into me is what's got into you. All of you, with you talk about wars and loyalty and rebels. I wants them good times back, like when Missy Ellen was here, like when the only trouble you had troublin' you was when some of them Cherrkees went to hell raisin' and you daddy went off all brave to fight with 'em and we all knowed he be comin' back and we jest be savin' up for it. I don't like these wars that starts out with men talkin' and writin' things down and givin' things away, and starts gittin' wuss with men gittin' hung and slashed to death. That ain't my idear war."

Sabrina was silent. After what had happened, a week ago, to Garlin Gresham, as if torture was antidote for shock, calamitous things happened to men, men did calamitous things. William Lyons' old uncle, Jedediah, awoke one morning paralyzed from the waist down and unable to speak, and people recalled that he had once courted Garlin Gresham's eldest sister. Up in the Little Dome territory, either by accident or design, Arley Hawkins killed a young Indian in a mountain defile. Over in Cantine, after the news reached them, one of the Briggs boys assaulted Elias Ward's ugly deformed daughter. There were several betrothals, several marriages, as if prodded by a compulsion to assure immortality, faced suddenly and horribly with the end which awaits all men, men declared themselves. It didn't seem much like war.

Jewel went on grumbling. "You daddy say this rain keeps on, the armies can't move. What armies is what I'd like to know?"

"It's not armies," Sabrina said, hotly now. "It's army. Army. Just one. Ours. Just because the Yancys went kiting off in the hope of getting one of those new-fangled long rifles you've no right to think they went to join an army. They haven't any army. They've only got a disorganized band of . . . of shopkeepers and things that've been fighting for five years now and only won one battle worth talking about. You know that, Jewel. You've heard father say it as many times as I have."

"I heard you daddy read Greek too," Jewel said. "Don' you go knockin' you Uncle Yancys . . . you half Yancy youself. I jest glad you pore mother ain't here to see you all takin' one side an' her brothers takin' another." She swung the pot away from the fire. Her long thin face was black as ebony under the white headpiece. "You know what I thinks, Brina, I thinks you ain't takin' no side with no sense, you's jest down with the irritations."

The two women looked at one another. The fire spoke comfortingly, with a soft sound. Sabrina said, "You know me better than anybody, don't you, Jewel?"

Jewel shrugged. "Whose milk you think you drank before you even knew you daddy's name?"

Tag came in with the milk pail. "Whoo," he said, "I'm wet as a drownded duck."

"Drowned," Sabrina corrected absently.

He made a face at her behind her back, good-tempered, mischievous.

"Stop that," Jewel said. She made a swipe at him with the flat of her hand. He ducked nimbly. "Stop it yourself, Jewel. You want me to spill this milk?"

He went down into the well house with the pail. He came back up immediately, having put the milk to set cream, his earnest ten-year-old face shining with rain and good nature. He did not look like his sister in any way, except that they both had the same mouth, a little too wide, with the full lower lip. He was a rather plain and unremarkable boy, but because of a brother eighteen years older and a sister sixteen years older he had been environmentally endowed with many of the qualities of both.

He went and peered into the pot. "Can I have some of that, Jewel?"

"You a pig," she said. "You a born pig." She got him a bowl and spooned some mush out for him.

He sat down at the table, not looking up or speaking until he had finished the mush and wiped his mouth surreptitiously on the back of his hand. Then he looked up to see if Sabrina was watching him and saw that she was not even looking at him but had gone back to leaning on her elbows and staring down the hall.

"Can I play in the loft?" he said.

Jewel answered. "You ain't got nuthin' else to do, you got some lessings in you room."

He made a face which said the ultimate in pain had swept through him. His mouth contorted; his eyes squeezed shut; he appeared to have been suddenly stabbed through the heart. He left the table. Both women knew that after an hour or so he would slip out the front door and find the sought-after hour of play; both women knew they would make no move to stop him, that they would smile, faintly, knowingly, at one another when they heard the door close behind him.

Sabrina and Jewel spent the afternoon in the little storage space under the stairs. When the sorting and discarding and saving and scrubbing were done, Sabrina went back to the kitchen table, lethargic, half asleep, filled with self-pity. She should have gone with Brant and her father; she could have spent the day with Lavinia Whiting, talked with Fraser, visited with Elizabeth Lyons or Charity Ashe. She put her face in her hands. Talked a lot of silly woman talk with Lavinia or Elizabeth or Charity, talked a lot of heaven knew what with Fraser. Within the darkness of her own hands her brow furrowed; the darkness made her mind heavy. She stood on a great curving stairway in a gown of iridescent satin, she looked through tall windows into the bustling streets of a city, the room she dominated was filled with finely dressed aristocratic women and men, lackeys hurried, there were flowers and a blazing of candles, she was . . . what was it . . . gracious and serene . . . holding out her hand to the handsome, famous young surgeon. . . .

She took her hands away from her face. She was going to have to do something about Fraser. She was going to have to do something about herself and stop feeling so dispassionate about a thing which demanded passion. And she had to stop feeling queer about some of the things Fraser had said that day, down by the spring.

When she looked up there was sunlight in the room. She thought she must have been asleep, must have dreamed. The door banged open behind her and there was Tag again, with a book under his arm so she'd think even if he had been in the loft he'd been studying.

"The gelding jumped the fence," he said, not looking at her, a little worried. "It went off toward the piney woods. You think I'd ought to go and get it before Brant comes back?"

Now he looked at her, and she returned his look levelly. "Did it really jump the fence," she said, "or did you forget to close the barn door?"

Confronted with his sin, he confessed it. Go study, she told him, and got her shawl from the back of the chair and went out into the sunlight. The wet ground was soft and yet crusty in the cold. She liked hearing it crackle underfoot. Overhead the grayness had rolled away; blue sky spread wide in the west.

The gelding was down on the fringe of the piney woods. It was a spirited, skittish creature, steadied down only when it carried Brant. She slipped a rope halter over its neck and turned to find the colt looking at her, its eyes curious and rather proud, its lovely slender face framed in wet pine.

"We are all of us getting careless," she said aloud. "Come on, you gelding. You, colt." The colt came to her. "Keep off my feet now," she said to it. "Just like Duke you are. Take my shoes right off my heels."

She led the gelding. The colt walked at her shoulder. It was still and clear. There was a light over the trees, etching them in gold against the pale sky. They left the marsh and came through a flat-land and then into a thicket of second growth saplings, where a thin path ran. Now the colt was forced to walk third. It nibbled at the gelding's flank. The gelding kicked at it spitefully.

"You all stop it," Sabrina said. "Here, colt, you go first, then. This gelding is all mule in the hind feet. Damn you, colt, go along now!"

Then the gelding went up, almost jerking the rope out of her hands, and made blowing sounds and skittered sidewise, and she looked where he had gone off the path and saw the man lying in the thicket.

She could feel her heart beating in her throat. She stood motion-less and the horses waited and she waited, but the man did not move. She thought, over the shock, it is someone from the Cross-ing, or one of the farms, and he has been hurt and his horse has wandered off and left him, and I am a fool. Resolutely she started into the thicket.

When she came close to him she stood a long time, thinking now that he might be dead, but while she stood, frightened and think-ing, he opened his eyes and looked at her and she saw he was a stranger and fell back.

He said, "Can you get help for me? I've got a gunshot wound in the shoulder. I've lost a good deal of blood."

She stood watching him numbly. He was not young. There were fine wrinkles about his eyes, a wrinkling of sun-and-wind burn, and the eyes were clear and tawny under heavy blond brows. The straight white-blond hair, almost silver, swept back cleanly, long on his neck but cut short at the temples. He was thin and wore a heavy linen jacket and deerskin breeches and boots.

She could think of nothing to say to him but the trite thing, the obvious thing. "Who are you?"

There was no strength in his voice; he simply lay there on the sodden ground, watching her levelly, unblinking, with the clear bit-ter eyes. "Mistress, who I am may never change the course of your life. The fact that I shall die here may, for then you can tell your children you once let a man bleed to death. Will you help me or won't you?"

She went to him. The white linen jacket was black with stiffened blood which flaked off on her fingers when she split the cloth and opened the heavy woolen shirt beneath it. Fresh blood seeped out and she tore a piece from the sleeve of the jacket and wadded it and stuffed it into the ugly hole the ball had made. He took her ungentle ministrations uncomplainingly. She stood up and said, "I will be back."

She swung on the gelding and struck him across the neck with the rope and he went off as if she had cut him with a switch. The colt ran behind.

Brant was back from the Crossing, unloading supplies by the kitchen door under Jewel's watchful eye. She raced down the path from the barn and pulled the gelding up short and slid off him. "Brant, there's a man lying down in the thicket. He's been hurt."

He rolled a cask of molasses down the wide plank he had set up against the wagon. "Who?" he said.

"I don't know who he is, but he's been shot and he's bleeding, and will you please come now? Now, Brant."

"Right," he said agreeably. "Watch your feet, Jewel." He rolled the barrel at Jewel, deliberate, sober-faced when she jumped clear. "I told you, Jewel. If your feet were an inch longer I couldn't unload at all."

"Brant," Sabrina moaned.

"Right," he said again, and climbed in the front of the wagon and started up so suddenly that she had to run to climb in. "You going to have to tether that colt," he said. "How'd you find this man? Who shot him?"

She shivered, half with cold, half with remembering. "He was in the thicket when I brought your gelding back. I don't know who shot him. I never saw him before."

He whistled softly, cheerfully, all the way to where the thin path led into the thicket. The first darkness was beginning to settle; the evening star came out directly over the path. "Can't git in there," he said. "I'll have to bring him out."

While she waited in the wagon the colt came up and waited too. "Go away, colt," she said, shivering uncontrollably now. Brant came out of the thicket, staggering a little with the weight over his shoulder. She helped him get the man in the wagon bed.

Brant still whistled, low and cheerfully, between his teeth. There were rectangles of light on the ground from the kitchen windows when they drove in the yard. Sabrina climbed down and Brant got in the back of the wagon and hoisted the man, and now, as if the comfort of help and the sound of human voices had restored him, the man stood, holding to Brant, and she saw that he was taller than Brant and slim through the hips. Then Alwyn was in the doorway, with a lamp raised, and Tag was peering around the jamb, and the man, swaying, holding to Brant, said, "Before I go any further I'd better tell you I am Major Orne Savage of Morgan's Riflars, First Virginia."

The hand holding the lamp remained steady. There was no change in Alwyn's face or stance, except for a tightening of the mouth, a straightening of the shoulders.

"Bring him in," he said to Brant, and Brant got him across the threshold and into the kitchen, and the light and the warmth were too much, so that the man fell forward against Alwyn. Brant slung him across his shoulder again and took him across the room and put him down on Jewel's pallet in the corner. Alwyn handed the lamp to Sabrina and said, "Hold it for me."

The new blood had saturated the wadding. Alwyn pulled the strip of linen out, and the blood followed it, clean and red. He took a knife and heated it in the fire until it was hot and sterile, and wiped it on a clean linen strip, cooling it, and probed for the ball. The long slim body arched a little; the face turned to the wall, not wanting to show itself. Alwyn found the ball, a heavy one, and deep, and took it out and looked at it curiously. He cleaned the wound. "Put some ash in that water," Jewel told him, peering over his shoulder. Now the wound bled freely. Sabrina brought fresh linen and Alwyn tore it into strips and made a new wadding. The man lay motionless, with his eyes closed and a bitter darkness of shadow at the corners of his mouth. "Feed him," Alwyn said, and got up and turned away.

"Father," Sabrina said, "is he going to die?"

Alwyn's face was weary, disturbed. "No. There are no bones shattered. He will not die." He looked down at the still white face. "Brant, get him some dry clothing. He will have to go to the barn, with the Brevards coming."

Brant whistled between his teeth. Tag said, "In the barn? But, Daddy . . ."

Jewel rapped him on the head. "Keep shet, Tag. You daddy know whut he doin'. You all hep Brant." She did not look at the door closing behind Alwyn.

Brant spooned out the hot broth, the rum, seeing the pain etched sharply in the pleasant network of lines around the rebel officer's eyes. But the man could not rise of his own will; it was Brant's shoulder he leaned upon again, and the little boy trying, wanting to help, and Brant full of the old indifference, but gently so, and Alwyn in the next room, not even reading now, but looking into the fire, not seeing the fire.

Sabrina, curtains clutched about her like a drape, watched Brant half lead, half carry the man up the path to the barn, watched the little boy run behind. Still nervous and shaken, she undermined her father's composure at last, questioning him until he could no longer keep the irritation and the concern from his voice. Still he was understanding, placing his hands upon her shoulders, speaking patiently, as though he explained to a child: he will not die, it is a clean wound; it is simply that it will take time for him to regain his strength. It is not my wish that this man should spend as much as an hour in the barn, but upon this night, or any other night of my life, I will not have the Brevards at my table, and a rebel in my house.

9

HE LAY ON HIS BACK in the straw, bedding down as a dog beds down, working a hollow in the dry fodder with his body. It was cold. He was cold all over, except for the arm, which burned from shoulder to wrist. Beneath him the horses stamped softly. It was so still he could hear them breathing and see his own breath in the air like smoke.

The cold wracked him, and he thought that he would go down and lie with the horses; he thought how good it would be to burrow into the straw and sleep close to the warm animal bodies. Because he felt Brant Quantrell had been wrong, bedding him down in a corner near the cows: anybody could see you bedded down with a bandaged shoulder, in a corner with the cows. After Brant and Tag had gone back to the house, he had managed to climb the ladder to the loft, clinging to the rungs with his good hand, blanket slung over his shoulder. It had been a mistake. He could almost feel the sleek warmth of the colt under his head, and he wanted to get up and go down to it but he could not summon the strength.

Sabrina said softly, "Major."

He mumbled something, he was not sure exactly what he said. He saw the top of the ladder in the dim loft opening, and then her head appeared, featureless in the darkness but with a faint light behind it.

"Are you all right, Major?"

"Yes," he said.

"I've brought you another blanket. You shouldn't have come up here. If you'd come down with the horses they'd help keep you warm. Can you get down all right, do you think?"

"Yes," he said. "I think I can." But he did not move.

"Come along then." Her voice was raw with impatience. "Come, I'll help you."

He raised himself on the bound arm, dropped back, clenched his teeth hard, but the hurt sound came out. Sabrina cleared the top of the ladder and bent over him. He looked up and saw the light around her hair and smelled woodsmoke and warmth.

"I wouldn't let a fox freeze out here, Major. If you can manage I'll steady the ladder for you."

"All right," he said then, stung by her straightforwardness. He did not remember getting to his feet, or swinging over on the ladder, or going down it to where the lantern burned. When he reached the barn floor he leaned against the ladder, spent and nauseated. Her weight coming down shook the rungs under him; then her hand was light on his shoulder for a moment and she stepped down. The lantern, with its tiny flare, seemed to exude waves of comforting warmth.

"Look," he said, "you don't have to do all this."

"All what, Major?" The words were clipped, broken off short. "Give you some straw to sleep on, and a blanket and a cup of rum. A lot that is."

He remembered what she had said about the fox. "You don't have to do it," he said again, clinging dizzily to the ladder. His head burned, and he was cold.

She touched his shoulder. "Please lie down."

He did not want her help. "No," he said. "No, I'm all right," and walked steadily, forcing himself, and went into the stall with the colt. The slender golden head swung around and the eyes looked at him, and then the eyes saw Sabrina, and Savage thought if it were a dog it would wag its tail. He let himself down gingerly, and Sabrina came and knelt by the colt. She put her hand on its head and it nuzzled at her.

"The mare died and I raised him alone. He's to be called Zeus."

"What?" he said. Her words came to him slowly, delayed, as if they were words in a dream, or he floated in some vacuum of delirium. But he knew he was conscious, knew he was cognizant, because her words amused him.

"Zeus," she explained calmly. "Zeus was a . . ."

"I know all that." He felt drunkenly rational now. "Someone translates for you?"

"My father. My father is self-taught. He can read Latin and Greek and French."

"And your father is a Loyalist and despises us."

"He doesn't despise you. He despises what you are trying to do." She sat back on her heels, regarding him gravely. "For as long as I can remember my father has been a patriarch. Not just for his own family, but for all the families miles around us. He's settled quarrels and officiated in court, though he's not a barrister. Not that he couldn't be, I guess, if he wanted to. It's a sort of saying they have around here: ask Alwyn Quantrell. Because somehow my father always knows. And he knows now. He would not refuse you, Major. I doubt if he would have put you out here tonight, except that friends are coming, and they would not understand."

He started to speak, but she interrupted. "Don't you mistake what I'm saying. You're a human being, and you've been hurt, and it's not that we think maybe you shouldn't have been hurt, it's the . . . well, it's the *pity* of the thing. You got hurt because you were riding the wrong side of the fence, maybe. But whichever side you were on, it wouldn't matter to my father, if you were hurt and needed help, because he is a gentleman. And an Englishman."

He looked at her intent face in the light of the lantern; her face swam in his vision, misty and beautifully somber, as if she spoke some terrible truth and believed it original with herself. He worked hard for control; he was aware of the hot tautness of his skin. "Let's get this furrow turned now, mistress. I too am an Englishman, and proud of it. I can't boast any self-taught business because I wasn't self-taught, I had the advantage of schooling in London. But I was born and brought up in Virginia of good English stock, and I am as English as your father. I shall say one thing more: you take yourself too seriously."

The cone of light from the lantern was golden on the too high cheekbones, the generous mouth, the wide gray eyes. She still looked at him intently and with beginning anger.

He said, "You could be beautiful if you would not let your face reflect your belief in your own efficiency."

That got her on her feet. "Good night. I would leave you the lantern but . . ."

"I know," he said wearily, "you're afraid I'd burn down the barn, along with Zeus and all you good Englishmen."

Now she could not help smiling. "You are so bitter, Major."

"And your father is not bitter, in his way? Well, what's the good in being a country oaf, full of bumptious gaiety and joviality and simplicity. Bitterness is a sort of seasoning, mistress. No realist can face life without it. It makes us see the horrible humor of the most mundane everyday circumstances."

"No," she said. "No, I feel life must be terribly monotonous for bitter people." She stood looking down at him. "Why are you bitter? Why are you fighting? What are you doing here? Have you a family, a wife, children? What made you come here like this?"

"You want to know a deal, don't you?" The tawny eyes were hard under the heavy blond brows. She came and knelt by the colt again, setting the lantern down. He said in a weary monotone, "I am forty years old, my full name is Orne Edward Savage, I am an Englishman by descent and a Virginian by choice, I have two sons, ages ten and thirteen, and I once had a wife who was also English and who remained English by choice. She divorced me in London three years ago and has since taken unto herself another husband, Frederick, Earl of Haight. I wish him joy of her." He gestured briefly with the good arm. "I live in a twelve-room house of white brick with my sons and my mother. My mother is seventy years old and weighs one hundred pounds and is about as frail and delicate as a full-grown oak."

He was talking too much. As if the rum he had drunk an hour ago was too dark, too strong, he was exhilarated, lifted, garrulous. And he could not stop himself.

"And I am here, mistress, because some months ago a friend of mine named Morgan thought it was time we did something about the war. He talks war well and he fights it better, and if I had to choose lots I decided it would be with him. Thanks to the excellent marksmanship of one of your neighbors, I am now in the position in which you find me . . . about to sleep with a colt bearing the impossible name of Zeus."

"You *are* bitter," she said, a little disbelieving. "I am sorry about it."

"Naming a poor innocent colt Zeus? You should be."

"About your wife. Did you love her?"

"Good God," he said, "that's a question young ladies don't go about asking total strangers." (And could not stop himself again, though he wanted to.) "I suppose I did. Only she couldn't stand it. The being alone. The no tea parties. The no people. Even the country wasn't beautiful enough to keep her." His eyes were brooding. "Even I wasn't. I can't blame her. There's no sense saying there are any two people in the world cut out of the same bolt, because there aren't. Somewhere, no matter how alike they seem, there's been a slip of the shears or a lopsided cut, maybe only an inch or two long, but enough to do the damage. And that's it, and you can't sew the two pieces together because they won't fit."

"I don't believe that," she said.

"I didn't expect you to believe it. I didn't think you'd believe anything I said. Why should you? Whatever I've thought and known must be completely alien to anything you've thought and known. How many times have you been in love?"

"Never," she said.

"Oh God, you're too honest to boot. That's one of the greater faults of efficient people."

"You are impossible," she said without anger. "What is it like, Virginia?"

"Like nothing here. Full of old trees, with a valley cut between the mountains that can't be talked about because there aren't any words, and a river in the valley. I live along the river, in sight of it, and you go down a dirt lane half a mile long, with a snake fence along it, and willows on either side, and you come to the house and there are willows there too."

"It sounds beautiful. I don't think you should be bitter. I think you are very fortunate."

He put his head back on the colt, turning to stroke its flank, not looking at her. The anger was white in his voice. "Why don't you come along with me? Marry me and go back with me and be a mother to my sons and perhaps raise a few sons of your own?"

She stood up and took the lantern. Her voice shook. "And if I should ever need you, Major, where will I find you?"

"Wherever the army is." He closed his eyes. "But don't look for me until you find out what you want to be in this world."

She went out quickly, so crushed that tears stung in her eyes. The frosty ground was cold under her thin slippers. When she reached the house she picked up the hem of her shawl and wiped ineffectually at her face.

Brant stood against the doorframe, inside, winding and unwinding a piece of string around his right index finger. He was whistling under his breath, hardly making any sound at all, yet carrying a formless melody which was clearly audible. He watched Sabrina put the lantern down and throw off the shawl before he said in a heavy half whisper, "The Major good and warm?"

She did not look at him. "I don't know. I don't even care."

"Father'd throw a fit, he knew you'd been out in the barn with that rebel."

"Well, why don't you tell him then, damn it?"

He said, shaking his head, "You only cussing because you think whatever it is you're sayin' sounds bigger when you say it cussing."

She whirled and faced him. Then she came across the room and put her hands on his arms and said his name, twice. She picked up her shawl and went into her room.

He did not see it coming, and so winced when Jewel struck him over the head with her thimble. "Now what did you do that for?"

"Cause you ain't too big to be thrashed, that's why," she said.

He felt his head gingerly and went on whistling.

It was full dark when they sat down to dinner in the family room, gathered about the white cloth and the bone china in the soft-moving candle flare. It was no special occasion; it was simply that out of long habit, years of habit, Alwyn's family dined at Brevard Hundred on the first Sunday evening of the month; Brevard's family dined at Brandyhill later in that same month on an evening chosen, plucked from the busy routine of people who worked their own land without the forced assistance of slaves.

This was an ill-chosen evening, Alwyn thought. The black un-shakable preoccupation stayed with him; he could feel the vacancy of his own smile, he fought the halting emergence of his own voice. He was blank and empty, looking down the length of the table at Sabrina.

She sat in the fruitwood chair which had been Caroline Aman-da's, a chair with elaborate carvings of grapes and vines and leaves on its high back and along the slender arms. Opposite her, at the head of the table, Alwyn sat in the big chair which matched it, but whose arms were heavier and wider and bereft of carving. He never raised his eyes to the little feminine chair without seeing first Sarah Ann Yancy's round figure and then, as if materializing out of a dream, the cool whiteness of Ellen Bowie's face against the mellow wood. Then he would realize it was Sabrina, grown, a woman, with none of Sarah Ann's roundness or Ellen's whiteness, taller than her mother or her stepmother, with those alert dreamless gray eyes and his own fine facial structure and Brant's clear dark skin. She had loosened the thick chestnut hair, letting it fall to her shoulders. She wore her best dress, a heavy China silk striped in gold and blue and white and fastened at the throat with a row of blue glass buttons. He watched her; her eyes held him, faintly, inexplicably reproving, full of a questioning which bewildered him, a strange and somehow anxious inquiry which he could not answer, since he did not know its nature. He did not like her looking at him like this; he did not like being carried, weightless and floating, on the direct onrush of her look. And he felt, out of the closeness, the intimacy with her, with these people, his own English countrymen, his own Loyalist allies, a bond, a tie visible and shining and strong as steel, and the tie bound itself to him and to his daughter Sabrina, and left his own English countrymen beyond the pale of bondage, ranged along the steel-sharp edges, outside, and father and daughter watched one another and the thin gray ghost of trouble, exorcised from the barn, stood balanced between them on the strong slender bridge of the bond.

With great physical effort he looked away from her, and the last thing of her his eyes saw in that moment was the final, closing, blue glass button at the base of her throat. And he did not see it again, because when he looked away from one woman he looked at another: Honora at his side in the lovely soft crimson dress and the roped pink pearls and the dark yellow hair piled high, with a soft cascading of curls on the nape of her neck. Her eyelashes were short and thick, and you could trace the delicate plane of bone in the heart-shaped face. He said, not merely to compliment her, not merely because he truly meant it, but because he could not help himself, "How beautiful you are, Honora."

She flushed. "Thank you, Uncle Alwyn." (He watched the pink bloom of softness and color come into her face.) "You're the only one's told me so!"

He took her fingers and squeezed them in his own, and felt how cold they were, and how nervously they responded to pressure. Why did I do that? What right have I to assure, to reassure this girl, this girl with her eyes and heart and mind set upon my son? And he saw her in that moment as Brant must have seen her all his life: saw how the restrained panic, the controlled hysteria which lay sometimes just under the sparkling veneer became instead a combination of the straining rigidity and high-strung skittishness which he admired in a good jumper; a quick shining of the eye under the thick golden lashes, a quick shuddering of the slender shoulders, and through it all the courage, the struggle to be brave, as if whatever she feared was a lance upon which she had impaled herself but stood upright, dragging the thing with her, through her, unconquerable and conquering. He released her hand, did not look at her again, did not look at Sabrina, strove to return to the blessed panacea of the blankness and emptiness which he had somehow lost. "Yes?" he said, turning his head so that the stream of Margaret Brevard's words poured directly into his ear.

Her voice was without sharpness, but somehow shrill, insistent. "I said it was a pity McLeod wouldn't tell us. He acts as if it was something which had happened to him personally and to nobody else, and I told John, I said, I think it's perfectly dreadful of him. . . . I know he's told the Quantrells all about it, and just try to get one word out of him. I told John, I can just see him sitting over here discussing it with you, and I think it's perfectly dreadful he won't discuss it with John. John always has something so definitely helpful to contribute at such times, don't you, John?"

Brevard said, "Eh?" not looking up. Alwyn thought the habit, the saying of the brief, meaningless word when he knew exactly, precisely what had been said, had developed in John Brevard simply and solely because of Margaret Brevard, his wife. She talked at times until both she and those around her were exhausted. Yet he did not dislike her. Say what you would, she had been a good mother to Honora, she had adapted herself well to the new life she had been brought to, and perhaps that was her destiny and now it had been fulfilled and that was all God or man could ask of her. "Yes?" he said again.

"After all, we have *got* to be neighborly with these itinerant Scots people, and the least they could do is tell us something about it. I've thrown all sorts of hints, and as I tell John, you can't be angry with the man because he's never mean or ungracious, he just won't discuss it."

"Discuss what, Margaret?" Alwyn said.

"Haven't you been listening? Culloden. The battle of Culloden Moor. I *know* McLeod was one of the boatmen who brought Flora MacDonald and The Pretender to safety. And he won't talk about it."

Brant said gently, pushing his plate away, leaning his arms on the table, "They don't call it Culloden, Aunt Margaret. The Scots call it Drummossie Moor."

No dismay touched her face. "And so? I am an Englishwoman and it is Culloden to me. Let the Scots call it what they will. Drummossie!"

Tag was old enough to suffer under his father's rigidly enforced rule that children at table were silent unless spoken to. He flashed a quick look at Alwyn and leaned his arms on the table as he had observed Brant do. "Brant knows all about Culloden," he said, and then was instantly downcast.

Honora saved him, leaping for the opening, shining, glowing, full of life. For Brant. "If you do know, it's because Ian's told you, isn't it, Brant? See, he does know, Aunt Margaret."

Brant shrugged. "Whatever I know's second time around. You just better keep reckoning on Ian, Aunt Margaret."

She sighed. "But he's so secretive. And I should like to know what she's like, this Flora MacDonald, wouldn't you, John?"

"Eh?" Brevard said, removing a splinter of bone from his mouth.

And she sighed again, the sound as much habit as her husband's monosyllabic unconcern. Alwyn looked at her, noticing the incipient mustache on the upper lip, the flesh beginning to fold on a neck which must once have been one of the loveliest in London.

Her pale eyes were so wonderfully clever, so wonderfully innocent; the ravaged beauty of her face forecast Honora's future ravaged beauty, as though Honora were truly her child rather than the child of her dead sister.

"Anyway," Honora said brightly, now as clever, now as innocent, now flesh-and-bone proof that simplicity is not necessarily simple, "nothing about Culloden could possibly be as exciting as what Mr. Shaver told our overseer today. He shot a man."

"My dear," Margaret said, "a *lot* of men got shot at Culloden. And you don't know whether Mr. Shaver is wholly honest about this . . . this tale he's telling."

"What's this?" Brant did not look at his father. "Who got shot?"

"Who was shot, John?" Margaret said.

"Eh? Oh, I don't know, some chap or other."

"Where? When? How long ago?" Brant said.

"A day or so . . ." Honora began.

Margaret looked fondly at her niece. "If what Mr. Shaver says is true, he was coming down through the woods north of here and saw a man on a horse. The man began to ride away, and Mr. Shaver hailed him and he didn't stop, so Mr. Shaver shot at him. He said he knew he hit him, because he fell over in the saddle, but he kept right on running. And then he found the horse, a mile or so beyond, but the man was gone and he did not find him."

"It was a rebel," Honora said shortly, looking at Margaret as if she asked Margaret's permission to speak.

Sabrina's eyes were hard, voice a little strained. "How do you know that, Onny?"

"Because Mr. Shaver has his gun, and he says it's a rebel gun, one of those long rifles with some sort of military carving on it. Mr. Shaver says . . ."

"Honora," Margaret said kindly.

Brant put his fork down. "Del Shaver says a lot of things. Most of 'em's through the top of his head."

"Why, Brant." Margaret fluttered her lids at him, feigning shock.

"It's true, Aunt Margaret. He's a braggart and a liar, and I wouldn't take any stock in his bein' one of us. When he's drunk I'll wager he's Whig."

"But he has the rifle," John Brevard said reasonably, almost disinterested. "Our overseer saw it. One of those Pennsylvania rifles, made by Deckhardt or somebody."

Brant was casual. He was good at this, this game, Alwyn thought. Alwyn Quantrell, trying to keep his hands steady, wondering if they could hear his heart, for he could hear it, moving unsteadily in his chest. His head jerked a little when Margaret spoke to him.

"What do you think, Alwyn?"

"Why . . . I haven't any thought on it, Margaret. It may be true and it may not be. If it is true there's little to be done about it. If it isn't true, no harm's done, except perhaps in the manner Shaver got the rifle."

Margaret shuddered. "You mean he may have stolen it, don't you? But from whom? I think we should get all the men together and make a thorough search, every thicket, every house, every barn."

Alwyn's knife rattled against his plate. His eyes met and held Brant's, and he thought, does Brant see me as I feel in this moment, helpless, guilty? Guilty, oh God, guilty, but you don't let another man suffer and die because his politics are not yours. Is the guilt in my eyes? Can my son see the guilt in my eyes? He felt sweat break out in the palms of his hands. But Brant had looked away and was laughing easily, with genuine humor. "Honest to catamounts, Aunt Margaret, nobody tells you anything, do they? Only way you're going to be happy in this world is to git right out there and see for yourself. Head this search party of yours yourself. Git up pretty and lead us on."

Her softly painted mouth made an O of horror. She loved to pretend Brant had shocked her. She loved to look at Brant, pretending, knowing he knew she pretended. Pretending or not, she loved to look at him, at the fine, hard young body and curving mouth and careless hair, to imagine him in her house, imagining him as Honora's husband and still imagining him not as Honora's husband, but in her house morning, noon, night, twenty-four hours a day. . . .

Alwyn said steadily, "I feel if Del Shaver shot anyone that would not be the end of it."

"Specially if he was wounded," Brant said, eating again, lifting the fork to his mouth. "Del'd want the pleasure of finishing what he started out to do."

Honora said, "But you say you think Del Shaver's a Whig? If he is, why would he shoot a man carrying a rebel rifle?"

"Because he shot first and asked politics after."

"No," Honora said, a frown settling between the bright blue eyes. "No, because after he got the rifle he'd know it was one of his own people carrying it, and he'd find him and try to save him. Wouldn't he, Uncle John?"

Brant could see she was getting glossy-eyed now, excited, nervous, feverish. She said, "But he might be out there right now, and not wounded at all, just making believe. He might be right outside this house. . . ."

"He ain't nowhere," Brant said tightly, mouth set. "And if he was, Del Shaver wouldn't look for him, Whig or Tory. He wouldn't give a hang. He's got himself a long rifle and that was all he was ever after to begin with." His dark head was bent over his plate. He raised his eyes without raising his head and saw that Tag was sitting bolt upright opposite him, his eyes round and expressionless and still so full of expression that Brant felt a hot flushing of blood in his neck. A vein began to work in his temple. Don't open your mouth, Tag . . . don't say one word . . . just say no when I ask you did you milk the goat.

"Tag, you milk the goat?"

"No," the boy said, starting at the suddenness of the question.

"You better, before it gits any later. You excuse him, Aunt Margaret."

She looked at Tag from the superiority of age and sex and Brevard. "You are excused to milk the goat, Timothy."

"Thank you," he muttered, and slid from the chair. Brant breathed easier.

"You avoid the question, my dear Brant," Margaret said. The eyelashes fluttered briefly at him, as if she would tell him they shared in some dark conspiracy, as if she would combat and defeat, by flutter of lash, the amusement in his clear gray eyes. "I think the men should search the area thoroughly. Who knows where the rebel might be? It might be dangerous for all of us . . . think, Alwyn, Sabrina's always off riding alone. It's not safe. We should find him."

"Now, now," Brevard said mildly, "rebels are men just like any other kind of man, Margaret, not monsters. We might turn him over to a court."

Alwyn shook his head. "After what has happened in Benton's Crossing these last weeks, justice may no longer lie in the court, John. We must ignore this. Brant is right."

Margaret tossed her head. "La, Alwyn, what you really mean is if there's a man out there somewhere fighting for his life, let him fight for it without either aid or discouragement. You are too soft, all of you."

"I ain't," Brant said, "but I say live and let live." He turned his head slowly, almost insolently, and looked at Sabrina, and little points of light moved in the pupils of his eyes. "You ain't opened your mouth all evening, Brina. You feel all right? You ain't scared or anything?"

Sabrina upset her wineglass. Alwyn saw that her expression did not change, even when the black-purple stain spread slowly on the linen cloth. Her face was white, strained, hard, rigid. Not even gratitude found its way to her eyes when Margaret said, "Of course she's frightened . . . we all should be. I didn't mean to upset you, my dear, with that talk of riding alone. Oh dear, I *am* sorry, Sabrina."

Sabrina said, "Forgive me," flatly. Brant rose and went to her, righting the glass and mopping at the stain with his napkin. Now Alwyn was suddenly irritable: it was that rebel. It was that damned rebel in his barn had got them all on the ceiling tonight. No wonder Sabrina was troubled: Margaret all for searching and her woman's tongue at them every second to do something; all of them filled with deceits and deceptions because he, Alwyn Quantrell, wouldn't let a man die alone in the woods. . . .

Somehow he struggled through the meal, thankful when John said they could not stay, he had work to plan with his overseer. Margaret predicted rain, assuming a knowing country attitude toward the weather which amused them all and prompted her husband to smile fondly if absently at her. Alwyn stood like a stick as they readied themselves for departure. He saw Brant, holding the crimson wool cloak to Honora's shoulders, turning up the beaver collar about her throat, looking as if, if they were not there, he would gather her up in his arms, looking as if he lied as he looked it. He turned from his son's face, but could not quite shut out the low voices. Are you riding back with us, Brant? And the, Not tonight, Onny, but soon. I'll see you soon. And the disappointment in the girl's face, and the hope that the soon was true. God, what was the matter with Brant, why did he put her off this way, why did it bother him so tonight? That rebel. That rebel.

He waited a long time after the carriage had gone. Sabrina went to the kitchen with Jewel. Tag went to feed the dogs. Old Jim came in and lay by the fire, licking his chops, watching Alwyn with eyes like steady yellow flames. Brant whistled under his breath. After a time Alwyn said resignedly, "All right, son. Go and bring him down."

10

H<small>E SETTLED HIMSELF</small> in the wing chair, moving the lamp close, and tried to read; the London papers were months old and it was the first chance he had had to get at them. But he could concentrate on nothing but sound. He heard the clatter of plates in the kitchen and Jewel's voice, steady, disgruntled. No word from Sabrina. He was tensed to outside sound, footsteps, rain, the wind, anything, so that it was with relief that he heard the front door open and Brant's laugh, and he put the papers down and waited.

Savage stood in the doorway, tired, lined, with his arm bound in the linen sling and a faint but in no way condescending smile on his mouth. "Come in," Alwyn said, a little gruffly. "I trust you were not too uncomfortable in the barn."

"I was most comfortable," Savage said. He moved to the fire and stood before it, letting the heat burn into him. He looked down at Old Jim. "Hello, boy." The hound touched his boot with an inquisitive nose. "That's a fine looking blue you've got there," he said.

"Well, sit down," Alwyn said. "The women are in the kitchen or you could eat and get some rest."

Savage sank into a chair opposite Alwyn. "You are very kind, sir. I won't forget this."

Brant spoke from the table, standing where the linen cloth with its dark wine stain was still spread. "The Major and I going to have a glass of brandy, Father. You want some?"

"A drop, thank you, son," Alwyn said. He shifted in his chair and looked directly at Savage. "You are a Carolinian, Major?"

Again Savage smiled, but Alwyn felt in this moment that the

smile, however easy, was rarely given. "No, sir. Born and bred in Virginia and eager to return to it."

"I can see that. Our country has not treated you well. My people were Virginians . . . my mother was a Wylie from the Shenandoah Valley."

"Is that so?" Savage reached up with his good hand and took the glass from Brant. He sounded so genuinely interested that Alwyn regretted divulging the information. It was as if he had something, much, in common with this man, this rebel. He sat in silence, and then Sabrina came with her sewing, and Tag, and he debated sending the boy to bed and decided against it. Let him learn if there was anything to learn. He said, "Major, you know you are in a Loyalist household. One, I might add, which is so out of the way that we know little of what's happened since our troops won Camden."

Savage said, "Then you are not active Loyalists."

"Active? What do you mean by that, Major? There isn't a Loyalist in Benton's Crossing or any like settlement in the province in any position to be active. Since Camden, it would seem our colonial councils move close to disbanding."

"So you sit at home with locked doors," Savage said dryly.

Brant said, "We got no defense, Major, either against you or our own troops." He avoided his father's face. "But we've had a heap of civil war in the back country."

"I thought your back-country people, because of their isolation, were indifferent."

"They fluctuate," Alwyn said. "One minute they blow hot and the next cold. As a consequence there have been all manner of scattered forays. But men get killed in them too."

Savage said, "You people are enough of a hindrance to be like a nest of wasps, stinging at us and never really doing any damage. Your organization is far too loose, like a torn spider web. In the North you're organized. But your Walter Butlers are few and far between, and your Indians here wouldn't stick with you long enough to hurt us, even if you could persuade them to stick at all."

"You put up a bold front, Major," Alwyn said evenly. "Why should we attempt military organization in our little territory? We have several excellent provincial Loyalist regiments in the field this minute. When Charleston fell to our troops I believe it was evident that we were needed only as a reserve, to supply those troops, to aid and protect them, to supplement their manpower in a position of secondary importance."

"Charleston fell in the summer," Savage said. "Last summer. And then we lost Camden. Do you know where these troops of yours are now?"

Alwyn said, "I suppose you would have us believe that they are all on men-o'-war bound for England?"

"They may be," Savage said, "due to make an appearance in your territory, as you call it, any time, Mr. Quantrell."

"What?" Alwyn said. He leaned forward in his chair. Sabrina had put her sewing down and was sitting very quietly, and Tag came and stood close to Savage's chair. Only Brant was calm, unmoved, going again for the decanter of brandy.

"You know about King's Mountain," Savage said. "You know we strapped you at King's Mountain."

"We know you murdered us at King's Mountain," Sabrina said, her breathing short and uneven. "We know that after we surrendered you massed us and fired into us and killed over a hundred of us, and many of us Loyalists, where we stood."

He looked at her for the first time. "That is true, mistress, and no matter what I say I could not make you believe that it was a terrible mistake, that those things happen in wartime. It happened because a British soldier accidentally discharged his rifle during the process of stacking the captured arms, and because when it discharged some of our troops lost their heads and fired on the prisoners."

"You condone that," Sabrina said.

"I deplore it, mistress. The fact that they were our troops does not make them infallible or guiltless, and I would like to see justice done, as you would."

Alwyn began to tamp tobacco into his pipe. He waited until he had lighted a taper and drawn several mouthfuls of smoke before he spoke, around the stem. "That, I think, is a mistake also, Major. I believe that because they are your troops you should forget all thought of justice. This, as you say, is war, and there is no justice in war. I say you should defend those troops because they *are* your troops, fighting in your cause." And he did not look at his son or his daughter, and he made himself believe himself.

Savage said, "Justice is something alien to war? It belongs expressly to peace?"

"Justice is something which sometimes exists only as a powerful and conditioning word. In war there can be no actual justice."

"Then you do not acknowledge it or believe in it?"

"Man cannot believe in God without believing in justice, Major. It is simply in time of war . . ."

"Yes, man can," Savage said. "Justice has nothing to do with God or war. You're making God and justice synonymous. And they aren't. Because when you speak of justice you aren't speaking of everyday human justice, you're speaking of some sort of Christian retribution. Or maybe of a moral justice. A fairness, let's say it that way. I don't believe in that kind of justice. It doesn't exist. I'm speaking of legal justice, the kind which would court-martial and hang the commander who let those troops fire on their prisoners, who made no attempt to stop them."

Alwyn's mouth trembled as he held back the anger. "I see that you are not only a traitor to your King but an agnostic as well. It does not please me that you should speak this way before my daughter and this boy."

Savage said pleasantly, "Whatever I do or do not believe in, whatever you believe in, it has nothing to do with justice. No angel with a flaming sword is going to descend to chastise man, the guilty, no matter what he's done or how he's done it. Maybe there will be some queer twist of fate ahead for him, some definite punishing circumstance which will make people like you, Mr. Quantrell, say that justice has been done. Which makes your conception of justice seem more like revenge. And an unchristian revenge at that. I say that the only justice for the colonel who let his troops shoot their prisoners should be the judgment of man, not God. And in this case it would be death. Just as I feel that is the only just verdict which could possibly be passed on your redoubtable Colonel Tarleton."

There was no weapon now. "I see you have succumbed then, Major."

"Succumbed. To what?"

"To this ghastly myth which is being perpetrated, by what means the Lord only knows, but I suspect by the rebels. It has come to me recently," he added distastefully, "that Colonel Tarleton has somehow acquired the sobriquet Tarleton the Terrible. I find this as galling as you would if I should refer to Washington the Warmonger."

Savage sat upright, looking at Alwyn uncomfortably. "I hope you will forgive me, sir, if I inform you that the name which so galls you was bestowed upon the colonel not by we rebels but by you Loyalists. You have remained more isolated than I thought. Would you be interested in hearing how the colonel got his name?"

"I would," Brant said, the corners of his mobile mouth flashing up into a crooked grin. "I'd be most interested. Specially since my father and I work on the colonial council which contracted to do all it could for the cause. But I reckon now they're all a little panicky Tarleton's come south."

"Brant," his father said, the pipe in mid-air, astonishment flaring into the strong old face.

"It's true, ain't it, Father? What's the use pretending. I reckon we're panicky, all but you maybe. It ain't we get this way because the colonel, or the rebels, moved South, it might be because there's troops in the South at all. Long as they stayed North we could talk and plan and be big about it, but once it started trailin' South we couldn't. I ain't hot on fightin' and I ain't ashamed to admit it. I just ain't hot on fightin'." He got up and refilled the glasses.

"A man can't be hot on fighting unless he believes in something," Savage said. "What do you believe in, Quantrell?"

"You're talkin' about the war, I believe we ought to win it," Brant said. "We're Carolinians first, but we're Englishmen too, and I don't see this tryin' to break away from it. It's what we are and what's the sense tryin' to be anything different. I don't want to go off and get killed fightin' you people. It ain't worth it to me, and I wouldn't risk it. If you win, I'll go with the times. But I don't think you're goin' to win."

"There's one thing you can do to help us win," Savage said, head a little lowered, the clear bitter eyes on Alwyn. "You can start believing it's true about your own troops. It's true how Tarleton got his name, he got it confiscating everything movable from you people, by sacking your homes and burning them, by ravishing your wives and daughters. We didn't name him. He never got close enough to us to do anything we could name him after."

Brant said softly, "And the only reason he didn't get close to you is you're running so hard, just like you run through the whole damn war."

"That is true," Savage said. "The underdog sustains himself in war by being always where the enemy is not."

Alwyn said suddenly, harshly, "But it is all so futile. What is it all for? We were content here, satisfied with our lot. What is it all about? What is all this talk of freedom? What do you mean by freedom? I have lived through the threat of Spanish invasion, and through the worst of the Cherokee uprisings, and never have I heard such nonsense as this talk of freedom, or dreamed that a nation and her colonies would go to war because of it. I say that I am an Englishman and that I shall die an Englishman, and no matter what you people do, even if you win, you will never be rid of us."

Savage said gently, "We have no wish to rid ourselves of you, sir. You misunderstand. I dare say you misunderstand the whole purpose of this war, because you are blinded by your own unrecognized fears. Tell me, which country do you love most, England, or your own Carolina?"

"They are one and the same."

"They are not. Not geographically or culturally or economically, in any physical or moral way. We are a new way of life here, a new people. I was schooled in England, but it is as far from me now as if I have never been there, ruled by a mad King and a Parliament which, with few brilliant exceptions, would beat us into a likeness of England, chain us forever into servility, feed off us, drink our wealth, uphold her own power as a nation through the fat of her colonies. We are no longer colonies, sir, we are states . . . united states, and we cannot go back to being colonies again."

"Do you hate the country which bred you?" Alwyn shot. "No, you hate the domination, the class prejudice, the idea that you are governed not within your own visible realm, but by a country so far away you can hardly conceive of it any longer, let alone accept it."

"I do not hate anything," Savage said, "but I am well satisfied that you admit English domination."

"Then why are you fighting us? Why in the name of heaven are you fighting this useless fight when you can't even hate?"

"For that freedom you deride," Savage said. "That freedom you look upon with contempt because you cannot understand it, because to you we are already a free nation, because you think only of the personal freedom which you as an individual enjoy. Independence is more than that, sir. There is a communal independence, apart from any personal freedom, and that is what we must have. The idea of hating comes easily to you? Not for yourself, but I see you think of us as a hating people. Perhaps that is true. Hate is necessary in us. Because the only way we can win is through the mass people, and to make the mass people fight you must make them hate. A capable man did that for them some years ago. His name was Sam Adams and he had a pulpit in Congress and he electrified the mass into hating. Our revolt is his seed. And it is people like you, you Loyalists, who force it into too early bloom . . . you much more so than your English troops."

"But you rebel," Alwyn said. "You rebel, and it is a terrible thing."

"What we are doing cannot be in any way construed as so simple a thing as rebellion, or uprising, or even insurrection. You call us rebels, but this is revolution in the purest sense of the word, and we are revolutionaries."

"You split hairs," Alwyn said.

"Not at all. Your dog, here, may rebel at the hour at which he is fed, may even snap at your hand. But he has nothing to suggest, no other hour in his mind when he would prefer to be fed. The true revolutionary revolts to replace, not merely because he is miserable."

Alwyn let himself smile a little. "You are a purist, Major."

"No, it is only that I would have you see the difference. If we rebel, we rise against existing authority without comprehensive thought as to what new authority must be created. If we revolt, it is with knowledge that not only must there be a new authority, but that the new authority has already begun to be created. Motivation for rebellion and revolution may be similar, but only revolution has some ultimate attainment for its springboard. However we are hampered . . . and we are hampered, because our armies are too small, too lacking in training, arms, equipment, supplies, to make but rarely any decisive gain in the field . . . we know what we want, where we want to go when the war is over. We are hampered mutually, you and I, sir, because our partisan guerrilla forces and your partisan Loyalist forces are both outside the pale of any organization and control by organized, controlled troops. You rebel, sir. We revolt."

Sabrina said, "And if you win, what will you have accomplished? What is to become of us, who cannot believe in your communal freedom?"

"In another hundred years, mistress, we will have the building of a new culture to show for our struggle, to make to the world,

116

culturally, some definite contribution, to explain, culturally, our reason for being here at all."

"If that is what you think, then you must set yourself above that mass which must feel hate to want to go to war," she said proudly.

"It is not what I think, it is what I know. Perhaps it will take longer than my hundred years, but to survive at all we must be free. I believe in the motives of this war. I believe fundamentally that freedom, any sort of freedom at all, is worth the price of this war. There, you see, is the difference between us. You have been taught slavery. Your father has taught you that your path in life, your loyalties, have been cut and dried for you, and that the slightest deviation would be immoral. I have not been taught. You cannot teach a man freedom. It must be in him."

"My father has taught me the value of loyalty," she said.

"Then you cannot condemn me, mistress, for I too am loyal to what I believe."

Brant said, "Tell us what you're doing about this belief of yours. Make it real, make it all the running you're doing. That's all I'll ever understand about it." But he knew. He knew.

"The running? That's simply told. After General Gates lost Camden for us our army reorganized in North Carolina under General Gates and General Morgan." He looked up and saw that Tag was pressing close to the arm of his chair. "At the moment, we run again."

"Will this man Morgan fight?" Alwyn said.

"He'd stand to the Mongol hordes. He's not a young man. He's a fighter, and he's got some good cavalry with him."

"You may think so," Brant said, "but no farmer on a work hack can look twice at Tarleton."

Savage was amused. "These are not farmers. These are the cream of the Virginia gentlemen under a cousin of our commander in chief, who, were they Carolinians, would perhaps be loyalists. But as it stands they are horsemen, and maybe they're good enough to take your Tarleton."

The boy's weight was against his arm. He looked at the boy and smiled and the boy smiled back, quiet but not diffident. He said, "Is that all true?" and Savage knew he spoke not to him, but to Alwyn.

Alwyn's voice was heavy. "The military picture is one which we will have to trust to the Major, Tag." And the boy knew he would not say more and was suddenly unhappy, for he felt his father had been bested. He did not know why or how his father had been bested; certainly he had in no way agreed with the rebel officer on any point. Truthfully, the boy thought, he had said very little at all, and it was puzzling to him. Then he thought maybe his father had deliberately refrained from speaking in the fear that Savage might pass on information, that he had been purposely close-mouthed. The rebel did not look like the kind of man who would make trouble for them. He wondered if, outside of Brina's and Brant's uncles, the Yancys, Savage was the only rebel his father had ever talked with before. This was a new thought, and it began a chain of thought which disturbed him. He could remember Uncle Joe Yancy saying there was two sides to a story. The only trouble was, he couldn't make heads or tails of the rebel's talk. Only his father's side made sense, but his father's side seemed archaic, something that had been told him far in the past, when he was still a baby, something he had grown away from in the space of an hour, hearing the rebel talk. His father talked that way sometimes, saying words which he did not understand, understanding only that they were things, those words, which he must abide by. He did not understand many of the things the rebel said tonight, but they had made him feel warm and secure and he was sorry Savage had stopped speaking. He wanted to stand against the chair like this and let the beautifully modulated voice flow soothingly about him.

"Major," he said, "what does it mean to be free?"

Savage looked at him for a long moment. Then he said, "I can't answer that for you, Tag. A collective freedom like the one we are fighting for I can perhaps explain. It means in that sense that we will be a united nation, that we will elect our own government, a republic, not a monarchy, and that the government will be chosen by the people themselves. The men in Congress will be chosen by farmers and shopkeepers and traders, and perhaps, in time, by Indians, and these people will have the power to remove their representatives if they fail in their work."

"Would I help choose?"

"When you are of age, yes."

"And that's what it means? That's what the war is about on your side?"

"Partially, yes. You see, Tag, you back-country people are so far away from it all that you've had no chance to observe British injustice. In the North it was different. The people there had to pay such unfair taxes that when they refused the ports were closed and their means of livelihood taken from them."

"Did they start the war?"

"Tag," Brant said.

"No," Alwyn said, "let him ask."

"In a sense they did," Savage said. "Recourse to arms was the only way they could protest. But that wasn't until the British sent some soldiers into the northern towns. Up in Massachusetts some soldiers fired into a mob, and that's how it began."

"Oh," Tag said seriously. He felt disappointed in the explanation. His father had said exactly the same thing, only his father had blamed the people for refusing to accept the taxed goods, for actually destroying them. The story . . . the story part of it was the same. Savage had said the same thing his father said. He drew away from Savage's chair, wishing that he did not like the rebel, because it was much more exciting to think of Tarleton's men in their fine uniforms and difficult to believe that this man was even a soldier. His clothes did not look like a uniform. But if he didn't have a uniform, maybe he was a spy. Maybe he was spying on them. He moved away.

There was silence in the room. Sabrina had gone on with her sewing. Her hands shook. They had not seen British injustice? But she would not tell him about Garlin Gresham. Tag went to sit by his father, scrunched forward on the edge of the cushion at Alwyn's side. Brant had tilted his chair back against the wall. His eyes were closed, but Tag knew he wasn't asleep. Then the silence was uncomfortable, and Savage said, "If I have said anything to offend you, sir, forgive me. You must consider it most unfair of me to speak this way before your family after you took me in. But I would prefer to be honest. Have I your permission to speak with your son?"

There was no sign Brant had heard. His chair remained tilted against the wall, his eyes stayed closed.

Alwyn laughed shortly. "You've nerve, I'll say that for you. I have no objection. Talk your lungs out to Brant, it won't do any good. And I'll tell you something else. Perhaps there is some basis in truth in what you have said tonight, I don't know. But if there is, this is not the time. You are too early, too headstrong, and you will fail. We at least know where our allegiance lies. You pledge your loyalty to a dream. And if you accomplish this, if you set yourself up as you believe you can, someday it will be too great, too huge, and it will fall out of hand and destroy you. Governments have destroyed one another and themselves since before the time of Christ. You will be no different."

Savage did not answer. Alwyn stared hard at him, seeing the knot of muscle moving in the throat, where his shirt was open. "You are in pain, Major."

"It is to be expected," he said bitterly, but Alwyn cut him short. "Sabrina, we must change the dressing. He needs rest. If he didn't talk himself to a nubbin he wouldn't be so tired. Come along, Major. It is past your bedtime, Timothy."

Tag went willingly, wanting to lie in the dark and think of the fine British troops, wanting to erase the troubling, incomprehensible words the rebel had spoken under his father's roof. He had gone to the room he shared with Brant by the time Sabrina had folded her sewing and risen, leading the way to the kitchen with her back ramrod straight.

Savage ate without hunger. They had made a bed for him on the floor, by the fire. The embers burned low and red, and seeing them, a great wave of loneliness swept over him, and of lostness, so that he hardly knew it when Sabrina unknotted the sling from his shoulder. His arm was so stiff he could not unbend it, and he did not feel that either. The longing for his own low-burning fire, for the willows and the red dirt lane was so strong in him that nothing else was felt, tasted, scented, nothing else mattered.

He heard Alwyn's voice from a long way off, saying the wound would heal and there was no infection, saying other things he did not hear at all. But Sabrina woke him to the misery of reality. It was her tone, irritable, impatient, which had alerted him, but it was the realization that it was to her father she spoke which wakened him fully.

"That's not right . . . if you place it that way the raw edge of the linen . . . here, Father, let me do it."

Alwyn glanced once at Jewel, huddled asleep in the corner. "Sleep too is medicine. I trust you rest well, Major."

"Thank you, sir. Good night."

"Good night." Alwyn turned and left the room.

Sabrina worked with a cool fury which he knew should have

amused him, but which instead sobered and depressed him. "How is it?" he said, looking down at his arm.

"It's all right. Try to use it a little, so it won't stiffen." Tying the final strip of linen in place, she said, "You surprised me tonight, Major."

"I did. Why is that?"

"What happened to all that ingrained bitterness and cynicism you were so proud of earlier this evening. Or do you reserve those for your conversations with women?"

"I like your father. It was out of respect for your father. And I like your brothers."

"I see." She laughed, without humor. "And you do not like me?"

"Why should I? What have you done to make me like you? Is it that you're so staunch a Loyalist you can't even be pleasant? You don't know what being a Loyalist is. All you know is this stuff your father's been pumping into you for . . . how many years now?"

"Twenty-six," she said.

"I wasn't inquiring your age, curious as I am. I know you're no child."

"No, I'm not." She turned from him, rolling up the leftover strips of linen. "Sabrina Quantrell, an old maid at twenty-six."

He caught at her wrist. "Why, Sabrina? Why?"

She tried to pull away, but he held her. "What do you mean, why? Why shouldn't I be? Who am I to marry? . . . The settlement men who look at me as if I were a brood mare when I cross the street before them? Don't you have to love, Major, or has the bitterness you profess eaten that out of you too?"

"No," he said, seeing she was surprised at his lack of anger, knowing she anticipated he would answer her anger with his own. "No, you're right. You have to love. But how do you know?"

He saw the full line of her features, as sharp and clear as frost, as she turned away. "If I did not know I would not be here, like this. Good night, Major."

But he put his hand on her face and forced her to look at him. "It's a shame, Sabrina, a terrible shame." Now he could feel her trembling, as if her whole body were crying. Because he did not want her to speak he moved his hand so that his palm lay against her mouth. "Sabrina, I'm sorry for what I said to you in the barn. Because I did not mean it. The only thing I meant was what I said about knowing what you want to be in this world." He took her by one unyielding shoulder and put his mouth where the palm of his hand had been, without passion, without tenderness, but with the sureness, the knowledge, the monumental rock steadfastness which would be with him all his life.

Nothing had prepared him for her face or her eyes. For a time after he released her, she looked up at him as if he had struck her. Then the color came back into her face, slowly, almost not coming back at all, and she picked up the scissors and the roll of linen and went out of the room.

Gradually, as if it hesitated, the tenseness left him. The pain was beginning to go from his shoulder, leaving the stiffness and the dull insistent ache. He went and dropped down on the pallet by the fire and rolled on his side, away from the hot red embers. There was no sound from Jewel, in the corner, but soon he thought, she is not asleep; she has not been asleep since we came into this room.

11

I T WOULD SEEM TO ME," Savage said, "when a man (or a woman for that matter) speaks overlong on spring or the coming of spring, it would indicate more than a simple concern for the crops or whether or not the dogwood will flower."

Three days had passed since his coming. She was learning not to be offended with him. "And it would seem to me," she said, "you spend too much time . . . waste it, in fact . . . seeking motives."

"But I've not got much else to do and I've an inquisitive mind."

She was cleaning and filling the lamps, sitting at the kitchen table. Savage sat as he preferred to sit, scorning chair, leaning back against the fireplace wall. Old Jim lay by him but did not sleep; Savage noted how persistently the hound would rise and leave whatever human he favored with his company and go to Alwyn whenever Alwyn appeared. He gave his company sparingly, being inhumanly true, therefore it was something of an honor, Savage felt, for the big handsome blue to lie at his feet this way. But the hound's ears were high, as if he listened, and the yellow eyes looked up now and then, watching. Savage envied Alwyn so faithful a thing.

"Well," she said, a little sharply, "aren't you going to tell me?"

"Tell you what?"

"Why it's more than a simple concern."

"Oh, that. It's just that I have heard you say several times that you wished it was spring, or last spring, or next spring, or in the spring thus and so."

"I see. Matters of the mind. I suppose you think this innocent allusion means some sort of reversion to my lost youth."

"Possibly," he said, shocking her, for she had believed he would deny so shocking a thing.

She looked up at him quickly, meaning to talk back. But she had begun to understand him a little. She sighed, letting the sharpness go out of voice and eye. "All I wish is that it *was* spring, so I could show you why I wished it. I'm sure you won't find a lovelier land in the world than our back country in spring. I'd like you to see the pretty things so you won't think badly of our country when you leave it."

"And would you come with me to see all this splendor, Sabrina?"

He thought she colored a little. "Only so I could show you."

"Well, that's something, little as it is. I'd as much like you to see my country."

"Why?" she said, remembering, not looking at him now.

"I suppose to show you how fine it too is, in spring."

"But that's different . . . it doesn't matter . . . your country's not been unkind to me."

After a moment he said, "You learn your first lesson in cold, hard unfeeling logic from me, don't you, Sabrina? I regret it."

She plunged, surely and without struggle, to a depth where no bottom lay. "But you only show things you care about to people you care about. If you don't care about the people, you don't care whether they like a thing or not."

And he said, only half amused, "Then why do you care if I like your country?"

Jewel saved her, coming into the kitchen with a duster of crow feathers in one hand and a sapling broom in the other. "Lord," she said, "I am listenin', but you ain't talkin' English. I don't know what you'se talkin', but it ain't English. Ain't you finish them lamps yit, Brina? Talk, talk, talk is all gits done."

"What else is there to do but sit by the fire and talk?" Savage said.

"That's all right for you, you got a hole in you shoulder. But it don't git the lamps clean, do it, Brina?"

Old Jim got up suddenly and stood facing the door. Alwyn was coming, Savage thought. But it was Brant, and the hound lay down again, making a wuffling, worried sound in his throat. Sabrina did not turn around until Brant put his hand, hard and cold, on the back of her neck, under the thick club of hair; then she got to her feet, laughing, striking out at him with a hand which had no strength or purpose in it. The hound moved closer to Savage.

"How come you went to the Crossin' so early this mornin'?" Jewel said to Brant.

"I thought if I surprised Aiken early enough he might not have time to load anything under the counter."

"Was you early enough?"

"I got some white sugar," he said.

"Enough for a cake?" Sabrina said, feeling the moisture gather in her mouth.

"I reckon."

Jewel said, "Cake. We'd ought to save her, jest in case. You never knows you might need a li'l white sugar. Ain't that right, Majuh?"

"Well," Savage said, "speaking purely as an impartial observer, my own feeling about it is that good things are to be used. Now you take that bag of sugar. There is, I suppose, some possibility mice might chew through the bag. Then too, in the dampness, the stuff might harden . . . be a lot of trouble to fine it down again. There's also the possibility ants might be wintering under the house. They could get in it. And as an extreme possibility, *Tag* might get in it."

They looked at him. His eyes were without bitterness though he did not smile. After a moment Jewel said, "Well, well, I guess you gits to make a cake, Brina. You's a disturbin' influrance on this house, Majuh."

"I hope that is so only when it comes to the making of cakes," he said.

Brant's head came up quickly. The two men watched one another. Then Brant said, "Reckon I saw the man who shot you this morning, Savage."

If he had thought to rile Savage, he failed, but his eyes did not mirror any disappointment when Savage said, as if he was incapable of caring, "Did you?"

"He didn't say he shot you," Brant said, more relaxed now. "Not to me anyway. He's been tellin' around he shot a stranger though. Braggin' on it."

"Had he my gun, do you know?"

"He wasn't carryin' it when I saw him."

"You think you could buy it from him?"

"The King ain't got that much gold, I reckon. Men are funny about guns, I reckon Shaver wouldn't part with it, not a fine rifle like that. Maybe the day'll come he'll use it on one of us Loyalists, so you can figger it's doin' the purpose it was forged for."

Savage did not answer. Again they watched one another, warily, not without anger, but with no dislike. Then Brant turned, almost spun and went out the door into the back yard, letting sunlight briefly into the room, letting Tag past him, letting the door bang flatly.

"I has tole you," Jewel said, "about slammin' that door. Go back and close her quietlike."

"But Brant did it," he said, bewildered. He obeyed, but his movements were hurried, impatient. When he turned again his eyes went to the rebel officer and his face was earnest. "Where's my father, Jewel?"

"He's writing," Sabrina said, "have you got to pester him now?"

"I saw Uncle John coming up the road." Again his earnest face turned to Savage. "I don't think my father would want Uncle John to know about you, sir."

Savage inclined his head slightly. "I have an uncomfortable feeling you might be right. If your sister won't forgive you for pestering, as she calls it, I will."

Sabrina had looked up startled at the boy's words. Now she rose and followed him down the hall without a backward glance, cleaning rag in hand. Savage stretched his legs out on the hearth, watching Jewel as she measured the white corn meal. "Why do they call him Tag?"

"He daddy call him Timothy," Jewel said. She appraised the level of meal in the glass with a practiced eye. "Timothy Bowie. The

125

Bowie was after his mother, died when he born. Brant begun callin' him Tag because he say Timothy too big a name, bigger'n the baby hisself."

They were quiet, companionable, easy with one another. "I'll go to the barn," he said then, half to himself, loath to leave the warmth, the talk, the mind-picture of the finished pone, taken from the oven, concocted through some never to be solved mystery from the pale dry meal which looked to him like sand in the bowl. "You waits and see whut Al'n says," Jewel told him. She cracked an egg on the edge of the bowl, draining carefully the last precious semi-liquid drop. "I can't see you goin' out there for John Breva'd. He won't know you's alive. He don't hardly know he's alive hisself sometimes. Lord God, it's wuss enough them pore animals has to be out in that mud. You hear that scratchin' and snufflin' down there? That's them dawgs under the porch. They do scrab aroun', don't they?"

He forgot about John Brevard. He said, "I like this mixture of dogs you've got, Jewel, the big blue especially."

"Old Jim git away with most anything," she said. "Al'n wouldn' part with him for all the gold in the world. Ain't you got no dawgs?"

"Some," he said. "Some hounds, black and tans."

Alwyn stood in the doorway. "I've just spoken with Sabrina, Major. She suggests you go to her room. It would be a good time for you to remain absolutely quiet. If you could sleep. . . ."

"If it would be safer I will go to the barn."

"Safer. Brevard is harmless."

"I was thinking of you, sir."

"Oh," Alwyn said, as if surprised. "No, we have nothing to fear, Major."

He got to his feet slowly, pulling the long legs up under him with effort. "Perhaps this is not the time to say it, Mr. Quantrell. . . ."

"It is not the time," Alwyn said. "This is Sabrina's room." He pointed with his pipe stem, briefly, and left. Savage heard him go down the hall to the front door, and moved without thought across the kitchen.

It was a small room, warm because of its proximity to the kitchen. Going to the window, he could see the tall pines at the end of the path, and the weathered rounded gravestones. The little plot looked neither excessively visited nor neglected, and the pines made a spreading shelter over it. He turned away from the window, looking about him with a first faintness of expectancy running pleasant in his veins. Sabrina was handy and had taste, he thought; there was a richness in the severity of the room: window hung and bed covered with a coarse black material stamped in gold and gray. The bed was of rubbed maple with a pretty raised carving of fruit, berries and blossoms, on the inner headboard. There was a heavy quilt folded at the foot of the bed, white with black stitching, and he saw her hand imprinting beautifully upon it pine tree and star. There were also a plain pine stand by the bed, a dresser of pine with a small mirror above it, and a chestnut ladderback chair near the window. The rug she had braided had been done in grays and blacks and ambers, and he found it restful underfoot. He was methodical and without guilt, looking vicariously where the cupboard was open, at her clothing: mostly the simply made day-to-day dresses, the striped China silk, a sheer flowered gown he thought she might wear well on a hot summer day, a heavier dress of some shimmering bronze material which nearly matched her hair, and beneath them the short boots, the fur-lined blue boots, the house slippers, the soft moccasins. He touched nothing, except a black velvet ribbon she had thrown carelessly on the pine stand. Nothing in the room was wrong. She had taken the individual components of its furnishings and welded them into a perfect whole. He could see her in the welding, and in the end result. He could see her neatness and her carelessness in the discarded black ribbon.

But the shoulder hurt badly. The kitchen fire had been kind to it, healing it with heat, and now the heat had been taken away, and merely looking out at the rain made him ache, like the rain was falling, stinging, cold, right into the raw wound. He had heard men say a gunshot wound was so sudden it didn't have time to hurt, but he knew differently. First shock keeps a wound numb, but the pain is there, as it must be in any tearing away of flesh. He sat down on the bed and took off the moccasins Brant had given him to wear, doing it awkwardly, with one hand. Then he got up and pulled the quilt up to protect the spread and lay down and wrapped the quilt about him and closed his eyes.

After a time he was aware of scent beneath his head, and the scent startled him, for in the first sensing of it memory flooded rudely upon him: flesh scent, sleep scent, of perfume and perfumed white powder and softness of thin slick-silky material and perfume in the hair. And he breathed it and knew it was none of the things he remembered, but a scent rather of soap touched faintly with violet, or perhaps rose petal, not sweet; smoky, like cold apples or dry oak leaves, like sunlight and south wind.

He heard the sound of a wooden spoon in the kitchen, as Jewel beat, beat, beat, softly, measured, like drum rhythm. Sabrina's scent came up around him in Sabrina's room, and he slept.

At suppertime Sabrina did not come to the table. For a time Savage wondered politely, waiting, but when Jewel dished out the meal pudding and Sabrina had still not come, he betrayed himself. "Your daughter is not indisposed, I hope," he said to Alwyn.

And Alwyn, who had spoken little during the meal looked not at him, but at Brant, as if he begged answer from Brant.

Brant lied. He knew Savage knew that he lied. "Brina's clever with herbs, Major . . . something she got born with, I reckon. She's gone to see to one of Uncle John's house slaves got took this morning."

Savage looked down at his plate, making not even the politic response, admired the boy, admired the lie, let himself stew in his own wisdom: Sabrina gone, missing mealtime, which was the hour about which all such farm families revolved. Not to doctor a slave, however valuable, which the slave's master and mistress were perfectly capable of doctoring. It was something else. It was, say, a prospective visitor to Brandyhill, a visitor who had heretofore been welcome, perhaps more than welcome, and because of his, Savage's presence, was no longer welcome; a visitor who, no doubt, had nearly unlimited access to all parts and portions of the farm. A visitor to Sabrina. A visitor Sabrina had gone out to meet. He went over it, with care, in his mind. While he had slept, while Brevard had been there that afternoon, the chance remark had been dropped: so-and-so, nameless, welcome visitor, would ride out that evening. And Sabrina had been sent as interceptor. Had been sent, or had gone of her own volition. Unsought, a black surging which he could define only as distaste and jealousy rose in his throat, bitter and thick as blood. Across the table he and Brant locked glances, not troubling to deceive themselves with the hope that they had deceived one another.

She waited under the oaks, as she had waited the morning Brant brought Hanson Stoner's body into Benton's Crossing; with the waiting she remembered that other waiting, that recognition, felt for a chilling moment the horror, the cold sweat in the fiery heat . . . *if Hanson Stoner had not been hanged, nor we, my people, called upon to pledge ourselves. . . .* Mosquitoes still hummed in the thinning November leaves. There was a deadness and a stillness and a sadness over the land despite the clear evening air and the brilliance of rain-crystaled sky.

Malcolm came around the bend on his young stallion. Rounding the curve in the road, the stallion sensed the roan and lifted his head, swung his head. Sabrina came down off the hill, seeing Malcolm had slowed and was waiting for her. He looked surprised.

"Hello," he said. "Didn't John tell you I was riding out?"

She nodded, forcing the brightness into eye and voice. "We ate early, Fraser. Brant's gone off and Father promised to help Ian this evening."

His hard black eyes searched her face, found nothing but a peculiar, almost glittering surface gaiety. It was the look she had cultivated that day in the park when she toyed with Ballentyne, and with him; he had seen that look on rare occasions and knew it was in no way natural. "Well," he said, "we've Jewel to see we conduct ourselves properly, haven't we?"

For a time they rode together, back along the road to Brandyhill. He let her set the pace, an uncommonly slow pace, he thought, a reluctant pace. Still she presented to him only a sidelong glance, glittering, animated, silent but bright; only once did he observe her with her head bent in that somber, contemplative gesture he knew. "I thought," she said finally, cheerfully, "you might treat me to something at the inn, Fraser."

"And I thought," he said irritably, "you might treat me to something in the kitchen of Brandyhill."

She laughed. "But it's not too late to ride into the Crossing, and there's not a crumb of supper left."

The stallion and the roan stood neck and neck, not moving. Malcolm said softly, "What a pretty mouth, and so full of protest. Tell me, Brina, how many times have you and I sat in your kitchen alone while your father went about his or somebody else's chores and your little brother slept the sleep of the innocent and just, and your big brother traipsed off into the mountains to kill some lumbering bear, or panther, or possibly even man . . . ?"

She flared at him. "Why do you say those things? Why do you speak of Brant like that, harping, harping, harping, worse than a woman?"

He shrugged. "It's all I've got to judge by. . . ."

"Don't judge then," she said bitterly. "You'd as good a head of hair as any to swing from a war lance if he hadn't killed Henry Deschamps."

"All right," he said, "what are we arguing about? I'm sorry. I'm sorry. I'm not really sorry, but as it's you I'll pretend I'm sorry." Then he said, "Truly, forgive me, Brina. Being I'm not wanted at Brandyhill, we could go to my house if you like. Emma Smallie's there, doing all sorts of womanly duties. Noisily. God how the floors quake under her."

She began to laugh again. "I should be more honest with you, Fraser. I wanted to talk with you. But not before Jewel."

His eyebrows rose. Something animal keen and knowing cut across his dark handsome face like a knife. He knew Sabrina too well. He knew something was wrong. She would go to his house at the coming of night, where she had never gone save with some member of her family; she would ride through the Crossing with him at this strange hour, unchaperoned, for any eye to see; she would . . . or would she . . . retain this unnatural brilliance and passion, like a woman under the stimulus of precisely the correct amount of liquor, or of love? The old hot hope moved in him momentarily and was replaced by a sense of dread. Suddenly he feared her.

But she had already swung the roan's head, reined the roan around. He saw, against the richness of evening sky and autumn woodland and harsh rising of grasshopper wings, the clean wide bar of her shoulders, the deep indentation of waist, the triumphant round of hip under the full rusty-colored skirt, where she curved to the sidesaddle. She turned and looked at him with a questioning in her eyes like flame. He swung the stallion before he knew he had done it.

When they came in over the wooden bridge the sky was red over the mountains. Black clouds lay heavily banked above the clear red, and the evening star shone. In the east there was still blueness and silver, and little puffs of cloud drifted slowly, looking as though they had been shot from cannon. They passed, acknowledged, Sam Ashe, the eldest of the Ballentyne boys, Opium. Men lounging on Sheller's porch raised their hats. Elizabeth Lyons, working beside her father and mother in the last yellowing foliage of the Lyons' vegetable garden, shielded her eyes as if a nonexistent sun had blinded her and noted their direction with vicious satisfaction. Sabrina squared her shoulders.

The room, left of the hallway, was chaste and plain, the walls washed dead white, bare of painting or portrait. A scarred cherry table pushed flush against the wall held a copper candleholder on a square brass base, a decanter and glasses on a wooden tray, and a mug of tapers. A chest against the opposite wall was piled with books. There were two chairs, one a wing back covered in a dark serviceable material, the other a high-backed rocker. There was also a curve-back love seat upholstered in red velvet. She had been in this room before, many times, but had never truly looked at it. Now, sharpened by something more than nervousness, she studied minutely, wavered between laughter and scorn.

Malcolm came in from the hallway. "That's strange, Emma seems to have gone. Housekeepers are so damned unpredictable. Listen, Brina, I swear to you she was here when I left. My honor."

She told him gently, "Now who protests?" She rose from the love seat and went around the room slowly, in a circle, not looking at him. "Fraser, this room."

"What's wrong with it?" he said.

"It's not like you, this room. Not like you at all. No complications. Nothing handsome. Nothing shadowed. Nothing flawless. No wonder you've such dreams of wealth and beauty and grandeur."

He went to the table and began to pour wine from the decanter. "One possible trouble with it is that you aren't living in it."

She sat down again. "That's to shame me, I reckon." She took the glass from him. "This is a wicked thing I do, Fraser."

"How so? I am your doctor. You are ill. Palpitations of the heart, trembling of the hands, nervous tic in the left eyelid, cold perspiration upon the brow, weakness in the lower extremities. All the symptoms of something. Inadvertently as I may have given them, perhaps of love."

"Love is an illness," she said, "there are symptoms." But she raised the glass to her mouth to cover her confusion. "You wouldn't dare broadcast such a diagnosis in the Crossing after all these years."

He set his glass down, the wine untasted. He leaned against the table, arms crossed. "I seem to be able to count at least eleven years. After eleven years you throw yourself into my path and come riding off to my house with me and display for me, unattended, your symptoms."

She laughed, but there was no laughter in her eyes. "Fraser, you're incorrigible."

"Not at all. In another eleven years I may suggest further and be rewarded relatively. Now what was it you wanted to talk to me about?"

She watched him. Her eyes mirrored suddenly a dumb apathy, a hopeless resignation, like an animal confronting the irrevocable doom of slaughter. He came across the room and sat down beside her and took her by the shoulders. "What was it we could not discuss before Jewel?"

It was no longer her voice speaking. Sound came from somewhere else in the room, from all around her, though she could feel the words forming, shaping, rising in her throat, hard and round as stones. "I have come to tell you that if you still want . . . if you still wish to wed me I will accept."

Over the shock of hearing herself say the words, of wondering if she had really said them, she knew that she had not contrived them merely to meet the exigency of the moment. Now she rationalized; truth made itself manifest in her with all the spreading potency of some deadly growth springing to life. In this chance meeting with the inevitable, brought to her before she was prepared for it, she had taken upon herself not only the simplest of temporizings but the most difficult of personal commitments. It had to be this way. All her life she had known this time would come. But it had been forced, thrust upon her, and she felt a passionate resentment. Not once, riding into the Crossing with Malcolm, had she thought ahead to her excuse for the meeting; whatever she had spoken had been spontaneous. And faced with the necessity of response to him she had continued in that same vein of spontaneity. That the day would have come when she would have made this statement to him, would have yielded at last, she did not doubt. It was the manner and time of its coming, and her own lack of continued resistance to him which shocked and frightened her.

She saw the grim amusement flicker and grow in his eyes. Her hands were unsteady, and there was a terrible massive knot of something slipping inside her body like a rockslide. He kept holding her by the shoulders, and she saw the amusement leave his eyes and the hard sharp penetrating blackness return. He said, "Sabrina, I want to know why you did not want me at Brandyhill tonight. Lies become a woman only if she is very very clever. You are not clever. Why didn't you want me there?"

She was limp, like a rag doll, like the beanbag she had made for Tag, when Tag was a baby. "Fraser, when haven't you been welcome . . . ?"

He began to shake her, lightly, as wind stirring faintly moves the brittle willow branches, but there was no gentleness in his hands. "Where did your father go tonight? Where's Brant? Where did they go?"

She tried to pull free; annoyance came into her voice. "But I told you. Brant found cat tracks in the piney woods this afternoon, late, and Father's gone to Ian's . . . they're putting up a woodshed against the barn."

"Tell me the rest," he said, still shaking her in that insistent, deadly manner. Wine spilled over the edge of her glass and stained her skirt. "Tell me how big the cat was, how many stone, how many toes, where the track led, tell me how much powder and ball Brant took, tell me how much wood Ian's drawing in and when he'll finish drawing and how many days the stacking will take. Tell me, Brina."

She wrenched away from him. "Don't be such a fool," she said. And then mirrored her fear for Savage, and for her father. "What are you afraid of?"

He dropped back against the seat and put his hand over his eyes. "I am not afraid of anything," he said. "I am not a painter to be downed by your brother's deadly aim, nor an ant to be crushed by your father's foot, nor a tree to be felled for Ian McLeod's woodshed."

She set her glass down on the floor beside her. "Oh, Fraser, I am sorry it turned out so badly." But there was a terrible relief in her; he did not take his hand from his face and so did not see the compassion, the affection in her eyes.

"I am only sorry you lied," he said.

"But I did not lie," she said awkwardly. "I only wanted to be with you, to tell you. . . ." Her voice died. "Anything, anything. . . ."

He put his hand down. He drew his breath in deeply. "Well, dear unclever Brina, I accept all your lies as Jordan's gospel. Now, as I accept you as you are, would you accept me as, say, a murderer, a thief?"

"Why," she said, "there would be other circumstances to consider." Then she said, "I would stand by you, Fraser."

"And you will marry me?"

She looked down at her hands, folded in her lap. Her voice was full of tears. "What has that to do with what you have just said?"

"A case in point," he said wearily. "Some other time, perhaps. But you will marry me?"

"I have told you so."

"I know. Your passion for me has stirred me deeply." He watched her, one eyebrow raised in the dark perfect face. "Tell me one truth. Wherever Brant and your father went tonight, had it anything to do with me?"

She was silent. As far as she knew Brant and her father . . . and Savage . . . sat at Brandyhill and waited. "What would it have to do with you, Fraser? I give you my hand on it."

For a long time her fingers lay hot and nervous against his palm. Still he sprawled upon the red velvet as if he slept, fighting to guess what she feared from him, fighting his own fear. "One thing more then, and I will let you go. For the sake of the obvious appearance I shall assume you came to me tonight to tell me that you had made up your mind. I shall assume you donned your original good cheer for my sake. Because you were full of something, some recklessness, some emotion, when I first saw you. Now simply say with nothing in between or around and about when you will marry me."

For a moment her lower lip lay trapped under the sharp white edge of her teeth. She said, "If you will wait until Christmas I will let Richard Jordan announce the banns."

He sat bolt upright. But he said, "Let? Let. Well, an honor for Richard, there's no dispute there. Christmas, then. When would you have me speak to your father?"

"Give me time," she said, pleading.

"I have given you some years."

"I want to talk to him first . . . please give me that, Fraser."

He nodded. Where triumph should have rooted in him grew misery. Still he knew he would take her if she should swear to die of her sorrow the day following their union. "We will go to the city," he said.

"Charleston," she said in a low voice.

"No, North. Perhaps Boston."

"All right," she said. Even then, she did not wonder.

"I will ride back with you, Brina."

"I must see Lavinia. Leonard will ride with me."

"I do not like you to leave my house alone."

"I would prefer it that way."

He looked at her. Then he rose and held out his hand to her. But she surprised him at rising, for she put her hands upon his shoulders and turned her face to him and kissed him upon the mouth. "I think we do need one another, Fraser."

"I too," he said wryly, holding himself in check, hands clenched at his sides, knowing for the thousandth time that he would hold himself always in check with this woman, if he wanted to keep her.

Darkness had fallen. Crickets squeaked tirelessly in the grasses. Lantern and candlelight frosted windows and projected into the blackness along the edges of the road. The park trees bulked dark on the sky. Malcolm tightened the girth and lifted her to the saddle. There was a creaking of leather, and the horse smelled hot and musty. She did not speak, but leaned from the saddle and touched him gently upon the cheek.

She did not stop at the inn, but rode slowly down the dusty track of road. She felt very numb and very calm, having come to believe that she had made a decision after great deliberation.

She paused upon the bridge, holding the roan in while she considered the possibility, or even the desirability, of weeping. Thunder rumbled meaninglessly over the mountains and the crickets spoke brightly to one another. The harshness of the air suited her; she drew it into her lungs, felt her face pull into hardness and acceptance, felt contemptuous of tears. And Brant volunteering her to head Fraser off . . . using her better than he, any of them, knew . . . how fine it would be to tell him this, who hated Fraser Malcolm. She too would have liked to hate: Brant, Savage, Malcolm, but not knowing which to hate, settled, in that moment, for herself.

In the autumn darkness nothing stirred but wind beginning. She heard the hooves, soft but very clear, under the wind, and she turned in the saddle, toward the sound, and knew by direction and silhouette and hugeness of horse, that it was Malcolm, taking the stallion at a steady, loping run across the park and up the mountain road.

12

H<small>E WATCHED THEM</small> from the thicket which crested the hill half a mile from the house, saw them coming along the road slowly, almost indolently. At each step the horses picked up their feet as if they would never pick them up again.

He surveyed them without excitement (for he had known sometime they would come) and with no fear. Nothing that they had ever done, or that he had heard they had done, or had surmised they would do, excited or frightened him. What was there of grown civilized man to excite or frighten a child who had done nothing all his short life but assiduously pursue the routine demands of his existence? And he had already sifted the essentials and knew that there was only a right and a wrong and that he was on the side of right, God's side, his father's side. I am a side. They are a side, he thought, watching them.

They would not come to the house. They were in a hurry. He knew that. They were in a hurry no matter how they dallied in the road. He would stone them if he had to, whatever it cost him. I am a side and they are a side. They would not come. He would stone the horses and the men as long as he could. If he had to.

He scrunched up on his elbows and looked at the bitch lying in a depression some yards away. She looked back, her glance half tragic, half comic, and then she sighed as if she knew what he would say.

"Go home, Belle. Git along."

He made shooing motions at her with both hands, lost his balance, fell flat again.

"Go along, Belle. Go home."

The bitch rose, snuffed the air without any genuine interest, and with dignified resignation went off slowly through the brush. Tag got to his feet.

He thought of his father. He would be his father now. He would be just and he would be strong in his knowledge of right. He tried, and felt nothing but a consuming curiosity.

They drew him down the hill and to the road. He did not move under cover, neither did he bid for their attention. As he went down he saw them amble around a turn in the road. There were seven of them.

From the bottom of the hill he looked back up and saw the scrub oak lying motionless after his passage. Pale sunlight glinted over the crown and got in his eyes. There were hummocks of old grass uneven under his feet, growing in wetness that had already seeped through his shoes. Where the little border of swamp began at the edge of the road there were stones aplenty.

He pressed close to the fence, looking for them, letting the brush surround him.

He could count the horses' ribs. There were worn hairless patches on their flanks and withers and bellies. One limped. Three of the men were Carolinians. He saw the green pine tree insignia on their buckskin shirts.

He held his breath, freezing as an animal suddenly alerted freezes. He sensed rather than heard the shift in the tempo of the oncoming horses, creak of leather, turning of men's bodies. Toward him.

"Poke outa there, kid," the man nearest him said.

He stood up straight, looking out over the sapling fence. He stared at them and they stared back, hands moving gently, hardly moving at all to their rifles and knives. They wore buckskin shirts and breeches and moccasins; all but two who had white linen smocks belted at the waist. The long rifles were slung over their shoulders on leather straps, barrels slanting skyward, or lay aslant the saddles. They wore powder horns about their necks. All of them were dark, burned dark by wind and weather, the faces, the throats, the exposed chests and upper arms dark no matter what the color of the hair. One had a coonskin cap pushed back on his head and a plug of tobacco stuffed in his jaw.

And three of them were Carolinians. Tag kept feeling it, thinking it, looking at them. They were soldiers. He knew they were soldiers, but he could not believe it. They only called themselves soldiers. Soldiers wore brave uniforms and shining boots. These men were a side. And three of them were Carolinians.

The man who had spoken to him was lean to the point of thinness and roughly handsome, with dark skin and long brass-colored hair. Tag thought maybe he would put a rock right on that dark forehead. If he had to.

"Hyah, boy," the man said, grinning, showing teeth white and even as a wolf's, making his horse dance a little. He was one of the Carolinians.

"Hello," Tag whispered. His throat was dry and he had not known it was dry, so the whisper surprised him.

"You've got no cause to be scared," the dark brassy Carolinian said, still grinning.

"I'm not scared," Tag said, and cleared his throat. "I'm not scared," he said again.

They clustered in the road around the blond brown man. One of them said, "Whatcha got, McDowell? McDowell's cornered suthin'." He wore the rattlesnake of Virginia painted crudely on his shirt.

The man they called McDowell was unslinging the long rifle, slipping the strap over his head. Tag's eyes widened. He felt with his foot and began to edge a stone toward him with the toe of his shoe.

"Ask the little bastid what's his name," the Virginian said.

"What's your name, boy?"

"Tag." The stone was under the ball of his foot.

"Tag what?"

"Tag," he said.

"No ma, no pa, no cows, no hosses, no pigs, no chickens, no good-lookin' sisters," one of them said. "Where's yer house at, boy, an' yer good-lookin' sisters?"

"I got no sisters," Tag said. He pointed off vaguely back down where they had come from, hoping they would think he lived off that way somewhere.

The man spat. "How them Tories can lie. Teach their boys to lie. Lie like hell. You a Tory liar?"

Tag stiffened. The man called McDowell said pleasantly, "Wouldn't reach for that rock if I were you. Hate to have to put a ball in that little boy belly of yours."

He knew now they were enjoying him. He was vulnerable and a diversion, and that frightened him for the first time. Because they might kill him. These Carolinians might possibly enjoy killing him. He pressed tight against the fence. His hands were sweating.

A hoarse rich voice said, "Leave him alone, McDowell." The rider nearest the center of the road came up, and Tag saw the biggest man he had ever seen, on a bay stallion. He wore buckskin, with the breeches thrust into moccasins that laced all the way to the knee. There was no rifle slung on his shoulder, but he had a cavalry pistol in a leather holster, and there was a turkey-bone yelper in his belt. He had long dark hair, graying, held back with a rawhide fillet, and there was a drawn white scar at the corner of his mouth. "Fan out and get going and leave him alone. I'm going back."

"All right," the dark blond man said. "Thatcher, you ride with the General."

Tag leaned on the fence hard. It creaked. The big man looked at him, not unkindly, and Tag saw there were heavy dark circles under his eyes. "Look, boy," he said in that same odd hoarse voice, as if he were trying to hold it under a shout, as if he were used to shouting and wanted to shout now, "Look, Tag, if I were you I'd stay off this road."

"Find out where he lives," McDowell said.

"No, we've got no time I tell you. Tag . . . Tag what?"

"Quantrell," Tag said, before he knew it, with the hurt and the defiance gone. He closed his mouth tight after he said it.

"Look, Tag Quantrell, armies don't get out of the way of children with rocks. Go home and stay home, and if you've got horses or sisters hide 'em, because your bloody-back protectors will be coming through. Keep out of their way. You hear, boy?"

He did not answer.

The man called Thatcher said, "You ready, Gen'ral Mawgan?" and the big man turned the stallion into the road again and went off, riding in a strange way, half bent over, as if something hurt him.

It meant something to him. General Morgan meant something, and the blond brown·man. McDowell meant something. McDowell's Rangers. These were the scouts, the men Ian McLeod said were so terrible and so fine.

He whispered again, looking McDowell in the eye with unblinking incomprehension. "But you're a Carolinian," he said.

"What?" McDowell's voice was full of astonishment.

He could not speak again. Nothing came to him. And they pulled out and left him and one of them said something he could not hear but he heard McDowell say, "Shut your goddamn mouth."

139

He had not told them about Savage. He was not to mention Savage. Even Savage himself had said he was to say nothing that would bring anyone to Brandyhill. It was funny he didn't feel so good all of a sudden. Half scornfully he rolled the stone over with the toe of his shoe, picked it up and sent it skimming down the road after them. After he had done it he wanted to cry. He dug a fist into one eye, rubbing the eye until it was red and teary. Damn them. Damn them. Rebels. Carolina rebels.

But he did not go home. He lay in the scrub oak the rest of the afternoon in a sort of stupor. Once or twice he thought, I am a side and they are a side.

They passed just at sunset, the tall men in buckskin with their long rifles; the weary men who looked like the men of Benton's Crossing, the farmers, the millers, the blacksmiths, without uniforms, weary, weary, weary; the slow-moving wagons he knew held forage and food and guns; the men, so many, he had not dreamed there were so many; the horses, not as worn as those the scouts had ridden, the horses with their riders in blue and one body in crimson with silver helmets; the long company of uniformed regulars; and again the endless, endless mass they called militia. He looked for the big man on the stallion, but he could not find him. He strained his eyes, running them back and forth over the stretch of road in a kind of desperation, searching, for the enormity of this army, this army his father called a handful was staggering, and he wanted to see again the man who led it. He had to see him again. He had to.

But he did not. He never saw him again. He stayed in that same stupor after they had gone, seeing the glitter of the helmets against the red sky and hearing the sounds of passage, of men, of horses, of wagons, until at last he stood up and the road was empty and the stillness struck terror to his heart.

He began to run, not caring Brant would be angry, or Jewel skin him alive. He ran blindly, wanting now to forget the big man with the scarred mouth, the lift of thin muscular backs and shoulders under buckskin, the slanting barrels of the long rifles. I am a side and they are a side. But those were his thighs grown suddenly adult and strong around the horse, his shoulders lifting so that the hard ridge of muscle showed, and he could feel the weight of the rifle on his back and in his hands.

13

THE DISPATCH RIDER came through just before darkness fell, galloping into the yard a bare few moments before Brant returned from Brevard Hundred, so that Alwyn, coming down off the veranda in his shirt sleeves, greeted both the messenger and his son.

Alwyn sized the messenger up quickly, accurately: thin, tired man, ununiformed but with a thick dispatch case bearing a gilt lion on the flap. Tory, or else a British regular with his scarlets put away for the moment of duty. Alwyn guessed the latter. The man had deep furrows in his cheeks and a lock of brownish hair showed under his tricorn. He did not dismount. His voice was almost indifferent.

"Alwyn Quantrell."

"Yes," Alwyn said, hesitating, holding his pipe halfway to his mouth, watching, waiting.

The rider reached into the dispatch case, sorted through a sheaf of papers, and produced a sealed letter. He leaned from the horse and held out the message, and Alwyn put his pipe back in his mouth and came and took it. "I thank you," he said. "Will you wait?"

The rider gave a harsh laugh. "If I waited for every back-country yokel to figure out the King's English I'd be a long time about my work."

Alwyn said, "You'll not have a bit to eat and rest your horse then."

"Not this time, friend." The voice was indifferent again. "In the King's name."

"In the King's name," Alwyn said. "Godspeed."

The rider put his heels in the horse's ribs and went off, going past Brant without a word or glance. Brant had not dismounted. In the falling dark he watched his father, turning the dispatch over

141

in his hands, examining the seal. Finally he said, "Ain't you goin' to open it?"

Alwyn glanced up at him. After a moment Brant sighed and threw his leg up and over the gelding and sat sidesaddle a second or two and slid off with slow grace. The gelding danced, as if to show its white stockings. "You want me to open it?" Brant said.

"Perhaps you'd better. The light's going fast."

Brant put his fingernail under the hard red seal, without haste, almost with a deliberation that made Alwyn want to cry out at him. The seal broke. I would have held it to the light, Alwyn thought. Good as my eyes still are, I would have had to hold it to the light. Brant read from waist level.

"'Alwyn Quantrell, at the place called Brandyhill. This is to inform you that officers and men of Tarleton's Cavalry will pass through this territory on Thursday in expectation of receiving succor at the hands of the loyal subjects of the King. As head of that body called the Provincial Council in the territory known as Benton's Crossing, the owner of the place called Brandyhill shall provide for and quarter twenty men for as long as is necessary to the success of our operation. I am, sir, your obedient servant, Balforth Waite, Captain, Tarleton's Cavalry.'"

"Ah," Alwyn said, letting his breath out slowly, so that the word was half question, half exclamation.

Brant said, "Good Christ. Balforth. Balforth."

"Ah," Alwyn said again.

Brant was looking down at his own hands, as if he had never seen them before. "You mean we ain't had enough of Tarleton's Cavalry?"

"Son, do not pose problems which may be nonexistent."

"What about the rebel?"

"We'll see, in time."

"Time's goin' to be sometime tomorrow."

"Is tomorrow Thursday?"

"By my lights," Brant said.

Then Alwyn said, "I cannot ask him to leave. He is in no condition to travel."

"He's been here two weeks. He'll want to go."

"Yes, I think he will."

"Or maybe he won't. Maybe he'll want to stay and learn things . . . that's prob'ly what he was doin' here to begin with."

Alwyn knocked his pipe out against the railing. "What will we do with him? Not Brevard's or McLeod's or the Crossing, certainly."

Brant nodded soberly. "Much as you've been to 'em all these years, they'd ride you out of Brandyhill on a rail."

"Well," Alwyn said. "Well. Why must men be this way?"

"Undoubtedly because they are men," Sabrina said. She stood in the doorway, light spilling yellow around her. "So they are coming?"

Brant looked at her, trying to read her eyes, her face, in the light which lay not in eyes or face, but only let itself trace the long slim line of her in the doorway. He said, "How you going to feed twenty men?"

She said with stern calm, "We'll manage." Then she looked away from him, not wanting to say more, not wanting her voice or her words to betray her in any way. She looked at the gelding, seeing the silveriness of its eye in the half-dark, seeing the way the light lay over the mountains, pale and golden against the purple sky, like an overlay of color on color. Alwyn too watched the day die before he turned. Passing his daughter, he let his hand lie gently, momentarily, upon her shoulder before he entered the house.

Savage was in the kitchen. Alwyn told him, briefly, noncommittally. "I want to go on," Savage said. "I've got to."

"I don't see how you can," Alwyn said.

"Look here, sir." Savage's mouth twisted as he watched Alwyn. "I appreciate more than I can ever tell you what you've done for me. But I will not put you in a position where you and your family are endangered. It is not your troops I am afraid of. It is what may happen to you and your children."

"We will arrange something, Savage. I will not have you go like this, I will not turn you out."

Savage said with great control, "You try my patience, sir. There is no need to protest your kindness to me."

Now Alwyn looked fully at him. If I could hate, I would hate him. He is younger than I and he is wiser than I. Surer of tongue. Surer of himself. Surer of what he believes in. As if he had thought treachery, he straightened his shoulders. "If you would go, Major, I cannot stop you. But I shall blame myself all the days of my life if anything happens to you. I will not say that I am not pleased at the coming of our troops, for that would be a lie. I am more pleased than I can say that Brandyhill has been singled out for such an honor. Those men and their destinies are important to me, important to all who embrace our cause. But because they are many and you are one, you are no less important as a human being."

So that's where she gets it, Savage thought, his clear bitter eyes still on his host's face, the line of his mouth still twisted and without amusement. He could hear Sabrina's voice again: I wouldn't let a fox freeze out here . . . it's the pity of the thing . . . Alwyn's voice in his daughter's mouth. And he is a good old man. But that's the trouble, he is old. Old and full of the old Biblical goodness, only half rejecting the hell-fire logic tells him isn't there but fearing to reject what dogma tells him is truth. Knowing the oldness was there, under the still broad shoulders and the height, in the brain under the flowing white hair, in the bones which would soon crumble in the vigorous seamed face, he felt his own half youth, half age stir in him, in the lean-hipped, long-muscled litheness and the fast-moving blood of himself.

Sabrina came to stand in the doorway, between kitchen and hall, not speaking, not moving, yet both men knew she was there, as if her presence was a pillar of fire which did not spread, did not engulf, but seemed only to maintain shape and substance and intensity on the threshold of the room. Too wise to speak, she only waited, one hand gripping the doorjamb with pressure to the point of pain, the other clenching and unclenching in a fold of her gray woolen skirt. Only once did Savage glance at her; her face was pale, but her face took paleness well. It was as if the color which left her skin concentrated on cheekbone and mouth. Out of that one hasty glance he thought her more than beautiful, for what he had known of beauty in a woman, his wife, had been in purity and perfection of feature; his wife had had none of this wide-eyed naïveté and strength. And he looked at her again, unable to help himself now, and saw that her eyes were clear and direct and honest on her father's, heard that her voice was still and untroubled, but emphatic when she spoke.

"Father, he must stay in my room."

Alwyn's face was surprised, but full of gratitude; the surprise was that he had not thought of this, the gratitude was that he could still save and preserve and protect. He, Savage, had to present the facile demurrer.

"Do you think I would subject you to that?"

Now she came into the room, laying her hands flat upon the table, looking from one to the other of them with a great weariness

144

in her face. Men were such fools. For the first time she spoke his name. "Orne, it is the only way. If there is room for those men there is room for you."

Jewel said, "Why can't he jest be one of us Quantrells when they come?"

Savage answered, not taking his eyes from Sabrina's still face. "Someone might come, from the Crossing or Brevard Hundred. You people can't risk it. I can't risk it."

He thought the arm was healed enough to go . . . two weeks, enough of healing. Now he did not want to go; now he fell back upon righteous weakness, now he waited with fierce hope for Sabrina's intercession, Alwyn's approval; now he searched himself in despair for the strength to protest and, decently, to leave.

But they were all against him. Jewel came to stand at his side, holding a ladle in her hand. "You's right, Brina. I knows it and he knows it too, whether he goin' admit it er not." She poked at his arm with the ladle. "You ain't goin' nowhere, Majuh."

He glanced at her, but he spoke to Alwyn. "I still say I endanger you."

Alwyn ignored him. The blood went away from his face and came back again, a flaring of color under the skin. He looked at Sabrina. "And what of you?"

"Father," she said, as if she explained to a child, "if there is one place on Brandyhill the British will not go, it is my room. It is the one place he'll be safe. He can always get into the clothespress."

Now Savage wanted to laugh, now he fought not to laugh: in his mind he crouched in the clothespress, while the British poked through the house with fixed bayonets, halting chivalrously outside Sabrina's door. It was all so damned simple it was probably workable. He took a deep breath, not even giving Alwyn a chance this time. "All right," he said. "Jewel, you'll move your pallet into Sabrina's room. Make up a bed for me on the floor, under the window." He turned to Sabrina. "Are your curtains heavy enough so they can't be seen through from the outside?"

She nodded mutely. Something strange lay in her eyes, and it struck him that whatever she felt had nothing to do with him, or the British, or where he slept. For a time he stood uncomfortably in a vacuum, planning, contriving, meeting with no response from the girl who had given him the plan.

"Your shutters bolt from the inside?" he said.

She started. "What?"

"The shutters. Do they bolt inside?"

Again she nodded.

"The door too?"

"Yes," she said.

Savage turned to Alwyn. "This needs more than your approval, I'm afraid."

Alwyn smiled a little wryly. "My blessing, perhaps. I won't give you that, Major, but you have my sanction." He looked away from Savage, as if he did not quite dare to meet Savage's eye, meaning to speak again to Sabrina, but Sabrina had left the room. They heard her step in the hall, the opening and closing of the front door. Alwyn thought, she is disturbed, terribly disturbed at all this, and I cannot blame her. Savage thought, she is disturbed, but not at this, at something else, and whatever it is, it is of her own making, and I blame her.

If you turned your head sidewise, to the right, more or less upside down, the profile of the mountain on the sky was a girl's head, straight-hair-of-trees drawn back, deep indentation of deep-set eye, nose slightly aquiline. Where the trees threaded down a ravine it looked almost like a braid swinging on the softly rounded shoulder of a bluff. Savage had discovered by chance what Brant Quantrell had always known. And had carefully avoided over the last few years.

This would be the last breath of freedom, before tomorrow, before he trapped himself behind the drawn, bolted shutters and waited for the British to come, and to go. You want a mouthful of air you better git it now, Brant had said.

The lilac leaves were a graying wreath all around the weathered barn. It was warm on the hill, though there were cold drafts in the low spots of land, and the twilight sky looked pinkish and dirty. The grass was green again, looking rich and healthy in the long-lying shadows, not yet full of the thick white frost which would glitter like diamond in the morning sun. If the sun shone tomorrow. Hooves would thunder here, scattering the bright diamond as if the frost were a broken necklace in the grass; hard hooves, British hooves, drumming up the earth in the morning, in the afternoon rain, in the first falling of darkness . . . when. . . .

Savage leaned on the top rail of the fence with his good arm. Brant's gelding wandered in the pasture, cropping steadily, hungrily. A little distance away the colt stood, not cropping, with his head up and the wind moving his young mane. He was almost above eating, Savage thought, spoiled little devil. He let his eye wander down the length of the fence and saw Sabrina swatting the flat-eyed spotted goat through the gate. No goat tomorrow. No horses. No chickens. No cow. I'd wager. I'll wager my sons' inheritance there won't be any stock left after tomorrow.

He walked along the fence, holding to the top rail with one hand. Old Jim came to meet him, and the goat gave him a yellow stare. Sabrina did not look up from closing the gate, but she said, "Should you be out here?"

He shrugged. "Your brother's judgment, not mine."

"I only meant that after all we've done to save your precious rebel hide, it would be a shame to have it all given away now." She straightened up and looked at him and he saw that she was not angry, only deeply depressed, sharply serious. The depression lay in her eyes like midnight trapped in a well.

"I suppose you think I'm not grateful," he said.

"Oh, I know you're grateful, it hasn't anything to do with that; anybody as sensitive as you must be grateful beyond all expression."

He said quietly, "I'd be twice as grateful if you'd take that knife out from between my ribs."

She let her arms drop straight at her sides, shaking her head a little, watching him. "What an evil-tempered shrew I am. I should make a poor martyr, I think."

"If you think that why do you work so hard to find out?" he said. "I wish I hadn't muddled up your life so terribly for you."

"You." She laughed a little with the saying of the word. "What an enormous conceit you have, Orne," and she would have passed him but he blocked her way.

"No," he said, "you aren't going anywhere yet. Not until you tell me what's wrong."

She looked at him levelly. "Nothing is wrong. Nothing that concerns you at any rate."

"I knew you'd say that. I could have told exactly what you'd say. So it will save time and words if you are as honest with me now as you were that night in the barn. Listen, that night you left, the night you went away and did not come back until late, something happened, didn't it? Somebody was coming here you didn't want here, because of me. It was a man and you headed him off, because of me, and ever since that night you've gone around in a deadly little world of your own. And because it was for me, I want to know."

"There's nothing for you to know," she said. "It was a man, it was Fraser Malcolm. I've known him for years and he's Father's right-hand man on the council, and we could not have him here. That is the truth. That is all."

But he would not let her pass, and his face had gone still and thoughtful. He said very slowly, as if he figured it out while he said it, "A man, one single lone man whom you have known so long, threatens your security, and your father, or your brother perhaps, throws you like a musket ball into the breech. You. You were thrown, you were used. But twenty men, armed men, descend upon you, and you keep me here, offer me your room, give me the collective planning of the good Quantrell brains. I'm bewildered, Sabrina."

"Well," she said, angry, "do they not use me now, then, just as they used me before? Or would you rather I rode to intercept these twenty men for you too? Do me one kindness, Orne. Tend to your own affairs."

"I would not see you so unhappy as you have been these last few days. Credit me with some perception, Sabrina. Whatever sadness you met with you met the same night you met this man, Malcolm. Why?"

"We are to be wed at Christmas," she said stiffly.

He was silent for a time. Then he said, "I see."

"No, you do not see. You can't possibly understand. If you knew Fraser Malcolm you would understand even less. There has never been any formal agreement between us, but there has always been a rather . . . rather tacit understanding. He is a fine man, a good man, with a brilliant future."

"I see," he said again. "He is not one of the Crossing men who looks at you like a brood mare, I believe you put it."

"Oh, why do you throw those things back at me?"

"I know, it's petty of me. But I know too that you had no more idea of marrying this man two weeks ago than you had of marrying me. Maybe less."

She gathered all her resources, not to pass him now, but to leave him. "No matter what you say, I still have the strongest argument. It is not your affair."

Now he put his hand out and took her by the arm. It was almost dark, and he could barely see her face. "It is a hard thing to admire a woman who so consistently fights against being admired. Or loved. You strive like hell to spare everyone else. To keep the truth to yourself. Can you stand hearing the truth now?"

"What truth?" she said scornfully.

"About yourself. About me. If I say it I might regret it, but if I leave it unsaid I will regret it more."

"Say what you will," she said icily, "but I would not have you regret one moment's time you spent with me."

"All right. Today you came into the kitchen and offered me, in your father's hearing, the sanctuary of your room. You knew I would accept it. And I protested. But I knew, all the while I protested, that I would accept it. More, Sabrina, you knew I was well enough to leave. I knew I was well enough to leave. And both of us knew the other knew it. Isn't that so?"

She was silent, standing with her head down. Something, perhaps her attitude, perhaps the tone of Savage's voice, brought Old Jim to her side quietly, protectively, head lifted to scent them both, breathe their trouble. But he found no threat; rather, he drew back, away from them, when Sabrina suddenly broke free of Savage, saying over and over again, first flatly, "no," and then, "no, no, no," with the note that was half joy and half terror rising and falling in the word. After a time the dog tested the wind again and turned and followed where Sabrina had run, on the narrow path to the house.

14

Tag said, "I'm going to wait until I see them coming, and then I'll run up to the barn so you can see me, and wave to you. So you'll know."

"I would rather you did not do that, Tag," his father said.

Tag scuffed his toe along the hearth, looking down at it dispiritedly. They stood before the kitchen fire warming themselves, while Jewel and Sabrina went about the preparation of breakfast. He said, "Why not? Then you'd be ready when they come."

"I would rather you did not," Alwyn repeated.

"Then why . . . ?" Tag said.

Brant said mildly, "I reckon Father don't see any dignity in havin' you stand on top of the hill wavin', like it was gypsies with a dancin' bear."

Tag went on sliding the toe of his shoe along the hearth, and then along the floor, following a crack in the wide warped boards. "Where's Major Savage?" he said.

Sabrina turned on him. "Don't you ever . . . ?"

"He's gittin' some books." Brant's voice was hard now. "And you ain't to mention his name again, not even in your mind, hear, Tag?"

The little boy nodded and went to the window. It had rained in the night, and the air was gray and wet, pressing dismally against the glass. The fire warmed the room, leaving a mist on the glass that was fun to run your fingers through and draw things and write your name in, except Jewel wouldn't let you. He pressed his nose against the pane and the pane was cold against his flesh. He looked out and saw the wet world and shivered, but he wanted to go out into it, to leave the fire which made him drowsy and the intimacy of the kitchen and the hot corn meal and syrup that would soon be set before him.

Jewel slammed a pitcher down. "I'd like to see one lil' aig agin. Jest one lil' aig."

"Perhaps this morning, Jewel," Alwyn said, "and if not, perhaps tomorrow. In time of war. . . ."

She flashed the whites of her eyes at him. "Well I ain't to war an' I'd like jest one aig."

"I still don't see why," Tag said, his nose against the window.

"You jest stop that whinin' an' complainin', boy, cause I ain't fixin' to hear no more of it this mornin'. Now you mind you father an' eat you breakfus'."

He got into his chair obediently, chastened, inhaling the steam from the corn meal. He pushed his spoon into the mush and made roadways and mountains and poured the syrup into the valleys and made rivers. Anyway, even if they would not let him wave to them, to let them know, he would go. He would go to the exact spot where he had seen that awful ragged little band of rebels and stand by the road and wait, and maybe they would bring him in with them, high upon a horse, before a fine officer. But the thought felt heavy and leaden, not because he thought it couldn't really happen; in his mind anything was possible, and riding with them would be fine and grand. It was something else. He bolted the mush and excused himself from the table and went to stand with his nose against the pane again. He made a hole in the steam with his finger and looked up toward the barn. It stood staunchly against the gray sky. He shivered again, looking now at the grove of pines, dark and tall, which sheltered the gravestones. He turned away and got his coat from a peg on the wall.

"Where are you going, Tag?" his father said, the mug of tea half lifted to his mouth and his mouth pursed to blow.

"Out," he said.

"Out to catchen more cold," Jewel said.

He was fretful at all the adult attempts to cross him. "I'm not either. I been stuck in this house and it stinks of smoke and I want to go out."

"Timothy," his father said.

"I'm sorry, Father. May I go out?"

"Don't get your feet wet."

"Yes, sir," he said resignedly, and pulled his cap down around his ears and opened the door.

He had to do it. Had to go to the road and wait for them, and when he saw them, strong and colorful, a whole army of them on sleek horses, with shining swords, it would erase forever from his mind any thought of that terrible, thin-shanked group of men who had threatened him in that same road, and after threatening him admonished him, and after admonishing him gone off as if they owned the world. Wearily, but as if they owned the world. They were in his mind constantly, kept there not only by memory but by the rebel who had slept in his own house, and he wanted to forget them because he felt guilty. As if he had done something wrong, something bad, something that his father would despise him for. When they came, the guilt would be gone, and he would feel clean and good and proud again.

Part of what he hoped for came true. But it was as if he had dreamed it. One moment he was watching for them and the next moment they were there and the next moment he was high up on a horse as he had wanted to be, sitting before a strange man who smelled of sweat and wet wool. Only once did he turn and look behind him, and although it was a fleeting glance it troubled him.

This horse he rode was as thin as any the rebels had ridden. A little thinner, maybe, he thought critically, disbelievingly. The same weariness which stamped the faces of those rebel Carolinians and Virginians was as clear-cut and white as cameo on these British faces. The uniforms were faded and dirty and wet, and he wanted to slip from the horse and run to the house, calling out to his father that it was not true, that they had been tricked. But the man held him firmly, and looking down, he could see the slash of gold braid on the green sleeve and the round tarnished eyes of the brass buttons.

The horses raced. They raced down the road and up the hill and into the yard, and Alwyn and Brant were there and Alwyn's face was like rock in his pride. Now Tag did slip down, falling to his knees and running from the laughter of the men. Even his father laughed, rumpling his head until the cap tumbled off. When the officer dismounted his father came forward, holding out his hand.

"Captain Waite. I am Alwyn Quantrell, and at your service, sir."

The officer took his hand limply for a second and then dropped it. Tag turned and looked at him and saw the white, white child's face and the high brow and the curling reddish hair under the steel helmet. The pale childish upper lip protruded, so that it appeared to be in a perpetual pout. The chin was softly rounded, that too like a child's, and the blue eyes were pale and looked as if they did not see well. The weathered brown face and arms, the strongly springing brassy hair, the keen eyes of the man they called Mc-Dowell flashed into Tag's mind. With what he did not, could not recognize as shock, he looked at the tattered band in the yard of Brandyhill and wanted to cry with disappointment.

"You colonials have been blessed with the most beastly weather on earth," Waite said in a thin voice. He turned to survey the landscape, hand on hip. "Little wonder nobody wants to come and settle."

Brant leaned against the doorframe, arms crossed. He said softly, "We Englishmen ain't too unhappy with our lot, Captain."

The eyes which looked as if they did not see well saw sharply now. A son of military age, fodder for any Loyalist regiment, stood at ease, at home, here. But he turned back to Alwyn. "Will you accommodate us immediately?"

"It is an honor, sir," Alwyn said, face softened with pleasure. "You will understand that we've not much space, but the barn is warm and dry and your men can rest comfortably. Brant, will you see they are cared for. We have hot food for you all."

Tag pulled at his father's belt. "Father. . . ."

Alwyn shook him off. "Tag, go into the house and help Jewel. You have been underfoot enough today." He smiled apologetically at Waite. "He could not wait until you came. I knew when he ran off after breakfast this morning that he was on the lookout for you."

Waite refrained from commenting. He stamped up the steps and Brant looked at him levelly and passed him and went to lead the dismounted band in the yard to the barn.

Alwyn followed the officer. "My home, sir, is yours, for as long as you care to make it so. My family is delighted that you've seen fit to stop with us."

Tag, inside now, thought it was mean of Waite not to mention the leaded glass panes by the door, or the glowing warmth of the house. Nothing changed in the Britisher's eyes until Alwyn said, "Captain, my daughter, Sabrina," and there was the swing of Sabrina's skirt as she cursied; only then did he remove the gauntleted gloves which seemed to Tag huge, so huge they did not fit properly, and take Sabrina's hand and lift it, and press her fingers with his lips and say, "Mistress, your servant."

Alwyn was excited, but working to retain an air of authority and calmness. "Come, Captain, come and eat. You will forgive us if we sit with you while you have your dinner, but there is much to talk of and I know you will be with us so short a time."

So they sat and watched him eat the two eggs which had miraculously awaited Jewel's searching hand, Sabrina upright and uncomfortable at the round table which had been covered with Caroline Amanda's best linen cloth, Tag leaning on both elbows, hungrily watching the eggs disappear, Alwyn rubbing his hands together, his eyes warm with anticipation. Waite ate silently, washing the eggs and mush down with an entire bottle of sherry, and eating the roasted hen with his fingers. Sabrina's hands tightened on the arms of her chair. Not a thank you, not a compliment for the sherry and the only eggs they had seen in days and were likely to see for a good many more.

When he had finished the meal he smacked his lips, and she took that for a compliment of some sort, wiped them on his napkin, and pushed back in his chair.

"Any more sherry?" he said.

"Forgive me, Captain." Alwyn was on his feet instantly. He got another bottle and uncorked it and poured, his hand shaking a little. Waite lifted his glass. "To our glorious cause. And to your daughter, Quantrell."

"I shall drink with you on both scores," Alwyn said, and got himself a glass and filled it with the clear yellow wine.

"And I shall drink the King's health with you," Sabrina said clearly, suddenly. Waite smiled his approval at her across the table, waiting until her glass was filled. Then he rose and toasted her, and her father rose too, and Tag slipped off the chair to his feet, no longer envious because of the eggs, wide-eyed at this display of British breeding. Waite, standing, holding his glass high, said, "The King," and they drank, and Alwyn refilled the glasses and said, "To our staunch Loyalist friends," and they drank again.

Waite did not appear drunk or even fuzzed by the wine he had consumed. When Jewel came and took his plate away he pushed back in his chair, crossing his legs in the muddy, once white breeches. "Very good," he said at last. "What's become of the boy in the yard, your son?"

"He will be in directly," Alwyn said. "Meanwhile is it possible for you to tell us something of your plans, something of what you will do when you leave here?"

Waite smiled a little. "You Tories. All alike. Anxious to learn what we're doing to protect you from your own neighbors but damn few of you willing to help yourselves. What we shall do when we leave this place depends alone upon Colonel Tarleton and not upon the whims of this peasant Morgan, as a good many of you provincials would have us believe. That lout runs from us as if he were possessed, but he cannot keep up this pace. He has nothing, no men, no arms, no food. We could be worse off. It's your vile weather has done this to us. But when we catch this . . . this man who has set himself up as some sort of militant god to these filthy rebels, it will be the last of it. Finished, for good and all."

Alwyn, stung, opened his mouth to speak, but the Britisher leaned forward, pointing a finger at him. "Let me tell you something, Quantrell. It's people like you who have hampered us every step of the way. Offered us your undying friendship when we travel through, but what happens when we need your physical support? That son of yours, for instance, what's he doing at home, tending the chickens? There are Loyalist regiments crying for men like him."

Alwyn said, "I shall never force my sons to do anything they cannot see themselves doing. Brant's sympathies lie with England, but he is not a fighting man. We do what we can to help. We pray for you, beset with obstacles every moment of the day and facing danger for us, who stay at home. I am too old. Tag is too young."

"I know. I know." He watched Alwyn, distaste pulling down the corners of his mouth. "We've heard that same story from Loyalists all through the South. We've heard it from closets and under feather beds and out of cellars, after the first gun goes off. We listened a little too long to this sort of thing, and when Colonel Tarleton's heard it too long he doesn't care what the speaker of those words pretends to be. It doesn't matter to him what you are. He has work to do and he does it." Waite drained the glass.

"No," Alwyn said evenly, determined to remain even. "There is no purpose in your calling us to fear. If it is true that Colonel Tarleton employs his own particular methods of justice with the rebels, I may not approve that, but you and I both know he has never molested a confessed Loyalist, and that any tales to that effect are lies spread by our enemies. I tell you that we are willing to give you all that we have so that your lot may be an easier one."

Waite stared at him as if he could not believe his ears. "Call you to fear. Fear." He began to laugh in a high childish giggle. He broke off when Brant came in; the laughter was broken neatly through the middle as he saw Brant shrug out of the heavy outer shirt and stand with it slung over his shoulder. In the light, firelight and penetrating gray daylight, Brant was dark and healthy and overpowering beside the pale, tired Waite. Abruptly Waite rose, striding with mock military sharpness to pull out a chair and fill a glass for Brant.

"Ah, at last, the older son, who assuredly must be in close touch with the political situation here. How do you find the talk of the war, Quantrell? Are there plaudits all about for we brave soldiers and our valiant Loyalist allies?"

Alwyn's calmness was in Brant, but there was a part of him that was not Alwyn and had not been the first Alwyn. "Talk of the war, Captain, these days at least, usually centers around gittin' it over with. Ain't that right, Father?"

Waite said, smiling, staring at Brant, "Well, we are here now. I dare say the day's not long in coming."

"That's our feeling too," Brant said.

Waite gestured at him with his elbow, but he looked at Alwyn. "He's an agreeable sort, this son of yours. But sickly, eh. I fancy I'm a tolerant man. If he's sickly we're all better off if he stays home." He broke into harsh humorless laughter.

Brant smiled quietly. "And are you a professional soldier, Captain?"

"Cavalryman, my boy, cavalryman." Younger than Brant or near Brant's age, Waite was in no way supercilious now, only patronizing.

"That's the problem," Brant said. "I'd like to be a cavalryman myself, not just a foot soldier. But I reckon, not having had the training and all, I couldn't fight from a horse."

"That's true." Waite nodded. "True. It does take training, no question about it. Strange you should bring it up at this time, but it's the professional soldier has made the British Army, no question about that either."

It all sounded terribly familiar, Alwyn thought, feeling a first little tremor along his spine. But Brant was only weary, prodding, gentle, relentless, seemingly without aim. "I met another professional cavalryman once, Captain. Maybe you know him, he's Tarleton's Dragoons too. Older than you, name of Galton."

Waite moved his head very slowly, as if his neck was stiff. Brant read him, read that what the captain feared most now was any comparison with the able Galton. "Why yes," he said, almost apologetically. "But you must understand Hal Galton was trained nearly from the cradle. Why he was an officer before he had a beard. In my own case, I was near twenty. . . ."

Brant stood up. "That's what I mean, Captain. I get to meet a man like that and I can reckon right off it's too late for me to make anything of myself, I mean to be more than just expendable in the field. I could've had all sorts of ambitions if I could have climbed out of my cradle and onto a horse, like you say."

Waite did not speak.

Brant said softly, amiably, "But I'll never be another Hal Galton."

"Well now," Waite said with equal amiability, "there's no need to fret about it . . . there's the privileged and the underprivileged, you know, and no possibility of one canceling out the other. As I say, I'm a tolerant man, accepting my side of the ledger with as good grace as I can." His eyes were full of his tolerance, and of something else, a queer extroverted pride. (He looked like a little ruffled banty rooster, Brant thought, chest out, eyes sparkling; he would be a very bad shot, but very brave, and if I put my fist in the side of his head, his head would go in mushy as a melon.) "I must say," Waite went on, not even feigning modesty now, "I must say it's a new experience to find a colonial er . . . countryman so humble. So openly envious."

He and Brant nodded at one another understandingly. Brant avoided his father's astonished face and looked at Sabrina, wanting to find something of amusement, of encouragement in her. But she was sitting bolt upright, eyes wide and serious, staring at and through Waite, not hearing him or seeing him, alive, in the room, with his pale childish face; not even seeing Brant, suave as a Jesuit, with his chair tipped back against the wall now. Waite, following Brant's glance, saw the girl's wide gray eyes upon him and smiled at her in smug expectancy. He kept glancing at her: her lips had parted a little. He brushed his hand along the side of his curling reddish hair. He would settle in early, so that the evening would be free. . . .

He rose cheerfully, quickly, striving to present to the girl youth and good spirits and confidence. Women liked confident men. "Where am I to sleep, gentlemen?"

Alwyn's face had not lost its look of astonishment. He was ready for talk. But he rose, heavily. "If you do not mind the inconvenience, Captain, you could share my bed, or my son's. Or we could make you a bed before the fire."

Waite glanced at Sabrina and thought the pallor of her face was magnificent, and the startling redness of her mouth. Looking at her made the slow blood begin to move in him. If there was any sharing of beds here it would not be with this sanctimonious addlepated old man, or his animal of a son. "Have you so little room, then?" he said, still watching Sabrina.

"There is only the women's room, off the kitchen," Alwyn said hastily, fumbling with his pipe, face turned from Waite.

Now Sabrina smiled, softly, directly, eyes a little downcast. "It is hardly proper to speak of such things, Father."

Waite bowed. His hand went dramatically to his heart. "Rather would I dethrone an angel in heaven, mistress, than turn you from your bed. I will share the barn with my men." He belched and looked at Tag. "My helmet, little boy."

Tag went to the table in the front room and picked up the monstrously heavy silver helmet with its stiff horsehair plume along the top. Standing alone in the room, he tried tucking it under his arm as the cavalrymen carried them. It was bulky and uncomfortable there and did not fit. He brought it to Waite.

"Could I try it on?" he said, looking up at the man whose horse he had ridden earlier that day.

"Come, come," Waite said, "I am in a hurry."

Tag handed him the helmet. He tucked it under his arm without any trouble at all. Then he made a stiff little formal bow again, crossing the room to where Sabrina still sat, with her lips parted and eyes averted. "Mistress," he said.

Her hand was like ice when he raised it to his lips. She looked at him, startled, and he saw the sudden leaping to life, the new fire in her eyes, and believed it was all for him.

They went down the hall with him, all but Sabrina, who had not moved from her chair. Then Brant came back into the room and picked up the little glass Waite had drunk from and looked at it thoughtfully and put it down again. "You know, one time a few years back Keoweh's father wanted to show me how to skin a bear and I told him I already knew and he said if a man ever stopped learning that man was useless, and then he showed me some tricks in taking off the head skin whole."

She waited.

"So I figure I ain't as useless as some people think, because I keep right on learnin' all the time. Learn a lot from these professional people, for instance. Learn all about the glories of war. When you're born to it. The glories of war, my boy, my boy, lie in sabering unarmed men, in stealin' from women and children. Why, I'm just learnin' what war is, and here I thought I knew it all this time, and it ain't any of the things I thought it was. It's noble brutality, splendid exaction, thievery on a majestic scale, murder on the grand plane of righteousness. Jesus God, imagine how I could've been so thoughtless all this time. Imagine."

"Brant." She almost moaned his name.

"You ain't imaginin' hard enough, that's your trouble. You stopped learnin'. And here I am goin' ahead so fast I reckon I could even learn what made all this happen, all this business of war, of revolution. Only thing I figure I'll never learn is how those poor dumb bastards in Boston took it as long as they did."

"Stop," she said in a low voice. "You will kill your father."

He shook his head. "Nothing will ever kill Father. Not even time'll wipe out his breed. Maybe thank God for it." He came and leaned over her, bracing his arms on the arms of her chair. "Don't you feel sick, Brina? You did that so bloody good you'd ought to feel sick now, by my reckoning."

"Please stop," she said.

But he forced her to look at him, ducking his head, holding her eye. The dark lock of hair fell over his forehead, sweat glistened on his face. "What's the matter with you . . . you liked Captain Galton? You like Captain Waite? Hell, and you ain't even sat on the council."

She sank back in the chair, shrinking from him. "Don't talk to me like that. It's only you're hungry to get off and go somewhere again, looking, looking all the time for something you'll never find, it's only you're sick of people, sick of us all. What does it matter whether I like them or not . . . would you have me side with Orne Savage and his noble brutalities and murders? Take your choice, Brant, but don't ask me to choose."

He stood upright. "I ain't choosing either side. And you already chose."

"What do you mean by that? What do you mean?" She looked up at him, white-faced. "Brant, don't quarrel with me. Don't let Father hear you."

He went to the fireplace and reached up and lifted down his rifle. "What are you going to do?" she said.

"I ain't goin' to do anything."

"You're going away again, aren't you?"

He turned and looked at her, holding the rifle. "I'm only goin' to clean it, in case," he said. "You don't think I'd leave you and Father here now, do you? But I ain't saying I wouldn't like to go. Because where I like to think I come from, where I like to think I want to end up my life, there ain't any war. There ain't any people, and that's the way I want it. I ain't as sturdy as those Bostonians, I reckon."

He left the room and went to the kitchen. She still sat before the fire, until Jewel's voice, vehement, full of complaint, called. When she went to the kitchen Brant sat at the table, working with the rifle. They did not speak to one another, and his face was as impassive as if this were a glade in the forest, and she was only another tree.

Waite had talked to the men. She knew it the moment she entered the barn, saw it in their tense courtesy and flushed faces. Far down at the end of the stalls, once, there was laughter, and she felt her face burn as if the not knowing what had been said made her know. A young lance corporal, his green cavalry coat open and his stock unbuttoned, came and took the sheet of corn cake and potatoes from her, bowing a little, smiling, and looking at this child's face she saw that Waite was not a child but a man. This was a child, who aided her now, truly a child, who had seen rank and perhaps title ahead and who stood now in her barn with the adventure and the hope dead in his eyes, thankful for the dry yellow bread. The slender vulnerability of him made her ache with sympathy. She smiled and felt his hands tremble as he took the pan. English gentlemen. She turned away, feeling their silence and their hungry eyes.

Waite came around the end stall and stood looking at her, holding his gloves in one hand and slapping them gently, decisively against his thigh. She walked firmly to the big door, and the lance corporal ran to swing it open for her, balancing the pan tipsily in one hand. She thanked him and went out and stood for a moment, drawing the cold air into her throat hard.

Waite had gone out the back door and come around the corner, so that when she started down the path he moved behind her. She turned on him, using her anger at Brant as a weapon. "Well, Captain?"

He had a shy smile, much out of keeping with what she had seen of him. "I would thank you for your many kindnesses, mistress. You have made us more than comfortable."

"I am sorry we have so little room," she said, without conviction.

"One cannot measure hospitality, mistress."

"We shall do all we can for you," she said.

He still slapped his thigh with the gloves. She led more nicely into his thought than he had believed she would, and, he was convinced, with less innocence. "There is much may be done to comfort a weary man," he said. "Your graciousness might be furthered, shall we say, with the giving of your charming company this evening."

She turned without speaking and started down the path. She heard his voice without surprise, saying her name twice, the second time insistently, and kept walking. He could not see her face, but he could remember, and when she did not answer, he put his hand on her arm, gently, his mind already full of the badinage which was a necessary prerequisite.

She whirled and struck at him viciously and with all her strength. Her hand glanced off his arm, and she pulled it back and struck him across the face. She heard him gasp, more in astonishment than anger, but once she had begun she could not stop herself, fighting him in cold, silent fury. He caught both her hands and forced them behind her, but she did not cry out, wrenching one hand free at last and clawing at his face and feeling his flesh under her nails before he caught her hand again. His weight forced her back against the barn; for a moment she went wholly limp, then she tore her hand free again and this time found his eyes, so that he staggered away from her and almost fell.

With the path between them, they stared at one another, panting. Then he said, "It is customary in most circles, mistress, that the method of attack be subtler." Now he smiled, but his voice was deadly. "You would do well to remember, if you speak to anyone of this matter, that it was *you* who assaulted *my* person."

On the way to the house she broke the skim ice from a puddle and rubbed it on her face until she could feel her blood begin to warm again. But she felt better, for she had done what Brant had wanted to do and could not. Because Brant would endanger them all, and she had endangered nothing, she thought, but Balforth Waite's pride.

15

EVEN WITH THE DRAPES DRAWN the moonlight shafted heavily into the room, the bold, shadowless moonlight of late autumn. Inured to the nebulous shadowy moonlight of the dry summer, Sabrina found the outpouring of light too brilliant, too hard, felt as if she must shade her eyes from the quickening mercilessness of flooding exposure; under the window light lay in her sight first a lemon pool, then amber, then darkening to pure brass.

Beside her, on the floor, Jewel's breathing was too irregular to be the breathing of sleep. She lay listening to the irregular breathing; in the darkness of the room with the light filtering through bolted shutter, through drawn drape, she lay stiffly, upon her back, hands locked across her belly; she lay as if dead, but did not feel dead, and after a time it was as though she could hear the moonlight falling. I will know when Jewel sleeps, she thought. I will know when Orne sleeps.

But he did not sleep. His voice came from under the window, low, almost reluctant, and she thought he knew too that Jewel did not sleep. "Are you awake, Sabrina?"

She nodded her head, as if he could see her. "I don't think I will sleep tonight, Major."

She gave off trouble to him like a scent. "Today," he said, "you called me by my given name. And there's not a doubt in my mind you'll sleep like a dog. What's the matter, Sabrina?"

She said, "Did you guess Uncle John came? And Aiken Sheller and William Lyons. All of them, with Father, up in the barn, talking with Captain Waite, saying as how they'd like to give a little reception for the troops." She laughed shortly.

162

Silence hung for a time. They were both aware that Jewel's breathing had become steady, the breath of unconsciousness, the breath of sleep. Still Sabrina lay upon her back, drawn-up knees pressed together, hands clasped now behind her head. Out of the darkness, out of the harsh light, Savage said, "And your betrothed did not come?"

"No," she said under her breath.

"Why is it you dislike him so much?"

"I don't dislike him."

Not needing more, he said, "Will the captain stay for this well-meant reception?"

"He says he must go in the morning."

He sensed her relief, but sensed also something more. "And did the captain speak pleasantly to you?"

She said in a tight voice, "He has red hair."

"Indeed. So did my wife."

"You won't tell me about her, will you?"

"I've already told you more than you've told me about Malcolm."

She drew her breath in and let it out slowly. "But you did not dislike her."

He laughed a little. "No more than you this man you are to wed." Then he said, "What have you to wager me, Sabrina, that you will wed him? Against my own wager that you will not, I mean."

She felt like crying. To save herself, to deceive him, she said, "You should have gone, you should not have stayed here."

He was quiet so long that she thought he slept. But when she held the thought most bitterly he said, "But I couldn't go. Something terrible has happened to me, Sabrina. Something unreal. I could no more have left now than I could have leaped off your barn roof and flown. And the weakness does not come from my wound."

"Whatever your weakness is, conquer it," she said shortly.

"Have you conquered yours?"

"I can't even identify mine."

Again he did not answer. Then he said, "If you turned on your side, Sabrina, you could see me, you could talk to me more easily."

She did not desire to see him, to talk to him. Again the tears came sharp to mind and eye, tears for Malcolm, for Waite, for herself. But *I hate self-pity. I do not want to know Orne Savage's weaknesses; I do not want to know whatever it is he wants to tell* me now. But I feel safe, I feel protected. And tomorrow Waite will be gone, and this man, this stranger, this rebel, and after him perhaps Brant, and I will stand alone in this world with nothing to shield me ever again from some sort of beginning with Fraser. I will hold this night in my mind forever, no matter what happens, what does not happen, for I can always go back to it if I wish, and it will be mine to share with no one else, one small corner of my body, one small corner of my mind where no one else can ever go. . . . In the morning, firmly, decisively, I will tell my father about Fraser. . . .

He said, beside her, from the floor, "Sabrina, are you all right? Are you comfortable?"

She felt her body rise and fall to the rhythm of her own breathing, felt relaxation spread through her like a warm washing of blood. She said, "I am comforted," and turned on her side and let her hand fall over the mattress, over the pine-star-imprinted quilt, and felt without shock his fingers find her palm and press and weave into her fingers and hold for a moment, so that the last thing she remembered before she slept was the flooding of moonlight in the room and their hands, not clasped now, but only touching.

It was still dark when Waite came down from the barn. He had shaved and brushed his uniform and freshened his stock, and the curling reddish hair was neatly clubbed. His boots shone, and the light struck off the newly polished helmet in the crook of his arm. There was a jagged scratch on his face. He looked directly at Sabrina when he entered the house, and she met his look evenly.

He bowed to Alwyn, spoke ingratiatingly to Brant, even to Tag. Tag stood behind Sabrina, looking out at the Englishman as if he peered around a wall, and she felt annoyance at the child underfoot. Alwyn was saying something, but she hardly listened, and the words sounded inane and servile and degrading. The honor of having you, success in the field, regret that we cannot do more . . . she wanted to stop him, even before Waite interrupted. He had not been listening fully either.

He said, "We are taking your horses."

Alwyn said, "We understand, Captain. Thank God we have them for you. Will you leave your poor tired beasts here?"

"They will undoubtedly be used in commissary," Waite said. "Who is your nearest neighbor with horses?"

"John Brevard," Alwyn said. "The gentleman who spoke with you last evening. His house is just off the main road, a brick manor house. You will find him as loyal. . . ."

"I know," Waite said, with great weariness. Then, more gently, "You understand, Quantrell, that it is not our choosing, that we must take every horse and egg and pan of milk in the country if we have to?"

"Yes," Alwyn said eagerly, gratefully, "yes, I understand that, Captain."

It was Tag who did not understand, whose throat was so filled with painful loss that he clung to Sabrina's skirt and at last swung around in front of her. "You don't have to take the colt," he said hoarsely. "You don't have to take him, he's too small. Besides, he's Sabrina's."

Waite turned and looked at her.

Tag said, "You can't ride the colt, what can you do with a colt?"

And Waite said, still watching Sabrina, "We have uses for all things, my child."

Nothing was left in Sabrina now, not even pride. She went across the room and stood close to Waite and looked him in the eye. "I ask you to leave me my colt, Captain."

And he bent and took her hand and raised it to his lips. "The fortunes of war, mistress," he said, and went out.

They were in the yard, waiting, with the old horses and the fresh horses. Alwyn hurried after Waite, face troubled, wordless. Waite had no words either. He was riding Brant's gelding, and he swung into the saddle and kicked the gelding hard and rode off without looking back. Sabrina did not see them go. She felt, numbly, Brant's hand upon her head for a moment, heard Tag sobbing in the kitchen and Jewel talking furiously to herself, but she saw only Alwyn, queerly stoop-shouldered on the veranda, holding to the iron grillwork, and the bare slender branching of the wisteria shutting him off from the world, so that he was alone with whatever he held inside himself.

Only Jewel was in the kitchen, eyes cloudy with anger, so when Savage saw the light of the lantern, moving up the hill to the barn, he went out into the half daylight and smelled the fresh wetness of the earth and went up the path. The light had disappeared, snuffed out by the barricade of the barn wall.

When he went in the barn, Sabrina stood squarely before an empty stall, in the middle of the floor, in the scuffed straw. She knew he was there, he thought, but she did not turn around, did not speak. He sank down on a broken bale in the corner, and the old bitterness came into his eyes.

"Well," he said.

She crossed her arms in a fierce, impatient motion. They were alone in a misty world lit only by the thin triangular flame of the lantern, set upon the barn floor. She began to walk back and forth, skirts swinging. "They took the horses. They took my colt."

"I could have told you this last night, Sabrina."

She bit at her lower lip. "My colt, which he has no use for, which he needed no more than he needed . . . damn him. Damn them all." She stopped pacing and put her hands up to the sides of her face, holding herself. "What did he want with my colt? What, what, what?"

Savage said quietly, "If it had been us, if it had been me, I'd have done the same. I'd have cleaned you out entirely."

But she only said "ah," sick with disgust.

He smiled a little. "The red-haired captain."

She looked at him blankly, as if she did not really hear him. "They've gone to Brevard Hundred. I hope Uncle John's got Onny under lock and key. If he'd as much as look at me, heaven only knows what Onny. . . ." She stopped. He had caught her hand and was holding it, with a queer gentle pressure of his thumb on her wrist, where the pulse beat. "Don't do that," she said.

"The things that must be borne. I'm sorry about the colt, Sabrina. What did you do to the captain?"

"I nearly tore his eyes out and I'd like a chance to try again. Now let me go."

He released her hand. She began to walk then, clear to the end of the barn, past the empty stalls. She walked with her head down, holding the shawl about her, biting at her lip; came back to him (but did not look up), started down the barn again. Halfway, she stopped. "Don't you see it's more than the colt? Don't you see it's part of something my father and my brothers and all of us have worked so hard to build and enjoy that's been violated?" She went on to the end of the barn and stood with her face against the timbers.

She was without form in the dimness, only a slim darkness, far away, to him. He said heavily, "Yes, I see. So much is being destroyed so gradually. Like a rock doomed to be worn away by water. Destruction should always be effected in one clean fine motion, tragic and grand. But it never is. The concept of cataclysmic destruction is erroneous. When you are living destruction, as you are, Sabrina, and as I am, it is always piecemeal, day by day. Little fragments splinter away from the whole and lodge in the heart, until the heart is so sore you pray to have it burst in you, rather than bear it. It's the detail of destruction, and the minuteness of the detail that is so terrible. Every hour we give a little more of our souls to it."

She came away from the wall and up the floor again. Still not close to him, but close enough so that he could see her face now, she stopped and kicked at a little clump of straw on the floor. It was a gesture made almost absently, without either anger or despair, and the futility of it tore at him.

"Sabrina," he said, "I love you."

She did not look up. "What?" she said blankly, as if she not only did not want to understand, but had not heard him.

"I wanted to tell you I love you."

Now she raised her head. He could see by her face how slowly the full knowledge of what he had said came to her. "But that's impossible," she said.

"If it were impossible I couldn't do it," he said quietly. "I think I loved you in that moment when you bent over me in the woods. Not just because I thought I was going to die, and you were hope. I began loving you then. I haven't stopped."

She came to him slowly, staring at him. Between them, the lantern threw its small flame upward; their faces were still and watchful in a fine pattern of light and shadow: the delicate silver planes of light shaded and sank into the rich dark planes of the shadow. For a moment her mouth contorted, then composed itself. But she could feel herself slip away from herself, as if not only physically but spiritually she had shattered and fallen, not explosively, but as glass will shatter and fall, in an ecstatic showering of herself. She was carried on a warm rushing softness, a heat as of the soft purple airless heat of August nights; she brought her hands up slowly, almost in an attitude of prayer, almost as though she would protect herself. "But I cannot," she said. "There is so much. . . ."

He only watched her, only thought that she must say something or turn from him.

She said, "It must have begun for me too, then. When I found you, when I thought it was fear had stopped my heart, and it wasn't fear at all, it was love. All these days . . . when I have been so full of you . . . *love* like a destruction in *me*, wearing me away . . . and I knew it, and could not, or would not, stop it. . . ."

He held up his hand to her. In it she read supplication and command. Her skirts brushed the lantern, heedless. For a moment only she bent over him, tracing the planes of his face with her fingers, as if she were suddenly blinded and could see him only by touching him; then she had shattered again, falling, crumbling against him, but restored to a wholeness of herself by the reality of his arm locking her close, by scent and vision, by contact. A season of perpetual summers flowered in the silky-harsh broken straw, enveloped her as his presence and touch had enveloped her, not crushing but transporting in a sharpness of fire and mitigation of cool wind; full of fire-forging and tempering flooding of still, golden waters and light raining sheer, soft, muted where there might never be darkness again.

The little lantern flame burned patiently, steadily. Outside, the pale shell of daylight rose, curving to the earth, burnishing itself against the mountains.

That night, in the kitchen, Savage said, "You got an easy life, Quantrell. A damned soft life."

Brant put his tongue in the mouth of the jug and pulled it out and listened to the soft, pinging, hollow sound it made. After a moment he said, "You gonna preach?"

"Hell no. Not to you anyway."

"Glad to hear that. I hate preachin'. You preach."

"Do I?" Savage said.

"You preached to my father."

"Preachers only understand preaching."

"Gentle," Brant said, "gentle. I ain't sure I like you, yet."

"You want to come back with me?" Savage said.

Brant tipped the jug up. "My Uncle Yancys make the best stump water in four territories. They ain't makin' it now, though. They might be dead for all I know."

"You know what I'm talking about?" Savage said.

Brant passed the jug over. "Here. You ain't got anything like that in the Shen'do. Sure I know what you're talkin' about. But like my father says, we ain't for what you're for."

"Your father is a good man, he should be in Congress."

Brant laughed. "That's a hell of a compliment, for sure."

"You aren't for anything," Savage said. "You aren't for anything."

"Wait a minute, now," Brant said, "that ain't exactly true, Savage. I'm for me. I'm for Brant Quantrell. This Brant Quantrell I'm talkin' about, this me, maybe he doesn't see the world the way other men see it, maybe that's why he keeps goin' along with the feelin' the world as he sees it is his world, a sort of personal world, if you know what I mean. There ain't nothin' in this world of his that conforms, or that's unified. This world you talkin' about now, this world you fightin' for, it's full of conformity, full of unison. Like armies. Like men marchin' in unison, like men killin' in unison. You seem to be buildin' up, in your mind leastways, a world in unison, a country full of conformity. I can't understand that: I'd like to understand it, but I can't, because either there's something at a lack in me or there's something stronger in you than I can reach out and take hold of. I don't want to march in unison, or kill in unison. I want men to be men, individual men. I want to love when I feel lovin' and kill when I feel it's worth killin' for."

Savage took a long, almost thoughtful pull at the jug. Then he said, "What's this about your Uncle Yancys?"

"My uncles. Brina's too. Joe and Luke and Darby. They went off with the rebels."

"They did." Savage half smiled. "Back country raise a little hell about that?"

Brant shrugged. "There's rebels around, I reckon."

The fire flared on the hearth. Now and then the rain dropped into it, down the chimney, having suffused with wetness the sunlight of the morning. Supper was over. Throughout the meal Alwyn had been withdrawn and uncommunicative. Tag, before he had taken a mouthful, had been violently ill and gone to bed. Jewel had been sullen, thumping and banging wordlessly as she went about serving the meal. Only Brant had kept up a steady flow of talk, small talk, talk they were grateful for, although they answered him in monosyllables. But after a time he could talk no longer, seeing his father's withdrawal, Sabrina's food untouched upon her plate, Jewel's fury. He had waited until the dishes were washed and put away and his father and Sabrina gone to the family room. Then he got the jug from behind the fireplace wall, and Savage had gone and dropped the heavy bar across the kitchen door. They sat together at the pine table while Savage accused him point-blank of living too well and too easily.

"So your uncles are rebels. Tell me about the rest of your family, your neighbors."

"No more family," Brant said. "Neighbors all Loyalist. Some rebels in the territory probably. They go along with us." He shrugged again. "They got to. Then we got Ian McLeod. Came over with the MacDonalds, from Scotland."

"Culloden survivor. Black Watch."

Brant nodded. "Used to try to git Brina to marry him. Lost his arm at Moore's Creek Bridge. Then there's the Ballentynes. Newley tried marryin' Brina too, he's off in a Loyalist regiment somewhere. And Fraser Malcolm. And the Brevards. Right from London, slaves and all. They'd shoot you in a minute."

"That's all right," Savage said, "I guess I'd do the same. What you're saying is that most of your neighbors are King's men who covet your sister."

Brant reached across the table for the jug. He said, not looking at Savage, "There's times I can't see any difference between Loyalists and rebels."

"Don't say anything more," Savage said, "I've still got one good hand."

Brant tipped his chair back. "You're a strange one, Major. Why you so hot to have me go with you?"

"I'm not trying to talk you into anything. I just thought maybe you'd like to go along."

Brant brought the chair down level. "Why? Why should I go along with you?" He leaned across the table, gray eyes hard and without expression. "I'll say one thing for you, Savage, you ain't full of fancy words like a lot of the lacy-pants rebels up North. Like the Adamses and the Hancocks. I'll give you that. I'll give you you know what you're fightin' for. But just because you're like you are and that pig Waite's like he is don't mean everybody on your side's like you and everybody on his side's like him."

"Who said it did? Don't put words in my mouth, Quantrell."

Brant stared at him, seeing the clean-featured mobile face half hidden by shadow, the falling of firelight on the white-blond hair. Unable to help himself, he said suddenly, "What about my sister?"

"What?" Savage said. "What in hell do you mean by that?"

"I mean you got intentions about my sister?"

Savage hesitated. Then he said, "I'm going to leave tonight."

"What's that got to do with it?"

Savage got to his feet slowly. Brant saw his arm move in the white linen sling, as if he would throw the sling off. "Listen, you self-centered, self-satisfied bastard, I'm not asking for any trouble with you. The understanding lies between Sabrina and me, and will lie between your father and me. Now, you coming with me or not?"

Brant was quiet for a time. Then he said, "Maybe."

Savage took a long breath. He sat down as slowly as he had got to his feet. "All right. I won't ask you to believe in anything. I won't ask you to like or dislike." His eyes left Brant's face and moved to the doorway from the hall, and told Brant without Brant's moving that Alwyn stood there. And Savage thought that this was how Moses would have looked coming down from Sinai, with this rich white hair and resolute mouth, venerable, self-disciplined, authoritative, fighting to not know the horror of condemning, crying in his heart for righteousness, not for any cause, but for mankind, which lived and died by causes.

"This is how you repay me," Alwyn said.

"I told you that I wished to speak with Brant before I left."

"I remember. I remember that even knowing how persuasive you might be, I not only gave my permission but derided you." His eyes held Savage. "You mock me, our people, our ideals, our way of life. You want us traitors to our King. You wish my son a traitor."

Brant said, "Wait, Father, wait, I got to live my life as I see it, you know that, you taught me that, and Brina too. You taught us that."

Alwyn said, to Savage, "He is my son, and I will fight for him."

Savage looked at him steadily. "I will not. I do not want him because he's your son, I want him because he's young."

171

Now Alwyn laughed, without humor. "I see. You would cast him in the traitor's mold, the rebel mold."

Savage's hand came out across the table, palm up. The fingers curved up and in; Alwyn saw the terrible sinewy lean strength of the hand. "You speak too easily, sir, of casts and molds. This is fine imagery, for yourself particularly, but it is impractical. I cannot see your son a traitor any more than I can see him a practicing Englishman. He is an American, and having listened to him talk, perhaps more American than you or I. I don't want to talk to you about your son, I want to talk to you about Sabrina."

"Sabrina," Alwyn said, "Sabrina." He gripped the back of the chair. He and Savage watched one another. "I want to come back for Sabrina," Savage said.

Brant's chair thudded on the floor as he brought it down.

Alwyn said, "You would not have gone without telling me this."

"No. I only wished to explain . . ."

"I know," Alwyn said, "I know. People are always explaining things to old men, as if by growing old they lost all power of reasoning for themselves, all knowledge of human nature, all sense of comprehension."

"I want to come back for her. Will you take my hand on it?"

"My daughter forfeits her loyalty."

"Your daughter's loyalty will win neither your cause for you nor mine for me. She will not let herself be unhappy because of loyalties or lack of them, and being a woman, especially so in matters of governmental ethics. You must take into consideration one thing: desire has no horizon. Neither wars nor family ties can erect a barrier high enough or heavy enough to surmount political and economic beliefs. No matter what happens, how this ends, I will look back at my knowing you with pleasure. I want not only your friendship but your guidance. I love Sabrina. I need her. I have two sons who need her."

Alwyn felt his heart thunder unevenly. For a moment out of time this was the Yancy cabin, and he stood in the moonlight, hearing the fox bark on the ridge, hearing his own voice telling the Yancys about Ellen Bowie. . . . He reached out and took Savage's hand.

"You will need a fresh dressing," Alwyn said. "Now we have no horse to give you."

"I'll pick one up somewhere."

"You will not take the road," Alwyn said.

"I'll strike for the river and follow it."

Brant said, "I got a pistol if you can use it, Savage." Without waiting for answer he swung off the chair and went down the hall. Alwyn had begun to change the bandage on Savage's shoulder when he came back with the pistol. He put it down on the table and began to load it, pouring the ball out of a leather pouch, measuring powder into an old scarred horn.

Alwyn worked silently. When he finished, Savage straightened his arm, flexing it, working it gingerly. "I'll do without the sling," he said.

Alwyn wound the roll of linen stripping. "Well, then, you will be back?"

Savage smiled. "Cornwallis willing."

"Good-by, then," Alwyn said brusquely, not holding out his hand now.

"Good-by, sir. I hope to find you as well when I come again."

Alwyn turned and left the room.

Brant still sat at the table. He held the pistol out, butt first, and Savage came and took it. "Thanks, it's damned good of you, Quantrell."

"No thanks to me. Good luck, Savage."

Savage picked up his jacket from the end of the table. He got the injured arm into the sleeve and slung the jacket over his shoulder, shrugging into it. He stuck the pistol into his belt. "Luck to you too, Quantrell."

Brant tipped the chair back again, watching him unbar the door. As the bar swung back he said, "You say you goin' upriver?"

"I'm going to try." Savage hesitated, turning back, watching him.

Brant raised his arms, linking his hands behind his head, careless, relaxed. But his eyes were very direct, very honest. He said, "Well, I got to get some cookin' wood drawn in first, but I got a feelin' you might see me up there, one of these days. Maybe."

16

THE FOLLOWING MORNING the child cried in the empty barn until he was sick, until he felt better, drained and weak, but better. When at last he rolled over in the straw and lay upon his back, he saw that the hound Dancy was beside him, burrowed down by his side, and that the great liquid eyes were full of sympathy; the liquid eyes of hounds are naturally sympathetic. But it was Dancy's first mature act, and he thought she wasn't a pup any more now, and that she'd probably settle down and be steady on trail and a good tracker. He gulped and snuffled and sat up, resting his arms on his drawn-up knees and his chin on his arms and wondered how he could ever look Sabrina in the eye again.

Because it had been his fault, right from the beginning. They had had no intention of taking the colt, but he had mentioned it and then mentioned it again, and they had taken it and now Sabrina was heartbroken. Only Sabrina was braver than he and had not cried.

How he hated them. The misunderstanding, which took the form of rebellion in him was so intense that he almost felt sick again. And what made him feel sickest was that his father could have been so wrong. All his life his father had told him lies, and he wondered how his father felt now.

He put out his hand and pulled at the hound's ears. "Dancy," he said. The hound crawled closer and put its head up against his leg and thumped its tail in the straw. "Good Dancy," he said, "good girl, good baby girl," and gulped again, a sobbing indrawn breath still full of tears. Then he stiffened.

He knew it was Sabrina even before she entered the barn. The tears gathered in his eyes again and he covered them with his folded arms. Dancy got up and went to Sabrina and jumped on her, and she touched the dog's head and pushed it down. "Tag," she said.

His voice was muffled, sulky. "What?"

She came and sat down beside him, drawing her knees up, like his were, and holding her skirts about them. "What are you doing out here alone like this?"

He apologized, lied, clumsily. "I left my knife in the loft."

She was careful not to touch him. "Do you know the last time I was up in the loft?"

"When?" he mumbled.

"The night you brought Major Savage up here, and he was hurt and sick."

He raised his head. "Why did you go up there?"

"I wanted to see if he was all right."

"Oh." He was disinterested. Then he understood. "I'm all right, Brina."

"So was Major Savage, but he was hurt too. And you know what he did?"

"What?"

"Well . . . it was awfully hard for him to do, I reckon, but he got up and went on, because that was what he had to do. Lots of times, when we're hurt, it's like that. We have to pretend nothing's happened."

He did not answer, staring ahead of himself, into gloom, into empty straw. Dancy came and nestled down at his side again. Then he said, choking, "But I did it."

"No," Sabrina said firmly, sincerely. "You did not do it. Nobody did it."

He burst out, "But why did Father lie to us about them?"

"It wasn't a lie, Tag, it was true, all the things Father said. He believes in all those things. Do you think just because they took the horses it was a lie? Tag, they're our people and we must believe in them."

Tag said, "Our people. Father isn't like them. They're not like Father." She was silent for so long he thought she had not heard him. He said, "Do you know who was . . . was strong like Father? Major Savage. And Mr. McDowell."

She closed her eyes. "What makes you think that, Tag? And who is Mr. McDowell?"

"You remember." Now he sat forward, eager and inspired, cross-legged in the straw. "You remember, Ian told us about him . . . about Colonel McDowell and his Rangers. I saw him. And I saw the man who is their general too."

She touched him now. She took him by the shoulders, her fingers biting into him, and shook him. "What do you mean? What are you saying?"

"I saw them. I was up on the hill above the road and I went down and talked to them." The heart-shaking childish bravado, the pride, came into his voice. "Colonel McDowell wanted to shoot me."

"What?"

"He did. I was going to throw rocks at them and Colonel McDowell said if I did he'd shoot me. And then the general came up and told me to stay out of the way because the army was coming, and I waited and saw the army go by. Brina, it was a big army. Captain Waite's is hardly an army at all."

She laughed uncertainly. "Why, Tag, Captain Waite's unit isn't an army. It's only a very small part of a very big army, much bigger than General Morgan's army."

"Is that true, Brina? Is it really, or is it just what Father says?"

"Why don't you ask Father that?" She shook him again. "You know how hard he has worked to keep us all safe, to keep us all united. Tag, do you know that your father has been a prime force in keeping us, you and I, out of danger? Do you understand all this?"

"I should, I guess," he said clearly, with innocent astuteness. "I've listened to it for so long now."

Blindly she reached out to him and took him in her arms. He put his head down on her shoulder, and the hound came closer and thrust its head against Sabrina. They sat for a long time, and the morning sun spilled pale gold through the warped boards of the roof and touched the straw around them with fire, touched her with the hot color of remembrance, and her arms tightened about the boy.

He said, "Did you like him, Brina?"

She would not lie to him. "I did not like him, Tag."

"I did. I thought he was strong and good. I felt safe when he was in the room."

"Do you mean Captain Waite?"

"Major Savage," he said sleepily, against her shoulder.

"Oh, the major. Yes, I think I liked the major." Again her arm tightened, a convulsive involuntary tightening. He protested the strength of her grip with a wrench of his body, sitting upright.

176

"Brant liked him too, didn't he? And Jewel. We all liked him. Why were the English troops like that?"

"Because they were tired and hungry. Because they are going to fight and some of them will die. Because there is a war and they must win it."

"You know what I think? I think Colonel McDowell won't die."

She laughed, for him. "Now why do you say that?"

"Because I just know it. I think Colonel McDowell and the general will shoot Captain Waite. Or maybe Major Savage will." Thoughtfully he said, "Brina, do you think Major Savage will get back to the army?"

"I don't know." Her voice was unsteady. "I don't know. I wish I knew." At last she was crying, and he got upon his knees, frightened, and tried to pry her hands away from her face. "Please, Brina, oh, Brina, please don't cry." He was terrified, clinging to her, begging, pleading, until she gasped at him, "Tag, Tag, leave me alone, just for a little while leave me alone . . . just for a minute . . ." and the words were thick and broken and he stood up in distress and went away, and the hound went with him, hesitating and whimpering.

He stood outside the barn. He could hear no sound from Sabrina now. He could hear no sound anywhere. Yesterday there had been the slow thud of the hooves, the rustle of straw, the soft snorting of the horses. Now there was nothing. The silence was awesome all about him, and he thought of the colt's empty stall and believed he knew why Sabrina cried.

Suppose it had been dogs they took: suppose they had taken Belle and Dancy and Duke and Old Jim? How would he feel? How Brina felt now, about the colt that she had raised all by herself and that had followed her about just as Dancy followed him.

He knew what he had to do. He had to get the colt back. He would go after Waite and when they camped he would turn the colt loose and the colt would follow him home, and the awful thing he had done would be erased forever. He could see Sabrina's face when he came back triumphantly leading the colt; he could see Brant's face, pridefully admitting him now to the full status of manhood. And he would never never speak to one of those English soldiers unless he had to, he would just get the colt and bring it home.

He ran down the path to the house. Dancy stepped on his heels, playing, and he kicked at her. "Go way, Dancy, I got no time to play now," he said.

Brant said, "Where you goin', Tag?" He was splitting wood in the yard.

"Nowhere," Tag said, watching apprehensively.

"Don't pester your father. He ain't feelin' good."

Tag came closer, hands behind his back, watching the swell of muscle in Brant's slender smooth-skinned arm as he swung the axe. "Is Father sick?" he asked politely.

The axe glittered in the still frosty air, came down in a great shining arc, and the length of log split neatly at Brant's feet. "Your father," Brant said, "has had something of a disappointment, you might say, so don't pester him."

Tag went into the kitchen. "Don' you mess with you daddy," Jewel told him. She was slapping dough in the palm of one hand with the pink palm of the other.

"I won't," he said agreeably.

She went back to slapping dough.

"Jewel, give me something to eat."

She banged a piece of cold pone down on the table. "You breakfus' ain't hardly over and you belly's groanin' already."

He took the pone in his hand and looked at it. "I want more than this, Jewel. Honest, I'm awful hungry."

She turned on him, one floury hand on her hip. "Jest in case you ain't heered, there's a war on. Everybody keeps tellin' me 'bout it and it's time you heered about it too. They ain't hardly no food for between times and none at all for the times they should be. And all I gots to say is if Brant take me into the settlement jest one lil' trip I reckon I rassle some food outen Sheller."

"I reckon you would, Jewel," he said enthusiastically, impetuously. "I just reckon you would. You're a wonderful cook, Jewel."

"All right," she said, turning away, "none of that smart stuff. You takes the rest of the pone, then, and git out from under my feets."

He reached over and lifted the slab out of the pan and it made him feel sick again to touch it. Suddenly he was filled with love for Jewel, for the big capable hands that made something out of nothing, that struck him and healed him in turn. And he loved his father and Brant and Sabrina. He loved Sabrina most of all, and he wanted to cry again now because he could not bear to leave, even for an hour. He wanted to sit here, on the hearth, and watch Jewel

178

making bread, to see Sabrina's hands flash under the colorful threads of her sewing, to watch the vigorous movements of his father as he built up the fire, and see Brant's dark face in the firelight as he cleaned his rifle. He wanted even to see Onny Brevard, so soft and so pretty, or Ian McLeod, whose gruffness frightened him.

On the way out he picked up Brant's skinning knife and hide sheath from the chair by the door.

Brant was stacking wood now. Tag watched him for a moment, holding the pone in his hand. Brant did not turn around, so he went on, past the barn and over the hill. He wondered if Brina was still in the barn. Anyway, he hoped she had stopped crying. When he was out of sight of the barn he tore off the tail of his shirt and wrapped the pone in it and went on, carrying the little package in his hand.

He knew that pursuit afoot would be futile, and they would have taken all the horses along the way. That meant if he was to get a horse he would have to go off the road, and the nearest place was McLeod's. He thought if he had a horse he could overtake them, not only because he knew a shorter route north, but because they would lose time by stopping in other settlements, like Cantine, for supplies. He wished he had thought to write a letter for Ian, so Ian wouldn't think his horse was stolen, so he'd know it had only been borrowed.

He lay in the stubble watching McLeod's cabin, and when there was no sign of life, went down and found the door was barred and locked and went into the barn and saw Ian's two work horses standing stolidly in the soft-cold gloom. He led out the horse nearest the door and climbed into the smooth-worn hollow of the swayback. The horse moved lazily, without surprise, so he snapped a thin branch off a tree as he passed under and struck the horse across the withers. It began to move, not fleetly, but with great sturdiness.

Urging the horse along the road, he figured: the way he figured, there were three units on this road now, the hunted and the hunters. There was that brassy McDowell and the big general and their army, hunted, and there was the English captain hurrying to join his colonel, the hunter. But if you followed back to him, Tag Quantrell, there were also the English captain, the hunted, and him, Tag Quantrell, the hunter. They were moving faster than he, but he knew he could move more skillfully, unencumbered and in familiar country.

If he cut cross-country, following close to the foothills, he reckoned he could catch up easily, say day after tomorrow, late. That was providing they stayed on the main road, and he thought they would, because the only good fords were in a direct line with the main road, and the rivers were so swollen from the rains he did not think they would chance fording at obscure points.

Encouraged by his own logic, which even then he recognized with pride as Brant's logic, he thought further. Sentries. Getting past sentries, which all armies maintained. Horses. Spread out, or picketed together. Being caught. Not captured, only caught.

It was very clear in his mind that if he were caught he would simply tell Captain Waite that he had only come to get back his sister's colt that she had raised all by herself.

The horse went through a low marshy spot, stepping stolidly into the cold water, and through a thicket of bare saplings, and came into a sandy pine barren. It moved at the same steady, even pace for an hour, two hours, three, and then panic came to the boy. No matter how hard he switched his gray bony lump, it would never be even a half starved edition of Brant's gelding. It would always be Ian McLeod's work horse. And anyway, it would tire soon. It was used to going up and down the rows of Ian's small fields. It probably hadn't waded through streams and sunk in sand and loped over hummocks in years, if ever.

That was when he made up his mind that if he killed Ian's horse he was going to get the colt. His lips were young and thin with resolve.

In the late afternoon the ridge of mountains was sharp and blue against the sky. He was cold and cramped and numb, but he was also sleepy, and he forced himself awake with the thought that he must, for a time yet, stay parallel to the road, that he could not sleep and let the horse wander. With a strange, homesick gratitude he saw that far off, at the foot of the mountains, there was a gray shack made infinitely small by distance, and that a thin thread of smoke lifted against the hazy background of the hill. It was the first house he had noticed. Long after he passed it, he looked back and saw the sky was the color of blood in the west, and the mountains gone black now. Again he choked down panic. He could not go on in the dark.

Then there was the brilliance of a star above the black upthrusting tip of a mountain, and he knew it would be clear. He took out the pone and tore a piece from it and wolfed it, almost with joy. And in the bowl of the sky once, twice, three times more he saw single stars. The last light burned gently on the sky, so that when night fell he was surprised to see not the spaced, single stars at all, but a pale powdering of them arching overhead. And he shivered silently, hating the blackness and the distorted bare trees and the inky depthlessness of the hollows, and he was sorry for Ian's horse, for he knew it was thirsty.

When they came to the creek, the water ran swiftly. The red clay bank went out from under the horse's feet and the creek came up around them, and he lifted his own feet upon the horse's neck to keep them dry. The horse slipped up the greasy far bank and hurried on with weary resignation.

He moved unfeeling through the long white path of the starlight, past the cold dark shadows which bordered the swath of light along the road. He slept. When he woke, shocked at sleeping, he found the horse had kept the road. Another stream lay ahead, and beyond it the road branched.

The stream was deeper than the first, and he wet his feet. The horse was forced to swim once. Back on the road, he took the horse down the left branching. While he slept he had dropped his switch, so that now, almost unconscious of the act, he leaned forward and patted the horse's neck. And the horse was consoled.

Dull as his senses had become, he thought he could see dawn in the east, and that served to wake him fully for a time. Dawn would be better than warmth, better than sleep.

And he loved the horse for the first time.

A watery yellow blob of sun rose in the cold sky. Then he dozed, unable to help himself, the weight of his falling head jerking him awake. Once when he woke, the horse had stopped and was resting, cropping along the ground, and he did not have the strength to stop him. He thought, the horse has to eat. I have to eat. When they came to another stream he slid down, throwing his leg over the horse as he had seen Brant do a hundred, a thousand times. But he did it unlike Brant, without bravado; he did it because it was easiest.

The horse went down and drank calmly from the stream, the gray old muzzle touching the muddy surface daintily. And the boy, watching in a stupor, thought, I can't feel like this and go on. I have to feel better than this.

He unbuttoned his shirt and took it off and went down to the stream beside the horse and plunged his head in the water and came up gasping. He splashed the icy water over his shoulders and arms and chest and back and felt as he had felt on a hot summer day when he had worked himself into a sweat and gone and plunged into the spring hole beyond the barn. He felt fine, and wonderfully hungry.

The horse had fallen to cropping. He kept his eye on it while he unwrapped the stale hard pone. He tried to limit himself, but it was no use; almost before he knew it he had gulped down nearly the whole remaining slab. He washed it down with the terrible water and put away the few leftover crumbs.

The horse, too, felt better. The horse was full of beautiful stamina and easiness and obedience and yes, even resourcefulness. He had a feeling that with Ian McLeod's horse, with himself, it was going to be all right.

By early afternoon he was not sure any more. He kept falling asleep, as he had done earlier. By late afternoon he let himself sleep, deliberately, not fighting it. When he did wake, he felt the dark chill in the air and the steady rhythm of the horse's gait, and knew that the horse too was weary beyond all knowing, that he would not stop; not knowing that in an old horse who works fields the dream of youth may not die, and when the time of youth comes back upon him he may reach for that time, as a man will.

He was no longer hungry, yet he choked down the last crumbs of the pone. But he did not feel any stronger or any better for it. Something terrible happened to him: the want to get off the horse and lie down, not caring what happened to the horse which was not his, or the colt which was his sister's. He lay over on the horse's neck and slept.

He did not know if he dreamed or remembered, but he was in the barn again and Dancy was beside him and Sabrina was crying and he tried to take her hands away from her face. He could not hear her voice, but he knew she wept for the colt.

When he opened his eyes again it was dark. The horse was still moving steadily, as if it were an automaton, as if he had set it going somehow and now could not stop it. He did not know how long he slept or how long it had been dark, so he thought the light in the northern sky was dawn again.

But the light was something else, though it bore the color of dawn. For a long time he watched it, and then he knew it was the reflection of fire on the sky, and he was no longer cold or hungry or tired, and everything came alive in him, sight, touch, smell. The path was a pale blur branching off the road, but he saw it and took it and came at last to the grove of trees and the fire.

He got one stiff leg over the horse and fell to the ground and could not stand up. When he gained his feet he leaned for a while against the horse, then the horse started off, investigating the stubble, and he let it go because he had nothing with which to tie it. Then he went off slowly toward the fire, not hesitating until he could see the billowing leap of flame and the shower of sparks blowing skyward. And he wanted to go and lie by the fire and let whatever happened happen.

The soft whicker of a horse made him lift his head, made him remember. Almost without knowing he moved, he found himself close enough to see the shapes of huddled men, the stacked arms, the single small tent which was Waite's. And between it and him was the string of horses, picketed in a line so that there would be no confusion if their riders had to reach them quickly.

It was absurdly easy. He went down the picket line slowly, with caution, and between the looming bulks of two sleeping horses, he saw the little lost shape of the colt, standing close to a saddled cavalry mount, and the tears came hot in his eyes seeing it. He stood still and listened and heard nothing but the horses breathing and twitching in their sleep, and the crackle of the fire. He put his hand down and felt for the hilt of the knife and drew it out of the hide sheath and went up behind the colt.

The big horse nearest the colt did not move, but the colt did. It swung its proud slender head around, and he saw the flash of its eye and then it backed out and almost into him and he put his hand on its flank and ducked forward and hacked at the rope around its neck. It kept side-stepping nervously, and then it tossed its head toward him again and whinnied in recognition, and he felt the rope part under the blade in his hand.

Then he saw the moving shape at his left and struck the colt as hard as he could and said hoarsely, "Move, colt," and one keen hoof cut across his leg as the colt moved.

He ran, in the direction the colt had run, and he thought he could see its hooves in the moonlight, flashing high and quick toward the road. Then he heard the sound, but he did not know he heard it, believing he had imagined it, and he opened his mouth to say something to the moving shape at the left. But before he could speak the sound came again, sharp and vicious, and he still thought he had only imagined it, even when he turned as if he had been pushed and saw the bright shower of sparks rising until they dimmed and merged with the arching sweep and fall of stars. There was an unfamiliar heaviness in his chest and he could not think where he was, or why, but it was warm and comforting and shining inside the lids of his closed eyes, and he thought he saw the powdering of stars again, and the rim of dark trees moving with the wind, and the colt's hooves flashing, before he fell.

17

WHEN MCLEOD FOUND THE COLT, coming toward him as independent as if it had been trotting strange roads all its life, his own voice came back to him, too loud, heavy with dread, in the kitchen of Brandyhill. "Aye, Sabrina is right."

He could see she had been crying: her face was swollen and her eyes discolored, and she seemed to have got thinner in the space of a few hours. He had stopped in just by chance when he found his horse was gone; he was on his way into the settlement to see if anybody'd seen his horse strayed or knew maybe it had been stolen. And here he found the Quantrells had been up all night, searching the woods and swamp, and Brant already been to the Crossing, and some of the Crossing men helping him look.

But she had known, Sabrina had known. She told him bluntly, incoherently, standing at the pine table while they sat (he and Brant and Jewel and Alwyn, still unbelieving) and watched her: "He blamed himself for the colt. He said if he hadn't talked about it, Waite wouldn't have taken it. I tried to tell him it wasn't so, but I was crying, and he didn't know it wasn't the colt I was crying about . . ." She stopped. "It had nothing to do with the colt, but I was crying, and I told him to go away."

"Where did the Britons go?" McLeod said.

She was instantly calculating. "They were going to Brevard Hundred, so they took the main road. They would cross the streams at the fords, wouldn't they, Brant? And into Cantine, probably."

"Do they night camp?" McLeod said.

"I reckon," Brant said, "they can't just keep ridin' themselves and the horses to death."

McLeod stood up. He was like a great shaggy lion, the empty sleeve of his shirt tucked into his belt. "I've my other work horse, Brant. You can get a horse."

I'll spit a horse if I got to, Brant thought. His nostrils flared a little, looking at McLeod. "I know John Brevard, he'll have had horses out of sight, time Waite got there. To hell with your work horse, we'll take Brevard's." He got to his feet.

McLeod came around the table and touched Sabrina's arm. He said, "It's all right, lass, we'll find him."

Outside Brant whistled and Old Jim came out from under the porch and followed along with them.

McLeod was sorry she had been so right, because sure as thunder that was the colt, coming down the road in the cold drizzle. He eased the sorrel to a walk, not wanting to frighten the colt, which he thought had probably had enough of various frights to last it a lifetime. Brant too had been right, about Brevard's horses: the loyal Englishman Brevard, hiding his choice mounts off in the woods, letting the cavalry unit think they'd cleaned him. The sorrel answered to the reins and stood steady, and the colt came toward it neat and quick as a thrust rapier, so proud he didn't even look, and McLeod reached his only arm out and dragged at the rope around his nose and stopped him. The colt danced, saying this was a game, that nobody really had him, that nobody could really hold him, and McLeod thought reverently, Jesus God, he's looking for her, he's looking for the lass, and felt the icy fingers of chill go along his spine. He halloed, holding the colt, and when there was no answer tucked the colt's rope under the stump of his arm and fired the pistol, like they'd agreed on, and after a time saw Brant coming down off the crest of the ridge to the right.

Brant was breathing hard, McLeod saw, and thought it strange because he had been riding easy, taking Brevard's big stud stallion up through the woods like it was fresh-laid eggs the stallion walked on. All he said was, "I'll take him," and got down off the stallion and hitched the length of rope through the colt's nose rope and mounted the stallion again and started off down the road where the colt had come from.

McLeod followed, so that he saw before Brant did that the colt wasn't going to follow the road. Brant felt the colt pull off to the left, toward the branching in the woods, and reined the stallion in. He let the colt lead him down the woods road, and when the colt stopped McLeod rode ahead. He saw the colt wasn't going to lead anywhere, any more. The colt was interested in snuffing the leaves, ignoring the rain which made mere humans so miserable and wet and cold, feeling himself better than the rain, maybe, McLeod thought, like a superior man who ignores unpleasantness.

Brant sat the stallion, letting the colt nuzzle, but the colt wasn't doing anything but nuzzle. McLeod said, "Fetch, Jim," and the blue hound moved ahead until he couldn't see him any more. But he heard him. He heard him cry like he had never heard a hound cry before, low, and so full of mourning that he knew. He followed the dog.

He stood over Tag in the rain and heard the sound of the silence. Not knowing what else to do, he took off his hat.

Brant carried the boy in his arms all the way back. The shot had been good. Maybe not the first one, it had gone a little high. But the second had been kind, landing where a heart would be in a small breast, quick and kind and unfeeling.

McLeod brought up the rear, leading the colt. At his side Old Jim padded, quietly now, not snuffing the ground any more, not doing anything but pad along as if he had grown old. Brant was stiff in the saddle. He did not speak, and McLeod said nothing to him.

They had been gone nearly two days, and that was two days without stop, except to let the horses rest, and to wolf down their food. At Cantine, nobody had seen a boy or a horse, but they had seen the rebels, and the British too. They had nothing left. The horses were gone, and the chickens, the oxen, the mules, the things which could be taken and carried and led easily. McLeod thought, now that it is over, we will not stop on the way home either. He will want to get home as quickly as possible now. He was practical. Seeing the blanket wrapped about the light burden in Brant's arms, he thought, Thank God it is autumn and cold, and not the hot summer and the sun, and the boy lying there in the sun-dappled wood. . . .

He was not a man slow to anger. But the anger was a long time coming up in him. He had seen dead people before. His dead wife and the dead of Drummossie Moor and the dead of Moore's Creek Bridge. Not too many months ago he had, indirectly, fought with these British troops, fought with and for these men who had killed a little boy, either deliberately or accidentally. Whichever way it had been, it did not alter the killing, and so was of no importance.

He had had enough of killing. He was too old now for anything but living, and he was poor, and it was brutal to think of it at such a time, but he was out a horse. He was out a good solid strong horse to work his little plot of land. He was alone in a dingy hut of a place and he would have to scrape to buy another horse. He began to feel the anger.

And he thought perhaps it wasn't the big things in life were so big after all. Maybe it was the sum total of the little things that were big. Like losing a horse. He was an Episcopalian, and it was against his teaching: God said you were supposed to consider your brother in his trouble. Well, he had considered, and it did not help the fact that he was poor and had lost a horse. Or that he was still not sure what he was doing here anyway, not only on this old dirt road, but in this country. That had been the MacDonald's doing, his being here at all: Flora and Allen MacDonald, and Drummossie Moor, and the House of Stuart, and Charles, the young Pretender. It was the doing of all those things and all those people, old battles and old loyalties leading him into new battles and new loyalties. And a child dead too, perhaps because of them. He had no feeling, like these Carolinians who thought they were Englishmen, about founding a new country, building a new nation out of the wilderness. The colonies were a haven, a retreat, a place of safety, for him, and the MacDonalds and the Highlanders who had survived what some called Culloden and some Drummossie Moor. Whatever they called it made it none the less real, far behind him as it was, the old cause and the old marches and the old battle, and the end of the House of Stuart.

The rumor in Benton's Crossing about Ian McLeod, Highlander and Scotsman, was true. In the black night, oars muffled, after the battle, he had taken the brave Flora MacDonald across the bay in the Hebrides. Flora and her maidservant, face hidden in the cowl and the Stuart clan plaid concealed under the long cloak: Prince Charles Edward, playing servant, playing a dangerous game which had been Flora MacDonald's plan, and which had saved his life for him.

When the MacDonalds fled to the colonies, into the Carolinas, McLeod went also, and what was left of his regiment and of the other Highland regiments. Into a new country and freedom, to worship as they chose and live as they pleased. He had had enough of war. But war had not had enough of him. He would not fight in the rebel cause; his allegiance lay with the mother country which had routed and whipped him on Drummossie Moor. And war was no less painful at Moore's Creek Bridge. He had broken a tooth biting down on the bullet, while the surgeon cut away the torn flesh and shattered bone of his arm and left him with a bleeding stump. And that was a different kind of pain. It had nothing to do with the heart or the spirit. It was a momentary pain, out of all pain, and a pain he could not recall, just as he could not recall the amputation, for there were times he could feel his fingers ache at the end of the arm that was gone.

He looked down from the sorrel. Old Jim was still plodding along, his tail down and his ears drooping and his eyes straight ahead on the road. The dog was tired, he could see, worn to the bone with the walking and the hunting, and perhaps by the finding. Did things go on in a dog's head? Did the dog know? He pulled the sorrel in and got down and lifted the dog and mounted and followed up the road after Brant. Brant holds death there. I hold life here. I could take the work horse, gather up my things and go on, keep going, down the Wilderness Road, maybe, into the place they call Kentucky, maybe begin away from this. Away from loyalties and killing, a place where you have nothing to be true to but yourself. . . .

The rain had become lighter. He thought the air felt a little warmer. The blue hound lay before him like a baby, half asleep. Once it looked up at him, showing the red underlids of its eyes.

He wondered if it was true about the Wilderness Road, and the land beyond the mountains: if there were meadows there like moors, and woods and lakes like the woods and lakes he remembered.

He looked ahead, seeing Brant's back and the end of the blanket hanging and the arrogant golden colt. The rain ran off his beard and dripped on Old Jim, lying across his saddle.

188

18

B RANT WALKED DOWN THE ROAD in the late afternoon, feeling the November sun across his shoulders, raising the dry brown dust of the road with his boots. There was still color in the trees, though the leaves were falling, and he could see the stark black outline of trunk and branch through the thinning reddish foliage. Leaves lay drifted in the rusty bent-over grass along the road. Birds teetered and hopped cheerlessly, not singing, making single, hard woeful sounds; but once, from a long way off, a phoebe sang, with the most distant, sad voice in the world.

His boots were heavy on the planking of the wooden bridge a mile from Brevard Hundred. Then they were back in the dust again, and the dust was rising, parching his lips with its grainy dryness, so that he longed, fleetingly, from somewhere in the back of his mind, for cold forest darknesses and the dark wetness of forest earth and clear water pressing over water-rounded stone. But there was only the dust. He consumed it, with his breathing, before it could consume him.

The last mile went faster than the mile before it; he had never expected he would ever in his life have to walk this road, but then, he had never in his life expected he would be without a horse. He went around a bend in the road, and there was the gate, with its high iron door, at the far end of the slope where the house stood.

He had never aspired to a house like this, with its brick walls and fan windows, its formal gardens going brown and lifeless now. It had too many windows and chimneys and too many other buildings around it, in the rear, where the cooking was done and the wood stacked and the slaves lived. He liked Brevard's fine acreage and the way he kept things, like he had to stand inspection before God every day, but he did not like the pretentious austerity of this house.

The sun swinging west filled the windows with fire; he thought that was pretty, it made the whole place look alive and glowing. He passed under the old oaks which had been so carefully left to line the crushed stone drive, and between hedges cut flat as a knife blade. Already he felt awkward, which, much as he had never liked this house, he had never felt here before.

The old Negro who had been old when Honora was born opened the door. But she was there too, and he saw her face, so flushed with pleasure that it too looked like the sun had filled it and fired it. He stood in the hall, looking at the girl he was going to marry. After all.

She was saying, "Why, we haven't seen you since the funeral. . . ." And stopping, gnawing at her lower lip, like he'd seen women do when they kept saying what they felt were the wrong things. He wished she'd finished it, said it, clear and honest.

Following her into the wide hall, under the falling pendants and looping crystal chains of the chandelier, he saw the high-strung movement of her head on the slim column of her neck, and the quick way she had with her hands. "Where's everybody?" he said.

She made a meaningless gesture with the nervous hands. "Aunt Margaret and Uncle John went into the Crossing early this morning. I'm alone." And she watched him as if she were waiting, but he made no move. Then she turned and went into the library off the hall. Her voice was forced and bright, flowing over her shoulder to him, a harsh-colored veil of sound. "What would you like, brandy, madeira?"

He sat awkwardly, resting his hands on his knees. "Whatever I'm supposed to drink at four in the afternoon."

She laughed, busying herself at the low mahogany sideboard. "There." She settled herself with the wine, not too close to him, smoothing the rich off-white silk of her dress with one hand, holding the delicate glass in the delicate fingers of the other. "How've you been, Brant? How's Brina?"

"She's doing," he said. "It's takin' her a while, after . . ."

She interrupted hastily. "Yes, I know." He saw her drain off the little glass. He sipped slowly, squinting through the liquid at the diffused sunlight in the windows.

Sunlight lay behind her, rimming her hair with fire, touching the smooth round of her cheek. He knew she would sit there, in the late-day sunlight forever, waiting for him to talk. She had always been quiet, controlled with him. He had always liked her quietness, if not her overt control. But he could find no small talk with which to either amuse or interest her; he was too preoccupied with orienting himself to the room, the sunlight, the wine, her beauty, her. So that he said it more abruptly than he had planned. "Onny, I came to ask you something. To ask you something and tell you something. I been a fool not to ask you years ago."

He thought she was going to faint, she turned so pale. "Oh, don't," she said, and turned her head away from him, and he felt astonishment sear along the edges of his mind. "Don't, not yet, please. . . ." Then she raised her head, higher, with that terrible control as evident as a blow upon the heart, and smiled. "Now. You have something to ask and something to tell. Tell me first . . . like a game."

Now she needs to orient, he thought. I scared her. She thought I was going to ask her and she near fainted she was so taken aback, and then she thought I maybe wasn't going to ask her and she feels like a fool for near fainting. "Onny," he said, and came and hunkered down in front of her and took her hands in his. He could see the little pulse beating in her throat. He had never felt so uncomfortable. He had never striven so hard for gentleness. "Onny," he said, "I wanted to tell you I'm goin' with the army."

The short, thick golden lashes swept down, lay passive over the soft, dreaming eyes. Then they swept up again and the softness was gone and her eyes were like hard bright stars, looking at him.

"You see, don't you?" he said. "I got no choice in the matter any more."

She disengaged her hand from his, raised it, brushed back the dark lock of hair on his forehead. The awful thought came to him that she only half understood him. He said, "I wish you'd say something, Onny."

It became more difficult. "I know what you prob'ly figurin' . . . how I can never git to feel too strong about things other people feel strong about."

He was never sure when her cool fingers left him, they left him so slowly. "What are you talking about, Brant? What army?"

Then he was on the defensive, instinctively, knowing this was maybe going to be harder than he thought it would be. "What do you mean, what army? You sure don't reckon I'd be aimin' to go off with somebody like Balforth Waite, do you? Now you bring it to mind, I reckon there will be folks won't understand, they been so wrapped up in what's right and what's wrong for so long. But I made my choice and I got to do it, no matter what they think. I'm sorry about my father, but a man's got to do what he reckons best and then stick by it."

She leaned back in the chair. He saw her lips open but nothing came out. She went on trying. Finally she said, "Are you mad? Is this what you came here to tell me, that you have defied your father, denied his teaching? That you are forsaking us and your heritage to throw in your lot with that foul scurvy little army? Is this what you are telling me, Brant?"

He stood up, looked down at her. "Onny, four days ago you and near everybody in the territory came to Brandyhill and heard Richard Jordan say the last words anybody'll ever say to my brother. You know how we found my brother and who did it to him. What in the name of God do you expect me to do, go find the men who murdered him and take their side of this?"

Her mouth trembled into a twisted little smile. "Everybody in this territory believes that was an accident. Everybody but you. Go on, talk yourself out of twenty-nine years of loyalty. Just don't ask me to bless you and pray for you and wish you well. Me, a Brevard."

The anger rose in him. But he fought it, watching her levelly. "Was Hanson Stoner an accident? Was Garlin Gresham an accident? I came here for a lot of things, to settle a lot of things. I knew when I came, I've known it all my life, I wasn't good enough for you, for any of you. But you let me believe all this time that didn't make any difference. I still don't think it makes any difference." Now he pled with her. "Onny, listen, I got nothing against killing. If it's me being threatened, or you, or even the Crossing, I reckon I can shoot a man quick as a coon. But I didn't think I wanted to do any killing in that disciplined, regimented way you got to do it in an army. I believe men and armies, no matter who or what they are, are pretty much alike, I think they're all bastards and it's just a case of reckoning which bastards you want to tie down to. But it ain't a question any more of what I like or what I want. Onny, *listen* to me, will you, those men, those English troops came here and *killed* my *brother*, what do you want me to do?"

All the time she watched him with the twisted little smile. "Will joining the rebels bring Tag back?" she said finally.

He turned away from her, picked up his glass, drained it. He should have known she'd say something like that, something futile and stupid and feminine. As if she read his mind, she began to cry. "We can't quarrel like this, Brant."

He turned back to her. He said sadly, "I ain't quarrelin'. I came to tell you I was goin' and to ask you to marry me before I go."

She made a hoarse sound in her throat, as if something had shut off her breath.

"Only I reckon I can't make you understand, and you were the one person I thought would understand. And instead you just want me to let what happened to Tag go by the board and keep on like nothin' happened."

"No," she said, "no it isn't that, it has nothing to do with that, nothing." She screamed it at him. "I'm sick, I'm going to die. O God, why didn't you ask me before this?"

He did not know where to put his hands. "You said, like a game, Onny. . . ."

She got up unsteadily. Then she pushed past him and stood with her face in her hands for a time. When she turned she was dry-eyed. But he did not like her eyes. He did not like the look in them. "I had everything to give you, Brant. I still have. I never cared what your name was, or what mine was. But I care now. I'd care you were not with my people. I'd loathe you and myself too." She moved away, leaning heavily on the sideboard, doubled over as if pain had cut her in two. "Because I can't believe you. You're using Tag as an excuse to sever anything that ever bound us together, you and me, and you knew when you came here that I would never sanction your treachery. Brant, you aren't going to do it?"

He shook his head. "Yes I am," he said, still in the same sad voice. "Because I got to."

She bent her head, for a long time, as if she were ill. He almost expected her to fall forward, clutching at the drawer for support. Then he saw she had bent to open the drawer. When she straightened and turned she had one of Brevard's dueling pistols in her nervous little hand.

"Onny," he said, amazed.

"I waited too long for you to let anything take it away now, Brant."

A lifetime of wilderness instinct saved him. He did not wait for her to speak again, or to act, but acted himself, dodging under the pistol muzzle and straining to reach her hand. When she saw him move she made a shrill sound which was half scream and half protest; the pistol jumped and discharged.

The powder flashed in the pan, searing the heel of his hand as he fought to reach her. He could feel the blackness and smell his own burned flesh. Then he was gripping her wrist, feeling through the amazement the bird bones in the thin quivering flesh of her. Then he was holding the useless pistol, looking at her, looking at her wrist where the tension and strength of his burned hand had burned her. He could see the marks of his own fingers on her, white first, then red, where the thin blood came back.

They stood staring at one another. There was a thick sickness in the back of his throat. He heard his own breathing, deep and torn, as though he had undergone some great physical exertion. He heard also the room as it closed in upon him, standing there with his hands hanging and the pistol hanging, where he still held it; heard the clock ticking with a measured sound of timelessness. In the sharp vivid colors which clothed this little reality the girl was a figure of single dimension pasted against the rich soft still room. Only the face of the pasted figure lived.

He was surprised to hear the clock, surprised at all the hours they must have stood there looking at one another. He began to back out of the room, clumsy and terrible as any wild strong beautiful thing when it is crushed and cannot fight back. The past, the sister-closeness of this girl to him, all his life, went by him in a deafening rush, like water over a fall. He kept backing out of the room. But he had to say something.

"Onny, I got to, that's all."

There were servants in the hall, discreet and shadowy; he heard them murmuring. He went out the front door and stood on the crushed stone. The sunlight smelled like brass, it struck him over the head. There was a trembling in the backs of his legs. But a powerful elation flooded through him: he had been close to death, and he was alive. He felt, also, guilt at the elation, but he could not prevent its hot flooding in his body.

He closed the gate behind him, with detailed care. He took one deep breath, accepting now with love the dry dust in his throat. On the road, walking again, a sweat he did not know he had exuded dried on him, and he felt cold. The pistol still hung in his hand. He wanted to talk to somebody, anybody; he wanted to say something to himself.

He went over the bridge again, not hearing his boots this time, or seeing the swollen water under him, and then the voice said, "Throw that pistol down here, Quantrell, and you foller it."

He was startled, but not as startled as he might have been if he hadn't been thinking about somebody to talk to. Now he could see the rifle barrel poked out from under the bridge, and the edge of a hat brim. "Who's that?" he said.

"I ain't tellin' the next time," the man said, "I'm shootin'."

He began to think, to function like a human being again. "All right," he said. "There's no ball in this pistol. Can I keep it?"

"Butt first," the man said, "and clumb down here."

He slid down the bank and ducked under the bridge, where there was no sun and the timbers creaked in the cold. There were about twelve of them, all mountain men he knew, squatting, holding their rifles in gnarled experienced hands. Before he could straighten up a rifle barrel had swung and knocked the pistol out of his hand. "Don't bend over for it," a voice said, and he looked up, hearing the voice was Malcolm's and said, "What's goin' on here, Fraser?"

The man who had challenged him was behind him and he felt the rifle barrel prod ungently into his kidney. "Was you in on it, Quantrell?"

"Was I in on what?" Brant said. "I wasn't in on anything."

"My house burned this morning, early," Malcolm said.

Brant looked at the silent men, the silent rifles. The nightmares were coming too close together, too quickly.

Malcolm's mouth was tight. "I never liked you, Brant. I never liked anything about you. Who burned my house this morning?"

"I didn't," Brant said.

The rifle was swung by the barrel now, and the stock of it crashed, flatways, into his kidney. The scream of pain came up in his throat. He choked it off, into a thin hurt gasp. "What do you bastards think you're doin'?"

"That's enough," Malcolm said to the man with the rifle. "I asked you, who burned my house?"

"I don't know," Brant said. The fingers of his hands were spread in pain; rage began to surge blackly in him, rising from the pit of his belly, boiling in his veins.

"How'd you like your house burnt?" the man with the rifle said. "How'd you like to see your Brandyhill burnt?"

"I wouldn't," Brant said, between his teeth. He fought himself to keep his hands away from his back.

Malcolm watched him steadily. "You coming from Brevard Hundred?"

"Yes," he said. "I been home all day. We didn't know about the fire."

"You ain't skeert," the man with the rifle said, "you better commence now."

Brant turned and looked fully at him and saw that it was Del Shaver. Saw the middling-height body deformed by work, the shoulders gone high and knobby, the pinched narrow head under the shapeless hat. The eyes were cruel with ignorance in the stubble-bearded face, and there was a wad of snuff stuffed under the loose wet lip. Dirt lay like a grease in the long furrows of line on his neck. Coarse black hair was matted like a cushion under his shirt.

Brant's eyes went back to Malcolm's unsmiling eyes in the gloom under the bridge. Malcolm, immaculate and stark in his black boots and white shirt, no more these men than they could be him. He was with them, but he would not soil the fine surgeon's hands with them.

A sadness came to do battle with Brant's anger. "I never reckoned you were a rebel, Fraser."

Malcolm smiled thinly. "Now you know it."

Brant shook his head. He could not feel his burned hand for the hurt over his hip joint. But he said steadily, "Maybe it's just as good I'm seein' you today then."

"What does that mean?" Malcolm said in the same thin voice.

"Because I reckon you're the man to tell. I'm throwin' in with the rebels. People change. You know, Fraser."

Shaver said, "Skeert makes Tory rebel any day, don't it? You start talkin' our side now."

"I ain't afraid of you, you son of a bitch," Brant said in fury. "I was on my way home to git my things and go find Morgan's army."

The men guffawed mirthlessly, brutally. There was a sound of saliva spat deliberately. Then the sun was down and there was a reddish light filtering through the planks of the bridge, and he could see the whites of their eyes and the light glinting off the barrels of their rifles. He held Malcolm's hard stare. "I didn't burn your house down, Fraser. If you want to come with me now we'll git our things and go. Take that rifle out of my back," he said to Shaver.

196

For a long time he and Malcolm watched one another. Then Malcolm said, "Load the pistol and give it back to him." He stood rigidly, remembering that ten years ago he was to have brought this man's brother into the world and that he had not done it, remembering this man's sister, leaning from her saddle to touch his face. "He wants to fight with us, let him fight. It won't be the first killing he's done. Killing comes easy to him."

Brant watched him, hands still spread. Not because he wanted to, but because of Malcolm, he thought of Jared Millikin lying in the inn at Hardington, dead; he thought of Henry Deschamps, spread-eagled before the Cherokee fire with the knife buried to the hilt under his ribs. Malcolm had chided him for those things a lot of years now; Malcolm, goddamn him, what had he ever killed? He hated Malcolm, and he admired him, like he had hated and admired the old man, Pomeroy Hollister.

Shaver went and picked up the pistol and began to work with it, holding it up against the light.

"You goin' to fight here, in the dark?" Brant said. "Who you fightin'?"

The carefully cultivated amiability lay bland and smooth in Malcolm's tone. "If they should come along, Brevards, or Quantrells," he said.

"I ain't shootin' any Brevards or Quantrells," Brant said, "just like you ain't fightin' any war. You're just takin' your burned down house out. You're just lookin' for a chance to shoot somebody over your burned-down house."

Shaver turned with the pistol in his hand and gave it to Malcolm. Malcolm said coolly, "Any way you want it, Brant. If the people who burned me out come down the road tonight there's going to be a fight. Say what you want to do."

"Suppose somebody comes down this road and it wasn't them that did it?"

"Say what you're going to do."

He looked at the doctor's dark intense face. He said, "Maybe you're right, Fraser, this is war. A dirty little murder under a dirty little bridge." He reached up and took the pistol.

Now the line of men under the bridge shifted, as if in relief. Brant got up and staggered off to the timber abutment and clung to it dizzily for a moment and vomited into the water. There was a sick sweat on his forehead; he let the cold air dry it, then he turned and went back under the bridge and sat between Malcolm and Shaver. After a time he put out his hand and took Shaver's rifle and looked at it closely and saw it was a Deckhardt, used, cared for, but with the stock scarred. Shaver stared at him all the time he examined the rifle.

"Where'd you git this?" Brant said.

Shaver said with pride, "It's the one I took off'n that horse, after I shot the stranger. It was strapped tuh the saddle. Got the horse too." He laughed in cracked rough triumph. "He won't need it no more, he's rottin' down in your woods somewheres, stinkin' rotten by now."

Shaver reached over and took the rifle back. They sat like a row of corpses. Shaver said, "Yore changin' over fer reasons like a little dead brother, huh?"

He did not say anything.

A man halfway down the line said, "Hear McLeod found him."

He heard the man spit and knew it was the same man had spat before.

"Heered McLeod wanted to buy that colt off'n yer sister," another voice said.

He did not say anything.

"She sell it?"

He took a deep breath. "No," he said wearily.

Shaver said, "She wanted it to home to keep her in mind of her little brother."

Brant sat up slowly. He said, "I can kill you, Shaver. I can kill you easy. I got a loaded pistol here, and you ain't got that rifle in my back now."

Malcolm's strong, skilled hand closed on his arm. For the first time in his life he responded to Malcolm, checked himself, said nothing further. He sat in his own little world, which was now full of things he could no longer think of clearly, and let them talk around him. Mercifully, no one mentioned Alwyn, though there was laughter at Lyons and Sheller and the Provincial Council in general. Then they spoke of women, and no one mentioned Honora Brevard or Sabrina Quantrell. He listened with one ear only, knowing they were amusing themselves, that they had half forgotten he was there. Then, like an explosion, like Savage's rifle which Shaver held had gone off in his face, like lightning had struck under the bridge and knocked him senseless, he heard Shaver's voice, thick through the wad of snuff, hoarse with lust; and he knew the explosion was in himself. Black and burning, it went off in his brain, blinding him, bringing the blood to beat agonizingly in his temples. Because Shaver had said, Women, hell, you'd ought to stick yer eyeballs on that Cher'kee squaw Pom Hollister's got up on Red Ridge.

He was on his feet in one powerful swift motion, like a cat gathering its muscles, springing. He reached down and took the front of Shaver's shirt, feeling the cushion of hair beneath it, and hauled Shaver upright. It happened in a matter of naked red seconds, but it seemed to him minutes, hours, before it was over. In the cold murkiness he saw Shaver's face, half astonished, half grinning at whatever he had been about to say and had not got a chance to finish. Brant held the rough hair-matted shirt with his left hand. He brought the pistol up past Shaver's lust-grinning face, holding it by the butt, and smashed the barrel full force down the right side of Shaver's face.

The face changed then, except for the astonishment, which was no longer a half, but a full astonishment. A glaze came over the eyes; it came in that first moment when the jawbone broke free of the skull. In a rapid, flashing movement Brant swung the pistol again and this time smashed the barrel down the left side of the face, and even the astonishment was gone then, and the face fell apart and teeth spewed out of the crushed bleeding head and he brought the barrel down again, this time on the protruding bone at the beginning of the spinal column, in the neck, where the head bent forward, toward him.

He stepped back. Shaver went down with interminable slowness, not toppling, but seeming to fall easily, full length upon the bank. Brant swung like a cat, cocking the pistol, covering the line of men under the bridge. His breath came up in him, painfully; he labored for it, distending his nostrils, fighting for the salvation of cold dark air.

He said, breaking up the words because of his breathing, "Anybody objects to this, say so now."

A man moved a little, as if he would rise. Brant swung the pistol up and down the line, silently, panting. There was a silence like he had never heard before. But he knew it was over. He could almost smell their wariness, and their respect.

Then he saw Malcolm's hands, very white in the falling darkness;

then he saw Malcolm's upturned face, and it too was very white. "Brant, he's dead."

There was enough air in his lungs now. He felt as clean and stark and white as Malcolm, standing under the bridge, resurrected, exonerated, absolved. Everything which had touched him these last days, today, had been erased; everything he owed had been paid back. This was for Tag, and in a way for Sabrina and his father. This was for Onny, today. And this, by God, was for Savage. The week's troubles had held him like a debt, building and building, each with its own foundation, but building, one atop the other.

The purity of original innocence lay upon him.

He took from Shaver's body the powder and ball and patches for the Deckhardt. When he stood up again he put the toe of his boot heavily and with strength exactly where Shaver's dead kidney would float and pushed Shaver's body down the incline and into the dirty creek. The sound came up wet and softly splashing; a few vague and impotent ripples came to lick at the bank. He stood there for a moment, then he came back and picked up Savage's rifle.

Men who had not bothered to address him, except by contemptuous laughter and spit, called him now familiarly by his given name.

After a long time, while Brant sat breathing evenly and cleanly where Shaver had sat, holding the rifle, the moon came up out of a strata of dark cloud, looking pale but brilliant. The wind had gone down with the sun and did not come back, and it was very still. Malcolm's breathing, at his side, was hurried and uneven, and Brant knew he listened. So he was not surprised when Malcolm said, "Listen."

They listened, and heard the footsteps, and Brant put his head back and looked up at the rifts in the bridge planking, where the moonlight came through. "Get up," Malcolm said, "don't let them cross the bridge."

They moved up the bank, with the light laying whitely on the rifle barrels. Brant moved with them, in a half crouch. Then he could not see them any more. They lay in the shadows on either side of the bridge, and the only thing he could see was the road, white in the moonlight, savagely exposed and vulnerable. He found his own shadow and lay in it, behind a boulder.

He saw the men come up the road, about twenty of them, on foot. He wondered briefly who they were and what Malcolm had done to give himself away, so that they would burn his house, and where they were going now. But his father knew nothing of this. They had gone beyond his father, beyond the counseling, and the dealing of justice.

The volley deafened him, roaring over the bridge. For a moment as long as eternity the little band stood in the road, suspended between heaven and earth, between moonlight and shadow, and before it could move there was another volley and he thought of dark branches dropping from a dark tree and knew Malcolm had done this well.

Something touched him and he saw Malcolm inching his way up beside him, a pistol in his hand. "They're going to try to cross," he said. A fragment of rock splintered off by his sleek dark head and he ducked and looked at Brant almost with amusement. "They shoot back," he said.

Brant hated to think of himself lying in the cold shadows for Fraser Malcolm. A dark figure ran up the road toward the bridge and Malcolm said softly, "Shoot, damn you, Brant," and he heaved Savage's rifle up and aimed, but did not fire, and the man kept running and Malcolm shot coolly and dropped him. The whole top of the rock went off in Brant's face; he felt the needle-sharp fragments of rock splinter into him. He sighted down the Deckhardt and fired and saw the man he had sighted go down.

There was silence. Men were panting, reloading; a few scattered shots came from the other end of the bridge, but there too men were panting, reloading. Brant thought, they are lying in the shadows, too, across from us, waiting; lying in the shadows, or inching forward. . . . All around him lay the rebel mountain men. He could not see them, but he could hear them, working with skill and desperation at their weapons. He reloaded the Deckhardt.

There were sporadic shots. Men fired back and forth, into the shadows. Behind Brant there was a short bitter curse as a Loyalist ball hit one of the mountain men. The shooting was like little bursts of wind running over the bridge. He did not once think, what am I doing on this side of the bridge? He put the rifle up again, waiting.

Then Malcolm was flat on the ground at his side. It was very quiet, and Malcolm said, "They're going to rush us."

The Loyalist band was in the road again, coming over the bridge, running, crouched low, weaving from one side of the road to the other, not in a mass, but each man a single, moving target which sought the shelter of the shadow along the bridge rails. Without thought, calm yet strangely excited, he sighted on a running figure.

His sight lay on the long barrel of the rifle, went down the long barrel, flickered past it. The moving target had swung away from his sight, and the barrel lay instead on a blurry, indistinct pale form at the end of the bridge. He held his eyes wide and straining, not letting himself blink, and thought of a dog, or a horse, or even a man in white, but remembered the heavy off-white silk Honora had worn in the library of Brevard Hundred.

He pushed himself up on his hands and said, "Fraser."

And Malcolm looked and said, "O Christ. O Christ."

Brant was on his feet. He meant to say Hold your fire, but he only said "hold" in a high, harsh, shouting voice before the Loyalist ball took him in the upper arm and spun him around and dropped him. He got up again and began to run, staggering and shouting, for the bridge. But the men did not understand; seeing him fall, seeing him now in what appeared a vain one-man offensive, they fired around him, across the bridge, with precision, elation, determination.

He heard Malcolm shouting hoarsely behind him. Not another shot was fired. He could feel his own blood running warm on his arm. He fell, abruptly, over a man's body, and did not know he fell he got up again so quickly. The bridge seemed a mile, two miles across, and there was no sound on it any more but the uneven pounding of his own boots. The Loyalists stood on either side of the bridge, exposed, holding their rifles, silent, as he staggered by them.

She lay half upon her side, half upon her back, at the point where the road and bridge joined one another, not twisted, but seeming to flow as lightly and coolly and narrowly as water flows between narrow curving banks. Her face was soft and without any expression save that of peace, and the corners of her mouth were tipped up, as though she had been smiling. She had been shot through the throat; standing, looking down at her still, smiling face, he saw the thin line of blood which clasped her like a necklace of some continuous unbrilliant red stone.

He did not see Malcolm until Malcolm was down in the road, lifting the girl in his arms; then he saw Malcolm, saw how the bright unbound hair streamed like a flowing of gold over Malcolm's crooked arm. He saw Malcolm rise, lifting the weightless weight which had been made for no part of this. He said in a terrible broken voice, "Don't lay her in the dust."

Dew was luminous in the grass. Malcolm put her down in the cool damp swath along the road, at the end of the bridge. She lay delicately, fragilely, a faultless fragment of palace Dresden smashed on a country road. Malcolm said, "Bring a horse." He stood up again.

Brant swayed; his whole stance begged support, but he kept his feet. Malcolm said, "Let me look at your arm."

He felt Malcolm's hand inside his shirt; his body urged him to lean upon Malcolm, to fall, to never rise again. He wanted to cry out, in anguish, in disbelief. But logic lay in him too, fighting its way to the surface. "Fraser, you got to git out of here."

"I'm going to take her back," Malcolm said.

"No, git out while you can."

Malcolm stripped off his own shirt and ripped the sleeve out. After a moment Brant felt something slice into his arm, felt a second warm running of blood, felt the strips of Malcolm's shirt stanching the blood. He was choked with impatience. "I'm all right, Fraser. Git out, will you?"

Malcolm shook his head grimly.

"I'm all right, I tell you . . . leave it, Fraser . . . I got to see to Onny. What about Onny?"

Malcolm said, "There is nothing to be seen to."

Again he wanted to cry out. The men on the bridge, rebel and Loyalist, held together now by the dark bonds of death, did not come near them. "I'll take her back," he said.

Again Malcolm shook his head. Brant thought he might be weeping but saw that he was not. "You didn't kill her," Malcolm said.

After a moment Brant said quietly, "Didn't I?"

Malcolm stepped back. "See Quantrell gets home. You, Halpern, and Scott. Get your horses. His wound isn't serious, but he's weak from loss of blood."

He stood swaying, looking at Malcolm. He knew nothing he could say would make Malcolm leave. But he turned in the road and stumbled across the patch of grass and knelt by the girl and took her hands and held them for a little time. Then he got up and started back across the bridge.

The men stood in the shadowy moonlight, silent, watching him.

The bearded, stubbled roughness of their faces was dissolved in the chemical of gentleness; their indomitable masculine attitudes had become the weak, sloping soft attitudes of women.

He could not mount the horse they brought for him, but was pushed up into the saddle. One of the men handed up the Deckhardt and he laid it across the horse's neck. Two rebel horsemen flanked him. His head fell, and he rode without control of his body or his senses, going home.

The sound carried in the still air as if it was in the same room with him: saw and hammer striking home in wood, on nail. He imagined it was Tenant, the carpenter, driving the nails in a Loyalist labor of love.

He sat at a table in the Bear and drank whiskey and water. He had nothing, not a coat to put on his back, only the white shirt without its sleeve and the black breeches and boots. The only thing he had left was the stallion Emma Smallie's boy had taken to the inn stables the morning the house burned.

He figured he had an hour, maybe two, and the only request he had made was that they leave him alone. They had given him that much. Even Alexander and Lavinia had given him that; the Bear was empty. He saw Authie Stoner, once, when she came through from the kitchen white-faced and said, "I reckoned you could maybe make it out the back, Doctor Malcolm, but there's three men with rifles out there." And he did not answer, did not look at her, he only nodded his head to let her know he'd heard. And understood.

Outside, a dog, ears gone beyond bearing of saw-sound, began to bark. He barked for quite a time and then the barking ended in a sharp yelp, and Malcolm figured somebody'd kicked him off. He finished the whiskey and poured himself another, but he drank it slowly, savoring it, letting it lie on the back of his tongue.

He thought it was odd how so much fell on Alwyn Quantrell, even this. There was a surging of affection in him for the old man. He did not let himself think of the old man's daughter. God help Alwyn Quantrell. Even this. Because the wealthiest and most beautiful woman in the territory was dead, and Del Shaver, and six men wounded and the Loyalist Johnson killed, back there on the bridge. (Either he'd killed him or Brant had, he wasn't sure which, but he thought it was Brant.) And when he stood surrounded, surrendered, he could think of only one thing to say: ask Alwyn Quantrell. Take me out to Brandyhill and give Alwyn the judging. And this too was a hard thing, for having sworn upon his son's death that he would never again set foot in Benton's Crossing, Alwyn found that Benton's Crossing would come to him.

In the yard of Brandyhill Alwyn heard the men out and asked Malcolm to speak for himself, and Malcolm shook his head and took the verdict with surprise, though he did not show it. Banishment from the colony was the last sentence he had expected. Death he was prepared for.

Benton's Crossing also was prepared for the supreme retribution. Almost before Alwyn had finished speaking the men had brushed aside such senile judgment and pronounced their own: Alwyn Quantrell was getting old and weak and no longer capable of logic. And Alwyn said, "You cannot do this thing," and knew they would do it.

Riding into the Crossing, they did not bind him or touch him or speak to him. He listened mutely to a peculiar debate on the return: it was whether they should hang him now from a horse or erect a gallows. The gallows won, for as Sam Ashe pointed out, now they knew where some stood in the territory and it might serve to stave off further trouble if they had a gallows standing in the park. The half smile had come to Malcolm's mouth unbidden, and to his brain the reminder. The gallows-reminder that death was repaid by death, and if they never utilized that gallows again the erection in itself would be justifiable. So he listened, but did not see, seeing in his mind only the thing he knew he would call upon, deliberately, as the last he wished to remember: Sabrina standing in the doorway behind Alwyn, saying through frozen lips, "O my God, Father, stop them." But that was all, all, and he imagined underlying the vain plea the release and relief of the girl to whom he had not even said good-by.

The inn door swung open. He was aware that the sound of saw and hammer had ceased. Sam Ashe stood in the doorway, and William Lyons and Richard Jordan. Behind them he could see sunlight and a faded blue flag of sky. He drank the whiskey and stood up.

Ashe had a length of rope in his hands.

"What's that for, Sam?" Malcolm said.

Jordan pushed forward. "Put that up, Ashe. You'd not bind his hands. What is he to do with his hands?"

Authie Stoner stood in the kitchen doorway. "Reverend Jordan, can't you talk to them . . . ?"

"I have spoken, Authie. It is not God's will that this be otherwise, for He has not given me the proper words. Fraser. . . ." (Ah, Fraser, Fraser, perpetual thorn in my side, I prayed for you, but I knew you would come to something like this.)

Malcolm said, "Thanks for coming, Richard. Will you go out with me?"

Jordan's shoulders slumped. "I had not thought to hear you say that, Fraser."

"Don't expect too much of me." The corners of Malcolm's mouth went up, half amused, half shaken.

"Let's go, rebel," Ashe said.

He walked toward them. Halfway across the inn room he turned, as if he had forgotten something, and looked at Authie Stoner. Her face was gray, perhaps with remembrance of another hanging, he thought. She left his sight as suddenly as Ashe's bulk shut her off from him.

It was, he thought, the ultimate in gatherings, in Benton's Crossing. He considered it. There was a possibility the Lamourees and Halpern and some of the others would try to get him out. It was a pale and bloodless hope, but he held it in his mind, walking across the road and into the park where the new gallows stood. Then he saw there was a half-ring of horsemen fronting the platform. Nobody was going to get to him, they'd seen to that. "By the way, Richard," he said, "see Brant Quantrell gets my stallion." And could find no answer in himself for the strange bequeathing.

Now the wind was heavy out of the north. The trees spoke to one another. He looked up at the gallows for the first time, and for the first time knew the desperation of certainty. What did Tenant, Ashe, know about building a gallows, building a gallows was an art, an intricate precise art. He would not have minded hanging, cleanly, in one last fine moment of surrender. But he knew, seeing their clumsy handiwork, that he had been condemned to strangle.

There was sunlight and a smell of fresh-cut pine. For a moment he thought, this is not happening to me, and then Honora Brevard's still dead face moved across his mind and his head cleared and he was standing on the gallows platform, grateful for the clarity. He touched the sunlight and the pine odor, he tasted and felt the leaf-strewn wind. And faced the crowd.

It was a quiet and stricken crowd, quiet because it could find no taunt to throw at this man who had consistently held himself above it, and continued to do so; stricken because it was this man.

"You got anything you want to say, rebel?" Ashe said, at his side, holding the noosed rope.

He shook his head.

Jordan communed with the heavens, eyes closed. The horsemen semicircled the gallows. Malcolm tried to remember, but he could only hear her voice. O God, Father, stop them.

"Clear that rope and plank off there, Tenant," Ashe said.

At the end of the line of horsemen, Tenant dismounted and walked toward the platform. The reins slipped out of his hands. Nervously, as if the pressure and tenseness of the air was too much strain to be borne, the horse picked up his feet and danced a little, swung around, faced the crowd.

Malcolm moved absolutely without thought, in an involuntariness of action he had seen in Brant Quantrell and other mountain men but had never believed inherent in himself. He flung himself back against Ashe, no match for Ashe, but Ashe was off balance and lost his footing; he fell with a hoarse cry, backward, over the edge of the gallows platform. Malcolm hurled himself into space of an almost tangible substance. Tenant's saddle came up between his legs so hard he half fainted in the agony of the impact. He lay over the horse's withers and dragged at the fallen reins and brought the horse up on its rear legs, clear over Tenant's still-stooping back, and rode down the screaming fringe of the crowd and heard and felt human flesh under the hooves.

The riders at the gallows were trapped by the crowd. They fought their way out slowly, cheated, in anger, shouting. But the earth blurred and lengthened under Tenant's horse, and the road ran north, to freedom.

19

Sabrina sat upon the doorsill, knees drawn up, shawl around her shoulders, watching. Brant could use his arm a little, but not enough, stacking the wood. The uneven rounds of log lay whitely, ringed with their own growth, fleshy, vulnerable, building a structure which gave forth a scent of sweetness and newness; however old they might be, whole with the tree they had been part of, had been, they were separate now; they bled, and were white and severed from the wholeness of tree. She breathed the sweetness emanating from the clean severing of them: her eyes went with much of longing to other trees, uncut trees, rising on the upslope of hill and mountain around the farm. A last color of leaf lay indeterminate and sporadic, single fires built upon the slopes, and the stark full mingling of bare trunk and branch and twig was blackly panoramic across her vision. The dry heat of October was gone; the still golden rain-washed November had passed. It was already the middle of December, the hardest month of all: all things died, and the inner knowing that the death was transitory, that another month, another season would triumph, did not assuage the grief in the transitory dying.

Brant half lifted with both arms, dropped the arm where the gunshot wound still healed, flung with his good arm, flung with unerring accuracy the bright-cut log. She closed her eyes: the human act of his moving, rising, flinging was a physical pressure upon her own body; she followed the rising and flowing of his movements with pain, feeling herself acquiescent but physically retarded, as he must feel. So that she was grateful for the sound of his soft polite strong affectionate voice.

"I reckon it's goin' to rain again," he said.

Old Jim was stretched out on the stone step, at her feet. She put her hand on his head, gently, touching him with love. She did not answer because Brant did not expect her to answer, looking up at the sky as if he had bid her do so, seeing the clouds mushrooming over the mountains. When she looked back Brant had flung up the last log, but was standing, looking, like there were, should be, more logs. But he said, "That'll keep us a spell." And turned to her.

She made room for him on the step, drawing her skirt aside. Old Jim's tail moved, soundless and full of meaning. She said, "Aren't you tired, Brant?"

"Sho," he said and dropped down beside her. He picked up a piece of pine shaving and chewed at it. He did not look tired, only thoughtful. His face was still marked with healing where the rock had splintered into it; one of the fragments would scar, just over his right eye. After a time he said, with intense masculine personal curiosity, "I keep reckonin' you got something you want to say to me, Brina."

Her hands came up and touched the sides of her face and her mouth shaped itself wordlessly. He turned and looked at her: she was too thin, long-flanked and sharp-breasted, and her waist pinched in as if she starved. He said, "I can't ever remember when you ain't been able to say what you want to say, Brina. To me anyway."

Her hand came away from Old Jim, lay in her lap, picked at the stuff of her skirt. She said, almost cautiously, "It isn't the saying's difficult, it's finding the words. It's only I've wondered all week why it is you get into a set routine pattern of living, and you live by that routine all your life, years and years of it, and all of a sudden, just overnight, everything's different, everything's changed. I don't reckon change in itself's so awful, it's just the speed of it, the way it comes visiting in on you in an hour's time, or maybe if you reckon your whole life as an average, a second's time."

He looked away from her serene, sad face. Looked away because he had seen that under the serenity, the sadness, there was a strange flush of elation, of fulfillment, that he had never seen in her before. "I know," he said. "I know more of change than you do, maybe. You talkin' about Uncle John. You talkin' about Brevard Hundred."

She nodded. Her hand lay still in her lap now. "I never saw Father look like that, not even when Tag. . . ." Her voice faltered, fell apart. "I just never saw him look like that."

They were silent; she began to pick again at the material under her hand; he still chewed on his shaving. Because there was nothing to say while they lived it all over again: Onny put down in their own pine grove, with Sarah Ann Yancy and Ellen and Tag. Onny with them forever now, and the cold stone over her within sight and touch, and the end of the Brevards for them, the end of Brevard Hundred.

"Well," Brant said finally, "Uncle John said he might send somebody on to run the place for him."

She made an impatient motion with the restless hand. "You know that was talk, that was for Father."

He nodded. "He told me, aside, that he was goin' to try to find a buyer. Either settle on the coast or go back to England. Except he thought it would be risky goin' back now, because even if he could get a ship nobody knows where the French fleet is. Or if they do say, they're likely lyin'."

They were silent again. A vast portion of their existence had been torn away, just as a vast portion of the Brevards' existence had been torn away with Honora's death. Sabrina remembered with pain what had passed as good-by to people with whom she had grown up: the fumbling handclasp, the awkward brushing of lips, Margaret Brevard, whom she had known as calculating but never cold, sitting proud and frozen in the carriage. Then the carriage was gone. Then that tie was severed irrevocably.

Brant said, "Well, I got my thoughts on it like you got yours, I reckon. My thought is that it's a damned decent ending. It's the sort of good-by you never come back from to say hello again. It's clean. I'm glad it happened like it did."

She did not answer. She, like the majority of people in Benton's Crossing, had not gone, the day Brevard Hundred burned. But she knew Brant knew who had had a hand in that burning: one of that ragged band under the bridge, seeking vengeance for Fraser Malcolm. Who had instigated it was of the least importance; the important thing was what Brant had said, it was clean and decent. Not only because it solved Brevard's problem of what to do with the place, but because it left no loose ends in the lives of Brevard's friends and neighbors, who might feel responsible. She put her hand on Brant's arm, gently. But he had gone away from her in his mind, and she could not see what he saw: what was left of that fine austere house, Brevard Hundred, in the last afternoon. The fire had gutted the main house and eaten out enough support to knock down a lot of the brick walls. One whole wall was out, lying in the smoldering ruin, and part of a chimney had toppled over. The other chimney stood tall against a clear winter sky, untouched and proud. But the other three walls had been hurt too, rising queer and lopsided and uneven where portions and parts of them had fallen. And all the outbuildings were gone, burned to the ground, mute proof they'd been set off, because it was a clear still day with no wind to carry the flames to them from the main house. And he had come away with anguish and yet with relief, trying not to remember the last hours he had spent in that house, riding for the last time through the still-intact gate on Fraser Malcolm's stallion, which had been bequeathed to him by a man condemned to death who still lived.

He was aware of his sister's hand on his arm. He said, "We do more than survive the changes, Brina. We learn to live with 'em."

Courage came up in her in a hot surging. She said, "Brant, maybe it's silly to dredge up things you once said to me and I once said to you and applying them to a given situation, but it's all I know how to do."

"What did we say?" he said.

"You said . . . you told me once you thought the only real test a person had to meet was finding out what he wanted. You said that, years ago. Orne told me that, only . . . only differently. Do you still think that, Brant?"

His strong white teeth lay upon his lower lip. He said, "You ain't goin' to wait for Savage, is that it, Brina?"

Her hand came away from his arm. "Yes."

He crossed his arms on his knees, looking up at the bank of rain clouds. "I knew it was something like that." He put the pine shaving back between his teeth and began to chew it. "I knew something was worryin' you. You told Father."

Now she wanted to weep. She crossed her arms, as he had done, and put her head down. "You know how Father was, you know without my telling you. He came into the kitchen, a little while ago, and looked at me for a while and then just said to me: Do you feel you must do this? Those were his exact words: Do you feel you must do this?"

"Well," he said, "I reckon you felt it or you wouldn't've told him."

She nodded quickly. Savage's living presence was upon her like a balm, an aphrodisiac to purpose. She said almost accusingly, "Father knew, and I think you knew, even before I did, I reckon. And Jewel. Because Father said to me: I suppose I should have known this the night the major left. And Jewel said: *I* could've told you the night he *come*."

Brant began to laugh. Then she laughed with him, suddenly genuinely amused and confident. They looked at one another fully. With his eyes holding hers, she said, "Brant, there were things we spoke of . . . Orne and I. When we first talked of *it* it was like a dream, and I didn't think on it much. But I think on it now all the time." Her voice was urgent. "Listen, Brant, it's not far . . . the army is up on the Broad. I can find it. I can find him."

"You told Father this too."

"Yes," she said. "Brant, it's not only I want you to understand, I want you to *want* me to go. Brant, Father wants me to go."

He looked away from her. "Yes, Father would." And she remembered Alwyn's sorrow and acceptance and gentleness and understanding and reassurance as they faced one another across the kitchen table, a bare hour ago; remembered her own willfulness and sadness and joy in the decision she had made; knew that the decision had been made in her long before she had voiced it. But she did not know as Brant did, did not want to know, that her father's approbation had been a supreme sacrifice, did not think as Brant thought: it is not that Father expects too much of us, it is that he expects like all parents do, a repetition of himself. The good, the steadfastness a parent strives for in a child is the good and the steadfastness he knows in himself, and any deviation from it is, to him, less than himself.

He nodded thoughtfully. He said, "Brina, I reckon it's just inevitable you got to go."

She looked at him. Her eyes glistened, as if with tears.

He said, "You know how I am. Every once in a while I got to pull up my roots, no matter how much it hurts to tear 'em loose, and go set 'em down somewhere else for a time. We're enough alike, you and me, you must have some of that in you somewhere, Brina. There's got to be other mountains, other country. I'm not sayin' I'd like you to just pack up and go off whenever you got the urge, that sort of life's nothing for a woman. And I know you're happy here, at Brandyhill. No reason you shouldn't be, it's been good to you, it's been your whole life. But you prob'ly got some of me in you. I ain't sayin' you're restless, but I am sayin' it's good to see what other people's mountains look like."

He had touched the one chord she knew he would touch, if she were honest with him. And she felt nakedly honest. "I know that," she said. "I can tell myself that. But I had to think it out, I had to take a long time thinking about it." She laughed with alien irony. "A long time . . . two, three weeks, a long time. A moment out of my life. And yet it seems a long time; the days and nights seem forever."

He nodded soberly. No, with more than soberness, she realized; with a grim concurrence. He looked almost as he had looked that morning, not long ago, when he had taken her face between his hands in the woods along the cold stream, when she had said, remember when you and Onny and I were children and we swore if one of us died. . . . But it was over and done. Onny was dead. Dead, dead, dear beautiful gentle Onny, who had never willingly hurt human or animal, or any living thing, who would not crush a flower or a spider underfoot, who had loved Brant. It was odd how you could know all your life that Onny loved Brant and never have it brought home to you with as much meaning as now: as if having her dead made her love him more. But that little vow had been made by children. It was as children that she and Brant had recalled it, in the woods, by the cold stream. If his face had been gentle to her that morning it was more than gentle now, softened by vision, by recall, by knowledges which she not only could not share because they were wholly his, but which she was only beginning to learn.

"Yes," he said, "yes. The days are forever. The nights are forever. Maybe it's the nights are worse. Because in the daytime you can look at things, sunlight, mountains, trees, anything to distract you and make you forget a little. At night there's nothing but the blackness, and whatever the blackness brings before your eyes."

His grimness had been momentary but his sadness came to her as gray and soft-springing as the rain clouds on the horizon. What he had said was true: in the daytime you busied yourself, achingly, with the terrible finite details of living and observing; in the night you lay with your eyes wide on the darkness and thought. She felt his rough shirt under her hand. Because she had a premonition of what was in his mind, because she did not want to ask, because close as they were, there were things sacred, things holy, things

213

upon which you did not intrude. Yet she felt, suddenly, that perhaps he needed to talk, perhaps talk was what he had needed all this time, all this long painful time. She said, not leading him, but trying to let him know in her own feminine incoherent way that whatever he felt, she was of blood and rapport bound to feel also, "I think if you love somebody, there's no good in waiting, waiting a day or even an hour. I think you have to take all the goodness, all the richness while you can."

Then she thought, I should not have said that, I have said the wrong thing. But he put his hand over hers, where it lay upon his arm, and said, "I know that, Brina. I know how you feel. But there's a difference. With you it's all different, the circumstances, the times, the other people involved. Like I said, it's what *you* got to do and what we want you to do." The little drawn scar over his eye, stitched as though with thread, where the rock fragment had scarred, was sharply dark with blood. "But you got to see too that sometimes waiting is all you can do."

She wept for him inside herself. She loathed her own exalted awakening, loathed almost love for the sake of love. She said, "I wish you'd tell me, Brant. You've never told me and I've never asked. What was she like?"

He let his breath out slowly. But he was without sadness. His eyes never went away from the moment, this last moment they would have together, alone, and she saw for this moment as clearly and as beautifully as he saw, in his mind. His voice, his words, painted for her, and she drank the colors into herself.

"She's little, Brina, much littler than you, and slight. Her hair's as thick as yours, and as coarse, but dark, and her eyes dark and a little slanted, like fawns' eyes look when they see you for the first time, coming up on them in the woods. And her face is like . . . like . . . you know how a pool looks, about sundown, when the sun comes in on it from the west, and there's no wind, and everything lies still and sort of gold-colored, and her cheeks are like high outcroppings of rock in the pool, and her mouth sort of like the columbines, red, with the goldenness lyin' around the edges."

His voice died. She sat with her hand light and trembling against him, under his hand. She did not speak, knowing he might not say more and wanting him to say more, wanting to know not only the girl but more of this man, wanting to know more of what had formed him to the long wilderness years, the now, the present.

And the old man, the old bearded man, no longer existed for him. He stood again in that dark garden loam, with the corn flowering green and quivering and his face against her bare sun-warmed instep, in the loam, and a bird hovered brown and silent above them, above the green, springing corn. He felt, momentarily, a magnificent calm of faith. He said, "She told me sometime I would see a wood thrush, and it wouldn't sing, and I could go close to it. And that's an omen of death." Suddenly he turned, looked at his sister with eyes gone wild and dark and crying for the faith he had felt so deeply, seconds before. "But she didn't say whose death, hers, or his, or maybe mine. She didn't say what I wanted her to say. She said she loved me; in her own way of saying it, she said it, but she didn't say whose death."

After a long time Sabrina said, "Oh, Brant, my dear, my dear, be logical, be practical. . . ." (But could she, loving, loved, be logical, be practical?) "Of course she did not mean her death, or yours, she meant. . . ." But she could not say it. She could not see the old man she had actually physically seen once or twice, abstractly; she could only see the old man as her imagination decided she must see him: gone at last, as if the wood thrush had sung him gone, no longer barrier, no longer existent.

He turned his head, as if he did not want her to see his face. He said, "So you see, I'm held here as hard as you're held to goin'."

"We are both of us right, then," she said. "Or no, maybe not right, maybe not wrong, maybe only what we have to do."

Then he said, "Brina, I wasn't goin' to be held, awhile back. Not after Tag. I was goin' upriver, not just to find Savage, but to do something for what was done to us."

"It's not too late," she said, but without hope, only to encourage, to comfort.

"I reckon it is. One of us Quantrells fittin' themselves into the new order of things is enough. I can't leave Father now. I can't leave off waitin', even if what I'm waitin' for turns out to be the biggest lie anybody ever lied."

She shivered. "Brant, these last nights, after I knew I had to leave, with all the things I thought about, I thought hardest about you, about what must have happened that night on the bridge. I remembered Fraser telling me once he knew Onny was going to snap someday . . . that was the word he used, snap . . . and how outraged I was at him. But he was right. I'll miss Onny all my days, because I loved her, because she was the nearest I had to a sister, but Brant, suppose it had been you dead on that bridge. I thought of that. I couldn't sleep for thinking of that, thinking of you dead. Because men were killed that night, and one of those men could have been you."

She could see how tense his face had got, and how full of remembering, and she who had never been, of herself, flesh-and-bone close to death, was close to it with him. He said, "I been close to it before, Brina, mighty close. But I never felt as close as that night. I don't think I felt it at the time, but in retrospect I do. It was different that night. Before, with Millikin, with Deschamps, maybe just with black woods around me and not knowing what was in that black woods, it was still me, all by myself, something to be met all by myself, and either strapped or fallen to. But it was different on the bridge because there were other men with me, other men to be reckoned with, other lives to be taken or spared, not man to man or on account of personal reasons, but for something the simple fact of my being there didn't obviate in any way. I tried, Brina, honest to God I tried, and I triggered off with the best of 'em, but it was still different, it was still something I had no individual part in. Oh, I did, for Tag, don't mistake me on that. But I knew all the time those men who came across that bridge at me had no quarrel with me, with Tag. If Balforth Waite had come across that bridge I would have stood up to him, horse and all, my own horse, and throttled him with my bare hands. But no man there, and I didn't recognize a one of 'em . . . after Onny . . . had a quarrel with me, nor I with them. You know what I mean, Brina? You know, don't you? I don't want you to leave me, not knowing."

"I know," she said, and she did. It reminded her how much of knowing, a lifetime of knowing, a lifetime of dear visual tangible knowings she must leave. Already she was pain-racked with nostalgia, with homesickness, with need for the salve of the familiar. To leave him. To leave the brother who had been not merely brother, but whole with her thought, her understanding, her spiritual existence, all the full rich lonely years.

They looked at one another. They loved one another, deeply and with an understanding of one another which was never to die in either of them. The sense of that understanding, of sharing what was in him lay sweetly, heavily, like the odor of wood lilies, upon her. The same lay upon him, but it was tempered by the odor of death, which smelled also of lilies: death was a dark moment upon a dark bridge, death was a dark bird which did not sing save to let you know it was there. And he could not say to her, if I had died that day it would all be gone: the still sunlit afternoons, the bright blazoning of autumn color and the smoky haze on the mountains, the dry apple-smelling beauty of the rushes and the swift black wings against the golden sky. And the hope, the desperate hot hope that there would come a moment, a moment when the bird song which is like no other bird song, so silver and incredibly pure it is, would ring within him like the pealing of a bell. And what are men, mere men, beside these, beside this . . . ?

She knew now, now that he had spoken, that he had loved longer and as intensely as she was only learning to love. She said, "I had to think, too, about Brandyhill, about what would happen here. Because I'm not just going away on a visit. If I ever came back, if we ever came back here, it would all be different. I'd search my mind expecting it to be the same, and it won't ever be the same. I had to think about it being exactly the same for all of you and so different for me. And I love it here, and I don't ever want it to be different."

"But it will be," he said. "Nothing stays the same. Nothing. Take all the good years, when Ellen was here. It was never the same when Ellen died. It's never going to be the same without Tag growing up here. Without you, and me, and Onny. Without Fraser, even. And it ain't only people changing, it's the actual physical surroundings they live in changing too, all the time."

"Because physical surroundings take their shape through the people who live in them," she said.

"And with them," he amended.

"And Father getting . . . getting along now," she said wistfully.

He nodded. But he said reassuringly, "Father's one of the few self-sufficient people I ever knew. Heart as big as the country for all humanity, maybe, but totally self-sufficient. Wasn't, he'd been dead long ago."

She said slowly, "I was thinking of Aunt Charity."

He looked at her. "You can't possibly remember Aunt Charity."

"No. In a way I'm glad I can't. Because I know her better not having ever known her."

He saw the parallel, but let himself smile faintly. "You ain't anything like she must've been, Brina. Just because she sat around here all those years and then finally got up and went off with a drummer. Maybe she did right. I don't know. Father never said what he thought, never passed judgment." His voice was almost reproachful. "You ain't exactly runnin' away with a pot mender, you know."

She laughed. Then she said, "No, I have managed to dignify a similarity is all. I'm frightened. I wonder if Charity was frightened."

"Sure you are and so was she. Real frightened. But wait'll you stand up to it and see how quick and easy you just walk right over your own fear. Like it wasn't even there. Charity must've, or she would've come home again. You will too, Brina." Then he said, "Not only because I think it, because I know it."

She drew from him a strength which she had been prone to draw from him all her life; a strength which was not peculiarly his, but which lay inherent in her also, and which she used as a strengthening of her own strength. She turned to him. He said, "Brina, I want you to go. You got to go."

It was what she had wanted to hear. And she knew that he had said it not only because he knew she wished to hear it but because he meant it within himself.

For the last time her hand tightened upon his arm. He felt it, under his own hand, and reached up painfully, slowly, with the arm where the gunshot wound still healed and took her face in his palm and kissed her high upon the cheek and then with love upon her mouth and looked at her until she drew away from him and rose.

And the coming of rain now was more than welcome in him; it challenged a drought of soul, and his soul stood unarmed to it. He sat quietly, no longer merely watching the sky, but piercing it with his gray young eyes, letting it grow up over him like a roof; not as if the coming cold shadow would wash him clean, but as if he would spring anew and grow again by its sustenance.

20

S HE THOUGHT AHEAD, to when the weariness would be a warm
flooding in her, and she would let it flow, feeling in its taut
ungentleness deliverance. It was the holding back weariness was
so hard; weariness in itself was not unbearable. The colt was weary
too, but had begun to prove itself of stern stuff with the softness
worked out of it and an end to pampering. It had grown used to
the young hound which walked sometimes at its side and rode
sometimes on its neck, when the streams were swift or the walking
hard in the pine barrens. The hound was still young enough so his
skull didn't fit all the head skin; the skin fell down in deep wrinkles
over his eyes when he lowered his head, and his under-eyelids were
loose and red yet, and he was long-gaited and awkward as a foal
in the hind legs.

She called him Battle, after the hound called Battle they'd once
had at Brandyhill, when she was a child.

They had gone miles beyond the crossroads where they found
the dog. There had been a woman sitting in a wagon, just outside the little settlement, a woman ugly as a toad, and with a sharp
thin voice. There was a man in the road too, half bent over, not
coaxing, hauling at the rope around the dog's neck, and the dog
braced in resistance, sliding on its long-tailed bottom. The colt
stood obediently still.

"What's the matter with him?" Sabrina said to the woman in the
wagon, the ugly toadlike woman. And the woman turned her sour
face, and you saw with surprise that her eyes were kind, and mirrored she had been nagged and beaten all her married life by the
man who dragged at the protesting dog.

"Got to shoot 'um," she said in her sharp thin voice, and it was
funny you heard so sharp and thin a voice come out in flatness
and acceptance.

219

"Why?" Sabrina said, holding the colt close to the wagon.

"Don't want 'um," the woman said, looking hard now, seeing this was a lady, riding sidesaddle and all, with fur on her boots and a blanket rolled on a fine-looking animal wasn't colt and wasn't growed up yet either. She sat stolidly on the wagon seat, looking at Sabrina, and Sabrina saw something else come into her eyes now, envy maybe, and maybe pity. Maybe pity for the hound. Maybe even pity for the man.

"But why don't you want him? Is there something wrong with him?"

The woman moved her head almost imperceptibly toward the man, and Sabrina looked and saw he had bent down and was trying to scoop the struggling dog up in his arms. "Vicious," the woman said with lethargic loyalty. "Bit 'um."

She didn't want them to know she had any hard money, she didn't know if it was safe, even if she was in Whig country. But even while she thought it she was sliding off the colt, cape swinging about her, and was running after the man and the dog.

"Wait."

He turned and looked at her, and she saw the narrowed eyes and the loose-lipped mouth and the brute strength of him. The dog was quiet now, as beaten as the woman in the wagon.

Sabrina said, "If you don't want him give him to me."

He said greedily, "For how much, mistress?"

She tugged at her skirt, holding up one narrow foot, showing him. "I will give you the boots. They are lined with fur."

He laughed. "I can't wear your boots, mistress."

"Your wife can, perhaps."

He laughed and turned away again.

"I will give you my boots for the dog."

"No."

"A dollar, then."

His eyes narrowed. "Continental." He saw confirmation in her face and roared with laughter.

So there was no other way. "All right," she said, "a sovereign."

He snatched the coin and bit it, and she saw the gaps between his teeth. She took the dog out of his arms and felt its ribs and the long ribbon of crusted blood over its flank. So it bit him, did it? It should have torn his throat out.

That was how they had come by the hound, and the hound went

with them, woman and horse, in sunlight and rain and coldness and wind. Once it snowed lightly. They stopped sometimes in settlements, and they spoke with people on the road, and they camped in the open at night if the weather was dry and not too cold. Christmas came and went; she had been on the road a week, and did not know it was Christmas; could not keep count of the days or the nights.

But there was another week of the ordeal.

The old man in the cart was very kind. He was drawing winter fodder, loose hay, behind a brace of oxen, and there was a setting hen on the seat beside him. His hands were big and square and work-worn on the reins, and his beard was stained and his voice cracked and funny. She went along with him all day. He let Battle ride in the wagon, and he talked a lot in his old cracked voice, not asking her questions, just talking about himself and the war and the weather. At midday she gave him some of her bread, and he shared his jug of milk with her. After he finished the milk he picked up the hen and took an egg out from under her and tapped a hole in the end, tapped it delicately for all his broad heavy hands, and sucked the egg out with relish. She liked him. She grew dependent on him, seeing that he was so kind, and not afraid of anything. So that all of a sudden she was talking to him too, telling him about Brandyhill and how she'd got Battle, and about her father and Jewel; telling him, when he said she should ride in the wagon awhile, that she'd almost been born on a horse. And saying it all merrily, like they were out for the pleasure of it. Saying at last what she had wanted to say right from the beginning. Do you know? Do you know where the army is?

And he laughed, not merrily as she had done, but in the funny old cackle, shaking his head, saying he knowed all along it was something like that, somebody she was looking to find, with such a tiresome journey up from the place she called Benton's Crossing. But he knew, he knew the river country. They was a road, up this road apiece, that turned off. Maybe a day's, two days' ride, if she kept at it stiddy. . . .

When they reached the road he said, "I'll take the houn' dawg off'n yer hands."

She looked back at Battle lying in the straw, his eyes amber and red-rimmed and trusting. She shook her head. "When you start over you have to have dogs. Dogs and horses. You can't start over without dogs and horses." And Battle got down stiff-legged with leisure, stretching and yawning, and followed her.

From the road-branching she watched kindness and dependability down the road, the old cart joggling, the old man humpbacked with work, the old hen still sitting unemotionally beside him.

Two days, if she kept at it steady. He meant without stopping, probably. But she had to stop. She would ride hard tomorrow, as hard as she could, and the next day she would give in to the weariness. Tomorrow did not count. Tomorrow was simply a small barrier which must be worn down and smoothed off and relieved of its sharp edges, so that you could find that world, not only the personal world of heart and mind, but the world of new country, new life, new beginning, which lay beyond tomorrow.

Because she knew this: it was a new country, which she had never seen before; it was a new beginning, the world which this man without whom she knew she could no longer exist, believed in; it was a new life, for which two generations of frontier permanence had prepared her.

She did not spare the colt that day, not as long as daylight remained. The darkness was cold and clear coming down upon her, and there was a thicket to camp in. She did not build a fire, but ate the thick burned edges of a corn cake she had brought from the last roadside inn and drank from her watered-down wine. She was self-reliant in the time she knew she must be, thinking she might soon perhaps be allowed the magnificent luxury of being cared for, protected. But she had been impatient with the day and so had ridden harder than the old man reckoned a woman capable of; now she was impatient with the darkness which detained her. Somewhere in the darkness was the cold running ribbon of the river, and the river had become for her a tangible goal, a thing to be possessed. She did not sleep well that night, curled under the old bearskin which she carried in her blanket roll; slept fitfully despite the warmth of the hound stretched at her side. She was awake and forcing the colt before dawn, before the last stars had gone down the sky. By sunrise she was weary, not thinking clearly, and hungry, but there was nothing before her, no house, no inn with its comfort of heat and food, only the dusty-cold road and the thin thickets and the rolling landscape of the country, and once or twice the flashing distant expanse of water which she knew was the river she sought, and which she followed.

When the sun was riding the mid-sky and her bones were warm again, she came out upon a meadow, having lost the road for a time due to its indistinct tracings and the indifference of the colt. At first she heard no sound but the soft thunk of the colt's hooves and the creaking of her own saddle; then, at the edge of the meadow, a mongrel dog growled and came out at Battle and jumped him. Battle fought back, but the hound's soft flews and gentle mouth were not made for fighting, and the mongrel was twice his heft. They rolled over and over, under the colt's hooves, and she heard Battle scream high, scream hurt, and she got off the colt and ran to the dogs and tried to pull them apart. The mongrel ignored her. He wanted Battle, and he had Battle now, and she cried out in fury.

The hands did not touch her. They were rough hands and they pulled the dogs apart and cuffed at the mongrel's face and sent him flying off his feet and pulled him up again and sent him flying a second time. Battle was up and limping, flopping down suddenly, licking at himself. Without looking at the hands again she went and picked up the hound and went over him carefully and saw that he was not badly hurt, and turned at last. Then she saw it was not one man, but several, battered, foul men in greasy buckskin. She could smell them; she could smell the sweat and the grease and the long-standing dirt of them.

"Thank you," she said, standing with the dog in her arms and the hood of her pelisse slipped off her head.

They stood looking at her, and she saw that beyond them there were other men, and some horses. She could see the tops of the tents beyond the upslope of the meadow, and old stumps lying in the swale, where they had cut the trees down long ago. She began to speak and stopped, not really knowing what she wished to say, and then the man who had driven off the mongrel was standing in front of her, grinning through his stubble of beard. Not looking at the horse or dog but at her. And she could not ask. Uneasiness made her hesitate. She heard herself say, "Is Colonel McDowell here?"

The man kept grinning. She thought, He imagines I know Charles McDowell, imagines God knows what. . . . She did not know what had put McDowell's name in her head. She faced the grinning man down, she wanted to stamp her foot at him. "Please, is he here?"

The men were all grinning now, looking like she'd seen Waite's men look in the barn at Brandyhill, except that Waite's men had been sober-faced. She stood her ground. Then the man who had rescued Battle took her by the arm.

Behind the men she saw the other men coming, and the man leading them, tall, with hair like brass and his sleeves rolled nearly to the shoulder. The man who held her arm saw too, and fell back, and the brassy-haired man said, "What's going on here?"

She said, "Are you Colonel McDowell?"

He ran a hand through his hair, the other hand on his hip. "What's that to you and how do you know it?"

"You knew my brother once." She kept looking at him, searching for a spark in the frosty blue eyes. "My brother. A little boy."

He watched her coldly.

Ah, she was doing this badly. "In the back country, when you were marching. A little boy. He stood by the road and was going to throw stones at you. And you said you would shoot him."

Far off, on the field, someone was shouting. The sound fluttered down to the edge of the wood like a torn banner in the wind. And she saw McDowell remembered.

But all he said was, "And?" He looked furious with her, furious with the world.

"I am looking for Major Savage."

"Oh," he said, and took a step back, his mouth open a little. "Savage, is it?"

"He is here?"

"He was here," the man who had rescued Battle said.

"Then he got back. You mean he is not here now?"

The man took off his torn stained hat, grinning with good humor and high spirits. "The Tiger ain't here. You can have me instead. All his mistresses been deeded over to me."

Before the shock and despair had time to rise fully in her McDowell said, "Why goddamn your filthy soul, Lessing." He moved once, short and sharp, so fast she hardly saw him move, and the Ranger was flat on his back with his eyes wide open and the blood coming out of his broken nose. She looked at McDowell in horror and gratitude; he saw her face, splendid in its open femaleness of terror and weakness; her face was bloodless, her mouth red as a winter sunrise. He did not understand, but he took pity on her. He said, "Try the third tent left, Savage might be there."

She could not even thank him. She swung up on the colt and put him up the field with the hound at a limping run beside her. She did not see men or hear sound or hesitate. But she had been heard. Already, when she slid off the colt, the tent flap had pulled back. She saw the white-blond head, ducked a little to avoid the inconvenient contrivance of canvas, and then she and Savage were looking at one another.

She was glad he did not look at her with surprise, that his eyes momentarily registered no emotion. Because she wanted to see his face blank and passive and dreamless before she found anything else in it; it was required of her by her own need that this face be as she remembered it, with its surface of lines around the clear bitter tawny eyes and its square planes of bone under the sun-wind burn and its terrible directness of purpose.

She felt the exhaustion and the weariness flow out of her as she had known it would. Her voice was as clear and serene as he remembered it. She said, "You told me once not to come until I knew what I wanted to be in this world. I know now. I know more. I know what I have to be."

The little space between them diminished and fell away. She remembered also, from a past which now seemed years gone, the taste of his mouth, a taste of hardness and gentleness and warmth, as of earth upon which the sun lies too long. Reaching to renew the remembrance, she felt his hands cup her face as though he held a chalice.

The colt moved off, cropping the stubble before the tents. There was a suddenness of clean sky above the rolling clouds, and the sun shone.

21

THE WIND CAME STEADILY from the south, carrying the sound of guns. The January dawn had been still, and so red that it was like fire in the sky, and sometime early, while the sky still reddened, the guns began. At first, in the stillness, the sound had been close, clear; now, with the deflection of wind and water, she had to strain to hear it.

She knelt at the window sill, head cradled on her arms, skirt belled around her like a green arching of boughs. The room was very cold; much of her lethargy was due to the insensibility of her cold flesh. When her knees would no longer support her she sank to the floor, still resting her head on her arms.

Madame Sevier came through the door like a bomb bursting. Her enormous bosom flowed and undulated and fought for a permanent resting place inside her heavy black dress; even the loose folding of shawl across her body could not wholly conceal the endless struggle. The floor shook under the weight of her mighty legs. But her voice was the sound of gray doves in twilight, of snow melting, of moonlight filtering.

"My dear child, *whatever* are you doing on the floor? How long have you been up and dressed?"

Sabrina turned from the window. A deep wave of the thick chestnut hair fell over her forehead. Shadow lay dark as ash under her eyes. "They're firing across the river. Didn't you hear?"

"Of *course* I heard," Madame Sevier said, "but it's no *reason* for you to be hanging out of the window like that. There's nothing to be seen but trees. Here now, Maria will have tea for us in a moment."

"I don't think I can get up," Sabrina said.

"It's no wonder, you must be *stiff* as a fresh oak plank." Her hands went out to Sabrina, lifting her, stronger than protest.

Sabrina said, "But something's obviously happening over there. Why don't they tell us . . . aren't they going to send someone to let us know?"

Madame Sevier's voice was soft and cheerful, yet under the cheerfulness lay a caution, a careful choosing of words. "Why, they're much too busy caring for themselves to care for us. Come down to breakfast now, Sabrina."

She tried to be calm, to accept, to humor the big sympathetic woman, but her face read otherwise. "Come now," Madame Sevier said, "come, come. All in good time, I'm sure. It's only *momentarily* men forget women exist. The wretched creatures *always* pretend there's something more important than women, but it's the women

226

they come to brag to. I found long ago guns are *music* if you listen to them as such."

Sabrina followed her down the staircase. In spite of herself she was aware of the house, a house as fine as Brevard Hundred and as richly appointed. It had also a warmth and graciousness which Brevard Hundred had never had: it was a house loved and lived in rather than erected and maintained to awe and impress. Structurally too it was like the Hundred, with its brick walls and center-hall design. But here ivy had been allowed to run rampant; sere and sleeping as it was now it was nonetheless there, clinging to the brick, and the gardens lying dormant outside had the look of being loved and grown for love, rather than for the formality and single end of having gardens. In this house were rich panoramic wallpapers with weeping trees and superbly plumaged birds; there was furniture as mellowed and graceful and time-honored as that which Caroline Amanda Wylie had passed on to the Quantrells; but there was also an air, in this house, that every inch of polished floor, of papered wall, of shining table, of tapestry-covered chair, of blackened fireplace, was used, lived with. Something of Brandy-hill lay here, materially richer, but with the same patina of tender love emanating like a fragrance. The dining room was warm and cheerful, fire talking to itself, table spread with linen, china thin and fragile.

She drew its hospitable warmth into herself. Esmeralda Sevier, whose late husband had been a cousin to the renowned rebel, Colonel Sevier, and who had been left financially more than comfortable, presented no other alternative than that she, Sabrina Quantrell, not only accept but become part and portion of this house, this hospitality. It was, save for the guns this morning, as if she had been born here, as if she had known this woman, thirty years her senior, all her life.

There were baked eggs and scones and preserves, but she could not eat. She drank the boiling tea dutifully, almost grateful for the tears it brought to her eyes, but she could not eat. She had been four days in this house, and what she could remember of coming to it was as vague and unsatisfyingly inconclusive as a dream. They had crossed the Broad, she and Savage, with the horses swimming astern, and ridden through swamps and up rolling country to the house which belonged to Savage's old friend, the cousin of Colonel Sevier. She remembered little of that journey, having journeyed so long, except the crossing of the river and the colt's sad eyes astern; and ashore, slowing one, two, three times to lean from the colt, while Savage's arm held her, while she gave herself up to the solidity and reality of embrace half awkward, half amusing, leaning as they did from horses. She tried to remember every hour, every moment, every word and gesture she had exchanged with Savage and could not, through apprehension and strain and the concentration on valiant attempt to adapt herself to a hardship she had never known before and was not yet done with: the hardship of fearing for this man and of being without him for however small portion of time.

She broke a scone and arranged it around the edges of her plate and said, "Madame Sevier, do you think it's our . . . it's the British troops fighting General Morgan's troops?"

"I'm sure it is," Madame Sevier said cheerfully. "It's what we've been *expecting*, after all, and the sooner it's over the better." And Sabrina, out of her own anxiety, admired this woman, saw beyond the cheerfulness, projected herself almost without effort into the personal and private world in which this woman lived. She and Esmeralda Sevier met now upon common ground: this hour of trial, of waiting, had been experienced by Esmeralda Sevier long before she, Sabrina, could have dreamed it would ever exist; this hour, all the hours of waiting, would have been the same for Esmeralda Sevier. And all the battles. And that last battle, from which her husband had never returned. Esmeralda Sevier had lived that battle, wherever it had been, had lived the dying and the finality of the dying, and had stood upright. Jed Sevier's death had not beaten her and she stood for him now, rebel to the core.

Sabrina looked down at her plate. "If only there was something we could do."

Esmeralda leaned across the table. "I suppose you *must* know I feel the same. Yes, today even, with the same intensity I felt two years ago, when Jed was gone, off fighting *God* knew where." Her eyes, surrounded by little pockets of flesh, were both shrewd and tender. "I knew in my heart when he was in danger, when he was in need. I knew he had died, even before they came and told me. I knew, the first time he went away, that one day he would not return." Her voice was calm, loving, soft.

Sabrina felt her body contract, refuting with horror the entire concept of death, shrinking from so calm an acceptance of the inevitability of the concept. Esmeralda Sevier's open fidelity to her dead husband was more shockingly mature than Sabrina could, now, comprehend. She knew that this huge woman with the beautifully soft voice, with the beautifully soft soul had loved Jed Sevier, that she loved him still. But it was *her* love, *her* burden of dying to be borne, and Sabrina was too full of her own love and the immediate threat of dying, across the river. It was a thing apart: love, when it is known, cannot be shared, and to the woman loving no other woman has ever plumbed the depths of love, no other woman has been allowed the privilege of loving. In spite of her sympathy she could feel no pain but her own.

In her wisdom Esmeralda Sevier knew this. She put out her plump ringed fingers and touched Sabrina's hand. "Sabrina, I have known Orne Savage long enough to know how skilled he is at whatever he undertakes. And how *fantastically* fortunate. He will be back. One way or another, he will come back. We must be ready. My dear child, *think* how very exciting it will all be. I had hoped so long to see my daughter married in this house. I raged against the unfairness of it when it did not come to pass. Now, you see, I am somewhat compensated."

Sabrina said, "Your daughter?"

Madame Sevier's eyes were misty and gone away. "She was about your size, though not as tall. She died at twenty-two with a sickness of the spine."

Sabrina watched the misty eyes. Out of this woman's body, out of a single throbbing emergence of love, out of the man now dead, then, had come a child, had come flesh-and-bone proof of that love. This knowledge too tormented her, brought up her blood in restlessness: she might not, now, know even that single comfort, flooding her strong young body in a paroxysm of release, seeding within her some final proving of love for the sake of love. Her mind begged her to weep; her pride in the face of Esmeralda Sevier's pride, would not allow it. She said, "What a terrible ordeal for you."

Madame Sevier nodded. "Yes. I've always been grateful we'd grown to know and love one another." There was a brisk factualness in the soft voice, yet the soft plump face seemed to float upon a river of tears long since shed and tears unshed. She said, "But there are the clothes, *lovely* clothes, my dear, in a trunk in the attic. And a wonderful dress, with white roses upon it. She never wore it. Why, Sabrina, as if it had been saved for you. Exactly. Exactly. I shall have the trunk brought down immediately."

Sabrina sank back in the chair. She wanted to refuse, to protest not only the proffered gift but the injustices of life which had been dealt Esmeralda Sevier. And later, standing in the drawing room with Madame Sevier and the maid, Maria, emotion conquered her. She stood in the center of the room, wearing the white dress, submitting numbly to the endless complications of fitting and adjusting and altering, and found herself trembling uncontrollably. It was as if the co-ordination of muscle and nerve had been incontrovertibly shattered; her hands shook; her balance was doubtful.

"You got to hold stiller, mist'ess," Maria said. "Madame, she shakin' like a leaf."

"And why shouldn't she?" Madame Sevier said. "Maria, we must take the whalebone out of the waist, the fortunate girl doesn't need stays." She was on the floor, on her knees. She said very slowly, from somewhere near the hem of the dress, "Before Jed and I were wed I was nearly prostrate for three days. I hadn't known him very long either . . . just long enough to know I couldn't *live* without him. Of course the actual business of *belonging* to him was another matter." She sighed. "I hear there are women with steel where their nerves should be, but I've yet to see one." She got up, with effort. "It's much too low at the bodice, Maria. Bring that bolt of lace and we'll fill it in." She got down again, with effort. "We women are quite amazing, you know, Sabrina. We are always masters of ourselves until some man comes along to beat down every last vestige of our confidence and self-importance. And we always feel, in these last hours of belonging to nobody but ourselves, that no other woman ever felt this way before and no other woman will again. It's a pleasant delusion. I still labor under it. I know how you feel now. Exactly as I felt. But you couldn't convince me of it."

In the hall the clock boomed with hollow and relentless certainty. Sabrina counted automatically. She said, "Eight o'clock. Only eight o'clock . . . Madame Sevier, can that be right?"

"I never argue with clocks," Esmeralda said. "Did you think it was later?"

"I thought it was at least noon. I thought we had been up for hours. I thought I had been standing here all morning."

"Maria," Madame Sevier said, "tell Aunt Loo to heat the irons. A large one and a small one, and not much more than warm, tell her." Again she got up. Her face was flushed. "Now, we shall have to be careful the pins don't scratch. . . . Sabrina, you look only *barely* conscious. I insist you go back to bed and stay there."

"But I'm not tired," Sabrina said.

"Of course you're tired, you simply won't give in to it. I remember, nervous as I was before Jed and I were married, I just simply *couldn't* seem to get enough sleep. It was a consolation. I *enjoyed* being nervous, but it wore me out. I'm getting so nervous now you'd think *I* was getting married again. Are you back, Maria? See the fire is banked in Mistress Quantrell's room, and the drapes closed. Come right back, we must see to the candleholders."

Free again of the white dress, standing in a thin long-sleeved wrapper, Sabrina said, "Madame Sevier, can you still hear the guns?"

Esmeralda did not make even a pretense of listening. "I'm sure they're still popping away even if we can't hear them. Perhaps the wind's shifted. Don't mention guns again, Sabrina. Don't even *think* guns. I want you to rest." Then she said, "My dear child, you must trust me. I shall let you know immediately there's anything to be known."

She stood with the white dress folded across her arm. Sabrina looked at her, knowing how right she was, relying heavily now on her wisdom. Either she is infallible in her judgments, or I desire to believe that she is, Sabrina thought. And was enveloped in a great and aching weariness. In gratitude she said, "I will do whatever you think best, Madame Sevier."

But alone, in her room, under the thick comforter, she was frightened of the silence. The nerve-wracking confusion of the morning had had about it a quality of reality. Nothing seemed real to her now, the warm bed or the whispering of falling ash in the banked coals, or the little glow of sunlight between the drawn curtains. I cannot sleep, she thought in anguish, and a moment later, slept.

In the depthless consolation of sleep, full and dreamless, even the gentle hand had about it a rudeness, an unnecessary strength. It took some time for her to struggle out of the black depths, to adjust to time and place. The hand, she saw at last, was Madame

231

Sevier's, resting upon her shoulder; she saw the plump full face, pink with anticipation, bent over her own. "Sabrina, they're coming, it's over . . . there was a young man here, a scout I believe he was."

She sat bolt upright. Her throat was suddenly so thick and dry she could not speak, not even the one word her lips formed.

Madame Sevier nodded. "Orne is safe and well." Her eyes were as bright as if she wept. She bore, suddenly, a great and stern resemblance to the portrait of Jed Sevier which hung in the hallway. "They have won a great victory, a great victory. The British have been routed."

Sabrina looked at her out of a steep cool well of relief.

"Now you must hurry," Madame Sevier said. "You *absolutely* must hurry. Maria is bringing hot water, and the dress is finished. Get up immediately. Orne is on his way, and there is a Colonel McDowell coming, and the chaplain. We've not a moment to lose. I shall be back to help you."

But after Madame Sevier had left the room, she dropped back upon the pillow. All the tension and ache and anxiety and nervousness of the day had drained out of her in sleep, and a warmth, a contentment, flowed in her veins like blood. She wished to lie forever in this blissful state; she wished to rise but did not dare move, even to breathe, lest the blissfulness fall away and smash around her.

Battle braced himself on the edge of the bed with his forepaws and looked at her. She looked back. His tail moved, almost circularly. "Ridiculous hound," she said. "Silly, silly hound." Then she had flung back the covers and gone to the window barefooted, hair loose on her shoulders. Looking between the curtains she saw that it was nearly dark outside.

Maria came with the hot water. "Ain't you undid yit, mist'ess?" Her voice was a moan. "Look to me like you ain't even hardly awake."

"I'm awake, Maria. Just leave the water. I'll hurry, I promise."

Outside, she heard Esmeralda's heavy footsteps, pounding down the hall and up the narrow stairs to the attic. Back again, and down the stairs. Again, up the main stairs, and down the hall. The feverish excitement of the big woman permeated the air, crept between the crack of door and doorjamb, floated up and down the stairs. At last she knocked, flung open the door, rushed into the room.

"I have pieces of wood where my fingers ought to be," Sabrina said. She was standing before the mirror, waiting to be buttoned. Her high cheekbones were suffused with scarlet in a long, upslanting line of color, as though the color followed the line of bone.

"The shoes," Esmeralda said, "I've forgotten the shoes." She rushed down the hall and rushed back. The shoes had high narrow heels and square glass buckles. They did not exactly fit, Sabrina found, but they would carry her for as long as she needed them. Esmeralda finished a frenzied buttoning of the dress. "The ribbon," she said, "I've forgotten the ribbon. And the ring. It's an old ring and worn thin, but it will do." And was gone again in a floor-shaking burst of agitation.

Alone, Sabrina moved the two lamps from the mantel and brought them to the table before the mirror. Framed in the soft yellow light, her face looked back at her, wide gray eyes luminous with something more than lamplight, lips half parted and tremulous. She stepped away from the table, still watching the mirror, wanting to believe the mirror. The stiff satin gown, despite its stiffness, flowed away from her, the embroidered overblown white roses shining as the light wavered upon them; out of the rich deep flowing of the skirt the narrow pillar of waist, line of breast and half-exposed shoulder were full of roundness and grace. The skin was very white against the creamy frothing of lace which masked the bodice. She looked at herself with wariness, as she might have looked at a woman she did not know.

Esmeralda thundered back. But she halted on the threshold. Sabrina, turning to her, thought she would burst into tears. She said, "My *dear* child, how very beautiful you are."

Sabrina crossed the room to her. "Madame Sevier, I'm not going to try to thank you. I only want to say perhaps we can make up to one another for things which should have been and weren't. All this . . . all this you wanted for your daughter. I never knew my mother, she died when I was very small. But I told you about Ellen, and how wonderful she was. Like you would have wanted your daughter here now, I would have wanted, on my wedding day, to have Ellen with me. I wanted you to know."

After a moment Esmeralda said, "It won't harm either of us to pretend a bit, will it, Sabrina?" She cleared her throat. "Now, here's the ribbon . . . Maria's sewn all these little plush flowers along it.

Do you think we should set it *over* your head or tie it around your throat perhaps . . . ?"

The clock began again. Together the women counted five. Then Esmeralda said, "They're here, they're here, I heard horses, I shall have to go down, you will *have* to hurry, Sabrina, I can't understand what is taking you so *long*," and was gone again.

Sabrina turned back to the mirror, holding the ribbon. For a little time she felt faint and sick and put out both hands to steady herself on the edge of the table. Through the closed door of her room she heard the sound of the front door, Esmeralda's high excited laughter, a man's voice, a stamping of feet, the voices again. Unsteadily she stretched the ribbon across her hair and took it down again. As if the performing of this small act, this decision that the ribbon did not belong there, had been the attainment of some peak of crisis, her heart steadied and a tremendous calm settled upon her. Now with deliberation, with composure, she brushed back the curling tendrils about her face, gathered her hair into its accustomed thick club, and tied the ribbon around it, letting the flower-strewn ends lie free. She knew herself, now, in the mirror.

Esmeralda came in, gasping for breath. "Sabrina, you have *got* to be ready . . . they are all in such a terrible rush, and the chaplain has been in the brandy *already*, and I would like him to at *least* be able to pronounce the words properly. Sabrina, I *know* how nervous and excited you are, but we simply *cannot* put this off any longer."

Sabrina turned, smiling calmly but with amusement. "I am ready, Madame Sevier, I shall come right down."

"Thank *God*," Esmeralda said, and rushed out again.

There was an extravagant bank of candles burning beside the stairs, in the hallway. From the top of the staircase Sabrina looked down, half concealed by a wall: Maria and a houseboy came across the hall, Maria with a candelabra, the boy with an enormous tray, and disappeared into the drawing room. Esmeralda stood in conversation with the chaplain, a short gray-haired man who nearly matched her in heft. Savage stood with his back to the stairs, talking with McDowell. His deerskin jacket was slung over his shoulder and he had a glass in his hand; she could see the long uneven tear across the shoulder of the jacket. And she resented, suddenly, these people, these strangers, who intruded upon a moment which she wished to share with Savage alone, whom she would not only have to face but to acknowledge and speak with sanely. The moment passed. She put her hand upon the balustrade and started down the stairs, still watching Savage, and saw him turn and look at her. For a time she moved evenly, smiling, but a few steps from the bottom she stopped, almost uncertainly, looking down at him.

He was hollow-eyed with fatigue, and there were raw patches on his jaw, where he had shaved too closely over the wind-roughened skin. His face, weary and strained, mirrored also an inner elation, a triumph, an accomplishment. Because she could see in these evident physical and spiritual scars with what haste and impatience he had come here, she felt for a time conscience-stricken at her own clean splendor. Then his eyes, watching her as if they had never seen her before, told her that she had given him, in a grim and unbeautiful world, the gift of beauty.

The white skin, in the upward flaring of diffused candle flame, was the color of spring sunlight. They did not speak to one another; their eyes locked, transmitted, received, communicated a language older than the spoken word. Then he turned and set his glass down and held out his hands to her.

Reaching to him, she was conscious of the black grime of powder imbedded in the chapped knuckles. Faint but clear, the gray smell of gunsmoke came to her, as though it had grown in him, in McDowell, in the very pores of their skin. She glanced at McDowell, saw that he too was powder-grimed, tense with weariness, elated; noted that he too smelled of the acrid bittersweet smoke. She stepped off the final step.

"Mercy on us," Esmeralda said, "you're not supposed to kiss her till it's all over, Orne. Orne, you're *squashing* the flowers. Come, Colonel, perhaps if we go into the drawing room they'll have sense enough to follow. I do feel, Reverend Carteret, you'd ought to say *something*. . . ."

Standing before the fireplace, where candles burned also, Sabrina saw for the first time that it was raining, steadily, evenly; small rivers flowed and joined and separated on the windows. She and Savage stood looking at one another.

"It is raining," she said.

"Yes," he said.

"I did not know it was raining."

"I either," he said.

Looking at one another.

"Major Savage," the chaplain said impatiently, "if you are quite ready. . . ." His bulk barricaded almost entirely the red glowing of logs on the hearth. And she who had told herself she would hear every word of this ritual heard not one word of it, spoke automatically, felt that the only reality in this room was the hand which held her own and the faint smell of the gunpowder. The soft light, sound of fire and rain, presence of sympathetic humanity, voice pronouncing destiny upon her, were a blur and rush as of some momentary surrounding, transitory, unreal, formed of the thin quick essence of dream. She might have stood naked on the top of the world, looking down, alone except for the gentle powder-scarred hand and the smoke taste in her throat. Once she thought clearly that she had known all the traditional emotions of this hour but one: the inveterate reluctance at the final moment, the desire for withdrawal, the need to retain herself as herself, the knowledge that she must preserve her own identity. Not once had she wished to turn away. Not once had she doubted.

Esmeralda said, "Now you can kiss her, Orne. I am going to kiss her. I think even Colonel McDowell is supposed. . . ."

It was over. So small a thing, so brief, so simple, to weave so strong a bond. She held her face up, a little stunned; the touch between them was brief, almost perfunctory, a duty imposed by the ritual. The chaplain said, "I may even kiss her myself."

Esmeralda was weeping. "Not just because it is *required* of me," she said. "Now, brandy. A toast *is* required." But she saw, as did Sabrina, the look which passed between Savage and McDowell. "Madame," McDowell said, "we've half an hour at most. I regret it."

Then Esmeralda said quietly, "I know. I knew it all along. Help yourself to brandy, gentlemen. I will help Sabrina to pack. But I would like to know more, before you go, of what happened across the river."

"I too," Sabrina said. She held tightly to Savage's hand.

"You, my dear, have the rest of your life to hear. Go up, Sabrina, Maria has laid out your things and Aunt Loo is putting up food for you."

Savage said, "She can't take much, Esmeralda, we can't travel with a lot of baggage."

"There's only a little trunk and a wicker hamper, you can manage that."

Sabrina moved with reluctance; long after Savage had released her hand she could feel the hard pressure of bone and flesh in her palm. To leave this house now, and this room, and the warm living presence of companionship she had dreaded only a few minutes before assumed the color of sacrifice. But Esmeralda was hurrying her again, quietly now, and with sadness. She said, "No, stay, Madame Sevier, Maria will help me," and went up the stairs alone.

She felt a pang as Maria helped her out of the briefly worn white satin, but there were familiarity and comfort in the fur-lined boots, the practical garments of travel, the hooded pelisse. Esmeralda came in as she locked the trunk; Sabrina sensed how close to tears the plump widow walked. Out of her own sadness she strove for cheerfulness.

"I wish I could say I felt different, somehow, in some way, but I don't. I still feel like me, Sabrina."

Esmeralda said, "I shouldn't like you to feel like *anyone* else." Then she moved forward and put her heavy arms about Sabrina and held her. "Come, my dear, they are waiting. You must write me, now, Sabrina, when you can. And I should like to write your father, to tell him how happy you have made me."

The houseboy came up for the trunk. For the last time Sabrina went down the stairs, where the men waited. The old cook, Aunt Loo, stood in the hall now too, and Maria. The men were impatient; their faces, through the strained elation, wore something harsh and restless; their hands made quick and meaningless gestures.

There was no wind, still the rain seemed to force itself into the hall; the last solace of light and dryness and warmth was swallowed in its relentless insistence. For the first time Sabrina was conscious of sound upon the road, the sound of men, the turn of wheels, the plodding of horses in mud, and once, a distant unmusical fragment of song. But she could see nothing in the blackness. The brilliantly lit house was an island haven in the dark night. Then a wagon came into the yard, drawn by two soaked, steaming horses; the steam rose from the sodden beasts like breath expelled warmly into cold air. Behind the wagon the colt walked, tethered to the tailboard. Sabrina turned in a rush and took Esmeralda Sevier's hands and kissed the plump soft cheek. "Thank you for everything, Madame Sevier."

Esmeralda said, "Thank *you*, my dear."

Savage lifted her and carried her down the steps and swung her over the tail gate of the wagon. She could smell the dry forage, straw and hay and old musty grass. Charles McDowell stowed trunk and hamper in a corner of the wagon, handed Battle up to her, took her hand for a moment, smiled and was gone. Over the tail gate she looked at Savage. Her voice was a dry whisper. "Where will you be, Orne?"

"Not far from you." Now he reached up to her and she put her hands down and leaned upon his shoulders. "I will try not to be afraid," she said, "but right now I am terrified."

He took her hands, cupping them together about his face. "Don't be, there's a trusted man with you. You aren't to leave the wagon of course, and keep the canvas down. We won't stop till dawn." Now he drew her down to him. "Obey me."

She laughed. "Martinet. Did you . . . did we really win a great battle, Orne?"

He teased her, out of his own overwhelming sense of victory. "This is no time to discuss your whipped friend Colonel Tarleton, Madame Savage. Another day. I'll try to see you in the morning."

She closed her eyes. Her hood slipped off and she felt the rain, cold and stinging, on her face as she leaned from the wagon. They clung to one another until the hound, whimpering, forced himself between them. When she looked up, Esmeralda Sevier was standing in the rain with a shawl around her head, holding a large and awkward-looking pistol. "Haven't you *forgotten* something, Orne?"

He took the pistol. "I was coming back for it, thanks, Esmeralda."

"Is that for me?" Sabrina said.

"You won't need it, but it's for you," he said, and passed it up to her. She took it gingerly.

"It's not loaded," Esmeralda said. "Really, it's so ferocious looking I don't think it will be *necessary* to load it. It was Jed's." Her soft face trembled and broke under the impact of tears; she turned and went hurriedly through the rain. From the portico she waved once, almost clumsily, and entered her empty silent house.

Sabrina leaned from the wagon again. "Try to come in the morning, Orne, try."

"I will," he said. "You try to sleep." He pulled down the canvas flap. For a time she crouched behind it, with Battle pressed against her, but Savage was gone. The wagon moved suddenly, throwing her off balance, so that she sat down hard in the straw. She meant to get up again, but it was very comfortable and dry in the straw, and she lay still, wide awake, listening. She felt the wagon turn into the road, and after a little she heard sound again, outside, the same sound of men in mud, of horses in mud, voices, shouting, clatter of metal on metal, creaking of leather, warped protesting of the wagon in which she rode, rain drumming on the canvas overhead.

Outside a man said thickly, with feeling, "Bloody stinkin' rain, bloody filthy rain."

And was answered philosophically. "It's rainin' on the lobsterbacks too. And they ain't got nowhere to run yet, even if they picked up the pieces."

And once again, song, voices lifted, comfortingly masculine in the blackness. "Lavender's blue, dilly dilly, lavender's green. If I wuz king, dilly dilly. . . ." And the breaking off of song, and the triumphant interjection: "If you wuz king, dilly dilly, I'd cut yer bloody heart out. . . ."

She sat up shivering, having caught a little of this mass elation, feeling herself secure but torn. In the dark she managed to open the little trunk and draw forth a blanket. But when she had made herself comfortable under it, an uncontrollable desire to cry came up in her. She closed her eyes, but the tears squeezed themselves out from under her lids and slid warmly across her face. Without reason, in the darkness, out of the strange sound around her, her father's face came into her mind, strong and gentle; she could see his hand, fine-boned under the blue tracery of veins, lifting, lighting his pipe. She saw him, asleep in the bed she had been born in, saw him rise to the dawn; saw Brant wake to the same chores he had waked to all winter, and the same waiting. The longing, the first homesickness, the nostalgia, the little lost boy, the myriad scenes and actions, colored out of all proportion by memory, were suddenly rooted in her, struggling in her. She wept silently, not wanting the driver to hear, not wanting to hear herself.

A man's voice sounded outside in a hoarse and vulgar shout. She lay listening, cutting off the tears and the convulsive shuddering as if she had cut off her own breathing. The voice did not speak again. She sat upright in the straw, holding the blanket around her. Dear God in heaven. If I am going to cry at least let me cry about a truth, however small. This is my wedding night and I am sleeping in a forage wagon.

But there was someone to talk to, one voice in the confusion which would speak directly, personally to her. She crawled to the front of the wagon and put her head out into the rain and looked up at the driver. There was a lantern on the seat beside him; in the upthrusting light she saw his seamed and stubbled face. He looked down at her without surprise or curiosity. She said, "Can you tell me what's happening, can you tell me where we're going?"

He held the reins in cracked shapeless knobby hands which had once bled and had healed and scarred over. He said, "We're goin' North, mistress, North, to git away from Cornwally's army. We beaten his cavalry this mornin' and now we got to git away while we can. You'd best stay out of the rain, mistress."

She waited for him to say something more, but he did not speak again. She crawled back into the wagon; the road was rough and the wheels jarred and jolted. She was drained of tears but the night was full of loneliness. In time she fell asleep, with the hound curled beside her.

22

S HE WAS AWAKE at dawn, stiff, cramped, with no true recognition of her surroundings for a long moment of nightmare. When she had come to her senses, remembering the night, the previous day, she went again to the front of the wagon and looked out. The rain had stopped; the wagon rolled in a gray and cheerless world of mud and dripping trees. There was a light fog in which phantom horses and the ghosts of men moved.

The driver was weary but in better spirits, seeing how many miles he'd managed to leave between himself and the British. He half dozed at the reins until he found her awake, just behind him. He was solaced at the coming of daylight and wanted to talk to her now. He was a Virginian named McCracken, and it was from him that she learned of the rebel victory at Cowpens.

"This here Gineral Greene is a right smart soljer," he told her.

"Right smart. He figgered he didn't have enough army to fight the whole consarned British Army. So what does he do?"

He seemed to be waiting for an answer so she said, "I don't know."

"Well, he figgers. He's a soljer fer figgerin', they say. So he gits the Old Wagoner Morgan to go kitin' off in one direction, an' he kites off in another, an' 'fore you know it, the British is kitin' off in all directions too, jest like he figgers. Cornwally goes a runnin' after him and this here boy Tarleton what's got everybody so scared they afeered to say his name, he goes a runnin' after the Old Wagoner." He chuckled. "That was a powerful sad mistake on his part."

She pushed her hair back. She was wide awake now. "And you fought Colonel Tarleton back there, along the river."

"Well, I didn't fight him personal," McCracken said. "I was in charge of wagons. You see these hands, mistress?" He held up the scarred hands holding the reins. "I'm all right with horses, but not so stiddy with a gun no more."

"What happened to you?" she said, moving so that she could see his face, see the hands more clearly.

"Ammyewnition wagon run over 'em," he said. "Why they was more weight in that wagon than God Hisself could hold up. I had fell down in the mud, you see, and there was them wheels asmashin' and acrunchin' over these hands, breakin' up all the bones and me hollerin' fit to kill and nobody to stop the wagon. So I hain't so stiddy no more when it comes to handlin' a rifle." He looked down at her, taking pleasure in her woman's face, refreshed with sleep, and the horror and sympathy in her eyes. "You got no cause to worry though, mistress. After I got healed and whupped up the boy let that ammyewnition wagon run over me, I figgered I was goin' to be a better wagoner even than Morgan ever was, an' I am. So as I was tellin' you, there we was on that field . . . used to be a old pasture . . . with our lines strung out across a slope, an' the British comin' at us near twice our number strong."

"It was at sunrise," Sabrina said. "It was just at sunrise." She shivered. In her mind she leaned again on Esmeralda Sevier's window sill in the red dawn.

He did not hear her. "So it seems Morgan's figgerin' too, or we hoped he was, because he done a peculiar thing, standin' on that slope with both his flanks wide open, just lettin' that infantry an' cavalry come pourin' down on him. And then he waits till they git right square into him, an' he calls in his own cavalry an' closes up them flanks jest as nice as you please, an' there was Tarleton caught right between 'em, hollerin' fer quarter an' gittin' the bejesus beat out of him. It was one mighty nice little battle, mistress, mighty nice." He chuckled again, shaking his head slowly in a crude appreciation at which she could only guess.

She said, "But what are we going to do now, Mr. McCracken?"

His face, in the dawnlight, sobered. "We got to keep movin'," he said. "Seems like Cornwally was kindee upsot about his fav'rit colonel gittin' whupped up like that, so he quit runnin' after Greene and run over to help the colonel git back on his horse again. An' now the whole bloody lot of 'em's after us. The officers' sayin' if we kin draw 'em fur enough inland they won't be able to git any supplies." He spat over the side of the wagon.

She sat back, her face gone almost as sober as his. She could remember Brant, hear his voice in the family room at Brandyhill: No farmer on a work hack could look twice at Tarleton. And Savage: But these are the cream of the Virginia gentlemen, and maybe they're good enough to take your Tarleton. And Brant again: Tell me about the running, that's all I'll ever understand about it. The running. The running through the whole damn war. A new terror swelled in her. What if they did keep running, like this, forever and ever, until they ran clean off the face of the earth?

McCracken spat again. He said casually, "You an' me's goin' to be together a fair spell, I reckon. They's talk around Major Savage took you right out of a whole fambly of Tories, mistress. It's some curiosity."

"What," she said, "where did you hear that?"

"Troops do talk an' gossip," he said. "Worse than ladies at a quiltin' bee."

She was indignant. "Well you can tell the ladies for me that I will end up a sturdier faster-running rebel than all of them put together. . . ." Then she laughed and his seamed face broke into laughter also, and into respect. "Look there," he said, "the fog's liftin'."

Daylight broke with no promise of sun. Ahead, now, she could see another wagon, lumbering in the mud and listing badly. A voice came from far ahead up the road, muffled by distance, then another voice took up the cry, and another, calling the order down the line and past her. Fall out, fall out, fall out. Until it disappeared somewhere behind her.

They had come to a clearing through which a swollen stream ran. Still leaning on the seat by McCracken, she saw Savage coming up the road on foot. McCracken touched his hatbrim sharply with a twisted hand. "Morning, Major." Out of the side of his mouth he said to Sabrina, "This means rations."

Savage said, "You hungry already, McCracken? Swing in here and see if you can locate some dry wood." Over McCracken's head he looked at Sabrina but did not speak, going past the wagon seat. She scrambled back into the wagon and reached the tail gate at the same time he did. But she checked herself; there were a wagon, and men, behind her wagon.

Savage smiled at her, but it was a strained tired smile. She knew he had not slept and felt guilty. He said, "You're in luck this morning, Sabrina. Morgan's orderly's heating water for you." He took her hands. "Don't get dependent on hot water, there won't be any most mornings. Clean up and we'll take a break."

"Do you want the hamper?" she said.

Now he grinned. "Listen, poor child, this is not a picnic. This is a rations break. Hang on to whatever Esmeralda put in that hamper like it was all you had between now and eternity. I'm going to get a fire going."

When she left the wagon he had started a fire on a big flat rock. McDowell stood near him, pouring rum into battered tin cups. With them was an enormous man in buckskin, hair braided like an Indian, single sidearm strapped to his belt. She went to the fire. "Good morning, Charles."

"Morning," McDowell said. He held out a cup and she took it and lifted it to her mouth. She made a face, sipping at it; it tasted worse than Joe Yancy's stump water. The big man watched her, half smiling. When she had lowered the cup he said, "Well, Mistress Tiger, how do you stand up to our little journey?"

"Very well, thank you." She looked at him closely. He had kind eyes in a gray drawn face which was scarred at the corner of the mouth. "You're General Morgan, aren't you?"

Now he came around the rock, and the fire, to her. He limped terribly, half dragging one foot. "Colonel McDowell reminds me of the incredible coincidence that I once spoke to your small brother. I am grieved to hear of your loss."

243

She looked at the ground for a time. Then she said, smiling, liking him, "Why do you call me Mistress Tiger?"

He, and McDowell, laughed. Savage did not look up from the fire. Morgan sat down abruptly on the edge of the rock. He said, "In the upper Shenandoah, where your husband and I grew to men together, there was a family called Davis. Notorious, the Davis boys. You remember, eh, Savage?" Savage still did not look up. "Now I," Morgan said, "am somewhat bigger than your husband. And I loved to fight. How I loved to fight. One evening, in the Red Lion Inn, in Winchester, I took on the three Davis brothers, one by one." He watched her, a figure of half shrewd amusement, half serious reminiscence. "Broke my toe, but I whipped those boys, whipped 'em all. Made 'em mad, too." He reached down beside the rock and came up with a stone jug and tilted it up and drank deeply. "So after I strapped 'em they went out to find somebody smaller. First man they found was Orne."

She did not want to ask, but Morgan was drinking from the jug again, obviously waiting for her to ask. "And did he fight them?"

Morgan put the jug down. "He ran."

She was not disappointed. "That was very wise of him," she said.

"I agree." Morgan was sober-faced now. "Of course after he'd run a few yards it developed he was only running to pull a paling out of a fence along the road. I tell you, mistress, he laid about him with that paling until the Davis boys were yelling quarter in the same tone of voice Ban Tarleton yelled it yesterday, and any one of 'em was big enough to pick him up by the scruff of the neck, just like that little dog you've got there. You can be proud of that man making your breakfast for you. He was Tiger to us that night, and me hobbling around the road on my broken toe yelling just as loud as the Davises. He's lucky to have a name the men can call him by, like they call me the Old Wagoner, and Charles . . . well, I don't want to say aloud what they call the colonel here."

She touched Savage's bent shoulder briefly, where he hunched over the fire. Then she went and leaned against the rock beside Morgan. "General, I've asked everybody I've talked to, and nobody answers. Where are we going?"

Now he looked at her a little narrowly. His good humor had passed quickly; he was ill and in pain, his body wracked with rheumatism. "Sick to death of it already, mistress?"

She shook her head, looking him squarely in the eye. "Only curious, sir."

"I apologize," he said. "I wish I could answer you, where or how long it will be or when we'll get there, but I've no more to say on it than that crow flapping around up there." She glanced up, to where the crow hovered, ragged-winged. She knew he had nothing to tell her, would not tell her if he knew. She said, "Is there anything I can do for you, sir, any writing, or mending?"

He looked at her for a long time. She was the wife of his old friend; they were to be neighbors, some day. His face changed, an almost childish gentleness came into it, and into the dark sunken eyes. "When you get home, see my wife. That's medicine. That'll earn you your keep."

At the edge of the creek a cavalryman rode, splashing up out of a shallow, swollen creek, crimson uniform muddied from the crossing. Morgan rose from the rock and limped off to meet him without another word. She and Savage and McDowell sat hungrily to the pork and rum and corncake.

It began to rain again before they finished breakfast, and she went back to the wagon. "It's a clearin' shower," McCracken told her. He pointed with his whip. "You see that little sliver of gray to west, enough to patch a baby's pants? That'll be blue before the mornin's out."

He was prophetic. After that morning the world, her world, her life, was an eternity of rainy mornings and palely sunlit afternoons, day after weary day. There were three weeks of dreary existence in the forage wagon, or riding the colt when the sun came; three weeks of constant moving, of short breaks to rest and eat, of rain spattering and pouring on the canvas overhead, of the chill sunlight and wet heavy air; three weeks of men moving and shouting, of streams to be forded and pine barrens to lumber through and roads so rutted and potholed she marveled that the wheels stayed on the wagon. The earth was a great sponge, filled and overflowing. They came into the river country, a country of minor tributaries, overflowing creeks and boiling streams. The rebel army had confiscated every boat it could lay hands on in this sodden territory, and the boats went with it, from river to river, from creek to creek, drawn overland on wooden wheels by cursing straining militia and Continentals.

In those three weeks she saw Savage only at rations breaks. In those three weeks, though she could call few men by name, she sensed a constant ever-growing change in this march, an indefinable air of pressure and strain. Savage did not tell her, and she would not ask: she learned instead to listen, to every scrap of stray word, when she rode the colt, from behind the flap of the wagon. She learned from listening that Savage rode ahead with the little army unto itself which was Morgan's crack Riflars, learned that William Washington's weary cavalry rode their flanks and advance and rear day and night, learned that the march schedule had been stepped up and that there would be now but one rations break a day, learned that men on special detail were allowed six hours' sleep out of forty-eight. Riding beside the wagon, at the end of those three weeks, she overheard Major Edward Giles, the General's aide-de-camp, say that they were covering thirty miles a day, an unprecedented daily march.

She had shared, dispensed the contents of Esmeralda Sevier's wicker hamper. Except for the brandy, which she hoarded for Savage, the basket was empty. And she regretted she had not taken Savage's advice, because the single rations break now was breakfast, and the pork was moldy and the corn-meal-and-creek-water bread, baked in ashes, was tasteless and dry as straw. The few small settlements through which they passed were sacked of supplies and livestock, but there was not enough for the hungry flying army of eight hundred men. She too was hungry.

She had become greedy about her morning cup of rum. Standing at the fire, before dawn, the liquor was more than fire, more than food. Still, the fire was an old friend, eating at the gray infinity of early morning, consuming loneliness. McCracken stood some distance away, doling out the near-gone fodder in the wagon to the horses. She said to Savage, "The British are very close to us, aren't they?"

He was sitting on a log, eyes closed. He said, "Very close. Our scouts say their advance is a day behind us."

She took a deep breath, coming to sit beside him on the log. "Are you finally going to tell me something, Orne?"

"We're going to be moving on, ahead of the army. The Riflars and Colonel Howard's Maryland."

"Where are we now?" she said.

"Clear across North Carolina."

"But why are we moving ahead?"

246

"Morgan collapsed last night. He's going on, to Guilford Court House. There'll be a junction of the armies there . . . us, and Greene's troops."

She thought about it. Then she said, "Does that mean the whole army, all the Americans, will be joined together? Does it mean we will wait there for the British?"

"I don't know," he said. He looked at her. "Your eyes look like you'd been crying."

"Well I haven't," she said. "Not lately, anyway. It's just I'm tired, I reckon."

"Don't apologize," he said. "Sometimes I feel like crying myself."

The smile began to move on her mouth. He said, "Hell, do you think I like this business, this sort of existence? I've left things the same as you have, good things, peaceful things."

He was leaning against her, not in weariness now, but deliberately; the hard lean hot pressure of his body told her that he had thought of her after all. She looked at him, seeing the concise, clean-bordered pattern of beard on jaw and upper lip. The lines about the eyes were deeper, older than she remembered them, and his face was thin and fatigued. But the face had lost something: it had lost the bitterness which had lain so long in the eyes, the set of the mouth; his face, now, to her, was as thin and strong and clear as if it had been taken from some smooth stone and chiseled into fineness. She said sorrowfully, "But you have something I haven't. Endurance."

He put his hand on her head. "What is it you call yourself, beautiful child, if not enduring?"

"But I ride," she said. "I am warm and dry and protected. And loved."

"You are also a woman," he said, "and there are men in this army should come and look at you." He sat up, linking his arms around his drawn-up knees. "Christ. Steal, desert, fight among themselves, whine, beg, weep, wheedle. God knows I don't blame them, I'm sick of it too, and I suppose they're allowed some sort of compensation for what they did back on that pasture, for being human and subject to all the human weaknesses. But they're obligated. They're committed, until Greene or Morgan or maybe God Almighty tells them they can quit. And they won't wait to be told."

She did not answer. She could not share this with him. From near the fire the hound, gone poor and gaunt, rose and stretched.

He came to Savage and nuzzled against him. "I've nothing for him to eat," she said wistfully.

"Well, he's an enduring sort then, too, isn't he? Would you feel ashamed he ate, if men were hungry?"

She sighed. Then she said, "Orne, look."

There had come a frieze of pale pink clouds over the grove in which the wagon stood. Her hands began to tremble. This was the hour her father loved, that he rose to meet. But he did not know this, nor feel what she felt. He said, "Thank God it's not going to rain this morning."

Far down the line a drum rolled, shortly, abruptly, with a sound like thunder. He picked up his cup and finished his rum. Then he got up and began to kick out the fire. She said, "Will we be riding on ahead today, Orne?"

"Not until Greene gets here. He's left his troops with General Huger. Morgan gives him two days to reach us and take command." He did not look at her. "Listen, Sabrina. Keep an eye on Battle."

"Battle. But why?"

"Men are hungry," he said briefly.

She made a small sound of horror. "Well," she said, "a fine lot of meat they'll get off him, poor thing."

McCracken was coming up with the wagon. Savage turned suddenly; she felt his mouth brush her cheek. "Maybe I'll see you later," he said. "Maybe tomorrow."

"Good-by," she said softly, emptily. She pushed the hound up into the wagon and untied the colt from the tail gate. Savage was gone, lost somewhere in the grove, when she turned the colt into the road. Over the trees a first edge of sunlight rimmed the morning clouds.

In the late afternoon she found the wagon full of fresh-cut pine boughs. "I cut 'em fer you," McCracken told her. "I give the last fodder to yer horse."

She thanked him. She looked at the colt. Pride was still in him, but his eyes were dejected and his ribs protruded. "All right, colt," she said grimly, "you're on your own wits now, just like the rest of us."

Sometime during the night she wakened, feeling a terrifying surge of blood, hot and fearful in her. Someone had come for Battle. Then she knew she had dreamed. But she was conscious of pressure and warmth at her side. Out of the darkness Savage said, "I didn't mean to wake you, Brina."

It was the word. Brina. Her name had lain always in his mouth as it had been given to her, fully; the abbreviation was a mark not only of convenience but of intimacy. It was his use of the word more than his presence which stopped her heart. She said, "Is anything wrong, Orne?"

His voice was low and clear. He said, "Not with me. Not with us." He smelled of smoke and sweat and leather and horses.

For a quiet time she was back in the barn at Brandyhill, except that her senses responded now not to broken straw, but to pine. She longed for the lantern flame of that yesterday, which had stood between them, which had drawn them close, longed for that impossible moment of ecstatic shock and knowledge which would either never come to them again or would come to them always, all their lives together. As the barn had taken on, into itself, the press and imprint and accustoming of flesh, so too the crude wagon had begun to be worn by the habit and continuing presence of the flesh which it sheltered; so too the wagon, for all its crudeness, had begun to give and form and mold itself to accept and assimilate the presence of flesh. Yet, if the woman was defenseless against the alarming quiet power of this man, she was also fearless, a vessel of deliverance, an instrument of infinite capacity.

Around and above her, there was a thin hard intrusion of starlight. Formed and formless, the essence of her being swelled within her and ascended, in some first-found revelation and interpretation of itself. She was at last heroic, significant upon the earth.

23

IN THE MORNING, as last night's starlight had portended, stilly, clearly, the sun shone. The wind was silent. She washed in a roily little pool, in a thicket. She could not see her own reflection in it; she longed for a mirroring of shining water to see herself, a scrap of mirror: to see if these are still my eyes, if this is still my mouth, for I have forgotten how I look. . . .

When she came up through the trees, whistling for the hound, she saw that Charles McDowell and two of his Rangers stood near the thicket and was no longer grateful for protection. She feared only the steadiness of her own voice this morning, shrank from contact with any world outside herself. But she was easy when she spoke, and poised. "Good morning, Charles, it looks like a fine day."

He bowed, watching her with those direct frosty blue eyes and his face like something hewed out of a cliff. He always looked so furious; she began to know a kinder man never lived. "You're to go down to the general's wagon this morning I'm told." Now he half smiled. "God that's a fine fat hound you've got there."

"Touch him and I'll have you court-martialed," she told him, seeing all the while he was drawing something out of his deerskin shirt, a little package wrapped in moss. "Don't give him this till you're down in camp," he said.

She took the package. "What is it?"

"A possum's backbone," he said.

She looked at him. "Thank you, Charles," she said softly, and set off down the line of wagons with him, the hound jumping and sniffing at the package in her hand.

The wagons seemed detached from the line of march, as if they had rolled ahead of the army, during the night. The groves of trees stood all about, branches bare but beginning to swell with hard-shelled buds. The wagons were drawn in a semicircle off the road, in a cleared area; little knots of men stood around them. In the groves, now and then, she caught a glimpse of dun-colored deerskin, a shattering visual blast of vivid crimson, as the scouts and cavalrymen came and went. The men around the wagons were ragged and unkempt, bearded, greasy, clothed in butternut and linen and wool and remnants of British uniforms.

There were several men around the fire. Morgan half sat, half lay on a pile of skins; his face was white and puffy, eyes black with pain. With him were his aide, Major Edward Giles, Colonel John Eager Howard of the Maryland line, and Savage. But she did not know the two men with them, one hunched forward on a low three-legged stool, the other standing at his side; she only knew that they looked incredibly clean and fresh-uniformed, the seated officer in full Continentals, the man with him in a white uniform she had never seen before. When she came to the fire the man on the stool rose and stood waiting and McDowell said, "General Greene, Madame Savage."

She curtsied, surprised and thankful that he was there so soon. Battle took advantage of her bowed position, snatched the package out of her hand and made off with it. When she straightened the general was standing before her, bowing a little, and smiling. He had a frank open face, ruddy in coloring, and pale blue eyes, and a sharp Yankee nose and light brown hair drawn back in a queue. His shoulders were big and a little rounded, and his paunch protruded in the tight buff breeches. His voice was flat and clipped and naturally hard, without any of the southern softness and slowness she knew, and was odd in her hearing.

"I am happy to make your acquaintance, madame. May I present you to Colonel Lee."

The man in the white uniform bowed. His face was round and shrewd, and he had thick, curly blond hair. "Madame," he said, smiling.

At the fire, a scout in the buckskin of Morgan's Riflars tended a pan of corncake. Giles came out of the wagon in which Morgan rode and set up a camp stool for her. She sat looking at the sun and the blue sky and the fine groves of trees and knew that this would be the morning of leave-taking. Her eyes were full of secret fire, she avoided Savage's eyes.

She ate hungrily, but listened. Once, looking at Morgan, she saw that he did not eat, but drank deeply from a copper cup, refilled it, drank again. His body was swollen and still somehow gaunt, he spoke only briefly. But the men spoke, Savage and McDowell and Howard and Nathanael Greene and the white-uniformed Light-Horse Harry Lee. They were preparing to send Morgan ahead, into Martinsville and the county seat, at Guilford, and Madame Savage must go too, of course (this from Greene, with a pleasant sidewise glance at her). But she saw that while the men talked, Greene's face fell into moroseness; he stuck out his underlip and pulled at it with thumb and index finger; he snuffed a great deal as though he suffered a cold.

Battle came back greasy-chopped, and lay by her side. When a little lull in the conversation came she said, "Is it out of place for me to ask what will happen when we reach Martinsville, General?"

Greene did not lose his morose attitude. He looked at her thoughtfully. "If I knew, madame, I'd tell you. Or perhaps I wouldn't, you've seen enough."

She laughed, and Harry Lee laughed with her. Lee said, "Were I in Nathanael's place, madame, only the fact that your husband is an old friend of Nathanael's old friend would save him from a firing squad."

Did they know? Did these rebels, these patriots, these gentlemanly, pleasant, competent men know I am the only daughter of a Loyalist household, seed of a King's man, and if they know, does it matter . . . her own voice, in the kitchen of Brandyhill, came back to her, hot with the passion of right as she told Jewel: They've only an army of shopkeepers and things. . . . She looked down at the ground, as if she had spoken those words directly, hotly, to Nathanael Greene, to Light-Horse Harry Lee. "I beg forgiveness," she said in a low voice, "for all the trouble I have put you to."

"Forbear, madame," Greene said. He was not awkward, but neither was he at ease in the giving of his little compliment. "The apologies must be ours. Had we known you were here we would have come sooner." He smiled absently; then his face fell back into its accustomed sobriety. "I am grieved that you will now be forced to go entirely upon horseback, and without the shelter of the wagon, poor vehicle that it is."

"Oh?" She looked at him questioningly, smoothing the red-and-white-striped material of her skirt with calm fingers. "Can the wagons no longer keep up with us, then?"

The men laughed. Savage looked up at her and felt a full and sudden rushing of pride in her ease, her interest. Light-Horse Harry Lee said, "You're outguessed, Nathanael. Or do you try little tactical problems for us, madame?"

Greene did not lose his morose look, but nothing of sullenness or displeasure showed on his broad frank face. "The British burn their wagons so that there will be no drag upon them. We do the same. And you, my dear, must ride with General Morgan's escort into Martinsville."

"But won't the British come to Martinsville too?" she said.

Greene said, "Here we are not ready for them."

A rickety chaise came down the road, drawn by two thin horses. A man in buckskin rode the off horse bareback. And this chaise, she knew, was not for herself, but for the pain-racked Morgan who slumped so patiently on the bearskins by the fire. Almost immediately the odor of smoke came thickly on the air, and it was no longer the smoke of the burned-out breakfast fire, but a choking smoke redolent of wet wood and iron and chaff. Men scurried and backed away in the road as the yellow flame ate at old rotten cloth and pine, slowed at the wet wood, took hold again, and poured the smoke blackly into the sunny morning.

The group at the breakfast fire was silent, watching. In their attitudes, standing, leaning, cup in hand, eye turned on the same singular immediate object of attention, there was an air of sacrifice without joy, sacrifice with a sadness to which they could devote no real hour of time, no real depth of themselves. There had been only a few wagons, Sabrina realized now: the British prisoners and arms captured a state away had been sent ahead of the rebel army; the wagons had been utilized solely to draw forage for the cavalry horses and a few commissary supplies. Nothing, even, for these ragged men, who marched with what they wore upon their backs and what they could steal along the way. She saw McCracken approach his wagon with a blazing length of pine. The fire was an enemy not to be repulsed, the red breath of destruction. She felt her face pull awry. There goes my home. There goes my marriage bed.

Nathanael Greene rose from his stool. She looked up at him with vision, with intuition, saw him now as the tight-knit nucleus of the country's instigators to rebellion must see him: hope of a cause, core of a future. What he did, where he went, whom he knew, how he conducted himself concerned her personally, for she was a component of that future. Like her father, he might lay out the path of her life for her now, simply by being there, simply by standing before her, surrounded by Morgan's tattered army. Whatever he did with this army, wherever he took it, she would be affected. And she found time to remember that he was more than a courteous capable soldier; he was a man, with a family and a home somewhere, with a life as private and intimate as her own. She felt that she whirled in the chaos of a country in the making, of time subdued for a timeless moment, felt that for the first time. She did not even wish for, in this taciturn big-shouldered Yankee, some outward visible sign of noisy, shouting, gregarious masculine strength, some brute earthy flashing color which demanded and inspired and lengthened and quickened the strength of other men. She could see simply by looking at him, at the morose open ruddy countenance, that he was himself and would never pretend to be any other man, any other type of soldier. Nothing of color or swift overt brilliance lay here: here was persistence, plodding perhaps a little heavy-footed across the red southern fields under the winter-turning-spring sky. Here were firmness, determination, patience, constancy; here was resolution.

She said, "I shall see you again, sir," and she believed it.

He shook the heavy head sadly. "I trust in happier circumstances, madame."

Light-Horse Harry Lee bent over her hand, raised it gallantly to his lips. When Greene took her hand he shook it gravely, as if she were a man. It pleased her.

Sidesaddle on the colt, the contents of Esmeralda Sevier's trunk rolled behind her in a blanket, she rode out of the grove on the wake of a small unit of men from Colonel John Howard's Maryland troops, from Morgan's Riflars, from McDowell's Rangers. Ahead, Morgan's big bulk was doubled in the old chaise. Down the Salisbury Road lay a mythical place called Martinsville, where there was a courthouse, where there was sanctuary. Or was it all lie, was it all legend?

She left the army, left a primitive existence she had never known before and would never know again, and was sorry to leave it. She was lost in herself, in the still daylight in which hooves sounded and men hurried: (The poor rough men rush upon this road and my marriage bed burns in the morning and I shall never see one charred plank of it again, and the pine boughs upon which we slept cried out when the flame took them and the yellow sap boiled in the branches and the sweet smell of it came to us thickly in the smoke. We leave legions to follow us down this road, or perhaps only remnants of legions. Are there legions ahead, men who wait for the legions which follow us, or are they too the same weary remnants, all cut from the same pattern, all cast in the same mold? Where are the splendid rushing dragoons of William Washington, blurring through the woods in their crimson and white; where ride the white-uniformed battle-hardened veterans of Light-Horse Harry Lee, leather-and-steel helmets black and silver in the southern light; where walk soundlessly the scouts in their worn-soft buckskin and moccasins, the men of the Maryland farms and towns, the green Carolina hills, the blue and golden Virginia that I shall know and call home; where is the glittering red line of the long-faced English-man, Cornwallis; where is what remains of Tarleton's green-coated cavalry; does the pale-eyed Balforth Waite stand prisoner at Salisbury or does he lie among the stumps, under my brother's gelding, on that field they called the Cowpens?)

She moved in sunlight, between two armies.

24

WAITING FOR the unidentifiable, watching for the unknown, Brant did not leave Brandyhill that winter, but searched for sign, and knew that sign, however vague, however preposterous, be it only a shooting star, he would use it to his purpose. And on a mild February day with no sun, no frost, and the sky low and leaden, Keoweh came to the farm with his sister Nadaminshik and her husband, Four Bears.

Brant watched them come into the yard, not from the road, but out of the foothills behind the barn, Keoweh carrying a rifle in the crook of his arm, the girl with a bundle upon her back, Four Bears armed with an old musket and a long knife. The girl wore yellowed doeskin, heavily fringed, both men wore woolen shirts and buckskin leggings. Keoweh spoke some English, badly, and out of respect for Alwyn he spoke it, but once Alwyn had gone to talk to Jewel concerning the midday meal, he lapsed into his own Catawba.

It had been a long time but Brant had not forgotten: the soft hissed s's of the Athapascan tongue came easily to his mouth, spoken as though through saliva; inflection of head, turn of eye, gesture of hand, the eloquent language which is not of the mouth, flooded back upon him. And the language in itself was not difficult; it was the ritual and formality of conversation through which he knew he would fumble and grope.

"You have not been with us in some seasons," Keoweh said. He was short but not stocky, a little round-shouldered, with soft direct eyes and flaring nostrils. His lower lip was thin and protruded. He was near Brant's age.

Brant shook his head slowly, once, in a negative motion. "A lot's happened to us since then, Keoweh."

The girl swung her bundle, rolled in skins, to the ground. Involuntarily Brant's eyes went over her. Nothing was left of the virgin child, the first woman he had ever taken, who had waited for him so long ago in the bay under the willows, who had shared his lodge in the long autumn nights upon the Broad River: she had grown heavy in both body and face, and her eyes were full of sadness that she had not yet borne Four Bears a son. If anything stirred in her at this meeting it was not apparent. Nor did any antique memory show upon Four Bears' square honest face, in the chunky, broad-shouldered set of his body. Nothing of the fierce pride, the brilliant hostility of the Cherokee was in these people; nothing of Dawn Star shone upon this girl's face.

Reading Brant's eyes, Keoweh said, "We will not enter yet." His voice was low and humorous. "Your black-skinned woman is no longer conscious of our red skins, but she knows we are curious as the lynx concerning her." He inclined his head toward his brother-in-law. "It will be Four Bears' first meeting with her, and he will disgrace himself." Four Bears' face did not change, but there was laughter, flicking-quick, in his eyes. Brant said gently, "How go all things with you, Nadaminshik?"

The girl had moved some paces behind her husband, not forgetting her position in the white man's lodge. Still, she was grateful. "Well, Brant. But we have missed you in our camps. Keoweh would see why you have not come."

He looked at Keoweh. "Like I said, there's been so much happened. . . ."

Keoweh shrugged. "Much has happened since you aimed truly at Jared Millikin's head, my brother. At this moment much happens. See, your father, who knew my father, beckons us."

As they turned to the house Brant admitted with reluctance the flow of single reminiscence: he had not thought of Jared Millikin, the bounty hunter, since the night before Sabrina left. But he thought of him now: thought of the inn at Hardington and Keoweh stoic as a wooden post under the white man's insult; thought of himself pressured at last out of his senses, until he had succumbed to the extreme of silencing Millikin forever. What was the use, in

256

remembering? Now the present was important, and perhaps the future. He was gladder to see Keoweh than he had been in many weeks.

The Catawbas ate with their hands, seated at the pine table in the kitchen, not speaking while they ate. There was plenty of venison, and weary of the jerked meat they carried, the Indians ate greedily of the fresh-cooked flanks and legs, devoured quantities of salt, licked the molasses from their fingers. Contemptuous, Jewel ate with glance averted, but once the meal was finished she stared around the table as if proud of their eyes upon her.

Alwyn rose first. "There are pipes for you if you would smoke," he said. "You will stay the night of course. Four Bears, would you see my land and my barn? Perhaps your wife would help Jewel and prepare your belongings in my daughter's room."

Four Bears grunted assent. With his mind set upon the exploration and acquiring of new land, westward, he felt deep interest in the acquired land of other men. With one of Alwyn's pipes in his mouth he left with Alwyn. Keoweh and Brant waited until Nadaminshik and Jewel had finished with the dishes and left the room. Then Brant said, "You want a drink, Keoweh?"

Keoweh shook his head. "I have seen drink and tasted drink. Man says many things he believes to be truth when he drinks, but it is not truth, only old grievances which emerge. What we say to one another shall be truth."

"You ain't goin' to winter grounds," Brant said.

"The winter is mild, there is much rain. The tribe has gone South. Four Bears and Nadaminshik and I went West in the hunter's moon. Many white men go West now."

"You find that bad?" Brant said.

"How find it you, Brant?"

"Bad," Brant said without hesitation. "But it's got to come, Keoweh. It's goin' to come harder, more steady now. Will you go West to stay?"

"Yes," Keoweh said, "but we go to trouble. We die out and the plains tribes are hostile to us."

"To us also," Brant said.

"But you will not die out. My father died in the late summer." He searched for the formal words. "My father will grieve, as I do."

"I know that. I find you much changed in your own house, Brant."

"Changed how, Keoweh? I don't find you changed a hair."

"You wear trouble upon your face. Worse, you let it be seen. Listen, brother, I would not see trouble upon your face. Your young brother, your sister who shared your house are not here."

For a time Brant was silent, hands folded before him on the table. "My brother is dead. My sister has wed and gone."

Keoweh said after a while, "The young go quickly and without delay to the final peace. Be assured, brother, there are many horses and fine lodges where he is, and no garden to sweat in. Your sister has traveled a great distance."

"She writes us from a colony away. She has gone with the army we oppose." He looked up at Keoweh. "Once I thought I ought to go too, either to the same army, or to the woods. I find I can't do it."

"Does your father hold you here," Keoweh said, "as my father held Nadaminshik and me to the clan?"

"I don't know. Do you find my father changed too?"

"At work in his mind, perhaps, but in face and body, no. This is a peculiar thing, for your father carries not only his own troubles, but the troubles of all men. Therefore I looked for change in him. But not in you. This is a good man your sister has taken?"

"The man I would have seen her take," Brant said.

"As I would see Nadaminshik in Four Bears' lodge. Then you should not mourn."

Brant stood up abruptly, one hand clenched upon the table. "I don't know what to do."

"Come West with us. I am certain nothing of feeling for you remains in Nadaminshik's heart, but she would be glad of your presence, as would Four Bears. And confident. Come West with us."

"I can't," Brant said. He did not look at Keoweh.

"Then something which is not father nor brother nor sister holds you here."

Brant did not answer. Keoweh said softly, "For a long time you came into our camps and were welcome. My father gave you my sister for your comfort and pleasure. You were taken into our clan because you understood us and did not know fear and accepted our ways, and you received with dignity our admiration for you. Have you grown away from us?"

Brant said, "I feel closer to you sometimes than to my own people."

"Then come with us. There is no trouble where we go but the honest trouble of the white man coming West. We may lose in the end, but the struggle occupies one's heart and hands." Keoweh reached across the table, picked up one of Alwyn's pipes, tamped tobacco into it from the tobacco bowl and held out a taper to Brant. While Brant lighted the taper at the fireplace, Keoweh said, "My father left me nothing but his wisdom, Brant. My father was a wise man, as is yours. When he died he told me that he had commended the wisdom of his soul into my keeping. I purified myself and fasted, and on the fifth day of my fast I lay upon a ledge upon my belly, and just at sunset I felt my father's wisdom enter my body."

Brant said dryly, "My father's wisdom won't ever enter me, no matter how many times he bequeaths it."

"There is something you feel which I cannot feel," Keoweh said.

"There is something I can't understand, Keoweh."

The young Catawba sat quietly for a time, smoking. Then he said, "What we strive to understand and cannot understand is part of some great plan for us. Much that I do not understand I accept, for acceptance, while not understanding, nonetheless comforts a man. You told me long ago, brother, just as you told my father, that you were at peace with us."

Brant said without impatience, "I'd like to go with you and Four Bears. I'd like, out of loyalty to my father, to go with the English Army. I'd like, out of love for my sister and respect for the man she's married, to go with the enemy army. I'd like, out of what's been bred in me, to stay upon my land. I'd like, out of a myth which was told me, to live out my life waiting for a woman who would probably warm my bed no better than your sister's done. I'd like to die tomorrow and I'd like to live forever."

Keoweh smiled faintly. "Then would you take my father's wisdom, which is now in me?"

Brant turned, violently. "Keoweh, if you could solve the things I can't for me, I would open both our veins and take in your blood."

"My blood was in you generations before you were born," Keoweh said, "just as it was in me. Listen, Brant, I speak of myself, but I speak of you. While I stayed with my people my father was well satisfied, as is your father. When I would have gone West, into an alien hostile country, my father was dissatisfied. While I stayed within my own lodge I longed for other newer things, and my father knew my unhappiness. When I walked under the very limb where the cat I stalked waited for me, I welcomed the thought of death springing cleanly upon my back. While I watched the sun rise in the eastern sky I prayed my fleshly form might never leave this land." He took the bowl of the pipe in both hands and looked at it; looked up; saw Brant's dark, tormented face. "Wait, brother. And if you find yourself waiting for this woman even in that happy place which is beyond mortal travail, wait there too."

In the silence they could hear the clock ticking in the family room. The grayness of the late afternoon daylight pressed into the kitchen. Keoweh said, "I would have you know you are welcome with us, but I desire you wait."

Brant drew a long breath. "All right," he said. "All right." The wisdom of Keoweh's father lay in Keoweh's soft black eyes.

"Four Bears comes with your father," Keoweh said steadily. "You will this night tell us everything of your past away from us, for at dawn we will go West."

They sat looking at one another. Keoweh's face was not without expression: he half smiled, calmly. Some new release lay in Brant's eyes; his face had relaxed and was as young as Keoweh remembered it. Almost Keoweh knew his thoughts, for their thoughts were parallel: but for some ancient turning of furrow, some distant-past sowing of seed, some long-gone hour of man's intent upon the body of woman, over which we had no conscious control, we would have been brothers of the same blood. And they knew they would never see one another again.

That night Keoweh slept soundly, having known fully and initially his inheritance. That night Brant slept deeply and without dream, having seen sign, having read it to his own interest and intent.

25

IN HER DREAM she was in the deep woods along the stream, beyond Brandyhill.

Coins of light dropped on the moss between the trees, rolled among the fallen leaves. It was green summer; the forest was a pure and shining palace, a dark cool palace with corridors which ran beneath the sky of trees, shutting out the summer heaven; the hollow where she sat was sheltered with the uncurling fronds of fern and the perfect rosy mouths of the lady-slipper spoke to her and the stream ran cold as death and sometimes wings glinted scarlet and brown down the dark corridors, along the layered shelves of rock overhung with white cataracts of blossom, and water slipped on the ledge of stone and shattered in the pool below. Light sifted, sometimes, like a showering of golden petals; light filtered, sometimes, and faded into the tomb of the woods. There was the crystal falling of water. Then the trees drew toward her, rustling, and a wind sprang up. There was a monstrous explosive sound and the scarlet wings were gone and all the blossoms fell and the water flowed away, leaving the smooth white, rounded stones of its bed exposed.

The act of opening her eyes was startling enough in itself, for she had believed herself already awake; looking into Savage's face, which seemed to hang, floating, over her, was even more startling, for he had had no place in dream. Little by little, she knew him, knew herself, found that she lay upon the ground, half upon her side, with her knees bent. Gradually pain came to her, insistent and steady, and with its coming she could not lie quietly, but began to twist and turn, even to attempt the gargantuan task of rising. Sound which she conceived as words died in her mouth, issued instead as a low broken moaning. The beauty and terror of the dream was still too real, too bright, so that she could not bridge the time between it and now. She fought the enfolding black cocoon of that lost time and at last freed herself.

"What's the matter, Orne?"

Hearing the thick drugged voice he slid an arm under her, half lifted her. "It's all right, Brina, don't talk now." But she shook her head, dumbly demanding. He said, "The ground was soft, and the colt sank, just his front feet. You went off him like a shot."

She tried to remember; she felt again the unexpected surge and projection of her body into space and sunlight as the bog cut away the colt's slim legs, just above the fetlock. "Did I break anything?" she whispered.

"You'll be all right," he said. Then he said quietly, "The colt broke both legs clean, Brina."

She bit her lip hard. She had heard the shot in her dream, the explosion which shattered the flowers and dried the stream. Poor colt. Poor golden colt, symbol of so much past, so much ahead, talisman, memorial, seal set upon the lost days, monument to the days ahead, epitaphic. She closed her eyes again, searching for the beautiful nostalgic reality of the dream, fighting to recapture it, holding back tears. But he shook her almost roughtly. "You're only bruised, Brina. We can't stop. You've got to get up. Listen, Brina, if you don't get up you're going to be so damned stiff. . . ."

She rolled away from him and before he could divine her purpose, got to her feet. For a moment she swayed. Movement and effort brought the pain up in her now. But she faced him calmly, already building a wall of strength in herself. "Can your horse carry double or will you walk?" she said.

Savage said very softly, "He'll carry."

She walked to the horse; she stood waiting. She did not look at the thin dead bulk of the colt, in the bog. Savage came and pulled his horse around and mounted and reached down for her. She put her foot upon his instep and swung herself before him, on the saddle. She felt his arm close around her, saying what he could not say, and then she let herself cry, achingly, bitterly, silently, not for her own pain, not for the little death in the bog, but for the futility of the act of the child, who had gone to save the colt.

Savage left her, left the road, at noon. The house lay a half mile in, hidden from the road by thick bare woods which sloped raggedly up a hill. It was a good substantial house, built of brick, with a leafless vine crawling over it, but it was falling into decay. Yard and gardens were a rough tangle, choked with brown grass and the skeletons of weeds. Wealth had lived here; now maybe wealth was gone, or didn't care any more.

He wasn't certain the house would be here, except he had seen what he looked for along the road: horse dung, leading up through a cleared place in the second growth. When he ran out of horse dung he kept walking, and there was the house. He waited for a while, in the woods, but saw no sign of life. He left the woods with caution but casually, letting his eyes be everywhere at once. A big oafish-looking dog came out from under the rotting verandah, looked at him, ran forward as if it had known him all its life and now welcomed him back from some far place.

The barn door yawned blackly open. He started for it and was halfway around the house when the voice said, "You take one more step and I'll kill you dead."

He turned and came back into the yard. The man was somewhere around Alwyn's age but not as big and vigorous as Alwyn, and he had a pistol in his hand. Savage thought one man with a pistol was better than several men with pistols, or slaves with clubs.

"Whatchu want?" the man said, face cloudy with rage.

"I just want a horse," Savage said.

"You ain't gittin' my horses."

"I don't want your horses. I just want one horse."

"Let's see the backa yore head. Move off," the man said.

Savage took one step forward.

"I'll kill you," the man said. "Nobody's gittin' any my horses."

Savage waited. The sweat came in a salty rush, starting out at hairline, armpit, palm. What set off the trigger: one small move on his part, fatigue at the argument, caprice of the man. While he sweated, waiting, a girl came out on the verandah and looked down at them. She was shapeless in an old wrapper, with a magnificent wild face and unbound dark hair. Savage's glance flickered over her briefly and came back to the man, held the man.

"Whyn't yuh give 'im a horse he wants a horse?" the girl called down.

"I wouldn't give 'im the sweat off my brow." Now the man made a derisive mouth. "Git, rebel."

Savage said, "The British will be through in a day or two. Their scouts or their flankers will find your house, maybe, and burn it, and take your horses anyway. I need one of those horses."

"I'll give yuh five counts to git," the man said.

"Oh dear Lordie God," the girl called, not in desperation, but wearily apathetic, almost bored. "Give 'im a horse, Bob."

"You mind your tongue, lady, you hear." He looked up at her.

Savage came in under the pointed pistol, landing with all his force on the side of the anger-thickened neck. The man dropped hard, dead weight sprawling in the tangle and choke of his garden, under the verandah. The dog ran over and began to play about the prostrate form, whining and licking at the face. Savage dug out the pistol which had fallen near the steps and imbedded itself in the leaves in the force of its fall.

"God's sweet land," the girl said. "You ain't killed 'im, have you, mister?"

"Not yet," Savage said. He looked up at her wild shapeless form. "I'll leave the pistol in the barn, in case you need it. And thanks."

"What you thankin' me for?" the girl said. She made no move to revive the fallen man, whether father or husband. She still called after Savage as he made his way around the house again. "Is that true the British is comin'? Say, mister, is that true?"

In the gloom of the barn there were two mules and several horses. Most of them were work horses, with sagging backs and great bellies. He ran his hand over the rump of a middling sized red horse with an almost white mane. It looked in pretty good shape, like it had been ridden rather than worked. He backed it out and pulled a saddle and blanket down off a peg and saddled the red. When he rode back around the house and out of the yard the man still lay in the grass and the dog lay by him and the woman was gone.

Back on the road, he kicked the red into running. It had taken an hour, and it would be an hour's hard riding to rejoin the little unit bound for Martinsville. But the horse was good, he knew he could run the horse hard.

He thought about the house he had just left: it had been something like his own house, brick and vine, although his own house was white and set in groves and in sight of the river, with a pond by it and ducks on the pond and his boys running ponies over the flat fields by the river. He felt a longing which was almost sickness, almost nausea. And with God's luck, now, there would be a woman, a child fourteen years his junior, but a woman. . . .

He pulled the red in so suddenly that it stood up panicky, on its hind legs. Sabrina came down off a lip of hill and fell in with him. She looked shaky but her eyes were tranquil.

"You endanger Morgan, yourself, and me by holding back," he told her.

"I only waited for you."

"But you're sick, Brina, you look sick. Why didn't you tell Colonel Howard or Major Giles, so they could keep an eye on you?"

She looked at him. "You don't think I'd tell them I fell off a horse, do you?" she said proudly.

Turning in beside her, he shook his head, half in astonishment, half in amused disgust. But he knew that it went, with her, far beyond so simple and small and understandable a thing as pride. And he was glad she had waited.

They were last to ride into Martinsville. Coming into the little hamlet on the Salisbury Road, they rode over a broken vale, a true ravine, and along cleared fields and forests of lofty oak. The ground rolled and dipped softly, but it sloped definitely, gently upward as it approached Guilford Court House. She liked, with an immediacy bred into her from a lifetime in Benton's Crossing, the people who offered their food and clothing and firewood, who opened their homes and gave their fields for bivouac.

The two-story house into which they moved belonged to a childless middle-aged couple named Hugh. The room was small and pleasant, and from its window she could see, a half mile or so away, the big stone rectangular bulk of the courthouse. While she stood, looking at it, feeling in some vague, intuitive vein that this building, solid and inanimate, was to bear upon her life with direct purpose, the doctor whom Savage had insisted she see grumbled his way up the stairs and came into the room, not disposed even to smile at her, but surrounded by some effluence of hideous concentration upon the matter at hand, faintly unpleasant, decisively unfriendly.

He was almost elderly. He was attached to Huger's troops and had been with the army nearly six years. Pummeling, pinching, probing, bending joints up and down, he lashed her with his impatience and ill humor. "Shouldn't let women near horses. Always maintained that. Never learn to handle either the horse or themselves properly. Never . . . there, that hurt, did it . . . ? Well, it's not broken, but why it isn't I can't imagine. Stay away from horses, young woman, my time's valuable."

Savage stood at the window; she saw the anger in his eyes. But she almost wanted to laugh at the irritable old man. He straightened, looking at her with disdain and superiority. "I'll leave some liniment for those bruises. I suppose you'd like to be bled, leeched, and plied with brandy, but there's nothing wrong with you and I've got my professional conscience to live with."

Savage took a step forward. But he saw Sabrina's mouth quivering with laughter, and when the doctor spoke to him the voice had lost something of its hardness and cynicism if not its brusqueness. "There's nothing I can do here, Major. I don't suppose you've got any hard money."

"No," Savage said. "I could give you a promissory note."

"Keep it. Congress has been paying me in paper money for three years now, and they might as well be paying me in air. Sick of it, sick of it all. I've seen more arms and legs and brains and guts in the last six years than most doctors see in a lifetime. Sick of it, sick of the army." He stood, a little wizened, a little crazy, eyes burning with near-fanaticism. "But I tell you something, Major, I tell you something, sick of it as I am, I'm going on. Till I fall down of old age, I'm going on. I'm going to patch you all up and get you out on that field again until you beat these filthy English, and if you come back I'll patch you up and put you out again, and if I can hold out long enough you'll whip the damned dogs yet, every last one of them, and drive the bloody hounds out. I'll keep right on getting paid in air, as long as I have to, and I'll keep right on feeding you poor damned rebels into the cannons as long as I can. You can depend on it."

He marched out, slamming the door behind him.

"Well," Sabrina said. "I see there are rebels and rebels."

"People and people," Savage said. "Unfortunately, we seem to need his ilk too. I'm sorry he was so damned beastly."

"Don't be sorry, you couldn't help it, and I'm sure *he* couldn't. He looked like a superannuated pickle." She laughed without restraint now. "Thank heaven there was nothing wrong . . . think of having to be treated by him. Why, he'd be feeding *me* into the cannons in no time, I'm sure."

He came and sat on the edge of her chair, leaning across her, bracing himself on the other arm. "Look, you stay in bed for a day or so anyway, will you?"

"It makes me restless to think about it. Tell me I must and I shall. But I should like to go . . . up there." Her hand moved toward the window in a gesture he could not interpret. "Up there," she said again. "I should like to see that building, the courthouse."

"All right," he said agreeably. "In time."

After a moment she said seriously, "Time. Time. How much time, Orne? How much time for what? Time becomes almost a physical entity, doesn't it? One day I hear it spoken of as if it were nonexistent, the next as if it were endless."

"Don't be cryptic," he told her. But he knew what she meant. He looked at her. "I can't answer any more questions for you. It's my turn to ask them."

"But you do know something," she said.

He was frowning a little, a cloudiness had settled on his face. "From here on in, anything I know you're going to know too, Brina, because we've got some decisions to make, you and I."

She did not answer, but sat watching him steadily, apprehensively. She was relieved when he rose and began to change his clothes, preparing to leave for an officer's council. As if his words had been chastisement, she thought, I will not ask any more, I will let him tell me, then.

She stayed quietly, restlessly in her room as Savage had wanted her to, for three days. But on the fourth day she rode the red horse up the road to the courthouse and saw the groves of oak and the cleared fields around it. It was a dark morning and threatened rain, but there was an alien warmth in the air; there was a green damp south-wind scent which might be the scent of spring coming early. Riding back into Martinsville, she observed deliberately, with great care, saw that the settlement was full of men and horses and tents, that the road already overflowed and the fields burgeoned with troops. On the march up from the South she had had no conception of the number of troops involved; now, wherever she looked, there were men: Continentals, militia, cavalry. She did not leave the house again after that; there was something terrifying about that encampment, the masses of men, the new troops constantly pouring in, their fires reflecting on the night sky; their shouting and laughter and argument was dangerous in the darkness. She, and the woman whose rooms she shared, Ellie Hugh, clung mentally and spiritually to one another, kept to the security of the little house.

March drizzled in, stinging and raw and wet, but the earth was turning over. Once the sun came out, even the air had a yellow look to it, which was water and paleness of sunlight and spreading softness. It made her think about spring and planting; she had learned that much of the trouble with the rebel army was that it was of necessity composed of men who thought a great deal about spring and planting.

She was awake when Savage came into the Hugh house near midnight. Stars misted faintly across the window; he did not light the lamp, and when he got into bed at last she sensed his reluctance, or inability, to sleep. Aware of her wakefulness he said, "Morgan can't walk any more. He's going home in the morning."

She had dreaded this. She said, "I'm not going with him."

"When did you make up your mind to that?"

"Long ago. Orne, today I saw a whole group of cavalry go down the road at a full gallop, and then there were shots, a long way off, but I heard them. What were they doing?"

"There was a skirmish. The British are camped near the New Garden Meeting House."

"Are they . . . did they attack us?"

"They're putting out skirmish parties. So are we. Feeling one another out."

"I've broken a vow to myself not to ask," she said. "Are you going to attack them?"

"Greene won't risk an offensive, he's chosen his defense here."

"Orne, if you do fight here, in Martinsville, what's going to become of these people, the people who live here? Are they going to go away, to leave their homes and a good share of their lives behind them? What about the women, what will happen to them, and the children?"

"Martinsville is to be evacuated," he said.

"What a temporary-sounding word. It implies that no matter what happens here they will come back, rebuild if they have to, take up where they left off. I will stay with the Hughs. I'll go with Ellie."

He raised himself on one elbow. "Why do you add to my responsibilities, Brina?"

She put up her hand and touched his face. "If I went away you would feel less responsible, perhaps, but you would also feel emptier, wouldn't you?"

He held her hand against his face; he did not answer.

"What is it, Orne? Was that ugly little doctor indicative of something? Did he mirror these people in this town somehow? Is it that perhaps they do not want us, like us, here?"

268

"Yes," he said.

"But they are your own people. You came here to make a stand, to . . . to free them."

"Reasoning principle in the face of fact is rather futile. Did you like your Captain Galton, or this man Waite? Waite, by the way, was killed at Cowpens I hear. But he was your people, in Benton's Crossing, in Brandyhill, ostensibly to keep you free."

"Oh, the parallel is too wide," she said hopelessly, staring into the darkness.

"The basic tenets are identical and exact. We are the same. I tried to tell you that, that morning in the barn. We will not turn out country gentlemen, guests, in these people's homes. We will confiscate, loot, take what we want, entertain ourselves with their women. No, they do not like us here or want us here."

"I am going to stay whether or not they like me or want me," she said, stubborn now. Then she said in a low voice, "What will you do, Orne?"

"We're going to fight, no question about it now, we can't run any further. Greene's played a clever game, gained us the time we needed. We've crossed rivers, waited till the British crossed behind us, recrossed, crossed, recrossed, were lucky enough to hit the rains right, so the rivers swelled and the British couldn't cross behind us. Time again, you see, time. We've been marching in circles, sending out Washington and Lee to hit Cornwallis' advance, taken every twist, turn, circle, devious route, and crossroad we could find. That's how precious time was, is, to us. And we've drawn Cornwallis further and further from any source of supply and reinforcement. I suppose too by sending out the cavalry in these delaying actions we've succeeded in giving the British the impression our numbers are far greater than they are."

"It seems to me there are at least a million men outside," she said.

"I wish there were, God, how I wish there were. The muster shows a hair over four thousand. Huger's in now with Greene's army, and Otho Williams has taken over Morgan's troops. Virginia and North Carolina militia just got in. We've even got a little Frenchman with a magnificent mustache and forty picked American horsemen."

"Then we have more men than Cornwallis, haven't we?"

"Yes. But unfortunately we're now largely militia and he's largely seasoned infantry. Mere weight of numbers doesn't mean much."

She said, "It has been rather frightening, all these troops and horses and guns going off in the distance and the cavalry pounding down the road like that. Everything seems so tense and frantic."

"We all are," he said. "All but Greene. What a tower of calm. Phlegmatic on the surface. That's another thing these mountain men have to reconcile to. They're used to Morgan's breed, shouting and cursing and forcing. Now all of a sudden there's Greene, just standing, just *being*, with that quizzical look on his face. Obviously not the soldier's soldier. Obviously the soldier's commander."

"He begins to remind me of Goliath," she said.

"And look at all the Davids getting up with their rocks. They've all had damned bad aim, though, thank God."

"I suppose," she said, "that he will one day be a truly great man."

"He's that now. More than that, he's a great soldier. And the strange thing is that he's not a politician and not army breed in any sense. I keep feeling that somewhere inside he's still the Rhode Island anchorsmith he was trained to be. And maybe the temperate Quaker too."

"Quaker. But I thought they could not bear arms."

"They can't. He sacrificed his religion for this war."

She was silent. Then she said, "How very extraordinary. It makes one a little sad, doesn't it?"

Before he could answer, Ellie Hugh's voice sounded outside the door. "Major Savage. I'm terribly sorry to disturb you, Major, but they're calling for you to come right away."

He got up. He saw in his mind the thin wispy mouse-faced woman in whose house he was lodged. "Who wants me, Mistress Hugh?"

"One of Colonel McDowell's men, sir. He says to go to the colonel's right away, if you will please, sir."

"All right, tell him I'll be down in a minute." Her footsteps fluttered down the hall. He said, "You're determined to stay with this meek creature then?"

"Don't condition things," she told him. "I don't know as I'm necessarily determined. I'm just going to." She lay propped on the pillows. "Do you think something's wrong, they're sending for you?"

He lit the lamp. "Something's always wrong." But he flashed her a brief smile.

When he had gone she could not, for the first time since she had come to Martinsville, sink easily and without fear into sleep. Lying awake in the darkness, with the stars wheeling across the window, she thought over and over, it is not just something wrong, some momentary crisis, whatever will happen at Guilford Court House is beginning, now, tonight.

Two days later, on the morning of the evacuation of Martinsville, she wrote her father (the fifth letter she had written since she left Brandyhill) and rolled her belongings into a blanket (this she had done many times since she left Brandyhill). Outside the house Rawleigh Hugh loaded the material possessions of his and Ellie's existence in a wagon. Sabrina came down with her blanket roll to help and found Ellie clutching to her wispy breast a huge family portrait in a gilt and cherry frame. Ellie wept.

"Ellie, you can't take that," Sabrina said.

"I can't leave it here." Her thin, gray, mouselike face was streaked with tears. "It's my grandma."

"I can't help it," Sabrina said, "you don't need it. What in the world have you got in that wagon, anyway?" She pushed the curtain back. In the yard, Rawleigh Hugh's tall bony figure teetered atop a load of chairs, china, chests. She made a despairing sound. But it was no use. The Hughs knew what was most important to them; if she had had any possessions of any kind she would have wanted to load them on too, except she knew Savage wouldn't have let her.

"Did you pack anything to eat, Ellie?"

Ellie snuffled. "Eat?"

"Is there any preserved food? To take along with us."

"In the cellar," Ellie said.

They carried pails and casks and stone jars up from the cellar. "There isn't any room," Rawleigh said, eyeglasses hanging from one ear. His bony nose twitched as if he too would weep.

"Then you've got to make room," Sabrina said firmly.

He made room. She climbed up on the wagon and Rawleigh climbed up too and took the reins. "Come on, Ellie," Sabrina called. But Ellie was standing in the open doorway of the house, looking down the hall. Rawleigh got down and took her by the arm and led her to the wagon.

Between hamlet and courthouse, beyond courthouse, the families of Martinsville moved in wagons, by horse, mule, afoot. Children clustered bewilderedly beside crates of chickens; goats and sheep, cows, dogs, cats formed a straggling, protesting portion of the march. A sheep dog ran along the edge of the road, barking sharply, herding not only his small flock, but children and other dogs. A boy carried a bright-eyed raccoon in his arms. Sometimes women wept, but they were for the most part stony-faced, holding themselves in, praying the houses would still be there when, if, they returned.

Rawleigh Hugh's wagon passed by the courthouse. Looking up at its blank walls and the expressionless eyes of its windows, Sabrina sat rigidly, hands clasped on her knees; the solidity of the building, in this moment, was awesome; its very presence spoke invincibility. Even so, she wondered if it would stand. Then the oak groves swallowed the wagon and she could no longer see the courthouse, or the settlement, though she twisted on the seat and looked behind her.

Coming upon the clearing far back in the oaks, she saw the long gray tent, with several smaller tents surrounding it. For two days now she had heard the axes ringing as the forest was cut away, but she had not asked. Now she thought Hugh might know.

"What are they doing so far behind the courthouse, Rawleigh?"

"It's a hospital tent," he told her. "Greene's set up good as he can, I reckon. He needs his men bad."

He would get them back, too, she thought, remembering the ill-tempered fanatic old doctor.

A man hailed them from the clearing where the tents stood. "You people have any rope you can spare us?"

Rawleigh pulled the wagon to the edge of the road. "We've some if I can find it, sir." Rawleigh called everybody sir these days.

Sabrina swung back over the seat. "It's right under that basket, Rawleigh, coiled up . . . I think I can reach it." She pushed the basket aside and worked the rope free. "Does he want it all, do you suppose?" she said, fumbling with the knot which held the coil, and then looked up and into Fraser Malcolm's hard black eyes.

She felt her own surprise burst warm and glowing on her face. But she had never, out of the years of knowing and the proposed surrender of herself to this man seen him look like this. The handsome dark mask which cloaked his face dissolved and disappeared as if it had been stripped away; his face was raw and naked. He seemed to falter, putting out a hand on the wagon wheel. And she thought in that moment what must be happening in his mind: of all the unlikely people in the world to be facing him squarely in the midst of the rebel army. . . . She laughed with honest pleasure and said his name. "Fraser."

His voice was very low. "Is it really you, Brina?"

"Truly." She held down her hand to him. "Is it really *you?*"

He nodded soberly. "I fear so. I fear I'm a bigger fool now than I ever was."

A wagon lumbered by them. Rawleigh twitched the reins impatiently. She said, "You and Ellie go on, Rawleigh."

Ellie was shocked. "Major Savage wouldn't like it, Sabrina, he said you were to stay with us."

But she was already out of the wagon, already reaching for the blanket roll. "Tell him, if he comes, I'm at the hospital. I'll get word to him somehow."

"You oughtn't to do it," Rawleigh said. His eyeglasses had slipped on the bridge of his nose.

"Go on," she said, "go on, I shall be safe; I'll find you later."

Together, they watched the Hughs' wagon out of sight, into the woods, watched Ellie turn several times and peer disapprovingly at them from around the load the wagon drew; together, they were grateful for the watching which gave them time to acclimate, adjust, find words. But when the wagon was swallowed at last by the trees there were still no words, no proper words.

She was halting, strained now. "I did not think to find you outside of . . . of Boston, Fraser. And hardly begging rope."

And he was disconcerted, elated, allowing himself the luxury of a small pretense. "But this is a limited country we live in, after all. And being a man of tremendous faith, in myself at least, I'd no doubt I'd find you again."

Now he reached and took her blanket roll from her, swinging it over his shoulder. His tone was no longer bantering, but heavy, disbelieving. "We'd heard there was a Loyalist woman came in with the troops."

Would she never be rid of that? Why did the identifying word, name, sound so odious, so like a stigma, on his lips. "Do they call me that, then?" she said lightly.

"The word has been used. A most incongruous situation, at least as I have heard it. The wife of an officer in Morgan's Riflars, so they said."

She watched him steadily, but with a look of old and sympathetic understanding. "That too is true."

He took a deep breath; his eyes had gone hard, expressionless, black as obsidian, as she knew them. "If I had known your preference for men of rebel politics, I should have told you much long ago."

"You never could do anything simply, Fraser," she said softly.

His mouth tightened. Then he said, "Come. You've stranded yourself here now, and I've no guarantee for you you've done the wisest thing. But I can use you."

She set off across the field, through the oaks with him. The hospital tent was very bare, with a fresh plank floor laid in it. Bundled along the walls were sheets, blankets, tablecloths, napkins, rolls of torn linen stripping, crocks and bowls of linen wadding, and cotton pellets. There was a strong smell of camphor and asafetida. She wrinkled her nose at Malcolm. "You'll get used to it," he said. "You can't keep that dog in here, take some rope and tie him outside."

Men were still felling trees around the clearing. She whistled Battle to a sapling and tied him. When she re-entered the tent Malcolm and two other men were moving a rough plank table into the center of the floor. She thought of the old doctor who had come to see her in the Hugh house; when the men had left she said, "You aren't working alone, Fraser."

"No, there's a Doctor Fenton here, an old man but capable enough."

"Yes, we've met," she said with distaste.

"And there's a British doctor, Stewart, who came in with the captured troops from Cowpens. If you want to sit down on one of those bales, you can start stripping and rolling linen." He strove for interest without personal involvement; watching him, she saw this, read the genuine effort in him, and loved him for it with the compassion and rapport which is also a plane of love. "And tell me everything," he said.

Seated on the bale, she told him the truth, thankful to keep eyes and fingers busy with linen. Nervous at first, she gained assurance quickly, and the words came easily and economically. Because of this, the honesty, the serenity, the ease of the telling, he did not

274

interrupt her, but when she looked up at last his face bore a crooked half smile she had never seen there before.

"Well," she said, after a long time, "aren't you going to say anything?"

He leaned against the rough table, bracing himself, with his arms behind him. "What is there for me to say? I've no doubt you've told me the truth. If I don't show surprise it's probably because nothing you ever did surprised me very much." He straightened, turning his face from her, looking down at the table. "How you develop, Sabrina." Then he said, "We ran out on one another, didn't we? If I were a religious man, if I were Richard Jordan, say, I would believe now that my running and your running and our meeting here again was all for a purpose."

"But you are not a religious man," she said. "Nor do I believe in such purposes as you infer. And you did not run from *me*, Fraser, you ran from everything and everybody. You ran from my father, and from other men who trusted you."

He said grimly, "My dear girl, I ran because I had a nasty suspicion hanging wasn't the pleasantest way in the world to die."

A man in worn soiled buckskin came into the tent. His hair fell from under a coonskin cap and lay upon his shoulders. He ducked his head at Sabrina, looked at Malcolm. "I'm goin' in to headquarters, Captain. You got any messages or requests to go?"

Malcolm opened a dispatch case which lay upon the table. "These are my reports. We've enough cleared area to take care of half the army, providing Cornwallis doesn't start lobbing shot into the woods."

"Please," Sabrina said, "could you leave a message for me also?" The scout looked at her with a faint smile. "I reckon as how."

"Then tell them, tell any of the officers to get word to Major Savage that his wife is at the hospital tent."

The scout ducked his head, scooped up Malcolm's reports, and was gone. Malcolm went to stand in the doorway, and after a time she followed. Only a few last wagons were on the road now, leaving Martinsville. The trees hid the tall stone rectangle of the courthouse. Two men came down a path between the trees, the old doctor, Fenton, and a younger man dressed in black and white, the Britisher, Stewart, Sabrina thought. She looked at Malcolm. Suddenly she shivered, in a violent convulsive motion. "Have we a chance, Fraser?"

Again the crooked smile. But he said, "I think we have a chance."

Late that afternoon Savage and McDowell crossed the field and entered the hospital tent. Already weary, hair disheveled, Sabrina looked up from the endless task of rolling linen and made a sound of surprise, ran across the floor. Over Savage's shoulder she caught McDowell's warning glance, which said that Savage was not pleased.

"You didn't come just because I am here," she said.

"Don't be arch, you disobeyed me, Brina."

"But I went with the Hughs." She looked down at the floor, looked up, shattered him with the candor of her glance.

"Do you feel yourself safe here?"

"Do you feel yourself safe on the field?"

"Don't beg the question."

Now she was serious, firm. "I want to do something, Orne, you can understand that. I want to help. I want to have something on my mind besides where you are and what you are doing. . . ."

He put his hand on her face, not letting her finish. They looked at one another. She moved into the bend of his arm as if she could not help herself, as if she no longer had any control over her body.

"I wondered how it was done," Malcolm said dryly. He stood in the center of the room. "You're Savage. You know my name, though we've not met." He offered his hand. "Fraser Malcolm."

Savage took his hand. "This is Colonel McDowell of McDowell's Rangers."

Malcolm nodded, turned away. "I had not expected this meeting any more than I expected to find Brina coming down the road in a wagon this morning." He went to the corner, picked up a jug. "There are some who hold, even doctors, that pouring corn whiskey into wounds is an outrageous waste. You'll join me, gentlemen."

Savage drank with him, but McDowell did not; McDowell, bursting as usual with energy and restlessness paced the floor, stared gloomily at the peak of the tent, looked out the door. Malcolm downed his whiskey in a quick draught, watching Savage. After a moment he said, "You know you don't need to worry about Sabrina, don't you? I'll get her out if I have to."

He came across the room again, suddenly, held out his hand again in an abrupt motion. "My hand on it, you know I won't let anything happen to her."

For the second time in the space of a few minutes, they shook

276

hands gravely. But Sabrina did not feel the gravity, the solemnity; laughter bubbled up out of her as from a well. "You look like two barn owls joined at the wings," she told them. "And for whose life am I accountable? Charles, come, let us swear we will let nothing happen to my Lord Cornwallis."

McDowell rewarded her with a humorless grin. "I'm in a hurry to see something does happen to the gouty old horse. You said half an hour, Orne."

"All right," Savage said. He had seen Sabrina, seen Malcolm, and was satisfied. "Walk to the road with us, Brina." The tawny eyes were level on Malcolm. "We hope to keep you at your leisure, Captain, unless you care for patching redcoats."

Malcolm shrugged. "My duty, they say, is patching men despite their politics. If you come back here don't come with any smashed bones, will you, smashed bones are hell."

Crossing the clearing between McDowell and Savage, Sabrina said, "Men are so cruel when they're smart, aren't they? Smashed bones."

"That was for you, not me," Savage said quietly.

She knew this, but thought perhaps he did not know it. She said under her breath, "Oh, Orne, be careful."

"I will," he said. "You too, Brina."

There were no more wagons in the road. One corner of the courthouse shone grayly through the lacy-yellow branching of the trees. The air was very still; it carried, from somewhere far down the road, the sound of a single drum. She stood stiffly at the edge of the clearing. "Good-by, Charles, take care." Then she said, "God keep you, Charles."

McDowell smiled briefly, but the frosty eyes did not change. He went off down the road. She watched him, not wanting to look at Savage, and found that her hands were balled into fists at her sides and that there was a terrible sick feeling in her. Her voice too sounded sick to her, and without strength. "Orne, I don't know if I can stand this."

She looked at him now. They faced one another across the greening patch of March grass. She was deathly cold, frozen, numb. His sleeves were rolled and his shirt open halfway to the waist, but he did not appear cold; he stood calmly, the rifle slung over his shoulder and one thumb through the strap. He said gently, "I don't know if I can stand it either."

"If I could go with you I could stand it."

"I too, perhaps," he said.

Then she cried, "But I want some assurance."

"We want the same things."

"No, I am selfish. Maybe I don't care about the country or the war or anything else any more. Maybe I only care about us, about you and me."

"I am the country," he said. "I am the war."

"We are the smallest things in this country, in this war."

"No," he said, now. "I am not one of those men who looks up at stars and feels humble. I told you this would not be easy, and you listened but did not believe. Keep your courage, Brina. You are not alone."

"I am always alone," she said steadily, "if you are not with me."

"I will be with you," he said. "I will be with you the rest of my life. Because I intend to reap something, some harvest out of this, I intend to go home. I want my sons and my land and my horses and my house. I want to know that I can carry my own life in my own hands, go West, go North, lie under my own trees in summer, sit by my own fire in the winter, be answerable only to myself and to what we make of our future together. I'm going to have that, Brina."

"If that is your assurance, then it is mine," she said. But the sickness was still in her. When she moved to him, pressing close, as if she would imprint his physical being upon her own, for all time, the cold upward slanting barrel of the rifle touched her hand.

She turned back to the hospital. She did not watch him down the road.

26

TWICE THE ROBBER JAY FLASHED blue and bright down from the lower branches of the pine, searching the ground, flashing back to the tree again. On the third attempt it screamed alarm and flared away. Savage stuck his head up out of the depression and rolled on his side. Deceiving a jay twice was better than not deceiving him at all.

"He didn't see you," McDowell said. "My powder pan swung over; he must've seen the flash."

They lay some distance apart in a hollow in the leaves, watching the road. Cool, milky, late-afternoon sunshine and windy sky rode over them. "Colonel Campbell know where you are?" Savage said lightly.

McDowell grunted.

"I heard him," Savage said. "Talking to Greene. Time the officers stopped lying under trees and going off on reconnaissance. That's what we have scouts for."

"Any time Campbell's riflemen match mine I'll listen to him," McDowell said shortly.

The jay shrilled at them. Savage looked up at the washed-out sky, squinting. Then he said, "You looking for something out here, Charles? Or waiting?"

"Waiting," McDowell said. "Lee let me in on something this morning. Colonel Carrington's got information there's about four hundred Loyalists answering Cornwallis' appeal for volunteers. Tarleton's on his way to bring 'em in. And protect 'em, Carrington says."

"Tarleton got enough horse left to do that?"

"He's been building it up ever since we smashed his original guts out."

"Did Carrington confirm this rumor?" Savage said.

"Look, you know damn well any medals handed out for this operation Carrington ought to get 'em all. You want to know something you ask Carrington, and if he doesn't know, which isn't probable, he goes and finds out for you."

"He knows where this force is, then?"

"Lee says they've collected under somebody calling himself Colonel Pyle, up on the Haw marshes. Last Carrington knew, they were near the Alamance River. Over the border in Virginia." Now McDowell sat up; the cold, direct blue eyes were like a knife thrust. "You like to go home a bit, Orne?"

Savage said, "I'll wait on Lee."

"I reckoned as much. I told Billy to bring your red." Then he said, "Get your head down. Horses."

They were Lee's horses, thin, steady, patient, brave, moving up the road. Lee himself rode in the van, white uniform spotless, leather-and-steel helmet squarely upon his forehead, eyes almost as cold as McDowell's, but with a glint of hard humor in them. Beside him was Colonel Andrew Pickens, whose troops had crushed the British right at Cowpens. Behind them rode the whole of Lee's Light-Horse and a picked unit of infantry. Halfway down the line Lee's little bugler cantered along the side of the road, leading Savage's red and McDowell's gray gelding.

They crossed the Virginia border in the morning, looking for Tarleton. They were up in the marsh country, along the Alamance River. But the British cavalry was not there, not yet, and two men in shirt sleeves, leaning on a timber fence, said they hadn't seen any British, or Continentals either. All they knew about the war, all they knew about anything, was they'd heard there was a considerable force about two miles north of the Hillsboro–Salisbury Road fork. And they spat and examined their broken nails uneasily, and their eyes were busy, awed, terrified, on Lee's white army of horse.

They kept to the road, save for some few who splattered down the wet meadows, and they rode without talk, silent, powerful, resolute. Now one or two broke free of the unit and rode ahead, losing themselves in the thickets along the road, searching, circling, riding back, turning, racing ahead again.

In the van a hand was lifted, and the horses pulled to a walk. A cavalryman came thundering back down the road, raced up to Lee and Pickens, conferred with a noticeable maximum of gesturing and pointing. But the horses only walked now, as if with reluctance.

Around a bend in the road, where willows grew, they came face to face with the advance of the Loyalist four hundred. Still the horses walked slowly.

The Loyalists too walked, but quickly; nerve, spirit, anticipation spurring them. There was not a uniform among them: they wore the homespun, the knee breeches, the rude shirts and hats of farmers, of small-townsmen. They overflowed the road and spread out into the marshy clearings, but banded together, bunched closely, tightly, like driven sheep. They had become, overnight, within themselves, soldiers, and they walked now to meet upon this road Banastre Tarleton's dragoons.

Down that stretch of road the civilian Loyalists and the veteran cavalry surveyed one another. The time of silence was incredible. Then both groups reacted simultaneously: the faces of the mounted men went tense and sweating and hard under the leather helmets, there was a mass loosening of sabers, unfastening of holster flaps, a clanking and rustling, a preparation; at the same moment a hoarse exultant shout broke from the massed Loyalists. They flung up their arms and cheered wildly.

They mistook Lee for Tarleton.

The shouting drowned the sound of sabers loosened in scabbards. After that first sustained burst the sound wavered, became hesitant, died slowly, except where men in the rear could not see that the cavalry still sat, watching them. In the Loyalist van a tall man in a green leather vest took off his hat and began to wave it high over his head, as if to reassure the mounted men he thought were Tarleton's. His voice boomed down the road. In its hearty strength there was that same note of reassurance.

"Hold your fire, Colonel, we're Loyalists." He shouted a second time, louder, jubilantly. "We're Loyalists."

But from somewhere behind him another voice sounded, high, shrill, almost wailing in recognition: "Oh, my God, rebels, rebels, they're rebels."

The man in the green vest still stood in the van, still held his hat, frozen, above his head.

Light-Horse Harry Lee's bell-clear call rang into the river meadows like his own bugler's horn. "No quarter. No quarter. Charge."

The Light-Horse flashed forward in a great rolling motion, flowing around Lee, leaving him to bring up the rear. The horses charged into the marshy meadows, throwing wetness and mud, raced down the road. In mass panic the Loyalists had begun a vain attempt to fall back; the advance lines pushed and staggered into the lines behind them; men milled frantically, pressed desperately against the milling men in the rear, fought to seize some avenue of escape, found no escape.

Except the man in the green vest, who still stood in the road. He was the first man to die. His face, insensible, turned upward to meet the charge of horse and saber, his stupified eyes followed in its most minute detail the rising and swinging of the steel; then he was down under the ironshod hooves.

The Loyalists made a frenzied endeavor to gain the meadows.

It was a useless, terrible, almost ridiculous attempt. The cavalry pounded down the fringes of the force, flowed around it, cut off its rear, circled, closed in. Not a Loyalist gun was discharged. The dragoons bore in with uplifted sabers, rose in their stirrups, threw the whole force of their bodies behind the stroke. It had become a time of absolute and perfect slaughter to which not even a token resistance had been, or would be, offered. Upon the road, caught within the circle of plunging horses and merciless slashing steel, the civilian Loyalists pleaded, screamed for quarter, were cut to ribbons. Here, men afoot looked up to an appalling height of horse and rider, stumbled, fell, rose, raged against one another in a boiling sea of blood in which no man stood long. Some held their arms before their faces as if to protect themselves; some stood dumbly, in shock so profound they could not move, and waited for the end of it all.

The Loyalists who gained the open reaches of the meadows were shot down methodically by the handful of Pickens' infantry sharpshooters who had taken cover behind trees and hummocks in the wet fields. Minutes after the charge Savage still sat the red in the center of the road, under the willows. When he finally unslung the long rifle it was with a gesture as automatic as breathing. He kicked the red in the ribs and set out into the meadow, riding the flank of the action, primed to pick off Loyalists who gained the marshes. He did not stay mounted long. A man stumbling ahead of him turned suddenly and threw up a musket. Savage lay over the red's neck and kept him running. Then there was a bursting sound and he looked up and saw the Loyalist's gun had blown apart in his hands, had blown head and arms apart. Savage swung to the edge of the meadow and threw himself out of the saddle, prone beside the red. Twice he picked off racing figures in the meadow. After a while McDowell came up in a half crouch, running from the upper end of the road; he had not unslung his rifle but was using a long-barreled pistol. He said something, but Savage did not hear him, did not want to hear him, did not know if he would ever hear again any sound but the harsh screaming and the soft cleaving of air the sabers had made, and the shrilling of the horses and the wet sucking sound of their hooves in the marshes.

But he heard the retreat call when Billy blew it. The thin metallic bugle sound lay upon the cool sunny air like a blow delivered to the heart, strangely shimmering and brilliant. Savage stood up and

282

watched the Light-Horse reform. This too was performed beautifully. The white uniforms were flooded crimson and the sabers dripped as they turned back into the road.

Lee was dismounted in the rear with a little clutch of cavalry officers around him. Savage watched him, standing coolly, helmet off, gesturing with one gauntleted hand, swinging his curly blond head, smiling, a young lion surfeited. Savage reached for the red's bridle and held to it. He could hear a single hoarse whining somewhere, like a dog in agony. There was a thick nausea in the back of his throat; he was running cold sweat.

He stood for a long time. He did not speak to McDowell and McDowell did not speak to him. A voice called clearly from the edge of the meadow. "Make it three hundred, Harry. That'll give you a hundred of the bastards got out."

McDowell looked at Savage. "That's three hundred we won't have to stand up to later."

A little ditch ran through the meadow and into a grove of birch. Savage walked toward it on the new pale greening which gleamed faintly under the sere dead grass. A man lay upon his back, head in the ditch water and therefore faceless, with his entrails spewed in a great red snakelike ball on the grass beside him. The water in the ditch, a tidal overflow from the Alamance, was thick and muddy; still it seemed to him reflective, mirroring with persistent, detailed clarity: he saw in it the filthy trampled snow on the Plains of Abraham, before the blizzard fell and he went over the walls of Quebec with the bells of the city pealing in the wild white night; saw for a fleeting moment the golden sea of the Saratoga wheat fields before Burgoyne's great redoubt fell to the colonies forever; tasted, bitterly, the frosty red sunrise over the sloping southern field of Cowpens. He had begun killing a long time ago and would kill again, but in this small time, retching over the ditch, with the torn faceless Loyalist body beside him, he knew he had today killed his wife's people, killed in essence Alwyn Quantrell, in the meadows of the Alamance.

In the clear weather Nathanael Greene was free for the first time in days of his old affliction, asthma. He sat at a table at the far end of the big room in Guilford Court House, turning a quill pen over in his blunt fingers while his aides checked the roll.

It was the morning of March 14. The massacre on the Alamance was two days old; he did not rejoice in it but accepted it. Before and around him were Colonels John Howard and Otho Williams of the veteran Maryland line; the Polish engineer Tadeusz Kosciuszko, who had planned the Continental defenses from Saratoga southward; Brigadier General Isaac Huger; Militia Generals Stephens, Lawson, Eaton, Butler; Artillery Captain Singleton; Colonels Greene and Hewes of the Virginia infantry, Gunby and Ford of Maryland; Colonel William Augustine Washington of Washington's Dragoons; Captain Kirkwood of the Delaware line; Colonel Lynch of Virginia; Colonel William Campbell of the North Carolina Rifles; Colonel Charles McDowell of McDowell's North Carolina Rangers; Major Orne Savage of Morgan's Riflars; Artillery Colonel Edward Carrington, courier and espionage officer now serving as Quartermaster General; the Marquis of Bretagne; Captains Fraser Malcolm and Carlisle Fenton, surgeons.

Present, accounted for, the men were glum, silent, did not talk among themselves, looked little at one another. When Greene rose they straightened in their chairs, crossed, uncrossed their legs, waited.

Greene cleared his throat, began unceremoniously. "Gentlemen, you are all aware that the British are encamped in a most advantageous position. Cornwallis is now between the Haw and Deep rivers where the Salisbury, Hillsboro, and Guilford roads unite. Consequently he controls the direct route to Wilmington, where we know his main depot and stores are situated. We know too that he is in dire need of those stores. It would seem the ideal time to dissuade him from resupplying."

Again Greene cleared his throat. The big head was thrown back on the thick neck, the direct blue eyes went over the room full of officers. "Before I continue I wish to read you a letter from General Morgan which Colonel Carrington brought in some days ago." He picked up the paper from the table, held it before him, read quickly and clearly.

"'I expect Lord Cornwallis will push you until you are obliged to fight him, on which much will depend. You'll have, from what I see, a great number of militia. If they fight, you'll beat Cornwallis; if not, he will beat you, and perhaps cut your regulars to pieces.

I am informed that among the militia will be a number of old soldiers. I think it would be advisable to select them from the militia, and put them in the midst of the regulars. Select the riflemen also and fight them on the flanks under enterprising officers who are acquainted with that kind of fighting, and put the remainder of the militia in the center with some picked troops in their rear with orders to shoot down the first man that runs. If anything will succeed, I think a disposition of this kind will. I hope you will not look upon this as dictating, but as my opinion in a matter that I am much concerned in.'"

Greene laid the letter down, looked up again. "I don't feel it necessary to tell so many of you who've fought with General Morgan how much I value this advice. I intend to take it, and I intend to use the same type line formation he used at Cowpens, with the riflemen on the flanks. I am using this formation for two reasons. First, the terrain before Guilford Court House is remarkably similar to that at Cowpens. Second, I now have under my command troops who won a decisive victory on like terrain. They will remember that. The two are contingent upon one another."

Again the massed men shifted, leaned forward, waited. Greene was silent a long moment, face gone a little morose as it was wont to do in time of stress, but still frank, open, ruddy, gentle. "In connection with the displacement of the riflemen, I am tendering a colonelcy to Major Savage of Morgan's Riflars. There are also some promotions among the junior officers which will be dispensed by Major Giles at the close of this council." Greene began to search through the papers on the table. "Major Giles will also see that written troop dispositions are given the regimental and brigade commanders. After studying them and counseling with your junior officers I would like you to bring to me any suggestions you may have. I want this done before sunset tonight. Your lines will form as follows: North Carolina, Eaton and Butler; Virginia, Stephens and Lawson; reserve line, which will stand at the courthouse, General Huger and Colonel Howard. Butler and Stephens will command the right, Eaton and Lawson the left. Washington's Cavalry, with Kirkwood and Lynch will stand on the right flank, the riflemen and Colonel Lee's Legion and Light-Horse on the left. At the present time our rolls list four thousand four hundred forty-four men, nearly two thousand seven hundred ninety-three of whom are militia. Our regular infantry numbers one thousand four hundred ninety, cavalry one hundred sixty-one. We are aware the British have seven regiments and two battalions, a probable total of two thousand five hundred men. Of these, however, Lieutenant Kreichdorf believes about three hundred are mounted. The disposition is now open for discussion."

Major John Howard rose, aristocratic face sober and intelligent. "I would like to ask, sir, when we may tentatively expect an opening engagement of any considerable force? In spite of Cornwallis' close pursuit of us and the skirmish parties he's thrown out, he does not seem to be massing for a total engagement. Are we to simply wait here?"

Greene shook his head. "Colonel Lee and Colonel Campbell will open an initial offensive in the morning, providing the weather remains fair. Our scouts report Cornwallis' advance is in formation, though not moving. Colonel Lee will ride to the attack at sunup."

Brigadier General Isaac Huger rose beside Howard, heavy-set, experienced, efficient. "But I assumed this was to be a defensive position. Are we then to await Colonel Lee's return? By that, I mean do you propose to stay in formation on the theory the British will move once their advance is attacked?"

"Their advance," Greene said dryly, "is Tarleton's Dragoons. When they are attacked they will be supported, perhaps by a regiment, perhaps by several regiments. From what we know of British tactical methods I believe the entire army will move once its advance and whatever supporting troops they put in the field are actively engaged. We will stay in defensive formation because we cannot otherwise maintain formation. I am relying on Colonel Lee's attack to draw the British out to us."

"How are we to know where Colonel Lee is?" Huger said.

Without rising, Harry Lee said, "You'll know where I am."

There was a little deep-throated laughter, nervous, repressed. Lee was not in the habit of doing anything quietly or secretly. But they knew he meant too that his whereabouts would be plain to the naked eye, even if he had been and gone again: his farriers rode with him, and his horses were shod with their own identical distinctive marking on the shoe. This ingenious device of Lee's had more than once served to mark trail for dragoons who became separated from the cavalry during action in unfamiliar territory. It also made obvious to rebel troops, and sometimes to British, that whatever particular havoc they might come upon, or investigate, had been wrought by the Light-Horse.

"If there are no more questions," Greene said, "you are dismissed. Pick up your dispositions, gentlemen, and call out your troops to prepare immediately. Colonels Lee and Campbell will remain with me to discuss tomorrow's action. I shall be at the courthouse until sundown."

The officers filed forward to receive their written dispositions. Seeing Savage still sat halfway up the room, McDowell picked up the Riflars' chart and brought it to him, handed it to him. "Let's go," McDowell said.

Savage rose. Outside the courthouse, in the sunlight, he stopped and looked at McDowell, eyes curiously hard and thoughtful. "All right," McDowell said, "congratulations. That what you're waiting for?"

Savage shook his head. The old bitterness lay upon his lean face. "No, I was thinking, Charles. About responsibility being for the chosen few. Godalmighty, I'm so knotted up with it now I haven't got room for any more."

"You won't need any more," McDowell said. "The Riflars only got you, now. Even if you were a sergeant-major with two left feet and a set of horns."

"Well look at us," Savage said. "You, Campbell, me. You need a shave. Not a wig among us. Too damn proud of this filthy old buckskin to get into a uniform. All we've got to our names is a reputation for being deadly with a rifle."

"That's enough for me, I never been choosy," McDowell said.

Savage still stood. "Charles, if anything happens to me this time around. . . ." He stopped. McDowell looked off at the sky as if he had ceased listening, more, had not heard. Savage's mouth tightened; he was silent, thinking: what *can* happen to a man who professes such personal verities: I am not a man who feels humble under stars; and if it does happen, what of the girl who must then start the long journey back to the strong old ghost of the man, the men, I killed in that river meadow? He looked at the sky, where McDowell looked. God, let me say the hell with all this, the hell with who wins or loses, God, give me one weakness, one weakness, one weakness. . . . Then he knew it was not the possibility of death to which he must adjust, but the thing he had done on the Alamance.

"You going to have any suggestions before sundown?" McDowell said.

Savage shook his head. "Whatever you say."

"Jesus, thanks," McDowell said, "I didn't get any promotions. Where you going, Orne?"

"I'll be back by dawn," Savage said. He went down the path, walking with hardheaded egocentric resolution, unhitched the red, set the red up the road, past the courthouse.

She was shaken, brutally astonished, perhaps even frightened to see him, he knew, having said good-by. He stood in the hospital door, feet braced apart, chest so taut with pain he thought it would burst. But the expanding guilt in him was repressed, constricted by the thick closing of his throat. His eyes went over the bare tent room. "Are you alone?"

"Yes." She almost whispered. Her face was two stratas of color to him: the luminosity of pearl shone through the harsh dark blood of garnet. Her eyes were already shadowed with fatigue.

He said, "Get your blanket."

She rose and followed him.

When the night came it came cool, and very clear, full of purpleness and filigree of branches softened by swelling buds and intense vivid swift-riding stars, they too succumbing to a softening which spoke mutely of spring. Along the marshes peepers had begun plaintive sound without substance. They did not sleep. The blanket was a token thing, a condescension to the proprieties of warming earth and the night which swelled and flowered upon it; sleep was a state dispelled, forgotten in the wake of the shattering time which had lain, measureless, upon them. The lost four hundred upon the Alamance was now also Sabrina's burden, accepted, understood, assimilated; her pity had been not for the lost four hundred but for Savage, as if she had only just learned that it is easier and more logical to proffer sympathy genuinely, warmly, freely, to a loved individual than to a mass concept. In the unburdening, in the moment of weakness he had begged for, he had not only absolved but regained himself. In the strange sharing she had for the first time driven straight to the core of the man, gained entrance to some heretofore sacrosanct country where she had never ventured before.

The trees sheltered, and the earth; the clear, flowing purple air did not touch them. When the stars went westward down the still-dark sky she said, "I will go back alone." And she was on her knees, against branch and sky and flying star: the heavy upcurving line of breast, triangle of rib, waist, hip, went across his sight like a momentary single object of original beauty, discovered, glimpsed, lost. He saw the lifting of her arms like slim twin branches. She said, premising, "I will be waiting for you." Her mouth touched the hollow of his temple. When he opened his eyes again the diffused tremulous colors of dawn shifted and pressed against the dying stars.

27

IT WAS A THING of crashing silence, after sound.
On this morning of March 15, early, Lee and Campbell had run into Tarleton at the New Garden Meeting House, south of Guilford, and in a brilliant little engagement killed one hundred supporting British infantry, forty dragoons, and nearly as many horses. The British horse was poor enough to begin with, taken from North Carolina farms and plantations, far inferior in weight and height and condition to the Pennsylvania, Maryland, and Virginia horse brought south by the rebel army, but Cornwallis needed that horse nearly as badly as he needed Tarleton's slain forty. Light-Horse Harry Lee, cold, capable, already a legend, knew what he was doing when he deliberately spent shot upon the British cavalry mounts.

As Greene had conjectured, an entire regiment, the 71st Highlanders, moved to support Tarleton. Lee disengaged and rode for Guilford Court House, leaving the whole of Cornwallis' army to follow.

Now there was the cruel, anticipatory silence, with the air clear, wind stirring, sun saying it was only an hour till noontide. The silence in itself was bearable, but relative to it, the forming and moving and advancing of so many men so silently was stunning. Not even hooves sounded now, nor music: no bugle, no drum, no fife, no gun. Only occasionally voices called, distant, hollow, faint, detached upon the cool bright air. The silence lay upon the American Army which waited, entrenched on the sloping terrain before Guilford Court House; the silence lay upon the British, even as they moved, by the hundred, by the thousand.

From the courthouse, Cornwallis' army lay within view for a full mile, spreading without haste, with that terrible lack of sound, into the cleared spaces which bordered the Salisbury Road. To the men who waited the silence carried with it a quality of dream, an implication of nightmare: a noiseless red tide flowing, undulating, with the same imperturbable, relentless, silent force with which lava flows on a mountain. They waited, stirred, restless, shifting, throats clotted with dread, attempting vainly to ignore the far flashing of sunlight on fixed British bayonets, concentrating whatever hope lay in them on the only visible resistance to the van of the spreading horde: Artillery Captain Singleton, his gun crews, and two six-pounders stationed in the center of the road.

Now there were drums, but even they were without the thing which touched, the thing which was sound, low, rolling, growling, soft, a mere plane in the gradation of silence. But they heralded the end of silence. Throwing as much residue of powder charge, as much thick smoke as sound and shell, Singleton's six-pounders lobbed shot down the road into the red wedge of the British vanguard. There was no reply, either from the advancing sea of men or from the Royal Artillery, and Singleton fired ineffectually down the Salisbury Road for nearly half an hour.

To the rear of the little artillery unit in a line whose flanks overlapped the British flanks, lay one thousand sixty North Carolina militia, partially concealed by felled timber and an old weathered timber fence. General Butler lay with them on the right of the road, General Eaton on the left. Staggered off the right flank were three separate units: Washington's eighty-man cavalry which had broken Tarleton's final charge at the Cowpens; Kirkwood's Delaware Corps, its ranks thinned by five years of intensive action; Lynch's Continental Virginia regulars. Widely staggered off the left flank were Campbell's riflemen, McDowell's Rangers, Lee's Light-Horse. With the cavalry was Lee's Legion, a small unit of highly trained infantry. Fanned out to advance and flank were the men of Morgan's Riflars, lodged in leafy depressions, dug in behind stumps, braced in trees.

Three hundred yards behind the North Carolina line lay the

sixteen hundred militiamen of the Virginia line, right flank under General Stephens, left flank under General Lawson, both inward flanks resting on the road. To its rear the reserve line, no longer utilizing the road as a demarcation point, was drawn up before Guilford Court House: the hard, tough, experienced Maryland troops under Otho Williams and his junior officers Gunby and Ford; the extreme right, Virginia infantry, under General Huger, John Howard and Junior Colonels Greene and Hewes.

With the reserve line was Nathanael Greene, a little ill of the old respiratory ailment, a great deal ill of worry, which in its way was also a chronic ailment with him. Mounted, he sat before the courthouse while Singleton's guns roared in the road.

The scouts and reconnaissance men came in. There was a little knot of men around Greene at all times, and his aides worked hard and fast and laid it all out for him to see: there was the British disposition, and in a little time, perhaps, from his eminence, he could see it for himself.

He knew, already, that these were fine soldiers, fine men the British had sent against him: Generals O'Hara and Leslie, Lieutenant Colonel Webster, Baron Bose's Hessians, not the mercenaries of a few years ago, but a splendid trained regiment, and the same with the German Jaegers. Eye might encompass a portion of that advance, mind might encompass it all: the Royal Artillery in the van, the 71st Highlanders, Bose's Hessian regiment, the First Battalion Guards aimed at his left; the 33rd and 23rd Regiments, the Jaegers, the Light Infantry, the Grenadiers, the Second Battalion Guards head-on at his right. And Tarleton, whipped clean once and hit hard only this morning, still eager, still willing, with his dragoons in reserve in the rear.

The thunder of the guns brought him upright, made him pull up the horse's head. The volley had come, raggedly, unrhythmically, from the North Carolina line. For a moment a gladness ran along his veins light and nervous as a thrill. This was the same: two months ago, at Cowpens, Morgan had told his first line: two volleys and retreat, and that line had delivered not two but many volleys before it broke. It would be the same today.

But it was not. Singleton, contrary to orders, had withdrawn his six-pounders and was retiring up the Salisbury Road. It was as if the withdrawal of those two poor futile guns had set a precedent, and the North Carolina militia never fired its second volley. With the bayonets of the British almost at their breasts, the line fell apart, broke, retreated, without covering its own retreat. Off its right flank Washington, Kirkwood, and Lynch poured a galling fire into Webster's 23rd and 33rd Regiments, and it was only this fierce defensive action which allowed Eaton's crumbling left to seek sanctuary on a hill behind Campbell's riflemen, and Butler's shattered right to pour through the opening Virginia line three hundred yards to its rear. A mass panic had laid hold of the North Carolinians: some would not be encumbered in their flight by their weapons and flung them away; some clutched their useless guns as they might have clutched the cross of salvation; some few stood so well on the left that the British General Leslie impatiently called the First Guards to break them.

The retreat of Eaton's line had left Lee's Legion exposed, but the little infantry unit held its ground, waiting, just beyond Campbell and McDowell, to see the turn of the British onslaught. The first line of defense was now formed by the Virginians under Lawson and Stephens, and the Virginians, standing, kneeling, prone, were far from ready to deliver a single volley and surrender the field. Stephens' line threw a withering and effective fire into Lieutenant Colonel Webster's infantry regiments; Lawson's line stood like rock, while the kilted Highlanders of the 71st and the ranks of Bose's Hessians poured across the field on them.

In the cool noonday sunlight the whole of the British command, cavalry excepted, was concentrated upon the Virginia line. Then the sunlight was gone, striking vainly upon a pall of smoke which lay like a strata of cloud, tearing itself at times to ribbons, shifting, rising, lowering, as the current of wind carried it. Beneath it, the hands of men blistered from the hot barrels of their guns. Beneath it, men untouched and whole fell into the grass and lay believing themselves dead, men mortally wounded stood in their own blood and fought, believing themselves untouched and whole.

On Stephens' wing, that dedicated exponent of the uses of cavalry who had lately proved himself Tarleton's equal, William Washington, called up Lynch's Virginians to fall upon Webster's flank. Lynch executed his command with precipitation and thoroughness . . . so well that Brigadier General O'Hara, who had been engaged in bringing up Webster's rear, rushed forward with a company of Grenadiers and the Second Guards. Seeing the hope of support, Webster, in a fine tactical maneuver, immediately turned his entire 33rd Regiment, already engaged, upon Lynch's Virginians and relieved his threatened flank. William Washington, having taken into his mouth a bit as hard and potentially painful as that which his horse wore, curbed himself and waited.

It was the savage Highlanders with their flared coats and skirts and flying regimental colors and impassive pipers who broke the Virginia left. The valiant line wavered and at last fell back, and for a time Stephens' right, half the line, stood by itself upon the field. But there was too much to face: the 23rd and 33rd, the Grenadiers, the Second Guards, in a monstrous bayonet charge. The whole Virginia line fell back, the left into the woods, the right to the reserve line before Guilford Court House.

Washington, Kirkwood, and Lynch, comprising the American right wing, Campbell, McDowell, and Lee, composing the American left, had moved back to corresponding positions on the Virginia flanks when the North Carolina line broke. Now Washington pulled his men back to form the wing of the reserve line at the courthouse, while the riflemen spread out in the woods and took their position on the left. Action between the woodsmen and Bose's Hessians became sharp and severe, although not at close quarters. All by itself, a distinct and separate action, it boiled and raged in the thickets and ditches. The Hessian bayonets were useless in the woods, the American long rifles priceless. Bose did not retreat, but was held at bay, and a little battle which was never to catch up with the main battle maintained itself long and hard upon the left. Savage lay here with the Riflars, and McDowell and Campbell, and Lee's Legion infantry, with Lee himself standing rear guard action with his Light-Horse.

Nathanael Greene, his big frame somewhat slumped in the saddle, had begun to ride up and down along his reserve line before the courthouse. From his vantage point he could see much if not all the immediate field of action, knew through the coming and going of his couriers exactly what had happened further out on the field. He did not despair: his strongest line had not yet been tested, and when he rode before it now it was in no way to strengthen or hearten the men who composed it, for it was not in him to ask their devotion by his presence alone. He knew these men and they knew him, they had fought together before. Nothing in his attitudes said to them, I am here, do your best that I may honor you, but rather, we are all here together, and I no more than you. The smoke drifting in upon him had given him a sore throat. His eyes were watering and he breathed with his mouth half open. The shouting and the guns, the shrilling of horses and the agonized sounds he knew were there but could not hear, pressed upon him like a weight of chains.

A boy with blood streaming down his face rode at full gallop down the line and threw himself out of the saddle, still holding the reins. As he did so the horse went down in a tangled heap of struggling legs, shot through the chest. The boy half fell over him, regained his feet, saluted, bringing his hand precisely into the torn mess of his face.

Greene's distressed eyes overflowed with tears of smoke. "It's nothing, sir, not anything," the boy said stiffly, thinking his commander wept for him. "It's only it looks badly." Greene could see a quarter of his head was gone. Between them the horse kicked feebly and made bubbling sounds and foamed at the mouth. Never had Greene felt so unbroken. "Yes," he said to the boy.

"I'm to report to you that Colonel Webster is personally leading against your line, sir."

"Thank you, boy. You're dismissed from the field."

"Oh, I couldn't do that, sir," the boy said. He reached over and took the horse's reins and tugged at them. The horse was dead. "Get up," he said. He said again, "Get up." He looked at Greene. "He won't get up, sir."

Greene fought to breathe. In a moment the same ugly yellow foam which lies upon this dead animal's lips will gush out upon my own. . . . The boy pushed past him and walked steadily up the line and lay down under a tree.

Greene said, "Clear this horse out of the way."

Sabrina had long ago ceased speaking to any of the surgeons but Stewart, the Britisher. Attached to Tarleton's Cavalry, Stewart had been sent on, after the Battle of Cowpens, to attend to British wounded and prisoners of war. He was a dedicated man; in the hospital behind the courthouse he awaited not only his country's wounded, but the wounded of those he termed the insurrectionists.

Doctor Fenton had not regained his patience, if he had ever had any; he did not speak to her out of contempt for her presence and her sex. Malcolm was equally impatient but emotionally torn, and she would not talk with him now because the friendly contact which they both knew was a necessity was impossible. But the British Stewart, lithely middle-aged, stark in his black, sternly aristocratic in demeanor, knew that she was the daughter of a Loyalist household, knew the circumstances under which she was here, because he had simply, interestedly, spoken to her.

In early afternoon she had grown accustomed to agony, self-pity, blood, bone, courage. The first sickness had left her; now she did not see or feel or hear, but regarded the work before her as she might have regarded the walls of Guilford Court House, and less curiously.

Malcolm stood resting in the doorway. His shirt was stained rusty and yellow. Seeing the weariness in his stance, the set of his head, she yielded and went to him and put her hand on his arm. She was filled with admiration for what he had accomplished today with the fine unfeeling hands. "Fraser." When he did not answer she said softly, "You look so tired."

He watched nothing. Guns sounded in the nothing, and a gray pall of smoke lay even here, under the almost-spring sky. He said, as if he had not heard her, "Did you know before what a terrible failure I am?"

For the first time she noticed the thin hard-carved lines at the corners of his mouth. Her hand still lay upon his arm, but it had already begun, as if of its own accord, to tense for withdrawal.

He said, "In Charleston, where my father was known and admired, we used to hire men to dig up graves, so that we could experiment upon dead bodies. In Charleston I let a child die because I wanted to know something."

She shook her head, sadly but with impatience. "Why do you tell me this now? Isn't it a little late, Fraser, for failure? For any of us. It's only other men who decide when a man is a failure, and everybody sets a different value on things, I reckon. Maybe Father feels Brant's a failure because he won't join a Loyalist regiment, and I'm a failure because I let my own path in life be the most important thing to me. But his feeling it doesn't make it so."

When he turned his head and looked at her the old intensity of the obsidian eyes was gone; she saw a dullness she did not know. He said between his teeth, "I think too much, of late. I think a few short weeks ago Richard Jordan would have risen in the church in Benton's Crossing and pronounced the banns which would have given you to me. I think a few short weeks ago you sheltered a man to whom you had absolutely no reservations about giving yourself. Do you remember that night you came to my house, Brina? Do you remember the evening you stood in the woods with me?"

She shook her head in anguished honesty.

He went on relentlessly. "You said to me yesterday that I betrayed your father. That is incorrect. I betrayed only myself. While I sat upon the Provincial Council of Benton's Crossing I aided you honestly, and you relied upon me. When I saved myself from you it made no difference, your Council would be as strong without me as with me. But I could have erased a whole lifetime of self-betrayal by letting them hang me."

She was angry, she could not follow him. "And you call all this . . . this sorrow for yourself, failure."

He said, "You know, of course, that I killed Hanson Stoner. With just about as much deliberation as other people get up in the morning and go to bed at night."

Now her hand left his arm. She could not speak.

"You, of all people, should have known," he said, "because I told you more than I should every time I got anywhere near you. That was why I came to the Crossing . . . I was supposed to work with Stoner. We hated one another; God how I hated that gross coarse man. And learned to grieve too, though you might not believe it, for that thin little waif he married. Poor Authie . . . she loathed him too, but she would have killed me for killing him."

"But Fraser, why, why? He was a rebel too."

He nodded. "That was it, the reason. He knew every rebel in the territory. Long after I came to the Crossing I had word from Charleston to seek out and organize those men. When Stoner decided he hated me, he would tell me nothing. One night in his cabin, Authie sided with something I had said, and that was the end, between us. When I left he told me, like it was the funniest thing anybody ever thought of, that in the morning he was going down to Brandyhill and tell your father . . . and the whole Council for that matter . . . that I was a rebel. I don't think he would have done it, but I couldn't take that chance. I picked my men that night and waited for him at dawn, and we hanged him." He turned on her suddenly. "And you know the most amusing part of all, now that I've had a chance to think it over? The most amusing part of all is that if he'd done it, betrayed me, nobody in Benton's Crossing would have believed him. Isn't that so?"

The guns made white sound in the distance. She drew in her breath, the anger was still sharp in her voice. "Do *you* know the most terrible part of all? The most terrible part of all is that everything which happened to us in Benton's Crossing, after Hanson Stoner, stemmed from Hanson Stoner, was instigated by you? By you, Fraser. Why is everything you do so wrong, not only for yourself, but for everyone else?"

"Brina," he said shortly, without preamble, "we could go now, go North. If you would go with me . . ."

After a moment she said, "I feel so sorry for you, Fraser. Not because you can't be honest with yourself, but because you won't be."

He began to laugh. He crossed his arms and looked at trees and sky, outside, away from her. "Precisely what I have always wanted from you, Brina, your pity. Accept my gratitude."

She left him, passing the old doctor, Fenton, gathering up a basket of pellets, going to Stewart, where he bent over a still and shapeless mass upon the table. After a time she looked around and saw that Malcolm had gone to a corner of the tent and was priming a small pistol. She did not think about it, tight-lipped, hurt, angry. Then thought struck her hard, and she turned and he was no longer there.

She went to the doorway. He was already far down the road, walking quickly toward the courthouse. She said, "Fraser," once, knowing he could not hear her, knowing she did not want him to hear her, knowing that a portion of her life had gone away and that it would never return.

28

WEBSTER CAME ON STEADILY, his forces moving over the bodies of men in blue, and green, and brown homespun, rebel bodies pitched queerly in the grass; over the bodies of men in scarlet and buff and green, men who had marched with them a scant hour ago and now were dead, nameless, already forgotten in the dreadful afternoon. Visibility was poor, under and over and through the drifting smoke, and men were tired, panting, greasy with sweat, cold inside themselves, flushed and burning with strain and effort.

At the courthouse the Grenadiers and Guards rushed Howard's right, the veteran First Maryland under Gunby. It was a close-fire action, without bayonets; the Maryland men stood up to it. They cheered, the first cheering which had been done on either side, when Webster fell back, repulsed. For a time that brief golden sound, half triumph, half derision, carried, muffled, in the gray smoke; then it died away. Webster charged again.

Again the Maryland stood. Kirkwood's Delawares swung in ready to close off Webster's flank; Hewes' Virginia infantry deployed off the wing in a sidewise-lying L crochet, protecting its own line with the long end of the L, throwing the short end of the L to the Marylanders' aid. Webster's ranks were suddenly, blackly full of gaps and holes; the red line wavered and could not close ranks. For the second time Webster fell back, desperate for reinforcement.

But the reserve line was under fire again almost immediately. The Second Guards and Grenadiers stormed Otho Williams' Second Maryland in an attempt to break the Maryland center. Almost before the First and Third Maryland could maneuver on the Second's flanks, the Second gave way. But pressing pursuit, the British were neatly trapped when Gunby's First Maryland, its commander unhorsed but still in the front, wheeled in a beautifully executed maneuver and closed the flank with a bayonet charge. At the height of the assault Washington's Cavalry thundered in from the Continental right, reinforcing Gunby, cutting off British retreat, relieving the Second Maryland.

In the detached battle to the left of the Salisbury Road, the riflemen still held the Hessians at bay, the Hessians still held the riflemen. For well over an hour Rangers and Riflars had maintained their position in the woods at the edge of the field, with the tide of battle swinging neither to the Hessians nor to themselves, save that they effectually prevented any advance of the Hessian force. By now Tarleton's cavalry had moved in support of Bose, and

Norton's First Battalion Guards had also come to his assistance. But the forest terrain was badly suited to the uses of cavalry. Tarleton offered no real threat, situated as he was in a completely unmaneuverable position. And even with Norton's added weight against them, the riflemen held, not wasting their shot, not letting themselves be seen, making every ball count. The woods were strewn with leaves, and the leaves now sheltered not only the defenders, but the mortal remains of a gallant enemy.

Lee rode in from the rear, incautious, somehow invulnerable. There was an iron strength in the set of his young body in the saddle, and his eyes were hard and narrowed against the circumstance of the moment. Nothing of his tight curly blond hair showed under his helmet; he seemed wholly composed of bone and steel as he rode into the riflemen's lines. McDowell got up from behind the bulwark of a dead horse and went back under the trees with him, stood while Lee dismounted, gobbled briefly on a turkey-bone yelper such as the Virginians used, and waited. After a time Savage came down through the trees, walking in a half crouch but unhurried.

Lee's white uniform was filthy, covered with twigs and bits of grass; the palms of his gauntlets were gray with dust and stiffened with his own sweat. He nodded wearily at Savage and said, "How the hell far out do you suppose their infantry line goes, Colonel?"

After a moment Savage realized Lee was speaking to him. He said, "I don't know, but I can find out."

"All right," Lee said abruptly. "We're holding our own, and there's damned small danger of them pulling any of their troops off the courthouse to come back here after us. Carrington says their whole bloody force is on Greene's neck. I want to take both the Legion and the cavalry up there."

"We've got cavalry on our neck," McDowell said. His eyes were rimmed with powder smoke.

Lee shook his head. "You've got Tarleton out there boxed solid. He can't get in here. And I can't get out through Bose to get to him. Well, Colonel?"

"All right," Savage said.

"See if you can locate their picket line, will you? If it's close enough to us it'll mean there's not another thousand of 'em spread out from here to hell and gone." He laughed shortly. "All we need's another thousand of the bastards. I'd send Carrington, but he's gone somewhere up the Reedy Fork Road." He looked at Savage. "I'll wait right here," he said.

Savage lay prone in a scrounged-out nest of old damp leaves, cut off completely now from any contact with the Riflars or McDowell. He was certain he lay within the British picket line because five minutes before a British infantryman had walked almost over him, leading a mule, bound on God knew what mission, ludicrous in all his clean splendor, with the flea-bitten mule in tow. Bose's line was in closer than he'd expected, which would please and re-assure Lee.

The Deckhardt lay beside him, not even in his hands, almost out of reach. He had no desire to touch it, he had no desire to return to his line, even as he had had no desire to send one of his men on this reconnaissance but had come himself. Things had changed. Four years ago, harrying enemy troops at Saratoga, he would have done what any good officer would do, stand up, be seen, not remain static, attempt to give off to his men that indefinable thing which is military leadership, which is heart, which is spirit, and which only a bare handful, military or otherwise, ever really possess. Even today, four years later, and a colonel now by some completely unexpected twist of fate, he should have done what Morgan would have done, blustered and walked the line and shouted and spoken encouragingly. But he was not Morgan, and what the hell anyway, the Riflars knew what they were doing. . . .

He froze. Leaves rustled, but the trees stood motionless. His hand moved imperceptibly, groped for the Deckhardt.

The voice said very gently, "I got a sight on you, rebel."

Then he located the minute spot of scarlet across the ditch from him. The Britisher too lay in the leaves. Savage said with the same gentleness, "I've the same on you, lobsterback. You want to trade?"

The voice was fresh and sparkling, full of contained confidence. "You've not even got a rifle. Your rifles are so long I could see it if you had it."

Savage found the barrel of the Deckhardt. His voice was still soft; he had no assurance the Britisher was alone. "Stand and trade," he said.

Now the voice was full of laughter. "I'll stand with my ten men if you'll stand with your five."

Savage began to move, to inch, not away as he could and should have done, but off to the left and forward; to the left there was leaf-free ground and a hollow, sloping upward toward the ditch. He did not speak again. He held the Deckhardt by the barrel.

The voice said, still full of confident laughter, "My ten men are five if your five men are none." And waited.

There was no sound. A branch snapped under Savage's chest. He froze again, waiting too, but the Britisher made no move. The little spot of scarlet stayed where it was, but now it loomed closer, redder, in Savage's sight as he inched forward.

The voice said, "You got your bloody guts movin' into our lines. Or did you get lost, reb? You lost your tongue too, like you lost your gun?"

Savage kept his silence.

The voice said, "Go on back, then. Go all the way back. I got a ball for you sometime before the day's out."

Leaves had long ago blown clear of the upsloping hollow. Savage kept his head down. The silk-fine humus of the woods tasted of its own blackness.

The voice was laughter. Savage lay on the upslope. He knew there were no ten, no five, only a man, like himself.

The laughter was wonderfully young and pleasant, the laughter lay all around the edges of the words. "How far back you think you can get, rebel? Here I am waiting for you and you keep backin' off. Yellow. Keep backin' off, you yellow reb."

The spot of scarlet, which had grown bigger, brighter, bolder as he inched toward it, filled the whole curved plane of his vision. He stood in one clean springing motion. He had still not dared locate the Deckhardt's stock and so swung, grasping the rifle at the end of the barrel. The stock came around in a fine low straight trajectory, like it had a heart and mind of its own and had only waited for this, and the sound was a hollow, low-key, wet smacking sound.

In the silence he stood breathing deeply, steadily, evenly; he wasted only one glance on the smashed head in the leaves. One half of the mouth still smiled, still echoed the brave cheerful laughter and disdain . . . no, more than disdain, echoed belief that all it had spoken was truth, and so proved that truth, after all, is what a man believes, when he dies believing it. The other half was grotesque in its composition of broken bone, and the normally hollow line of the temple was more than hollow, was caved in completely, was running red and still strangely blue and white at the same time.

He could still taste the woods soil, and leaves, and a small movement of wind. The earth was very friendly but he could not bring himself to lie upon it again and so walked back through the woods.

Lee still waited, standing with his horse in nearly the same spot and attitude he had stood in when Savage left. Savage wiped the dirt from his face with the sleeve of his shirt. Lee did not even ask, so he said, "They're in close. However many there are, they're all concentrated right here, on us. Go on up to the courthouse if you've a mind to," and turned away and started up through the woods to his own men. When he was aware Lee had not moved or spoken he turned again. Lee was not looking at him, but at the rifle slung on its shoulder strap. Now Savage understood, but did not glance down, knowing the British blood would already be setting up, like a thick gelatin, on the stock of the Deckhardt.

Lee's resolve to take his Legion and Light-Horse to Greene's aid was further strengthened by the withdrawal of Norton's Guards from the fringe of the wood. The Guard commander, in view of the indecisiveness of the action had decided that Bose was capable of holding his ground and that his, Norton's, presence would be of more value in the main battle at the courthouse. He withdrew, intending to join and reinforce the twice-repulsed Webster.

But Webster had already started up the field again toward the Continental right. Heartened by this spectacle, General O'Hara, wounded but still in the saddle, effected a connection of the 71st and the 23rd Regiment and also moved to join Webster in a final offensive.

In a swift change of tactics, Light-Horse Harry Lee committed his Legion to McDowell and Campbell, seeing Norton's withdrawal and estimating the possible defeat of Bose's Hessians now that they were supported only by Tarleton's terrain-hampered cavalry. But Bose was fighting hard; the tenacity of the German was that of a game, limping pit dog, and Lee dramatically changed his mind again in that hotly contested plot of woodland. It was a decision which was to end the day for Bose.

The Legion infantry withdrew and joined the Light-Horse. Rushing to junction with the beleaguered line at the courthouse, Lee's cavalry overtook and fell upon Norton's Guards. With slashing sabers and weight of horse, the cavalry drove Norton back upon Bose. Bose had been sucking at his wounds for some time; now he was faced with the impediment of the routed Guards thrown rudely upon him, the majority of them no longer capable of action, and worse, without hope of getting back through the Light-Horse to reinforce the main British assault.

Howard's Virginia infantry and the three Maryland regiments stood as though sworn to protect that austere edifice of stone which loomed over them like a gigantic window-eyed face. The reformed North Carolina and Virginia militia stood with them now, but the two original lines of defense were badly hurt and incapable of rallying with any strength. From a little knoll before the courthouse Nathanael Greene took his round gold watch from his pocket and held it up to the light. It was nearly five o'clock in the afternoon, and the hands signified the ending of the longest five hours of his life. And this before him, this back-breaking, bone-tearing, flesh-piercing chaos would go on, and on, until there was nothing left. . . .

Already most of the horses were dead. He was still mounted, as was Lee, but the over-all perspective of the situation proved to him the sad fact that there was scarcely an American horse left on the field. Arms and ammunition would be running dangerously low now; they had been none too plentiful to begin with.

To arbitrate, to decree. . . . He was a plain-spoken, plain-thinking man. When he reached Guilford Court House he had had three logical and possible choices: give battle to the British advance only and retire before it; move on into Virginia by the upper fords; stand where he was. He had chosen. To sting at so small a portion of the British Army as Cornwallis' advance would have availed nothing, wearied his already weary troops, cut deeply into his supplies. To have moved into Virginia would only have added to the deplorable condition in which his troops had existed for so many weeks now and would in no way have prevented the British from following. To stand at Guilford would perhaps mean the rendering of a mortal wound to the exhausted British lion.

But what of his own? If this army was permitted to stand today, to fight until some ghastly finish to it all evinced itself, when it was gone, unequivocally, shadow-vanishing into the wraithlike smoke of all its old battles, when it had dropped to mingle its muscle and sinew and vital juices with the red earth of a cause-lost country, where would he ever raise another? What men were left him in the southern field but these men who moved from battle to flight, from flight to battle, as though they knew no other way of living? Better the chance he had inflicted that mortal wound today than see his army annihilated.

Before him his reserve line still held. Cornwallis had not been able to break it. The British walked now in the running streams of their own blood; it would take a while of bandaging to stanch that flow. The men who held his line would die here to a man without thought, not so much blindly dedicated as physically and mentally unable to stop themselves in the dazed moment of crisis.

The northern general looked once more down the long sloping field of Guilford Court House, into carnage, into smoke through which the late-afternoon sun now slanted. Death stood upon that field, but hope stood also. He knew instinctively that he had slashed deeply into the lion's tough old hide, severing perhaps some tendon without which an essential and active co-ordination was impossible, and which might never heal. He would not now sacrifice his saber.

He lifted one gloved hand. From a little distance Major Edward Giles saw him and hurried to the knoll. The young aide leaned close, listening to Greene's flat heavy Yankee voice.

"The Virginia militia has done well. I will rely on it again, to cover us. Tell Colonel Lee to sound retreat."

29

SABRINA SAT UPON A BALE in the hospital tent, eyes closed, longing for sleep, having pinched a week of calamity into the frame of five interminable, unconscionable hours. In the room and outside the tent and in the smaller tents surrounding, the wounded made sounds of pain and despair. There was a hot, sickening stench of blood and flesh laid open, of sweat and camphor. The old doctor, Fenton, stood in the doorway; Stewart sat on a bundle of blankets beside her. At his side a British officer, foot sawed off at the ankle, lay staring at the ceiling, wig immaculately in place upon his narrow, unbelieving head.

"What's happening?" Stewart said to Fenton. The old doctor did not turn around; the back of his neck was gray as death.

Sabrina said, "If only they would all be quiet." She pronounced the words carefully, unsure of each individual syllable, tongue-thickened by stupor. Stewart got up and came back with a cup of rum. She shook her head but he made her drink it down. When she closed her eyes now the darkness lay all around her, warm and fuzzily comfortable. There were little red lights in the darkness, like swaying flowers at the far end of a black corridor.

Stewart's voice sounded thick and distant. This time Fenton answered, but she could not distinguish between their voices and all the words ran together.

"—What are they doing now?"

"—I don't know, I can't see anything, why the devil do you keep asking me?"

"—I've smashed my watch. Have you the hour?"

Gruff, irritable old laughter. "—Near sundown I should say. If you really care."

"—Why do you suppose it's got so much quieter down there?"

"—*Will* you stop these asinine questions, Stewart? I am not clairvoyant."

"—You are not even human."

"—Keep your arrogant British opinions to yourself."

She opened her eyes and looked down at the footless British officer. Dying of shock, his mouth had gone beatific in smiling.

The old rebel doctor had lurched out the door. He made an exclamation which brought Stewart to his feet and carried him also to the doorway. Troops were streaming past, on the Reedy Fork Road which intersected the Salisbury Road. Fenton watched, uncomprehending; it was Stewart to whom realization came first. He spoke quietly but could not entirely keep from his words the nuances he wished to avoid.

"There goes your army, Fenton."

The old man took refuge in pretending. "A redeployment merely, obviously, Stewart."

"A retreat," Stewart said calmly. He looked to see Sabrina at his side, white but controlled, face apprehensive and twisted with conjecture. Past his kind shoulder she saw the unhorsed cavalry, the staggering Continentals, the unsteady columns of militia supporting, carrying, dragging their wounded. "We have lost," she said.

"It would seem so," Stewart agreed cheerfully.

"But what . . . what will we do now?"

"You and Fenton can do what you like, I suppose. I can do nothing."

"But the British will come here."

"Yes," he said. His mouth looked as if it would whistle.

She stopped herself on the edge of disaster. They would come. Stewart would be free. To be free. The old loyalties surged in her like an infusion of new blood; for a torn time she wavered in a matter which she thought was long ago decided; the patriarchal Quantrell chauvinism built towers of strength inside her exhausted body. Home. God, home, the spring turning Brandyhill green and silver, and the cool woods, and the loved faces in the still, dawn light. . . .

But she knew she had not grown apart from all that, nor severed the antique ties, but grown closer, strengthened them. She put her face in her hands, suddenly terribly excitedly grateful for what she was and where she was. For the first time she felt the stirring of a new loyalty, not to Savage but to what Savage was loyal to and believed in. And she was filled with pride at her discovery of this new depth in herself: this new knowledge that she could not only accept this patriot movement but understand and support it with her own courage and abilities.

Outside, under the trees, British and American wounded stirred restlessly, inquisitively. There was still a sound of gunfire far off down the road, where the Virginians covered the rebel retreat, but even that was dwindling. Fenton stood stunned, his irascible head turned as though to listen to some stupendous British lie. Stewart did not spare him a word or a glance. Watching that endless river of withdrawing enemy troops, his eyes were brightly misty and speculative. He felt paternally aeons older than the girl and bound to protect her with the solicitousness which he had lately given genuinely, but which he must now revive with effort from the

306

depths of his own inner gladness. He put his arm around her shoulders. "So, Sabrina, what will you do now?"

She too was filled with herself and no longer thought of him, or of the chaotic world outside. "I will wait here for my husband," she said.

She watched and waited. Shadows lay long and murky now in the clearing. Men in buckskin passed the hospital, went on up the road. But at last she knew. When she stood up from the stone where she had been sitting, Stewart knew too, and in a moment of sadness took her into his arms, thanked her, promised to get word to her father if he went South again. After that she ran, stopping only to untether Battle from his sapling, moving out of the clearing with the bone-crushing weariness reduced to memory in her.

For a long time she and Savage clung to one another in the road, and not a man saw them, not a man spoke. Then Savage said, "You must have a horse."

"The red." But she knew.

He shook his head. "Dead. They are all dead."

"I will help you."

"No, go with McDowell."

She went, half running down the Reedy Fork Road, asking once, twice, three times for the Carolina troops. After a time, having lost track of hour or daylight or of anything but confusion, she remembered unevenly that she had not seen the Hughs again, or found if the houses still stood, or said good-by with a final look to the courthouse, which had become a dear landmark these last days. Then she found a group of McDowell's men and stayed with them. There were some other women on the road, but she passed them without curiosity. Around her, in the woods, in the road, men walked and faltered and died, but she felt her own strength as she had never felt it before. With the thin hound at her side, powerful, fragile, serene, weary, renewed, she kept pace with the Rangers.

By some strange, quiet, intuitive knowledge which lay uniquely in himself, Nathanael Greene effectively communicated not only to his country but to England the victory which lay in his defeat at Guilford Court House.

As quickly as couriers could ride, the Continental Congress knew that this long and seemingly indecisive engagement had been unaccountably costly for the British, and that Greene had saved the American Army. Yet Cornwallis truly believed he had won, and so reported. The day was not long in coming when Lord North would stand in Parliament to announce bitterly that another such British victory would ruin the British Empire, but Greene could not know this nor did he need to know it.

At nightfall, before Guilford Court House, the British gathered their dead; the rebels left their dead upon the field while the living were saved. Cornwallis had no choice but to turn to the sea, where reinforcements, supplies, and salvation lay. But salvation was a nebulous dream which would never materialize, and his shattered army was never to recover from a blow dealt by men who had thrown down their arms and men who had stood like mountains.

April lay upon the land, green, and filled with shadow and sunlight, when Sabrina and Orne Savage came home, leaving behind them the long magnificent path of the Shenandoah Valley, riding the forested foothills of the Blue Ridge. In the woods where they lay at night, violets folded their petals in the darkness and the triangular blossoms of the trillium gleamed whitely. This was a new woodland, full of new darknesses and mysteries, and when they left the woodland the river lay before them in the morning light.

They turned off the road under pale yellow-green willows, so tall and thick she thought they must be as old as the world. Leaves were fragrant in the moist air, and the house gave off so tangible an aura of power and solidity that she thought, This house has shaped Orne, and will shape me. To her who had known of water only still meadow pools and wood streams, the river was blindingly beautiful and majestic; the river instilled in her a doubt that man who lives out of sight of water is fulfilled. Everything of house, land, trees, garden, spoke of comfort and security, of grace and ease and elegance. But when the Negroes met them on the road, running, calling out, and the dogs barking, she tensed, already anticipating the strain of homecoming. But held up her head.

From the mounting block she looked at a wide verandah flanked by four columns, and the columns ringed and held in a delicate-clinging of wisteria. Courage came to her: a loved and familiar thing sprang from this earth as it had sprung from the earth of Brandy-hill. Going up the steps, she paused to touch briefly a tendril of the encircling vine.

In the square hallway, from which rose a wide circular stairway, a little Negro maid waited. She was very young, and a little nervous, Sabrina saw, and as if to reassure herself smiled reassuringly at the girl. Still smiling, she looked up and saw the old woman on the stairs.

Not as she would have thought her, all in black, and very stern. Rather, in some sort of dressing gown which needed smoothing but was still neat, and quite feminine with its pattern of exaggerated pink flowers. The hair was bluish-white, but the eyes were the same tawny eyes she had given her son, and they were without surprise. Yet when she spoke it was as if she had only at this moment recovered a composure she had obviously never lost.

"Well, Edward," she said, looking at Savage.

Savage did not go up the stairs to her, as Sabrina expected he would do. Rather, he caught Sabrina's hand in his own and stood with her, as if waiting. His voice was very decisive, almost matter of fact, but underlying it was a heavy recurrent darkly emotional chord of amusement and pleasure.

"Mother, this is Sabrina. We were married two months ago and she has been on the road a long time and gone through a battle with me and she's tired. You look well rested, so we'll let you do the talking."

The old woman came down the stairs, looking directly at Savage. When she reached the last step she began to smile. Then she came and took Savage's face between her hands and said, "Welcome home, Edward, welcome home," and turned to Sabrina and held out both hands for a moment and turned to Savage again. "Thank God someone has at last melted that stubbornness of yours."

Sabrina stood stiffly. The words were a reminder that another woman had stood in this house with Savage, had inculcated in him that reserve and terrible calm of which his mother now accused him. But she could not maintain discomfort in the face of the old woman's amiable acceptance. She said, "Madame, I would beg leniency . . . my appearance . . . the shock Orne must cause you. . . ."

The old woman looked down at her wrapper. Her face was soft and wrinkled, like a peach gone overripe. "And I should not beg yours," she said. "Never mind, I have always found Edward a shocking creature, from the day he was born. Molly, we shall have refreshment in the drawing room. Edward, your sons are down along the river, building boats or devising some other terrible adult pleasure for themselves. Go and find them."

In the drawing room, richly appointed but starkly simple, the old woman's eyes were kind and uncritical. "Well, Sabrina, sit down . . . such a lovely name, with Biblical overtones, hasn't it . . . ? I've forgotten my Bible for being so busy . . . or is it the Sabine women I'm thinking of . . . never mind, names are so unnecessary and so essential all at the same time. Edward, for instance. He was christened Orne because that was his father's name, but I've never liked it. I always suspected his father had Dutch blood somewhere, but I never wanted to know for certain. I couldn't have stood it if he had."

The little maid came with a tray. The old woman said, "Tea. *Tea*, Molly. Go and warm up the scones left from yesterday and get us some cheese. I should like some whiskey. You, Sabrina?"

Sabrina said in astonishment, "If you please, I think it would warm me." Her hands were very cold.

The old woman's face said, good for you; the old woman's eyes were busy but not overtly so. "So you will have much to tell me and I to tell you. How tired you must be of those rough clothes you are wearing; haven't you trousers to wear with your skirt? Well, never mind now, Edward says you have been in some battle or other, so I suppose there's reason enough."

Molly came again with the tray. Sabrina took a long hot drink from her glass and relaxed. Something told her that Savage's mother, for all her surface lightness, was a strong and formidable ally. She said, "I feel I must apologize for having come unannounced into your home."

The old woman said, leaning forward, holding her glass, looking at Sabrina with Savage's tawny eyes, "My home. Edward's home, which I have kept for him through necessity, to preserve him and the future of his sons. I tell you that I am sick of running homes and would like to stay in bed for a month or so."

"But I know nothing of running a house," Sabrina said, "only our little farm. . . ."

"Well, you can come and ask me then," the old woman said. "But don't bother me unduly. All the servants are most co-operative

. . . you'll have no trouble. Richard's wife is a little lightheaded, but she'll help."

Sabrina thought, And the crops and the field hands and the myriad problems which beset a landowner. . . . Savage's mother had not deceived her. Savage's mother had run this place like a man, with only token help from her older son, Richard, who would after all, have his own land to care for.

"Ah," the old woman said, "so much to catch up with, isn't there, and neither of us fit to do any running now. We shall rest, and when you feel up to it we shall look for the prettiest materials and bonnets, and some flowers to trim them with. . . . Here now, why do you look at me like that?"

Sabrina said honestly, "Because I cannot help feeling that you are not as astonished at my appearance here as you should be, madame, no matter how consummate an actress you are."

The old woman took a long but delicate drink from her glass. She said, "Isn't it pleasant how nicely we begin to understand one another? Richard and I had driven over to see Dan Morgan right after he came home. . . . He and Edward have known one another near all their lives, you know. Dan's wife may have been a little intemperate, she was so eager to give me news of Edward."

"She told you," Sabrina said.

"Yes, bless her. So I enter the field with an advantage over you. Don't be unhappy, I'm seventy now and need a head start at times. How terrible for you to come into this house almost as a guest. Get over that feeling, Sabrina. It's your house now, I wash my hands of it. I will not get in your way, and I will not advise you, unless you ask it. I shall also not let Richard's wife advise you, or Dan's wife, or anybody else's wife. Edward won't be here long, I suppose. I know about your battle, of course, however much I pretended not to . . . everybody in Virginia who can read or is not stone-deaf knows about it. The war is not over, but I assume it shall be one day, as all wars come to a standstill if not an end. I believe we shall win it, but the work isn't over. Forget I am here and spend as much time as you can with Edward."

She rose from her chair. Sabrina saw that she must have been very fair once, and tall, and that the bluish-white hair would have been as silver-white as her son's. She said, "You will have enough problems here without considering me. Two of them are young growing boys who have been without a mother for a long time, but who are mature and sensible, too much so perhaps for their years. Dependence upon oneself is an astounding builder of character, you know. I might suggest that it would be a warm and generous touch to meet them somewhere besides in this stiff room. The path right of the house runs straight to the river."

Sabrina stood up. For a little time the two women looked at one another; then Sabrina went into the hallway and out the door and saw the path and took it. The morning sunlight was strong and hot now; she felt its strength burning into her and walked quickly, seeing the sun-hot, wet burning of the river in the distance. Where the path curved the willow branches grew low, framing earth and river and sky in a tracery of pale leafing. She bent the branches aside, stooping a little, feeling the brittle-pliant wood and narrow foliage spring back from her hands, and went on down the path to the river.

30

THE SPRING SOFTNESS unfolded on the land like clouds unfolding in the morning sky, tenderly pale and silver. The nights were still bracing cold, but the stars had traded their hard winter glitter for a mistiness that made them more spark than fire in the warming heavens, and when you looked toward the mountains you could see plainly the rolling stretches of new budding lacing the dark stands of conifer, the startling whiteness of birch just beginning to cover its nakedness again. The swallows had come swooping clove-tailed back to the loft and the peepers filled the evenings with thin wistful song and the maples were full of red blossom and bees. Up by the barn the mare and her foal moved across the greening land side by side and stood under the bud-swelling lilac.

It was not too early to think of planting. Peas were in already, and it was getting time to set out onions. Jewel came out on the stone step, shaded her eyes with her hand and sniffed the softness in the air. "Look at that, Al'n," she said. "Rabbits gittin' so bold they comin' right up in the broad daylight." She stepped down off the stone and the rabbit fled.

Old Jim raised his head. Alwyn half turned in his chair.

"You see that, Al'n?"

"I didn't see any rabbit," he said.

"Only cause you didn't wants to see it." She came across the yard to him.

"Where did Brant go?"

"I told him see if he could find me some wild onions. Reckon he stopped to see if the fish was hungry nuff to eat his worms."

He did not answer.

"How come this a holiday?" Jewel said. "Ain't you gonner put in the onions?"

"Tomorrow," he said. "The weather's going to hold good for a spell now."

"Al'n, you ain't fussin' about that letter, is you?"

He smiled. "What is there to fuss about? It's a fine letter."

She stood by his chair. "You thinkin' on it too much," she said.

"Well, and why not? It makes me wonder how things are and what they look like."

"Don't make me wonder," she said. "I already knows. She's set it all down an' I can see it in my eye and you'd oughter be able to do the same."

"I can, in a sense. You'll tell me, eventually, when you feel I've goaded you into it, so tell me now what you think, Jewel."

She shrugged. "I thinks you'd oughter go."

"I supposed that. Where are your doubts, wise judge?"

"I ain't got no doubts. You makes everything so hard, Al'n, you makes sides to everything all the time. There ain't no sides to this, it's what you wants to do."

He sat back in his chair. "Does it seem to you we settle too easily into the old routine, with all that has happened to us?"

Her face was outraged. "And why shouldn't we is what I'd like to know? Why shouldn't Brant go on jest like he always has, and you, and me too? What's to be diff'rent about it?"

"They are all gone," Alwyn said, looking at her.

"Al'n, nuthin's gone, less'n it gone out of your mind."

He nodded slowly.

She said with indignation, "Miss Ellen say for you to go. I can tell you jest what Missy Ellen say. You makin' trouble for youself you look for roads you'd oughter travel an' roads you'd ought'nter. They's only one road, an' that's the road where you insides tell you to go."

"It would be too much for Brant," he said.

"I reckon not. You got to give Brant he work hard on this land, since he were a little feller. It's what Brant likes, is his land."

Again he nodded, but said nothing.

Jewel said, "You try a body, Al'n."

She went away. After a time he got up from his chair and Old Jim rose too, hesitating until he saw where Alwyn's steps turned. But Alwyn stood, looking at the house in the soft spring sunlight, at the broken earth of the garden, and the weathered barn on the hill. The blue hound touched his leg questioningly with its graying muzzle. "It would be hard to leave you," Alwyn said aloud, not looking at the dog. "It would be hard."

Brant had four fine trout. He gutted and cleaned them in the barn doorway, and the gray cat feasted and sat in the sun and washed its paws with great concentration and curled its immaculate paw around the triangle of its ear, bending its head to the curling.

He took the fish to the house. "Where's my onions?" Jewel said. He opened a roll of wet moss and showed her the feathery green spears and tiny pearls of the fruit. They smelled strong and good. "Them fishes looks nice an' milky," Jewel said. "I'm gittin' sick to death of deer meat."

He went outside and doused his head in the wooden bucket of water and washed his hands and cleaned his nails with a skinning knife. When he went back in, his father was in the kitchen. He thought his father hadn't aged much, considering all the aging he should have done, logically, these past months. He sat down and tilted his chair back against the wall and watched, for a moment, Jewel rolling the trout in corn meal. He closed his eyes.

"What are you figuring, son?" Alwyn said.

He opened his eyes. His father sat at the head of the table, smoking. "Wasn't figurin'," he said. "Wonderin'. You know how in the summer you git a terrible honing to go out and lie in the woods by the cold water, and in the fall you git a honing to pick up your gun and git out to the marshes for the ducks . . . like a fever it is . . . and in the winter you git a honing to sit by the fire and read all day. Well, I was wonderin' how come it is in the spring a man gits a honing to go do something, only he can't put his finger on what it is he hones to do."

Alwyn said, "Men have known that restlessness since the dawn of time."

"I know that. But it don't explain it. Father, I got a feeling this is going to be a good spring for you."

Alwyn smiled. "I believe that is the first prophetic observation I've heard you hazard in some time."

"Well, a man don't just quit short growin' up, does he?"

"Some does," Jewel said.

"Why don't you say right out what you want to say?" Alwyn said.

"It was just I figured you ought to go up and see Brina."

Alwyn smoked quietly for a time. Then he said, "Pressure from all directions."

"No pressure. It was just in case you needed help makin' up your mind."

"It's riddy," Jewel said.

They ate silently, the three of them at the table, and the room full of quietness, of familiarity, of routine. It was early and the spring light lay outside and made to lie an hour or two more, with the lengthening of the days.

Brant said, "I tore the shoulder seam in that blue shirt, Jewel."

"I seen it when I put it away." She rose from the table. "You wants to bring it out I'll mend it after I wash up."

He finished eating and went down the hall to his room. When he picked up the torn shirt his eye fell on the little wooden box on the shelf above the row of clothes pegs. It was made out of fruitwood, apple or pear, he couldn't recall which; Darby Yancy had made it for him when he was about twelve, to keep his fishing line and round lead sinkers in. It had become the inevitable catch-all: there were odd buttons and a broken quill pen and some loose rifle ball in it. He didn't use it any more because he kept his willow poles and lines and sinkers and flies in the shed where he could pick them up easy on his way to the creek. He took the box down and held it in his hands. It was fine-done, rubbed until it looked like yellow satin. The hinges on the back were loops of leather with a wood peg slipped through, so when you raised the lid the wood peg turned neatly inside the loop. He opened it and spilled the contents toward the front edge and Dawn Star's braid bands fell out in his hand. It sort of surprised him; it wasn't he'd forgot them, it was he'd forgot they were there. Thin little circlets of blue beads. They felt cool and tearful in his hand. He put them in his pocket and went back to the kitchen.

"Where's the shirt?" Jewel said.

He went back and got it, where he'd thrown it across the bed, and brought it back to the kitchen. He took the jug out from behind the fireplace wall.

"Now what?" Jewel said, not turning around, lifting the kettle of hot water from the hook over the fire.

"I reckoned I'd sit out on the step and clean my rifle," he said.

She didn't answer. He took a long swallow from the mouth of the jug and put the jug back and got the Deckhardt down off the rack over the door and went to the corner cupboard for the dish of grease and the worn soft doeskin rag. Jewel looked at him once and he was sitting on the step, looking off at the sky and not cleaning the rifle at all, and a ways beyond him there was Alwyn, back in his chair under the tree, facing the garden, and he too just looking off. She shook her head and started to put the fresh-washed plates away. After a time she began to sing, without any words, voice as thin and high and musicless as the peepers shrilling up along the spring hole.

There was a fine filtering of sunlight, like the sun strained to shine, not wanting to go down behind the mountains. It lay soft and gold-red, like the patina on old wood, or old copper. Rich damp scent came up off the turned earth of the garden, and faint flower scent came down off the hill where the cherry trees were coming into bloom. All the crispness and brittleness and dryness of winter-scent had blown away like smoke, and the softer scents, the green scents, were everywhere.

For the third time that day Alwyn unfolded the letter and held it so he could read it. Like the rustle of the paper had disturbed him, Old Jim got up and wandered over and lay down by Brant on the doorstep. "Orne has not yet returned to the army, but must soon do so. He would have me say to you that you are to come.

Then he says I must not say you *are* to come, for then you would accuse him of commanding, so he amends it to we would have you come. And we would not hear one argument you would make to this, only to say you need not stay forever if you do not wish to, or that you may stay forever if you so wish."

Here was the troublesome part, the writing as if he were still a young man could tear up his roots, even for a little and transplant them confidently to some new-prepared soil and set them out again and be asked to decide whether it was an annual or a perennial planting. Alwyn raised his head and saw Brant was rubbing down the Deckhardt and that Old Jim was wide awake, looking up along the ridge and smelling the air complacently. He lodged the scene hard behind his eyes, imprinting it against the rosy evening sky, with the sun going down and a thin golden line of light lying along the broken border of the mountains and the first amethyst mists beginning to rise in the hollows.

"Father, say you will come, if only to see that I am safe and well and loved, if only to make me happy. Orne speaks much of the country to the westward, where so few men have gone . . . does not commit himself, but speaks, I think, overmuch on it, and speaks of you in connection with this land, so that I am not sure what is in his mind, except that it is something I think he would talk of with you. So we urge you will come, for homesick as I have been for Brandyhill, I adapt myself to the new life here and the homesickness would be only a very small ghost, raising its head less and less, if you were here with us a time."

The last gold went out of the sky, but the rosiness lingered. It was very quiet, and he thought Brant had finished with the rifle, though he didn't look to see. He wondered if Brant thought of him as an old man . . . certainly Orne Savage didn't . . . more, he wondered if he should think of himself as an old man. And what would they say in Benton's Crossing, if he just picked up all of a sudden and went off all those miles, if he encouraged in himself some young-man enthusiasm for whatever his son-in-law had in his mind about the land westward.

And it astonished him, so warm and welcome was the rising knowledge in his heart, that with fortune he had twenty good years yet, and who cared what they thought in Benton's Crossing?

High up on the ridge, where the rosy light still burned in the young leaves, a bird sang once, piercingly, with a single note, and was silent. From the long tangent of sidewise vision, Alwyn thought it was only Old Jim had got up, then he realized Brant too stood, and the old Cherokee omen sent the blood cold along his veins: death riding palely in spring's saddle was beyond comprehension; all the senses cried out against it. He saw Brant walking, slowly at first, as if he listened, up the path to the barn, and then the walk lengthened and haste came into it, and the blue hound ran at his side.

Alwyn stood up, meaning to call, wanting to call, but he could not speak. Unwilling, he found the path in the twilight, and the haste came to him too, though he could not have told what he did or why he did it, save that he would have spared his son, save that he felt the thrush's song, if it was for one of them, was for him.

Then he said his son's name, hesitatingly but with gentleness and understanding, not calling, only saying it, as if to himself.

Brant turned, faceless, featureless in the coming dark, standing against the red-turning sky with the rifle slung from the palm of his hand. He stood hard, the wiry, powerful body black on the last lingering light, and the hound black at his side, but his voice was not hard, his voice was clearly broken, as if by fear, or joy. "I got to see," he said. "It's just over the mountain. I got to see."

Night already lay in the cool hollow of the hills, but the stars had not come yet. Alwyn thought he could name the tree, a young birch with round green coins of leaf, where the thrush had called, but when he reached the crest of the ridge Brant and Old Jim and the brown bird were gone.